The Pussy Trap 5

Family Ain't Family: Blood Ain't Blood

"We are living in a time where we are burying our friends and our enemies in the same place."

~NeNe Capri~

Dedication

To my Daughter Princess Khairah. Everything I do is for you.
Thank you for giving me the best job ever, being a mom! I love you!

Acknowledgments

I am so blessed to be able to do what I love and share it with all my 'Reading Bosses'. Thank you, Mommy and Princess, for all your support and patience while I build our legacy. I can't do anything without both of you. Thank you Tiko and Tiombe for forty-two years of friendship. No matter how far we are in distance, we are always joined by spirit. I love y'all! AT&T Forever.

Shout out to my baby sister Angel. You are a true inspiration! I love you from a special place in my heart.

Shout out to my sister Keisha, my 'KeKe' you are the bomb.com thank you for always listening and guiding me! I love you.

Thank you so much Lashonda Johnson my editing genie. You are the gift that never stops giving. We are about to set the industry on fire.

Last but never least, To my 'Trappers' you are the heat in my pen. Because of you, I write. Thank you for over ten years of love and support.

Stay tuned we are just getting started.

Prologue

Kayson stood tall over his father glaring down at him. Then he glanced around at all the death that scattered the room and pride swelled up in his chest. He'd finally put their enemies to rest. Today everything would start over, he just needed to put his wife and family back together piece by tattered piece.

Kayson turned and looked into the eyes of his men, then passed out orders, "We start this shit over today…" he paused staring into their eyes. "…my wife is no longer in charge. She will be my personal advisor, that is it. Y'all bring everything to me and me only. And your disobedience comes with a penalty of death…" he paused again. Each man stood firm and nodded confirming their allegiance. The silence was thick in the room as Kayson held their gaze. He then moved towards KoKo. "You're done, baby. I can't live with you on this end of our business. Am I clear?"

"Yes, and you owe me," KoKo said unable to hold eye contact with Kayson.

"I'ma spend the rest of my life paying you back." He pulled her into his arms and KoKo rested against his chest.

Kayson turned and looked at Baseem who was now kneeling next to Goldie trying to lift her into his arms. Baseem rose to his feet and held Goldie close to him. Tears ran from his eyes and onto her face. He whispered in her ear as he caressed her golden, blood-soaked locks. His heart sank to the bottom of his dark, black soul with every word he uttered.

"No regrets, Bas. She chose her path, now you have to choose yours," KoKo stated with ease looking over at Baseem.

Baseem choked back tears and inhaled deeply. He thought back to the day Kayson saved his life and the many days he took the lives of others. Death

7

was his destiny, and he would live from this day forward in its painful shadow.

"My loyalty, my honor, and my gun will always be for y'all." Baseem looked at KoKo then firmly into Kayson's eyes.

There was an eerie moment of silence then Kayson spoke, "Today our allegiance is stronger than ever." Kayson held their gaze. "We will take all the pain and hatred we have for our enemies and put it in our sons. They will settle every score we leave behind."

Kayson knew there was no getting out and there would always be someone lurking to be at the top, someone to challenge his power. He vowed to protect his throne at all costs and only relinquish it to the grave. Until then, they would all live each day in the shadow of death.

****

Seventeen Years Earlier

Tonight, several men were gunned down in a warehouse in the Ironbound section of Newark, New Jersey. Of the victims was Malik Barnes husband of Sabrina Barnes who was killed just a week earlier at the couple's Seven Oaks home. The investigation is underway. As to why these families were robbed a life, twice? We will have more on these stories at eleven. Back to you, Robert.

"Muthafucka!" Tyquan threw the remote control across the room as he jumped up and headed for the door.

Tyquan busted out the exit and stepped swiftly to his vehicle. He hit the locks, jumped inside, and sped off leaving smoke and black marks on the concrete. He drove from one block to the next with heat filling his veins. When he reached his destination, he barely turned off the engine before the locks were popped and his door was open. He rushed into the building and sped past the doorman to the elevator as he rattled off questions at Tyquan's back.

Tyquan ignored the young clerk as he pounded the up button impatiently watching the numbers decrease. Once the doors opened, he stepped inside, then leaned against the wall as he ascended to the 27th floor.

Bing! The doors slid open and he rushed down the dimly lit hallway.

"What the fuck is going on!" Tyquan busted into Smoke's office slamming the door behind him.

"Calm the fuck down and have a seat," Smoke spoke smoothly from his reclined position.

"Man, fuck that! How you let that nigga touch Malik like that?" Tyquan's voice boomed as he moved closer to Smoke's desk.

"It was out of my hands, Tyke." Smoke picked up his cigar from the ashtray and pulled evenly, then exhaled thick clouds into Tyquan's direction. "You need to let it go."

"What the fuck are you talking about? A feeling of peace! They touched that man's family. His wife and children are in danger. I told you to let me handle it!" Tyquan was now towering the desk with heat rushing through every inch of his body.

"You didn't do a good job handling it," a voice crept from the dark shadows of the room.

"Who the fuck is you?" Tyquan moved towards the darkness.

Click! Clack! The sound of a round being pumped into the chamber paralyzed Tyquan's movement.

"Keep yo' ass right there and take that fuckin' base out of your tone," the voice grew darker with every word.

"What the fuck you mean take the base out of my tone?" Tyquan took another step then felt the heat of a bullet whistle past his head and hit the wall behind him.

"Move again, nigga. You and Malik will be having this conversation face to face," the voice ordered as another bullet was pumped into the chamber. "This one won't miss."

"Smoke what the fuck is going on?" Tyquan's chest heaved up and down as he waited for a response.

"Tyke, I told you, this shit is way outta my hands. And from the looks of it, it's way out of yours, too." Smoke took another pull on his Cuban looking up into Tyquan's bloodshot eyes.

9

"This is a lot of blood you trying to have on your hands," Tyquan gently warned Smoke. "They touched that man's family."

"Well, since you're so fuckin' loyal, make sure whoever is left is taken care of," the man spat coldly from the corner as he rose to his feet.

Tyquan looked at Smoke's emotionless gaze and thought, *This was once a man I respected.'* Now he'd been added to a list he kept tucked tightly to his heart and from the tone in the room he and his dirty ass team had been put right at the top.

"Anything else?" Tyquan forced the question through his lips like hot glass.

"Nah, just remember, that blood you speak of is on your hands, too. You just make sure the money don't get fucked up while we're exchanging blood from one hand to the next."

"Is that right?"

"Yeah, it's right," the other voice answered for Smoke.

Tyquan put a small smirk on his face, fixed his eyes towards the dark corner, then turned to exit. He reluctantly snatched the door open and moved swiftly slamming it hard behind him. He hurried to the parking lot, jumped in his vehicle, and rubbed his hands back and forth over his face.

"Fuck." He slammed his palms against the steering wheel. "These muthafuckas wanna play. *Let's play!*"

Tyquan pulled his emotions together and began plotting his plan. He was about to show them what it looked like when blood was no longer blood. He turned the key in the ignition and pulled off headed to the only ones he knew would bring heartache and pain.

Chapter 1

Deadly Ink

Tyquan pulled in front of the tall glass building and silenced his engine. He sat thinking about the last conversation he had with his friend. It had only been a week since he'd been in Malik's presence, he was now preparing to bury his comrade in a dark space. His mind shifted to that final conversation and all that was put in place...

Tyquan pulled into a parking space right next to Malik's red BMW. He eyed the area then closed his sunroof and stepped out. He walked over to the bench where Malik sat playing with his small daughter.

"Daddy duty I see," Tyquan announced walking around to take a seat.

"Sheeiitt...you know, Sabrina, don't give a fuck who I think I am. She be like, nah, fuck that you a daddy first," Malik joked extending his hand to Tyquan.

"I hear you." Tyquan shook his hand then took a seat next to him. He tickled Ce'Asia's chin as a smile took over the curves of his mouth. "She looks just like you," he added enjoying the sparkle in her bright, brown eyes.

"Yeah, that's what they say, Daddy's, KoKo. I pray she has a different destiny than ours." He looked over at his friend.

Tyquan had witnessed the hit being put on Malik's head, and it was eating him alive that he couldn't find the money trail to stop it.

"I know you know what's up. I am not asking you for any loyalty you are not expecting to give. I know what this is. I know who I am and what the fuck these greasy ass niggas want..." Malik paused to kiss Ce'Asia's chocolate cheeks. "I just need you to make sure my family is good. I laid my

suit out the day I signed up for this. It is a dying man's wish that his family is spared." Malik looked into Tyquan's eyes searching for whatever remnants of what was human still inside him.

Tyquan thought about Malik's words, then his own position on the board. He then did the only thing he knew. "You have my word." Tyquan put his hand out and Malik shook it firmly.

Malik reached into Ce'Asia's diaper bag and pulled out an envelope and a small black bag. "This is all I have left. Wait until you get to a safe place then open it. Instructions and contacts will be all laid out."

Tyquan took everything into his hands as he rose to his feet, he nodded in agreement as he plotted the curveball to the enemy's plan.

Malik also stood grabbing his princess firmly in his arms as he threw the bag over his shoulder. "Take care of my family, Tyke," Malik said as he walked off toward the side of the river rocking KoKo, taking what felt like his final walk.

"You have my word."

Tyquan watched as Malik walked over to the water. He had made his vow then moved to his car, hopped inside, and took off headed to set shit in motion. If he hadn't kept his word to anyone else, he was going to keep it to Malik. He owed him more than just his life.

Tyquan pulled over to a phone booth, jumped out, dropped a few quarters in the slot, and punched in the numbers, then waited for an answer.

"Hello," the sweet voice bellowed through the line.

"I need you to get the team."

"Doing it now," the woman confirmed then disconnected the call.

Tyquan hopped back in his car and took off with a heaviness and a thirst for vengeance locked deep in his heart.

****

"Put that on the pile over there and let me review those documents one more time." Monique extended her arms toward her assistant who looked as if she was about to fall over from exhaustion.

"Here you go." She handed her the documents and a fresh cup of coffee.

"This is the last stack we have to go over ladies and gentlemen." She took a sip of her coffee then placed her mug on the conference table.

"I pulled the bank reports for the clients we signed this morning. If we move right, we can close all deals by tomorrow afternoon," Karen said as she passed a few folders around the table.

"Thank you, my heart. I promise we will be out of here in the next few hours." She looked down at the floating arms of her Rolex praying she was right. It was now midnight, they had been at it for the last eight hours.

Monique walked to the end of the long table filled with contracts and folders, surrounded by her dedicated team. She sank into her chair and began flipping through the documents. Time seemed to tick by slowly as each person in the room shuffled through the paperwork and keyed in figures.

Monique rotated her eyes between the computer and the documents. As she was about to key in a few figures, Jade busted into the conference room holding the cordless phone tightly in her hand and a look in her eyes as if she was holding back severe pain.

"What's the matter?" Monique's brow creased.

"It's for you, it's urgent."

"*Urgent?* Who is it?" Monique said as she took the phone from Jade's hands. "Hello?" she asked with intense concern.

Monique rose to her feet and crossed her free arm over her chest as she listened closely. When the caller completed their last words, Monique grabbed her throat trying to calm the forming lump as she pulled at the tears threatening to leave her eyes.

"Yes, I'm on my way," she mumbled staring at the wall stiffened by the shock lingering from the caller's words.

"Mo, you good?" Karen asked jumping to her feet rushing over to where Monique stood.

Karen put her hand on Monique's shoulder as she stared at her lifeless, color-drained face.

Monique choked back her breath and swallowed her spit. "Yes! Can you wrap everything up? I have to leave town," Monique stated slowly turning to place the phone on the table.

"Sure, we got you. Do you need someone to come with you?" Karen asked trying to relieve some of her agony.

"No, I got it. Just make sure you go over everything several times and forward me all reports before they go in," Monique said making no eye contact as she headed to the door. When she pulled it open her assistant was standing there with distress in her gaze. "Jade, call my driver and book me the first flight to New York."

Monique hurried past her and down the hall to her office. She threw on her jacket and quickly grabbed her purse and keys. She closed the blinds, then hit the safe grabbing a few envelopes, some cash, and credit cards, then tucked them in her purse. She locked it back and secured all cabinets and drawers. Monique stood still, took one last glare around the room, then exited slamming the door on her way out. Her heart and mind raced as she vigorously pushed the down button on the elevator while trying to make sure she wasn't forgetting anything.

When Monique exited the elevator, she sped past security out the doors, then jumped in the back of the limo awaiting her and slammed the door shut.

"LAX, Mrs. Wells?"

"Yes," she answered then took a deep breath as she struggled not to crumble. Monique put her head back in exhaustion, dreading what was waiting for her on the other side of the flight.

As Monique stood quietly in the airport bar waiting her turn to board the plane, she stared at all the movement through her dark shades anxious to board and get the flight over with. She put the glass of Bourbon to her lips and downed the shot in one gulp. She was on her fifth glass and still craving more.

14

Just as she was about to try and quench the thirst, she heard the agents announcing they were now boarding first-class. Monique put two hundred on the bar, grabbed her leather bag, and headed to board. As Monique stepped onto the plane, a heaviness took over her heart. She pulled her hand up to her face just in time to catch a few tears that had gotten past her lids.

"Are you okay, ma'am? Can I get you anything?" the flight attendant asked as Monique took her seat.

"Yes, bring me three bottles of something brown, then again in thirty minutes," Monique requested passing the young woman a hundred-dollar bill, then she fastened her seatbelt and pulled her collar close to her face.

When the flight attendant returned with the bottles and a cup of ice Monique quickly poured the small bottles into the glass and began drinking it down. She crossed her legs, turned toward the window, and prepared for what felt like the flight to hell.

Monique closed her eyes and thought about Malik and all the conversations they'd had, and the water she'd threatened to stay where it was disobeyed and flooded her flushed red cheeks. An aching pain filled her gut as she thought about the last time he was in her presence. Monique closed her eyes, gathered all her memories, and let her favorite one play out in high-speed definition.

"Who is it," Monique asked wiping her hands on the dishtowel.

"Malik," he answered then waited to hear the locks click.

Monique formed a big smile on her face as she looked in the mirror by the door then fingered through her hair. She smoothed her hands over her figure-fitting dress then reached for the knob.

"Hey, you," she said pulling the door open wide for him to enter.

"What's up, Mo?" Malik asked as he moved through the opening, kissing her forehead as he passed her.

"Just working, you know me," she said then put her attention on the little chocolate dream in his arms. "Awwww... she is getting so big." *Monique took Ce'Asia from Malik's hands, closed, and locked the door. "Come in, dinner is almost done." She rocked Ce'Asia and swayed her hips to the music.*

"Yeah, she is getting big and driving daddy crazy." Malik closed the door behind him. He placed Ce'Asia's bag on the floor by the couch and followed Monique to the kitchen.

Malik inhaled the aromas in the house, and a smile came across his lips. The soothing sounds of R&B played lightly in the background causing peace to take over his soul, making him feel right at home. To Malik, Monique was the only peace he had, unlike many others in his life all she wanted was true friendship, and her loyalty earned her that.

"She is so precious, she didn't do anything wrong. Ain't that right, Asia?" She nuzzled her nose into Ce'Asia's neck and enjoyed the sweet smell of baby lotion and Dreft detergent. She was so sweet and chocolate with China doll eyes. "Damn, I miss this feeling." Monique hugged Ce'Asia tightly.

"I can leave her here. Or I could hook you up, I don't miss," he joked.

"Yeah, right, and the first time the baby cries, I'll be in my car heading to your house to drop it off. Like fuck that, with my hand out and pay me for my pain and suffering." She busted out laughing.

"I'll just add them to the tribe, nigga need a team." Malik laughed along picturing her pulling up just dropping his poor baby on the porch and driving off.

"Nah nigga what you need is dick control, and stop talking slick before I resend my invite," Monique joked as she sat KoKo in the high-backed chair and snapped her in snug.

"Whatever. Damn, it smells good as hell up in here." Malik was rubbing his hands together and licking his lips as he eyed all the dishes on the table. "Where is my hug?"

"If you stop fucking with them birds, you could get a real nigga meal," Monique joked as she kissed Ce'Asia's cheeks then stepped into his embrace.

"Why you always popping shit about my stable?" Malik squeezed her tightly.

"That weak-ass stable. You need a real rider in your corner if you plan on winning the race," Monique taunted enjoying the exchange.

"All the real bitches are taken." He looked at her like she could melt in his mouth and his hands.

"Don't start shit you can't follow up on. Besides, you know that bitch Kisha would be sleeping on my fuckin' porch if she knew you was up close to

16

the realest bitch she will ever know." She chuckled then broke their embrace pushing him a few inches back.

"Is it like that?" He raised his eyebrow intrigued by the possibilities.

"Boy, bye, go sit down!" She went back to the stove to give them some distance.

"Scary ass," he mumbled as he took his seat.

"Yeah, okay." Mo twisted her lips as she grabbed their plates. "Kayson!" she yelled out.

Within seconds he was right there. "Yes, mommy." He popped in the kitchen full of life with his hazel eyes beaming brightly. "Uncle Malik." He ran up to Malik and Ce'Asia.

Ce'Asia lit up when she saw Kayson and wiggled her little body in excitement.

"Heyyyy...Asia! Asia." He grabbed her little hands and waved them in the air.

"What's up, nephew? You being good?" Malik asked as he ruffed Kayson up a little.

"Yesss..." Kayson giggled as he twists himself free. He punched Malik in the arm a few times then ran to his chair.

"I see you, little man. Gonna have to watch what I say." Malik chuckled at young Kayson trying to assert his strength.

"That's right," Kayson stated boldly as he hopped up in the chair.

Malik laughed as Ce'Asia danced and giggled in the highchair. "Daddy's girl." He tickled her ribs.

"Did you wash your hands, young man?" Monique asked placing the big silver tray in the middle of the table.

"Yes, ma'am." He got up on his knees to peek inside the pan as she removed the lid. Kayson closed his eyes and inhaled deeply. When he opened his little lids, he smiled and rubbed his hands together.

"Damn, ma, that's what I'm talking about." Malik did a slow shuffle with his shoulders.

"Wow! You got two bitches and you still be hungry," she slickly stated as she filled his plate with the tender meat and sides.

"That's why I come here on Sundays. I know you gonna feed me."

"Whatever! Don't get used to it, I'm about to start charging." She giggled as she made the other plates then took a seat. "Can you say the prayer, Malik?" she requested.

"Yes, I can." Malik bowed his head and Monique and Kayson followed his lead as he began to speak a good word over the meal, "In the name of the beneficent, the most merciful. We continue to thank you for all your many blessings and mercy. Please continue to protect the beautiful soul that has prepared this meal and the family we have built, and if any dirt should fall from our hands, please show mercy to our children. Amen."

"Amen." Monique opened her eyes and instantly connected with each person at the table as his prayer rang truer than it needed to. She quickly forced a smile forcing the rising emotions back to the pit of her stomach.

"Amen. I'm ready." Kayson wiggled as he placed a napkin on his lap.

"Let's get it." Monique picked up her utensils.

"I'm about to hurt this food, y'all playing," Malik said as his eyes roamed over the thick chicken breast smothered in onions, peppers and gravy, and glazed baby carrots.

She had topped it off with fresh mashed potatoes with sour cream and chives, grilled string beans, and homemade butter biscuits. Monique smiled as she watched her best friend enjoy every bite. Once they'd all had a few bites, Malik started joking back and forth with Monique and Kayson. Little Ce'Asia giggled and screamed as the laughter in the room escalated. Monique smiled widely watching Kayson enjoy what he called his favorite day of the week. For those short hours' life was regular for them all. They had what each of them loved the most in one room, untainted.

Kayson ate his last bite and ran to put his plate in the sink then headed over to harass Malik. Monique cherished their relationship. It was one she could depend on. Malik had been taking up the slack for Tyquan for years, and that was what brought him her loyalty.

"Get ready to have your bath," Monique instructed Kayson as she began clearing the table.

"Okay, mommy. Thanks, Uncle Malik!" Kayson hugged him tightly.

"Always, little man. You know you, my partner. You six, right?"

"Yup and I'm strong." He flexed his muscles.

Malik reached into his pocket and pulled out a small stack of cash. *"You need to go get you some shit you can flex on these niggas in."* He handed Kayson the cash. *"Count it out."*

"One…two…three…" Kayson counted the hundreds until he got to the last bill. *"Ten, thanks, Uncle Malik."* He jumped into his arms.

"You know I got you," Malik said as a tightness took over his chest.

"See you next, Sunday," Kayson said breaking their embrace. He then ran over to a dozing Ce'Asia and kissed her little cheeks. *"Bye, Asia! Asia,"* he said as he ran to his mother and hugged her around her waist then took off thumbing through his riches.

"You don't always have to give him money every Sunday. You know when I invite you here it is to relax, have peace, and enjoy yourself. You don't owe us nothing." Monique crossed her arms over her chest.

"That's my buddy. You know I'ma make sure he good and you as well." He looked sternly in her eyes.

"Thank you," she stated grateful for all he did for her and Kayson.

"Always," he confirmed his loyalty.

Monique became overloaded with emotion as she stood before the only man she could say she truly loved. *"Let me go get him situated. I'll be right back,"* she announced as she walked off to check on Kayson.

Malik started to walk behind her and was reality checked by the sound of his baby girl, *"Da, Da,"* Ce'Asia called out with her arms raised.

"Yes, Princess?" Malik walked over to the high-chair and took Ce'Asia's limp body into his arms.

"I'ma change her in your room!" Malik hollered just when the water began to run.

"Go ahead!" she yelled back.

Malik retrieved a few items from the diaper bag then headed down the hall. He entered Monique's bedroom and laid sleepy Ce'Asia on the bed. She rubbed her little eyes as Malik adjusted her clothes.

"Awwww…Daddy's Princess is sleepy." He smiled as Ce'Asia's heavy lids lowered.

Malik got Ce'Asia clean and dry, then changed her into a spare outfit. Once he was done putting her together, he patted softly on her back until she was sound asleep with her mouth open. When he heard a light snore, he placed *a few pillows around her then eased off the bed and out the room pulling the door slightly closed.*

On his way back into the living room, he stopped and stared at the new photos on the wall Monique had put up along the hall. "Damn, ma," he said as his eyes zoomed in on the fat pussy print in her jeans.

Malik always flirted but never crossed the line. Monique was the type of woman that most would say was way out of his league. She was wise, wealthy, powerful, and older than him.

Monique had become someone whose friendship was very important and valuable to him but the desire to see what that pussy do would creep to the front of his mind every so often. He shook off the sensations, then peeked in on Kayson who'd also closed his tired eyes. Malik pulled the door closed and headed to the kitchen where he heard Monique shuffling dishes.

"Where is little mama? She can't hang, huh?" She chuckled as she rinsed the last few pots.

"Shit, I'm the one who needs a fuckin' nap." Malik laughed as he picked up the last two plates from the table and brought them to the counter.

"I got it, sit down and relax," Monique said as she pushed him toward the chair.

"You know I don't mind. You be hooking a brother up." He grabbed some grapes from the bowl on the table, popped them in his mouth, then took a seat.

Monique rinsed the two plates and cups then added them to the dish rack. "So, what are you going to do about the change of hands that's about to take place?" She dried her hands then turned to receive his response.

"This shit gonna be messy, Mo," Malik said as he thought of everything that had been put into play.

"I don't want to lose anybody else I love." She got choked up at the thought.

"We just gotta move smart, Mo." He smiled at her in an effort to ease her mind. "Let me give you something before I gotta get up outta here." He rose to his feet and headed to the living room to retrieve Ce'Asia's backpack.

Monique eyed his chiseled frame in that fresh white T-shirt and crisp blue jeans laying on all that sexy chocolate. Malik placed the bag into the chair and grabbed a few yellow envelopes and a folder. He looked through the

20

contents then slid them out onto the table. Monique walked over to his side and stared down at the money, passports, and jewelry on the table.

"What is all this stuff?" she asked as their eyes connected.

"You are the only one I trust, Mo." He put his hand on her shoulder. "I need you to protect my babies throne."

"I can't..." she said a little over a whisper as the reality of his request sank in.

"Mo, I already know it's a target on my back. These niggas know they gotta kill me, cause I ain't gonna stop," he asserted.

"Malik, I'ma do whatever it takes to make sure that doesn't happen." Monique tried to comfort him as the water that was building up in her eyes began to slide down her face.

"I know, Ma, but listen carefully we don't have much time," Malik began running things down and explaining the money and property that was to be allotted to each of his kids. He instructed her on what to do for his mother and what to do for his wife and Kisha. He had everything laid out down to the penny.

Monique stared blankly as she tried to process what he was asking of her.

Malik placed his finger under her chin and brought her gaze back to him. "Listen, Mo, I need you to make sure you also give each of my daughters one of these when they get eighteen." He held up two gold and diamond necklaces. "And this is for you and Kayson." He pointed at an envelope that sat slightly to the side. "This one, you look in only if something happens to me," the words left his mouth and a pain shot up to his heart as he passed her a black sealed envelope.

"Malik, this shit we are in is fucked up," she uttered wiping the water from her face.

"It's all good, Ma. I'm just covering the bases just in case. And you are the only one I trust." He strived to ease her fears.

Malik reached out and pulled her into his arms. Monique closed her eyes and rested against his chest while recording his scent and every bit of comfort from his embrace.

"I got you, Malik. You don't have shit to worry about. I got you," she mumbled through her tears.

"I know, Ma and I got you," he confirmed.

21

Monique broke their embrace then turned her attention back to the items on the table. "Okay, run this by me again?" She asked as she wiped her eyes and really paid attention this time.

After Malik went through everything the second time, she was now secure in her mission. She gathered everything from the table organized it well and headed down to the basement to her wall safe. When she returned, Malik was sitting on the couch with his hands folded staring down at a spot on the rug. She opted to not disrupt, instead walked over to the kitchen, grabbed a shot glass, and filled it to the middle then headed back in his direction.

"You good?" she asked, passing him a short glass of white liquor then took a seat beside him.

"Yeah, I'm good now, Mo. I'm about to get little mama home." He swigged down his drink in two swallows.

"Yeah, you don't want to be on punishment. Those bitches be on yo' ass." She laughed at the thought of him having two women with babies the same age.

"This is grown man dick, I run shit," he said as he stood placing his empty glass on the table.

"Whatever, you run your mouth that's about it." She stood also.

"You better stick to what you used to. Fuck around and need ya pussy replaced." Monique's mouth dropped as the last word left his lips. "Just like I thought. All that mouth and nowhere to put it," he returned.

"Shut up and go get little mama." She pushed her hand against his chest. "And trust me, you don't want this mouth on you. Fuck around and have God mad at me 'cause you fucked up your chance to get into heaven," she seductively reminded him.

"Sheeeiitt…I know heaven is between those bowlegs. I'm sure I can make both of us find God with every stroke."

"Like I said, nigga, you don't want it," she quickly responded. "Let's go, sir, it's getting late." She kept walking putting needed distance between them.

Malik walked behind her watching as her round ass rotated in that tight body dress, rocking with every step. He just shook his head and calmed his dick.

"You better hit me when you get home crazy…" Monique paused and turned in his direction.

"I will, and just remember everything is going to be fine, beautiful." He stepped a little closer then leaned in and wrapped her in his arms. Monique held a firm grip as if it would be her last time. "Remember what I told you. And know, I love you, Mo!" He took a deep breath as he prepared to let her go.

"I love you, too," she confessed as the gravity of everything they'd been through took over her soul.

Malik pulled back, put his finger under her chin, then placed a single kiss on her lips. Monique gave up the struggle and released a flood from her eyes as she enjoyed the softest kiss she'd ever tasted.

She squeezed his arms as she pulled back. "Thank you." She ran her tongue slowly over her lips. Monique felt heavy on her feet as she battled with the on slot of emotions that flowed hot through her body.

"Stay here, let me get the baby," she said as she backed up, headed to retrieve Ce'Asia.

"No. Thank you. I owe you, ma," he confessed as he watched her put more space between them.

"I know you do," she shot back as she turned the corner.

Malik took a deep breath, ran his hands over his face, then turned back to the couch. He grabbed the baby bag and stood silently waiting for her to return.

"She is still really sleepy," Monique spoke softly as she placed her on his shoulder. "Don't forget to hit me when you get in," she requested and grabbed the knob pulling the door open.

"See you in a couple of days," Malik said as he passed through the open space.

"Get home safely," her voice lowered as the door closed shut.

Monique wanted to yell out, "Stay!" Instead, she closed the door and secured herself on the other side.

She stood lifeless staring around the living savoring all the memories of the night. She walked into the kitchen, hit the light, turned off the radio, and checked on Kayson before heading back to the basement to review the contents of the envelopes. Her hands shook as she twisted the dial on the safe.

When it popped open, she grabbed everything into her arms, headed over to the table, and laid it all out. Monique shuffled through the envelopes all *except the one she was instructed not to touch. She took one of the necklaces and held it in her hands, then brought it to her nose.*

A light trace of Malik's cologne filled her nostrils and her mind with so many happy thoughts. She took one last look over the paperwork recording all she could then she began placing each document back into its place. When Monique went to put the necklaces back, she saw a few pictures stuck to the inside of the envelope. Quickly she fished them out and thumbed through them. She could see him, and the little girls who she knew were Ce'Asia and Star. But confusion set in and her brow ruffled when she read the back of the last one. "My son?"

"It is now safe to take off your seat belts. Thank you for flying with Delta Airlines. The weather here in New York City is eighty degrees. Please enjoy your stay!" the loud voice of the flight attendant broke Monique from her thoughts.

She sat up, pulled her hat down over her shades, grabbed her Louie, and exited the plane. Her legs moved swiftly as she headed to the front entrance of the airport. Monique stepped out of the double doors, and her eyes settled on her brother Rabb.

"You okay?" he asked coming around to her side to open the door.

"I will be," she stated coldly as she hopped in the front seat.

Rabb closed her door, moved swiftly to his side, eased into the seat, and sped off.

Monique looked in the backseat at Kayson fast asleep and for a mere second, her soul felt peace.

"So, what's the plan, Mo?"

Monique didn't change her expression or her mood. "There is only one thing to do…" She paused and looked over at Rabb. "I'm about to spill blood."

Chapter 2

Family or Foe

Tyquan sat patiently waiting for the ladies to arrive, he pulled hard on his cigar while rubbing the pearl on the handle of his .45, as he eyed the area. Tyquan looked out over the water at the darkness covering the city. A light drizzle played on the hood of his truck and the moonlight danced along the river.

The days Tyquan prayed would never come had just kicked the door in and put that same foot up their asses without a handshake or introduction. He knew there was no way to stop the hell that was coming, and the only way to survive was to be the grimiest player in the room and ready to kill friend, family, or foe.

Tyquan brought the Cuban to his lips and prepared for another pull when the glare of headlights approaching brought him back to the here and now. One car after another came to rest next to where he was parked, and each engine quieted as the ladies exited their vehicle. He looked over Brenda's long, slender frame adorned with all black to suit her mood. Her short-tapered cut accented her high cheekbones which were slightly covered by dark designer shades.

Tyquan looked in Pashion's direction as she swayed her thick hips towards him, with each stride her dark red, leather ankle boots dug into the blacktop. He could see trouble guiding her every step. Tyquan put his cigar in the ashtray and tucked his gun in his waist before stepping out of the car. He adjusted the buttons on his jacket and prepared to pass out everyone's fate.

"What the fuck is going on?" Pashion was the first to speak her mind.

"Calm down so you can hear me."

"Fuck you mean calm down? My whole fuckin' family is in danger!" She escalated the mood.

"Lower your fuckin' voice," Tyquan warned as he stepped forward slightly.

"You better watch your fuckin' tone!" she spat back.

"We can't start fighting each other." Brenda grabbed Pashion by the arm.

"Fuck that, they took my child!" Pashion snatched away from Brenda then removed the shades from her eyes. "The only thing I want to hear out of his fucking mouth is how he's going to make this shit right," she barked as tears of anger and rage flowed down her cheeks.

Tyquan thought long and hard about his next words as he stared into her eyes right into Pashion's pain-filled soul. "Pashion, I can't say I know how you feel because I don't…" he paused and gauged her mood.

"I know you don't fuckin' know. They didn't touch your house, they touched *mine.*"

Pashion stood only inches away from his chest, with her aching heart pumping against her breastplate wanting to release its venom from her lips. She quieted her voice behind shivering lips and waited for him to dig the hole she was going to bury him in.

"Look I didn't come out here to fight with you. We are all we got. This shit we are up against could cost all of us our lives," he spoke plain words. "What we need to do to make this shit right is going to take clear minds," he stated calmly before things reheated.

"Pashion, please just listen to, Tyke. You know he got us," Brenda cut in.

Pashion cut her eyes over at her. '*Brainwashed ass,*' she thought then looked back at Tyquan. "Say what you gotta say," she responded with an icy chill hanging from every word.

Tyquan watched her attempt at restraint then continued with extreme caution. He ran down each part of the plan and what needed to be done immediately. His empty, hazel eyes rotated back and forth between Pashion and Brenda. The coldness that stared back at him let him know his enemies were about to die a slow horrendous death.

Pashion listened closely as he planned out her future. She could not believe that within a weeks' time she was about to bury her daughter and son-in-law and lose more than half of her family. Her mind rotated back and forth between what had been done, and what must be done, then the bow broke the water she was protecting so safely behind her lids, causing hot steam to fall uncontrollably down onto her jacket.

"This ain't no time for fear. We in the middle of a muthafucking war zone." He looked in Pashion's eyes and then in Brenda's. He paused slightly as he choked back his own brand of pain. "Most important we gotta keep the kids safe."

Brenda stared out at the moon shining down on the water as she too listened to their whole life change.

"Are you done?" Pashion asked through tight lips.

"I need y'all to chill the fuck out and let me handle this." Tyquan flipped into attack mode.

"What the fuck are you talking about?" Pashion stepped even closer to him. "That's my child laying cold muthafucka," she gritted with fists balled tight.

"You don't think I know what the fuck just happened?" he barked back.

"I don't give a fuck what you know." Pashion looked into his dark soul. "You go ahead and complete everything on your little laundry list. I'ma go ahead and clear up mine," Pashion spat on the ground next to his feet. "And stay out my fucking way." She threw her shades back on her eyes, then turned in the direction of her car.

"Pashion, we gotta trust, Tyke, right now." Brenda grabbed her arm.

"Bitch, you fucking trust him." She snatched away from her. "As long as y'all still got kids breathing, you ain't on my fuckin' level." She straightened her jacket then continued as she pointed in Tyquan's direction. "You better do whatever it takes to keep your promise to Malik. But just stay outta my way while you are doing it," she warned then turned her back on them both.

"Pashion, we gotta stick together!" Brenda yelled out.

"*We are together!* Y'all just stand the fuck over there." She jumped in her car and sped off.

"Fuck!" Tyquan pounded his fist into the palm of his hand. "We gotta slow her the fuck down."

"What do you expect her to say or do. They touched her house," Brenda barked at Tyquan. "They broke us, Tyke. We fucked up, right now."

Tyquan bit into his bottom lip as he chose his words wisely. Things were moving way too fast and all outside of the scope of his plans.

"I just need y'all to carry out your part and let me engineer this big shit. Y'all got to sit still until I can put my foot on the line," he tried to convince her.

Brenda touched him gently on the arm. "You can ask us to sit still all day. But you know good and fucking well, you ain't going to be able to calm Pashion. And you will never be able to stop Mo," Brenda reminded him.

Tyquan took a deep breath as the reality of her arrival burned in his belly. "I'll handle Mo," he replied as an entourage of thoughts crowded his mind.

"You better make sure you do," Brenda stated as she stepped back a few feet. "*Make sure you do,*" she repeated as she too headed to her car.

Tyquan watched her sashay away and the words she left behind played in his head like a scratched CD on repeat. For a moment, he had pushed the thoughts of what Monique was about to do to the back of his mind but because karma is a crooked bitch, he was about to face every demon he created.

Tyquan moved to his truck and jumped inside. It was murder season, and his list was yearning to be satisfied.

****

Rabb pulled up to the pool hall, parked, and hurried inside. "Yo, did y'all hear what the fuck just happened?" he asked as he threw his cards on the table. He nodded at J-Bone as he continued to his office not breaking his stride.

"Hell yeah. What the fuck we gonna do?" J-Bone asked as he rose to his feet. "That's game niggas pay me." He threw the rest of his cards down snatched the stack of twenties then followed Rabb to the back of the club.

"Y'all niggas tighten up!" he yelled as he exited the open area.

Rabb and J-Bone entered the back office and closed the door behind them. Once on the other side, Rabb enforced his orders.

"We gonna chill and wait for instructions," Rabb enforced as he walked over to his desk and pulled open the top drawer. He reached inside and got his gun, then tucked it in the small of his back.

J-Bone watched as Rabb suited up and played with what he was about to say. Then decided *fuck it.* "Man, I think we need to let this be the situation that we move on," he said with a slight bit of hesitation in his tone.

"What the fuck you mean make a move?" Rabb asked as he came from around his desk.

"Fuck it, let's put this shit on the table. We have been loyal as hell and we still have only one area to work out of. If we make a move, we can have our pick of whatever the fuck we want." He stood silent waiting for his comrades' response.

Rabb stared at the defined lines in J-Bone's face. He studied his body language as he filtered the disloyal hand he wanted him to partake in.

"Allow me to put some shit on the table as well…" he paused then moved a little closer. "Ain't no fucking moves to be made.

29

We have been good from day one. I don't have more territory because I never requested any. And no muthafucka ever gonna ask or fight for no shit on my behalf." He looked J-Bone in his eyes with an intense glare that caused his friend's knees to buckle just a bit.

J-Bone calmed his raging spirit and chose his words well. He could tell that now was not going to be the time to make a friend an enemy.

"Cool." He threw his hands up in surrender. "We gonna chill and wait for instructions. Anything else?"

"Nah, ain't nothing else. I didn't ask for the shit you just gave me." Rabb was getting increasingly heated by the second.

Malik had barely been introduced to his grave and this nigga wanted to war over a chair still tainted from lethal injection.

"I know me and you ain't about to fight over these other nigga's shit?" J-Bone turned his head to the side shocked that his brother was speaking to him with such venom.

"Nah, we ain't fighting over shit. You are asking me to step in the middle of the road when traffic is coming just to sit on a dead man's throne." He tried to jolt his friend back into reality.

"I'm just saying we need to be sitting at that fuckin' table not waiting for the orders to hit the kitchen."

"I have always been at the table. Even when I'm not in the room. What the fuck have you been paying attention to?" Rabb's voice deepened as he became more aggravated with J-Bone's audacity.

"Look my bad, I'm on your side. But no worries, I'ma play my position." He again threw his hands up but this time decided to head toward the door.

Distance was definitely needed before either man said too much and went too far. "I'ma get everybody on point," he continued as he pulled the door open and headed back to the pool room.

"J-Bone!" Rabb yelled.

"What's up?" J-Bone stopped and stood in place without turning back in Rabb's direction.

"Just fuck with me, I got us." He tried to calm the situation before they parted.

"I know, but I promise you Malik's camp didn't think they would need coffins after he said he had them."

J-Bone's words hit Rabb in the center of his chest. He was thrown off balance briefly then he enforced who the fuck he was.

"If you have not been welcoming death from the first day you signed up for this shit. You in the wrong fuckin' game."

J-Bone stood still a little longer pondering Rabb's last sentence. He wanted to respond but figured since his back was already turned he needed to keep it that way. He left out with the same energy he'd entered with closing the door hard behind him.

Rabb walked over and clicked the locks then headed back to his desk and picked up the phone. He paged Rashaad and waited for him to call back.

"What's up?"

"I need you to up security and keep a good eye on J-Bone."

"Is there a problem?" Rashaad went right into attack mode.

"Not yet, I just need your eyes and hands-on everything," he gave firm orders.

"On it," Rashaad replied then disconnected the call.

When he turned around, he scanned his mind trying to see where each man's heart was. The loyalty of his crew had never been tested. But today there would be an amendment to all rules and freedom, equality and opportunity was going to rest at the end of his gun. Rabb came around his desk and plopped hard onto the highbacked, leather chair. He rested his elbow on the armrest then laid his head on his hand.

Rabb looked over at Kayson. "You, ready little man?"

Kayson's young eyes rose from his homework and he nodded as he reached for his book bag.

The crown had just become heavy it was only a matter of time before the head that was wearing it would have death attached to its neck.

Chapter 3

The Shit List

Monique moved quickly through the city hitting a few banks emptying the safety deposit boxes and withdrew all cash from the open accounts. She headed to her Manhattan apartment and tucked everything in a safe place, all except the envelope she prayed she never had to open. Monique's heart skipped against her breastplate as she contemplated what could be inside. She ripped at its seams, pulled out the four-page document, and eyed all the names, accounts, favors that needed to be rendered, and the dirty evidence she needed on each person, so she could make things happen.

Monique's eyes and mind raced as she processed all the input hitting her at once. When she got to the last page and saw a list of his enemies, her eyes widened, and her knees buckled as each name echoed in her head.

"Oh, shit," she mumbled as a hard lump moved up into her throat.

It was no turning back after today. She took one last look at each page and as she began folding the last page over, her eyes went to the first name on the list *Smoke*. Monique always felt he had cross in his heart, but she also understood that whatever lies he had to say, she needed to hear him say it.

"I'm coming for that ass," she spoke aloud.

Monique tore off the last page then placed the document back in place, grabbed her purse, put the single sheet inside, and left the apartment with all the ammo she needed to bring pain and suffering.

"I got you, Malik," she mumbled to herself as she sauntered off the elevator moving quickly towards the thick glass.

The doorman pulled them open as he eyed her elegance in an all-white Gucci pants suite, accented with Platinum and diamonds.

"Enjoy your day, Misses Wells," he said tipping his hat.

"Thank you, Russell," she responded and pulled a few bills from her bra, then placed them in his open palm.

Russell's smile widened when he saw the neatly folded hundred-dollar bills. "Thank you. Thank you so much as always." He brought them to his nose and savored the sweet essence she left behind.

It was something about Monique that always earned her an unspoken loyalty among everyone in her surroundings.

"Have a nice day," he yelled as the limo door closed.

Monique waved her hand then turned her attention to what was in front of her. "Take me downtown." She ordered as she stared out the window. Malik had put a big ass ball in her court, and she had to paint the right illusion before they realized she could barely dribble. She reached in her clutch and checked the contents one last time then snapped it closed. There was no back-peddling from this day forward, she was in this shit knee-deep, and the sacrifices of having such power was what no man wanted to pay.

****

"Pull up right in front," Smoke said as he eyed the area.

"You want me to come inside?" Skully asked as an uneasy feeling filled his gut.

"Nah, I'm good. Just stay close," Smoke responded as he stepped out the back of the Navigator. He slammed the door closed and headed into the hotel.

34

Skully busted a U-turn in the middle of the street and stole a parking space right across from the hotel. He lit a cigarette and eased the window down just a bit. As he reached over to adjust the radio, he saw a black Mercedes pull up and come to a stop.

When the driver jumped out in a crisp black suit, white shirt, and hat, he figured that was their honored guest. He watched as the man walked around and opened the back passenger door, then out stepped what he could only describe as an angel dressed in all white that hugged and accented every curve and sway.

Monique pulled her jacket on her shoulders then headed inside.

"I guess when you losing pull out a pretty bitch." Skully chuckled at the idea that she was the one they sent to put the deal on the table. "Fuck it, we kill pussy, too." His brow crinkled in anger as he thought about the betrayal coming from the very niggas he trusted.

Skully sat watching the mirrors keeping his eyes on all angles while he waited.

"Do you have a reservation, Madam?" The host asked as he came around his station to greet Monique.

"Wells, party of two."

"Yes, your guest has already arrived. Please follow me."

Monique pulled her shades from her face and focused her gaze on the array of people in the room. She scoped out two exits then met eyes with Smoke. She held a serious continence to her face until she reached the table.

Smoke rose to his feet and stood until her chair was pulled out.

"Good afternoon, Miss Wells, please have a seat." He extended his hand.

"Thank you." She took off her jacket and sat on the edge of her chair.

"I appreciate you coming at such short notice."

"*Short notice!* A man was killed, I don't think he got a notice before that," she got right to the point.

"I hear you. So, why the fuck you here?" he also got to the point. Then stared intensely awaiting her answer.

Monique gave no space for fear as she showed him her balls were hanging just as low.

"Hi, I'm Lucy, I will be serving you this afternoon. Can I offer you something to drink?" The waitress cut in as she sat a wine menu in front of them.

"We good for now," Smoke announced not taking his eyes off Monique.

"Okay, well, I'm Lucy just give a wave when you are ready." The woman tried to remove herself from the heated exchange.

"Look, I know you have a hand in more than you will say or admit..." she paused then folded her hands together as she proceeded with her point. "The only thing I need you to do is back up. Tell the connect you can't work the angle of his numbers, then sit all the way the fuck down."

"Are you fucking serious?" Smoke started laughing. He leaned back and held his stomach as he tried to gain composure. "Wow." He sat up and dropped the smile from his face then proceeded with his verdict.

"First of all, tell whoever sent you over here *fuck you*. Then I want you to get up from this seat and get that wet pussy back to the nigga whose dick you sucking and both of y'all to get the fuck on." He shewed her from the table.

Monique cracked a smile. "I knew you would bring dick and no balls." She reached into her clutch, pulled out a white envelope, and slid it across the table.

"What the fuck is this?" He grabbed it and tore it open. Smoke read over the document line by line. When he got to the last page his heart sank to his feet. "What the fuck?" He flipped the pages back and forth.

"Yeah, I thought so." She stood up and threw her jacket over her shoulders. "Looks like the dick you wish I was sucking is up yo' funky ass." She pulled her clutch close to her body and pushed her shades up on her face. "This ain't no bitches game strap up,

I'll be in touch." She turned and walked away from the table praying with every step he was not up and on her heels.

Monique moved quickly to the exit and just as she approached the door, her driver pulled up. She didn't even wait for the car to come to a complete stop as she snatched the door open and jumped in. "Go!"

As the car sped off Skully sat forward and watched the mist from the tailpipe in the rearview mirror. Skully fixed his gaze on the entrance to the hotel. Smoke was storming out and heading in his direction with flared nostrils and tight lips. Skully turned the key in the ignition and popped the locks. Smoke hopped into the front passenger seat and slammed the door so hard the window shook in its place.

"What the fuck happened in there?" Skully asked as he pulled into traffic.

"That fucking bitch is way more dangerous than we thought." He looked over at Skully.

"What the fuck did she say? Who is she working with?" He rotated his eyes from Smoke to the oncoming traffic.

"I don't know yet. But I will say this that bitch is dedicated."

"What the fuck is that supposed to mean?" Skully stopped at the red light and clicked his turn signal.

Smoke took a minute and played with the answer he wanted to give. He stared out the front window then looked over at his friend. "Remember this when a nigga is about to fall and he puts all his trust in a bitch. It's because he knows when he does that bitch is gonna come back with a bigger bank and stronger army."

Skully looked over at his boss and for the first time and saw worry on his face. He turned the corner then pumped the radio all the way up. It was killing season and it seemed that the pretty bitch in the white had just passed out the permits.

****

Pashion pulled up slowly and darted her eyes at the water dancing on the streetlights in the distance. Reluctant to dead her engine, she sat watching the wipers glide against the glass. Tears filled the slits of her puffy eyes forcing her lids to close as distorted visions filled her mind of the pain and suffering her child endured.

"Why God, why? What did we do to deserve so much pain?" she humbly asked and listened closely to the universe, but there was no comforting sound that could ease her bleeding heart.

The money, deceit, and power had earned them a price of death that had missed their heads only to force the penalty of their sins onto their children.

Pashion opened her eyes as she choked down her saliva, then forced the love she had left to the bottom of her soul. She turned off the ignition, popped opened the door, and extended her umbrella. She fought against the wind and rain as she headed to the covered porch.

Pashion threw the soaking wet umbrella in a corner by the door then turned her key in the lock. She stepped inside securing the door behind her, then stood still as an assortment of floral scents filled her nostrils.

"Sis, where you at?" Pashion announced herself as she eyed the dimly lit sitting room off to her left.

Pashion pulled off her trench and threw it over the banister then headed down the marble hallway. "Sis, upstairs?" she called out as she flipped a light switch and ascended the stairs.

Pashion slipped the .38 out of her sleeve and rested it in her palm. Slowly she eased toward the bedroom door taking a deep breath with every step.

When Pashion got close to the last door on the left, she heard the faint sound of muffled whimpers. She laid her head against the door for a few seconds then turned the knob and proceeded to enter. Her eyes settled on her friend laying on the floor with a pillow clutched tightly in her arms and tears streaming from the corners of both eyes.

"Awww…Mama." Pashion put the gun on the dresser, walked over and kneeled beside her, then pulled her head onto her lap. "It's going to be okay. We will get through this," she tried to convince them both.

"They took my son…my king. They took my heart!" she cried out from the pit of her stomach.

"And they took my child, too," Pashion's voice cracked with every word.

"What did we do? What did we do?" Malika mumbled as she stared at the wedding picture of Malik and Sabrina.

The reality of everything they'd done flooded from her soul while memories of one evil deed in exchange for the next caused vomit to rise to the back of her throat.

"Whatever we did we didn't deserve to have our children touched the way they touched them."

Malika jumped up and ran to the bathroom slamming the door behind her. She barely made the toilet as she released everything she had left. She gagged and held her chest as her body locked up with every violent motion until there was nothing left to give. She shuffled slowly to the sink and attempted to wash her hands and face avoiding the mirror and hideous sight staring back at her.

Malika threw some mouth wash in her mouth, spat, and rinsed, then dragged her grief-stricken body back to the bedroom. She walked back to where Pashion sat and dropped back to the floor.

Pashion took a deep breath as she too thought about how badly their children had suffered, and now it seemed they would have the same fate. She rubbed the sides of Malika's face in an attempt to calm her weary spirit.

"We painted their future in tainted blood. They never stood a chance," Malika whispered.

Pashion's heart skipped a beat as the reality of what they had done took root. "Well, now they owe us."

Malika wiped the back of her hand across her eyes and nose. "The only thing they can pay me back with is the souls of their sons."

"And they will," Pashion vowed. "Come on get up, ma. We gotta get you showered and in some fresh clothes." She helped Malika up to her feet.

Malika sat on the edge of the bed and watched as Pashion gathered her things. She slipped off her shoes and began pulling her shirt over her head.

Ding! Dong! The bell rang and jolted them both out of their thoughts and movement.

"Who the fuck is that?" Pashion said as she went to the window.

Pashion peeked out the side of the curtain but the tree limited her vision. "Stay right here," she ordered. She grabbed her .38 from the dresser and headed downstairs.

Malika wiped her face with her shirt, grabbed the sawed-off from under her bed frame, and followed Pashion down the stairs.

Pashion gripped the handle tightly ready to bust anything moving. She eased to the door as the bell rang again.

Ding! Dong!

Malika positioned herself in the middle of the staircase. She pumped a shell into the chamber then nodded at Pashion to go for the door. Pashion gently placed her hand on the knob and used the end of the gun to move the curtain. Malika stood breathing heavily as she awaited the chance to transfer some of her pain.

When Pashion saw the side of Monique's pretty-red face, she let out a sigh of relief and waved at Malika to stand down, then quickly popped the locks.

"Y'all good up in here?" Monique asked as she passed through the entrance.

"Yeah, we good," Pashion responded, she looked out the door, then locked it back.

"Shit, Mo, I was ready to go," Malika said as she lowered her gun.

40

"That's the way I trained you," Monique reminded as she headed to the living room.

Malika trotted down the steps and entered right behind Pashion.

"So, what the fuck are we about to do?" Pashion went straight to the point.

Monique pulled off her wet jacket and scarf and threw it on the chair then took a seat. "We gotta take everything they own, then everything they love." She looked up at Malika and Pashion the hurt that stared back at her only fueled an already kindling fire.

"That's what the fuck I'm talking about. Let me get us some shit to drink so we can get to business." Pashion walked over to the glass chest and opened it wide.

Malika placed her gun on the coffee table and plopped down on the couch. As her body sank into the cushions, she shook her head at what was about to take place.

Pashion walked over and passed each of them a short glass of something dark and strong. She poured herself one a little taller then joined Malika on the couch.

"Let me start by saying, I'm sorry for your loss." Monique took her time with her words. "I can't say I know how you feel because I don't. But I will say this…" she paused. "I will not stop until they all feel the pain that I imagine you are feeling, plus some." She looked at the anguish that choked the spirit out of two of her best soldiers.

"I just want to make sure none of us buries another child," Malika said as the tears ran down her soft brown cheeks.

"Every tear you shed they will shed over ten of theirs." Monique laid it on the table as her gaze connected with theirs. She downed her drink in two gulps then eased the glass onto the hardwood.

"Let's make these muthafuckas pay."

Monique began running down a few levels of her plan leaving out what she needed to. When she was done Pashion ran down all she had put into place, then brought her up to speed about her little meeting with Tyquan.

41

Malika sat there looking back and forth between them both. She was mentally and spiritually exhausted. She was hearing them but not really hearing them. She was there, but not there. She watched as her two comrades put pieces in place that could possibly get them all killed.

Malika had only dealt with a few people, and the ones she trusted, took her son's life. She sat battling with the thoughts of who she could actually trust, and which one of the people she did trust would turn on her to save their spot at the table? Her head was about to explode when Monique stopped and looked in her direction.

"Malika, I know everything is fucked up, right now. But know that I made your son some promises I am *not* going to fail at keeping. I promise you that. Them niggas gonna feel me," she asserted.

"So, what about Tyke?" Pashion asked and waited patiently for Mo's answer.

"Don't worry about Tyke. I will take care of him," she reassured them both. "Just stick to the plan and everything is going to be good." Monique stood to leave.

Pashion nodded her understanding but inside she was a little afraid of Monique's words. Tyquan had power over Mo that nobody else had, and it was that tiny element that could stand in the way of everything she'd just vowed.

"Just know." Pashion rose to her feet. "At any point if I feel shit is going left. I'ma make it right," she stated firmly.

"And you know if it goes left. I'ma kill anyone standing in that direction," Monique confirmed.

"Then let's fucking get it." Pashion extended her hand and right there in that room the exchange of power had begun.

Chapter 4

Bad Hand

"Aahhh…oohhh…my, God!" Zibra called out as she felt her walls stretching with every stroke.

Smoke stood firm in place behind her pounding her insides. He gripped her ass and spread her cheeks so he could hit every corner.

"Nah, come here, Ma. You said you wanted to fuck me…now *fuck* me." Smoke tightened his grip and quickened his stroke.

Zibra clutched the seat belt as her knees pressed against the edge of the chair with each deep forceful push. She closed her eyes and imagined she wasn't there as his thickness felt as if it was filling her stomach.

"Smoke you too deep, baby!" she cried out just as she felt him pick up the pace.

"Shut up and arch this muthafucka," Smoke growled pushing his hand down on her back causing her breasts to press against the cold leather.

Smoke's Tims pressed into the concrete as he fucked fast and hard. His garage was filled with loud sexy moans and the faint sound of music from the car speakers. His belt buckle scratched the ground at his feet accompanied by the sound of her ass cheeks smacking his thighs.

Zibra placed her hand on his wrists in an attempt to have his mercy. But it was no such negotiation. Smoke felt a nut rising in his gut and her tight wet pussy was not going to allow him to stop.

He stared at the drops of sweat as they landed on the small of her back. He leaned in and nibbled along her spine grinding deeper and deeper before rising for his attack.

"Daddy, you all in your pussy." She tightened her grip while trying to breathe through all those inches he was feeding her.

"Damn, baby," Smoke moaned as he felt her pussy pulling him into her womb. "You trying to fuck a nigga up," he huffed taking a few more deep strokes.

Smoke slid out briefly admiring her juices covering his dick. He reached down and played in her wetness then eased her off the seat and bent her all the way over. He spread her legs wide and pushed each inch in slowly until he was all the way back inside her. Zibra braced her hands on the floor as she felt him enter her.

"Smoke…" she purred as the slow easy strokes hit her spot.

"What you need, Ma?" he asked watching her cheeks jiggle and bounce to the rhythm of his stroke.

"I wanna cum, Daddy!" She looked over her shoulder and right into his bloodshot eyes.

Smoke didn't respond with words he let one G talk to the other as he let the head speak the language her pussy was used to.

"Yes…yesss…right there, baby! Spoil your pussy, Daddy!" Zibra cried out as her body began to shake against him.

Smoke didn't miss a beat. Her juices were what he craved, and she was spilling them all down his thighs. He held her in place until her body went slightly limp, then it was his turn.

"Now, Daddy wanna cum," he said in a devious tone.

"Smoke be gentle," she whined.

"I can't," he hissed pushing her dress to the middle of her back.

Smoke gripped her hips, pushed up on his toes, and drilled every inch hard and fast. He worked her pussy quick and deep hitting everything coming and going. Her moans drowned out the music and all his thoughts as the tight, wet feel of her walls took over his mind.

Zibra's nails pressed into the garage floor as she prayed that the nigga would cum quick. Just as she felt his fingertips dig into her flesh, and his breathing quicken, she pulled forward, turned toward him and kneeled before his glory, then put him to the back of her throat.

"Oh, shit!" Smoke took a deep breath as he watched her bob and suck along his rock-hard dick.

Zibra filled her mouth with saliva and got sloppy with it as she jaw-gripped the head while two-hand stroking along his shaft. Smoke grabbed the top of her head and fucked her mouth pushing him deeper into her throat.

"That's what the fuck I'm talking about," he mumbled just as he prepared to release.

Zibra quickened her pace and grip. She opened her legs wider and rubbed her clit. Moaning loud as she played in her wetness, giving Daddy exactly what he needed.

Smoke's dick felt as if it would bust as he watched her play in that pretty, pink pussy. His mouth watered as her juices slid down between her lips and she circled that sweet pearl. He could no longer hold on. He pulled her mouth back and forth along his length until he felt his seed ease out into her throat.

Zibra played no games with it. She sucked and swallowed every drop gripping harder as he tried to pull back.

"Fuck," he barked wanting the same mercy she had just begged for.

Zibra ignored his plea and held him in place as she stroked and sucked the swollen tip without mercy. She felt his fist tighten in her hair as his knees buckled in their place. She slowly eased him from her mouth jaw-gripping his inches along the way. She eased him past her lips then sucked lightly on his balls.

"Mmmm…" she moaned as she looked at him with both lust and greed in her eyes.

"Damn, Ma," he slurred, watching her lick his essence from her pouty lips.

"Smoke!" Swift yelled popping the garage door open entering a kill zone.

"Hold up!" Smoke yelled out as he tried to adjust his semi-hard dick.

45

"My bad, nigga. Do you, I'm in the kitchen," Swift announced as he backed out of the door closing it tightly on his way out.

Zibra rose from her squatted position adjusting her fitted dress until everything was back in place.

"Thanks, Ma." He smiled, then gripped a hand full of her ass.

"Well, you said you wanted to get fucked," she purred as she reached into the back seat and grabbed her bracelets and purse.

Smoke just smiled and rubbed his dick as he watched her sashay by him.

"Here, baby." He reached into his pocket and passed her a small money roll. "Get some fly shit for Daddy to look at."

"Thank you, baby," she cooed tucking the money in her Louie.

Smoke closed the car door then followed her out of the garage palming her ass one more time before they entered the kitchen. He slipped his hand between her legs then brought it to his mouth.

"Damn, and it tastes good! I'm fucking you all night. Let me finish this meeting."

"You so nasty." She looked over her shoulder with a low gaze.

"Yup and I'ma be nasty all in that pussy, too."

"Hey, Swift," she spoke as she headed to the nearby bathroom.

Swift didn't respond he just held a tight lip and low eyes.

"Hurry up." Smoke pulled her close and kissed her lips as she passed him.

"What's up, nigga?" he asked Swift as he walked over to the sink and began washing his hands.

Once they heard Zibra cut on the water, Swift started his spill. "Yo, I found out that fucking bitch you saw the other day is connected to Tyquan, Malik, and the Spanish cat uptown." Swift counted off each name touching the tips of his fingers to drive home his point.

Smoke rested his frame against the counter as he played back the letter Monique showed him trying to see how all the shit was connected.

"Just give me the word, I'll put somebody on all them niggas and their bitches, too."

"Don't do shit, I'ma smoke all them niggas right out to the frontline," Smoke quickly cut in.

Swift nodded his understanding as he tried to control the voices in his head that screamed, *"Just kill that bitch!"*

"I'ma be cool..." he paused. "...for now," he continued while pulling the blunt from the back of his ear.

He turned on the stove and put fire to the end, then pulled deeply as he too tried to capture what this bitch's angle was.

Zibra pressed her ear hard to the door trying to hang onto every word. When silence fell over the room, she threw some mouth wash in her mouth, gargled loudly and spit, then turned off the water. She adjusted her clothes and headed out the door with all she needed.

"You ready, baby?" She smiled and ran her tongue over her top lip.

"Yup," Smoke confirmed then reached his fist out to his brother. "I'll see you later," he confirmed then headed back to the car.

Swift didn't speak a word he just watched his friend exit the room grinding against what he felt was a soulless bitch. He remembered what Smoke had said just several hours ago.

"When a nigga losing he sends in a bitch," But Swift knew when a bitch starts losing her weapon was poison and from what he could see the venom was already running through Smoke's veins. It was just a matter of time until his whole situation would seize up and become numb.

****

Tyquan pulled on his black sweatpants then strapped his boots uptight. He tucked in his white T-shirt then threw on the matching sweat jacket and zipped it halfway up his chest. He walked over to his desk, picked up each weapon and loaded the chambers, then turned them back and forth in his hands. Tyquan laid the steel on the table and took a deep breath. It was the time he prayed would never come. It had been over a decade and he had been able to keep all the lions at bay. But today the den would be tested the heads would knock hard and any sign of weakness could turn you from boss to victim.

Tyquan walked over to the file cabinet and thumbed through a few folders. He grabbed an envelope full of cashiers' checks and stuffed them into his hoodie pocket. He slammed the cabinet doors then stood glaring at his distorted reflection in the wall clock just above the cabinet. He frowned at the man staring back at him. It was that beast...that monster within the man he fought so hard not to be.

"This what the fuck y'all wanted? Let's fuckin' go!" he said aloud then turned to strap up.

Once his guns were firm in place, Tyquan grabbed the small black duffel bag and headed out the door. He jumped in his truck and pulled out of the garage. As he drove, he began pumping himself up with visions of how dirty they did Malik and Sabrina. His blood rushed hot through his veins as he sped through the busy New York streets. He needed to be anything but human when he pulled up to the devil's door. The heat was waiting, and he was about to deliver its fury.

Chapter 5

Pain & Fury

One car after the next pulled into the factory opening driving past the heavily armed men strategically placed throughout the large dimly lit space. They were waved in each car passed through the gate and came to rest. The large iron doors slammed closed just as they began to exit their vehicles causing an eerie chill to ease across their necks.

The men made eye contact just before heading to the empty seats with the look of fear and death on all their faces. There they were all in one room the head and second in command from each family. All twenty pieces on the board at one table. Now the big question was who was going to walk away and who wasn't? Security double-checked the perimeter as the men exchanged salutations before taking their seats.

"What can we get you to drink?" a young woman asked as she placed glasses in front of each guest.

"Whatever you recommend," Kingston responded as he eyed the candy in the room.

"Okay, I got something hot, sexy, and slippery you can put in your mouth." She grabbed the Jamaican Rum by the neck.

"Let me find out." He chuckled. "Do that then," he responded as his eyes roamed over her fat ass in those tight jean shorts.

The young lady poured him a shot glass of brown then moved around the table adhering to each man's request.

Scarie leaned over and whispered in his thick Jamaican accent, "Stay focused." Then took his glass into his hand.

"You got it, Boss," Kingston answered as he took the shot to the head.

Once she filled the last of the glasses she cut and lit the ends of their cigars. "Can I get you anything else?" she asked.

"No! Thank you, beautiful," Carmine responded then pulled a small stack of cash from his jacket pocket. He held it in the air until she reached him then placed it gently in her palm.

"Thank you," she said flashing him her girlish grin before disappearing like she was never there.

Tyquan was the last to pull up. He eased past the gates nodding at security as he drove through. He watched the gates close and lock behind him as he parked in the back. Tyquan walked up to the doors, performed his series of knocks, and was let right in. All eyes were on him as he proceeded toward the seated men dressed in all black and a dark spirit to match. He walked right up to the table and just stood over the shoulder of one of his most trusted men.

"You good, Tyke?" Loco asked as he secured the locks.

"We will see," he responded as he walked to where Scarie was seated.

He looked over at Big John and his accountant Mr. Jacob Stein who were the only two men standing and nodded in their direction.

"So, what is to come of this meeting?" Raul asked as he dutted the ashes of his cigar onto the floor.

"I think we need to let Tyquan put the first cards on the table," Bison stated smoothly.

"Nah, don't extend me the courtesy now. I know you have been in a conversation when I wasn't at the table so by all means. Let me see your hand," Tyquan stated locking eyes with Bison.

The air became thick as eyes met from across the table then tongues followed.

50

"Look, I think we need to hurry up and get a handle on this shit we are all losing money. The connect knows we are hit. We need to make them niggas comfortable," Sanchez cut in.

Raul touched Sanchez on his arm, and he sat back.

"Nah, let the little nigga talk," Tyquan asserted.

Sanchez looked over at Raul then at Alex and Antonio before he continued, "Look this shit is a young man's game. We need to move the old pieces off the board and let the new energy make the next moves."

"Oh, is that what you think?" Tyquan cut in looking at him then at Alex and Antonio. "And you two niggas think it's a good idea?" He paused. "What this little nigga just said, *get rid of the old?* You feel comfortable with that?"

"I'm just saying, it seems like we losing with y'all in charge," the young nigga's heart began to pump fast as the free words flowed through his lips.

Tyquan formed a smirk across his lips as he looked around the table checking each man's soul.

"Then that settles it." Tyquan put both arms out as if he was welcoming the idea.

Confusion eased across the once confident face.

"Come over here and join me with all your great ideas."

"Don't mind if I do." Sanchez got up and took the floor.

He stood next to Tyquan like he was the man as he prepared to rattle off the demands, he had for what he called the *Old Blood.*

"First order of business me, Antonio and Alex are gonna take charge of each borough that we are currently allotted…" he paused. "No more of that weak ass shit. From this day forward anytime we hear of treachery we kill it on-site ask questions never," he boldly stated.

"And you said Alex and Antonio feel the same way you feel?"

"Exactly," he stated in his smug Spanish accent.

"This shit is interesting. Alex and Antonio come 'mere." Tyquan waved them over.

Raul fidgeted in his seat as he watched his young Lieutenant make a mockery of the reputation his crew had built.

"Tyquan, if I may," Raul requested.

"Nah, we gonna see this shit through." Tyquan clutched his fists as he waited for the other two idiots to take the stage.

"I belie…" Alex tried to make his point.

"You believe nothing. I want you to come take a seat!" Bison yelled in his Russian drawl.

"Shut the fuck up!" Tyquan yelled. "And you…talk," he based at Alex.

Alex looked at his boss practically foaming at the mouth then up at an impatient Tyquan and knew he had no other choice but to make his move.

"I was just saying, I believe new blood should be in the seat."

"Well, here's to new blood." Tyquan pulled his gun from his lower back and shot Alex in the forehead, then shot Antonio in the leg.

Sanchez jumped as he watched his boy's head crack against the cement floor.

The men shuffled in their seats as the armed men pulled their AKs and pointed in their direction. Antonio wailed out in pain holding his hand over his gaping wound.

"What the blood clot!" Scarie yelled as his mind flashed to the other night where he had just taken Malik's life.

"Shut the fuck up!" Tyquan's voice boomed through the warehouse.

"You muthafuckas wanna rule but don't wanna pay no dues." He pointed his gun in each man's direction. "Tonight, the debts will be paid."

Scarie reluctantly raised his hands in surrender and nodded his head in agreement.

Tyquan held a firm gaze with Scarie before looking over at Sanchez and began his lesson. He placed his arm around Sanchez's shoulder allowing the gun to dangle right over his heart.

"What was it again you thought should happen?" Tyquan peered down at him.

Sanchez looked over at Alex's dead body and the thick, red puddle he now lay in and choked down the little bit of spit he could form before he spoke his next words. Sanchez slowly rose to his feet feeling like he had just been asked to read aloud. *Fuck it* echoed in his head then left his mouth.

"Fuck it." He straightened his posture and proceeded, "Like I said, we need to put fresh faces at the head of the boroughs let them see ain't shit weak about us." His eyes connected with his adversaries.

"You ready to take this shit to the next level?" Tyquan asked then waited for the proper response.

"Born ready," he stated firmly.

Tyquan looked in each man's eyes and decided their fate. He raised his arm and pointed at Carmine, Kingston, and Antonio.

"Kill the heads," he spoke a little over a whisper.

Sanchez wasted no time, he pulled out his gun, then shot Carmine in the throat and Kingston in the chest. He aimed his gun down at Antonio.

"Please, we planned this shit together. You supposed to be my brother."

"Family ain't Family," he uttered then let off three shots into his body.

When his gun came to rest he laid it against his leg. Heat surged through his body as the feeling of power filled his hands.

Tyquan leaned in and mumbled in his ear, "And Blood ain't Blood…" Then he pressed the steel to the back of his head and pulled the trigger.

Sanchez's body dropped inches from Antonio causing their dark crimson fluid to mix and puddle beneath them.

Tyquan looked at the terror in the eyes staring back at him and took great pleasure in each fear-stricken glare. "Does anyone have anything else they want to suggest?" He waved his gun around the room.

Silence was the verdict the jury handed, and Tyquan took that as their nonverbal agreement to whatever was about to come out of his mouth.

"Bison you now have, Harlem. I will be sending over Jimmy to assist you.

Bison nodded his understanding as he glanced over at Alex. "I will be ready, Boss," he slurred out barely able to part his lips.

"Scarie, I want you out of the city. I need you in Detroit. There will be two men waiting to greet you. You have twenty-four hours."

Scarie ran his hand over his face then also nodded his agreement.

"Loco will run Queens until further notice and Big John will run the Bronx."

Tyquan tucked his gun then continued, "All business will run as it always has. If it's a fucking problem, you get that shit to me." He made firm eye contact with every man in the room. "From this day forward. If I even think there is an evil thought I'ma blow your fucking mind," he barked then turned to leave the building. "The shipment will be here in a few days. Get right!" he yelled as the doors opened and he left the same way he entered.

Chapter 6

Hidden Intent

Tyquan ran the towel over his head and face then threw on a pair of Versace boxers. He moved around his bedroom with a certain ease to his heart. Tonight, couldn't change what he lost but what he gained could not compare. Tyquan pulled on a pair of sweatpants and headed to the living room. He ran his new power through his mind and his dick hardened at the thought of the empire he was about to build. Tyquan pressed his bare feet against the cold, wooden planks as he headed to the kitchen. He eyed the new decor with the hues of platinum and navy blue as he moved through the semi decorated space. He passed through the living room, into the kitchen. His mind was heavy. The crown was in place but now with it on, the tight fit made his brain feel as if it was about to explode. He pulled the stainless-steel doors of the refrigerator open and grabbed the orange juice from the shelf. As he reached in the cabinet for a tall glass the intercom alert rang from the wall unit. He set the juice and cup on the counter then headed to the phone.

"Hello?"

"Mr. Wells, Monique, is on her way upstairs," the husky voice announced through the line.

"Thank you. Hold all calls and no visitors for the rest of the night unless it's an emergency."

"Yes, sir." He disconnected the line.

Tyquan returned the phone to the base, headed to the door, and opened it wide then prepared for Monique's bullshit. He walked back into the kitchen, poured the juice into his cup, and calmly waited for her to enter.

"What the fuck is going on, Tyke?" Monique asked as she stormed in, slamming the door behind her.

"Lock it," he ordered in a soothing tone bringing the glass to his lips.

Monique turned on her heels, marched back to the door and hit the locks then proceeded back in his direction.

"It's locked. Now what the fuck is going on?" Monique rested her hands on the counter.

Tyquan kept his back turned until he was able to speak without losing his cool.

"So, who are we dealing with?" she asked pulling her jacket off, throwing it over the bar stool.

"There are only ten to deal with."

"Then ten more must be taken," Monique asserted.

"Is that right?" Tyquan's brow lifted.

"Tyquan, I'm not sitting across from a nigga that could slit my throat when I turn my back. I gotta worry about my son," Monique's voice echoed through the house.

"Ain't nobody touching my son," a lump rose in his throat as the statement left his mouth.

"You can't promise me that." Tears threatened to leave her eyes with every word.

"I killed all the innocent, so the evil could grow. Let it show its face, Mo."

Monique stood silent fighting to control all the turmoil that was brewing in her soul.

"Mo, you know what the fuck this is. And you know I got this shit under control," he reassured her.

"How the fuck you got things under control? Malik is fuckin' dead," her voice echoed against the walls.

Tyquan again remained silent unsure where Monique's heart and loyalty had shifted.

"Malika and Pashion gotta bury their fuckin' kids. Tell me again how you got this shit under control? Cause it don't fuckin' look like it," she raged as she pulled off her leather jacket and threw it over the barstool.

"Yell one more fuckin' time," Tyquan gently warned placing his glass on the counter.

Monique stood breathing heavily out of her nose trying to find a calm place to lay her anger. She was ready to slap fire out of Tyquan's mouth. Monique took a few deep breaths then proceeded with her demands.

"Talk, Tyke, you got to tell me something more than I got this."

Tyquan rotated a few things around in his head before giving Monique what he thought would be enough to calm her down. "Look, you know more than anybody how I fucked with Malik. This shit is on my mind every muthafuckin' second!" his voice raised slightly. "I made that man some promises and gave him my word. Trust me, I'ma make this shit right. I need you to keep the girls and you on ice until these deals go down."

"What deals?" Monique cocked her head to the side.

Tyquan looked into Monique's eyes and carefully read her moves then continued. "I sat down with the heads."

"Oh, here we fuckin' go." Monique threw her hands in the air. "What are they saying? Who authorized the hit?"

"I cleared the air that's all you need to know."

"No, that's all you need to know. Who...authorized...the...hit?" she asserted.

"Look, we got this shit under control."

"We?" She folded her hands over her chest.

Tyquan just shot Monique a half-smile and shook his head. "You really think you are a player in this game, don't you?"

"What the fuck are you talking about?" Monique spat. "You brought me into this shit. You put me in the room even when I didn't want to fuckin' be in there."

"Well, you can leave the room now. You have my permission, I got it from here."

"Well, let me say this shit real calm like so it can stick to your fuckin' bones." She leaned in. "The shit I'm about to handle is out of your control. I made that man a promise, too, and your punk ass can sit on yours, but I'ma make this shit right."

"Stay out my way, Mo," he warned her.

"No, you stay outta mine." Monique grabbed her jacket and headed for the door.

"Who the fuck you think you talking, too?" Tyquan sped up on her and was right on her back as she reached for the knob.

Monique turned quickly and pressed her hands against his chest. Her jacket fell to the floor as her back slammed against the door. "Tyquan move." She peered up into his bloodshot, hazel eyes as his body towered over hers.

"Stay, the fuck out of this, Mo! I got it," he spoke firmly through gritted teeth.

"You gonna have to make me." She gritted back at him.

Tyquan grabbed her wrists in one hand and her throat with the other hand. He pushed her against the glass cabinet, raised her arm high above her head then spread her legs with his feet.

"Is this what the fuck is wrong with you?" His nose met with hers.

"Get the fuck off me!" Monique grabbed his wrist in an attempt to loosen his grip on her throat.

"You gonna have to make me." Tyquan squeezed tighter on her neck as he plotted each move, he needed to make, to break her.

Monique took labored breaths as his grip became even tighter. "Let me go," she uttered as she squirmed between Tyquan's heated frame and the chill of the glass.

Tyquan moved his hand from her throat, pulled her skirt above her waist, and slid his fingers between her thighs.

"Tyke, stop." She dug her nails into his arm in an effort to stop his fingers from entering her.

"Damn, my pussy is still tight."

"Move your fuckin' hand," she gritted as he played inside her.

Tyquan knew all her spots, every wiggle, and every moan. It had been years since she last let him touch her. Tonight, he was going to answer the thirsty animal inside of her. He ran his tongue over her lips, then enjoyed the taste of her chin and neck.

"You feel so good, baby."

"Tyquan please," she slightly moaned.

"Please what?" he asked pushing deeper.

Tyquan's warm breath and soft lips caused her thoughts to shift as he gave her body what it craved. Monique looked up through the slits of her eyes and her pussy began to melt in his hands as his intensity stared back at her.

"Ahhhh…" she cooed as he tickled her sweet spot.

Tyquan kissed her lips sucking her tongue and bottom lip before releasing a few passionate moans of his own. Monique moved and squirmed turning her face away from what felt like the kiss of death. Tyquan stood enjoying every bit of her heated resistance which soaked his fingers with each stroke.

"If you don't want me touching you. Why my pussy so wet?" he taunted as the soft kisses turned into nibbles and bites along her neck and collar bone.

"Tyke…sto…" soft moans left her lips as her pussy gave in to his pleasure.

Tyquan moved his fingers faster as his teeth played with her erect nipples through the silk of her blouse.

"Tyquan, move, let me go," her quivering words slipped through her lips.

"I can't," he whispered as he rotated his thumb on her clit.

Tyquan stared into her eyes as he gave her pussy what it was asking for. Monique's mouth had uttered no, but her kitty was in full cooperation with every caress.

Tyquan adhered to her request only long enough to slide his finger out and his dick in. He let go of her hand, pulled down his boxers, and released the beast.

Monique pressed her palms against his chest and attempted to close her legs.

Tyquan pulled her up to his waist and forced himself into her tightness. Monique grabbed him tightly around the neck as he went deeper.

"Mmmm…" she moaned as his forceful strokes got faster with each entry.

Tyquan held her legs open wide and began breaking through the resistance.

"Ssss…damn," he mumbled as her pussy responded to the power of his stroke.

Monique held on tighter as he pinned her to the China cabinet showing no mercy.

After a few more power strokes Tyquan pulled her closer to him then proceeded to his bedroom with his stiffness deep inside her.

"Tyke, no, put me down!" she begged as she turned to see the king-sized bed in the middle of the room.

Monique struggled to be free knowing once she was in his little playground, he was going to make her play all night with all his big boy toys.

"When you gonna learn, Mo? I'm the one in control," he taunted as he climbed onto the bed and even deeper into her pussy.

"Tyke, don't," she moaned as she felt his teeth sink into her neck.

Tyquan ripped at her shirt tearing it from her body not missing a stroke. He released her breasts from the lace of her bra, placed her nipple in his mouth, and sucked gently while he stroked hard.

Monique's cries filled the room with a symphony of pleasure and pain as all the feelings she had for him came rushing to the front of her mind. They were both on the brink of death and even in darkness he was giving her life.

"I fuckin' hate you," she moaned as she felt her body ready to release.

"This pussy don't hate me, though," he teased as he bounced from side to side against her walls. "Your pussy is whispering, Daddy, fuck me," he moaned then kissed her deeply.

Monique held on for a few more strokes then released years of built-up frustration. "I'm cumming…"

"Say that shit." He hit her spot faster as he felt her pussy tightening around him.

"Baby, I'm cumming!" She held on as he rocked her soul to sleep with every push.

"Mmmm…" Tyquan slowly slid back and forth in her wetness. "I need you to do what I say," he said, pulling just the head in and out.

"Tyke," she moaned as he slowly dipped the head in her opening.

"We gotta do this shit together, Mo. It's just me and you. Help me protect our son," he uttered, picking up speed.

"Ahhhh…yessss…I got you," she cried as he hit that spot like only, he could.

"Help me, Mo." He pulled her legs onto his shoulders and stood up in her pussy.

Monique closed her eyes tight as a wave of pleasure took over her mind, body, and spirit. She took in every touch, every taste, and his every intent.

Tyquan closed his eyes and thought about nothing but how good she felt with her legs fearfully clinched to the side of his neck. There he laid between the legs of the only woman who gave him life and with one blink of her pretty eyes could also cause his death.

As their movements took them from one distorted position to another, Monique charged this small amount of pleasure to the fucked-up game they were playing. For Tyquan, Monique's pussy was only for play, not for power. However, he had surrendered the moment he slipped into something hot and dangerous.

"I wanna ride it, Daddy," she purred, nibbling along his chest.

"Is that right?" Tyquan gave her that devious smirk as he positioned her on top of his throne.

Monique rode slow and easy, then placed her feet firm into the bed and bounced to the beat of both of their treachery.

"Get that shit," Tyquan mumbled as he assisted her in her glide pulling her into him hard each time she slid down.

"Oh, my God!" she yelled as her pussy took the heat he was offering.

Monique placed her hands on his chest and continued to take in all of him with every push. Waves of energy surged through her body as her pussy juices rained down on him.

Tyquan allowed her to bounce until he felt her legs wobble, then he let the tables turn.

"Daddy gotta get some now," he teased as he flipped her over and positioned her body to receive him from the back.

Monique looked over her shoulder as she produced the perfect deep arch. "Be gentle, Daddy," she purred.

"In the morning," he responded stroking his throbbing thickness back and forth until he fit just right.

"Baby, please… make me cum…" she moaned as the speed and depth of his stroke caused her body to quiver.

Monique dropped her head and rocked into his movements increasing the pleasure for them both. An onslaught of emotions took over and tears formed at the corners of her eyes. Here she was in her enemy's bed enjoying every inch of him. She blocked out all her hate and replaced it with the love to win. The board was set and now the only question was who had chosen the wrong pieces.

Tyquan took full control and fucked Monique until she couldn't see a foot in front of her. He laid her on her back positioning himself between her soft ass cheeks, then grinded until she begged him to stop.

When he was done making sure her pussy knew who owned it. He came deep inside her womb. Their mouths met and his tongue danced perfectly with hers.

"You gonna always be mine," he whispered, pressing himself firmly against her.

"I know," she uttered as she felt him once again stiffening inside her.

In Monique's mind, she had a win, she had him right where she needed him to be, deep in distraction. However, in Tyquan's mind, she was just giving a General good pussy right before the battle. His only hope was that she remained a friend and wouldn't become his most regretted casualty.

Chapter 7

It's A Blood Sport

Pashion stepped out of the black and yellow cab firmly placing her black stiletto boots onto the concrete as she eyed the tall buildings. She took one last pull of her cigarette then dropped it to the ground and with one step crushed it into the concrete as she sprung into motion. The block became thick with unknown tension as the men standing close to the entrance of the building watched the tall thick woman sway her hips towards them.

"You sure you in the right place, Ma?" A voice boomed in her direction.

Pashion looked up from her shades right into his eyes. "Only a worker would ask a dumb ass question. Have somebody alert your boss to my presence." She slid her glasses back up on her nose then pushed on as if he said nothing at all.

"I'm so sick of these bitches," he grumbled under his breath as he signaled the doorman to let her in. Jay spat on the ground then nodded at his men to stay alert.

Pashion approached the tall-bearded gentleman then strutted right up to the open elevator and hopped on. As she rode, she thought about what the old wise one would reveal. She steadied her breathing as the ride came to a stop. When the doors opened again, she was greeted by another one of his faithful crew. She looked hard against the glass of her shades as the cold pair of eyes stared down at her.

"Go down there and knock twice." The man's baritone pressed into her chest as he stepped slightly to the side to let her by. His breath left his nostrils hard and warm as he gave her not an ounce of space for error.

Pashion wanted to punch that nigga dead in his throat but didn't respond. She tucked the experience knowing the next meeting would end differently, she used the space provided and headed quickly to her objective. Pashion knocked twice then stepped to the side. When she saw the door crack, she peeked into the open space.

"Tell Fred it's, Pashion," she spoke firmly ready to learn the intent of her enemies.

The door closed hard in her face and after a few seconds of silence, she heard the chain slide and drop. There was one twist of the knob, the door swung open and a female appeared wearing a tight, white, leather bodysuit with her hair tucked in a neat bun on top of her head.

"Put your arms out," the woman commanded as she positioned herself in front of Pashion.

Pashion complied putting her arms out to the side as her eyes wandered over the woman's perfect frame. She allowed the woman to do her work as she stood firmly in her spot.

"You done?" Pashion looked down at the thinly built woman and chill bumps covered her arms as the cold empty stare glared at her from this beautifully broken young lady.

"Go down the hall, last room on the left," she uttered stepping to the side clicking each lock back in place.

Pashion dropped her hands, and straightened her jacket then proceeded down the dimly lit hallway. The strong aroma of black love and cigar smoke filled the air as she ascended the hallway. Faint Jazz and muffled moans played against the thin walls as a backdrop to her already miserable life. When she got to the hard-wooden door, she knocked twice then turned the knob and walked in.

"Why would you come to this door?" Fred bellowed from his high-backed chair.

"Because a phone call won't do it." She closed the door then stood directly in front of him.

Fred pulled on his cigarette then blew thick smoke in her direction as his eyes roamed over her frame.

"It's just me, your bitch already checked," Pashion said opening her jacket.

"Be seated," he mumbled as he brought the cigarette back to his lips. Fred watched Pashion closely as she took the seat in the chair across from him. "Speak."

Pashion took a deep breath and carefully began. "I need you," she pleaded removing the shades from her face.

"You need something but it ain't me." He chuckled.

"Fred, you are my last stop. I don't want to touch anything that belongs to you and believe me, I'm 'bout to get reckless," she warned with clenched teeth.

"Let them handle it, Pashion." He sat up looking her right in the eyes.

"I let them handle it. Now I am forced to wear black. I need the next bitch to mourn with me," she uttered holding tightly to the water that threatened to leave her slightly swollen eyes.

Fred sat back taking the drink from the nightstand next to him. He brought the glass to his lips and drank the hot liquid down with one gulp. He sat the glass down then folded his hands across his chest.

"This is your only time you get to question me. It is also the last time you get to walk through my door," he spoke his words without fear or regret.

"Agreed," she quickly accepted his offer.

"Ask your question," Fred responded holding a tight jaw.

"Who killed our children?" she got right to the point.

"Who has the most to gain?" he spat back.

"Everybody has different greed in their heart. It's hard to tell," she shot back leaning slightly forward in her chair.

"What does your gut tell you?"

"That the men who say they are protecting us are really fucking us raw."

"Then make 'em bust," he returned with a half-smile.

"Who am I up against?"

"It's not who, it's what..." he paused then sat forward. "When you put aside all the grief, and pain. You will see exactly what you are up against. Then you will find the who." He sat back again folding his hands over his chest.

"I don't want to play this game, Fred. I need you to be straight forward with me," she pleaded as her patience with his wordplay was wearing thin.

"I just answered your *one* question. You need to hurry up and make your moves. Time is already against you."

Pashion dropped her head as she rubbed one hand in the other. She tossed around Fred's coded message trying to see his angle. She was living on the memory of the last time she heard and touched her child. That same feeling was also fueling an evil deep in her belly that all her enemies was about to feel.

Pashion slowly lifted her head and with tears in her eyes she spoke, "Just remember when the shit spills over into your house. You could have prevented it." She rose to her feet then turned to exit. "Thanks for your time."

Fred watched this wounded woman storming away from him. In that moment, he knew he had to break the street code. "Sit closer to your enemies than you do to your friends. Because sometimes Family Ain't Blood and Blood Ain't Family."

Pashion paused to think then clutched the knob in her hand as Fred's words echoed in her mind. She pulled the door open as several names replayed in her mind. She knew exactly what he was saying and was about to make everybody's blood curdle.

"Thank you, I'll remember if you ever cross me to show you mercy first," she spat pulling the door open then heading back the way she entered.

"Ain't no mercy for men like me. The trap don't owe no nigga, and it definitely don't trust no bitch," he projected his voice in her direction then chuckled as the last word left his lips.

When Fred heard the apartment door slam closed, he got up, shut his bedroom door then sat back in the highbacked chair. He relit his cigarette, poured a full glass of Brandy then took it straight down placing the glass back on the table. Fred crossed his legs and thought about the fallout and how to make sure he protected his men.

As he pondered his moves, he heard a few light taps on the door.

"You good, Boss?" A strong voice bellowed through the door as the knob began to turn.

Conard peaked his head in. Fred waved his right hand into the room. "We need to call a meeting. Get all our frontlines to my house in Yonkers in an hour. We may have to close some things up and move around."

"What the fuck is going on?"

"The glove is changing hands." Fred gave his partner a stern look.

"I know that bitch that just left out of here is not the problem." He pointed over his shoulder.

"The only thing worse than fucking with a nigga's bitch is fucking with a mother's child. There is not a revenge more powerful. We just going to get the fuck outta the way," he spoke firm orders.

"I'm on it." He hurried out of Fred's room to round up the family.

Fred sat back in his chair thinking back to his humble beginnings. He had been involved in many wars and was the only one left to tell a dead man's tale. He knew that the only way to survive was to get as low as a snake and hiss at anything moving.

****

"Monique are you sure?" Malika asked as she covered her furniture with white cotton sheets.

"Yes, Ma, I can't keep you safe here. I gotta move you now." Monique went from one suitcase to the other packing the things Malika placed on the bed.

"I hate this shit." Malika sighed as she grabbed her jewelry and dumped everything into her makeup case, then placed it near the other bags.

Monique zipped the bags closed and hauled them downstairs. She loaded them by the door and ran back up to hurry her along.

"Come on, Mama. You know they on my ass," Monique announced, darting her eyes around the room to make sure they had everything covered.

"Do I have everything?" Malika looked around the room a final time.

"If we miss it, fuck it. We can get back everything but life," Monique reminded her of the times they were living in.

"I know," Malika's voice cracked as her heart became weighted in her chest.

Monique walked over to her and put a hand on each of her shoulders. "I promise you, just as I promised your son. I will not rest until each person involved feels a lifetime of mourning."

"I am depending on it," Malika uttered as the tears rolled down her face.

"I got you." Monique pulled her into her arms and squeezed her tight. "I got you," she confirmed then pulled back. "We gotta go." She took her hand, snatched up her purse, and headed down the steps.

When Monique opened the door, she looked up into a pair of bloodshot eyes that were sunken into dark black skin. There he was...her savior...the deliverer of death and regret.

"Is this all?" Lux asked as he grabbed the two hard-cased traveling bags.

"Yes!" Monique hurried past him pulling Malika to the car. She snatched open the door and helped her inside.

When Malika fixed her eyes on KoKo sleeping away tucked nicely in a car seat, she covered her mouth to avoid the release of her screams.

"Oh my, God, my KoKo," she mouthed at Monique who only nodded to avoid the tears threatening to leave her face. "But where is my, Star?"

"Safe."

"Okay," she whispered as tears of joy rained down her face.

"I got you. Listen to Lux he will not fail in keeping you safe." Monique reached in her purse, pulled out three cashiers' checks held together by a paperclip, and handed them to Malika, then passed her two passports.

"I will make a deposit once a month to this account." She then handed her the last of the paperwork. "I will see you in a couple of weeks. Stay off the phone, all messages will come face to face."

Malika nodded then looked down at the information. Her eyes almost left their sockets when she read the amounts. "Nah, Ma, I can't take this," she calmly stated.

"You have no choice. That's blood money, your son paid with his life. Now give her one." She squeezed Malika's hand.

"See you soon." Malika returned the courtesy then tucked the papers into her bag.

"Let's go," Lux ordered then closed Malika's door and escorted Monique to the other waiting vehicle.

"Thank you, Lux," Monique stated as she slid into the back seat. "Take care of my family."

"With my life." He slammed her door shut then headed back to the truck. When he hopped inside, he remained silent as he pulled off zipping through the city traffic.

Malika looked over at KoKo and smiled. "We gonna be okay, Mama. We…are…going…to be…okay!"

Chapter 8

Bury The Truth

Tyquan drove eagerly down the highway with thoughts of the murder and mayhem that had just shaken and turned over the cart. In a matter of weeks, everything they had built was falling apart body by body and brick by brick. The sun shined brightly against his face as he thought about the lives that had been placed in his hands and what he was going to do to keep each one safe. He pulled in front of the hospital and looked down at his watch. As his eyes rotated toward the sliding doors, he saw Kisha being pushed in a wheelchair toward his car.

Tyquan jumped out and met them at the curb. He tried not to stare at her scars and bruises but couldn't help but to look and cringe at the sight of the trauma that had replaced the shine and happiness of her once vibrant chocolate face. With a look of defeat and sadness, she was an empty shell and what was left on the outside was hanging on by a very thin thread.

"Mr. Wells?" she asked as she extended her hand.

"Yes ma'am," he confirmed as he gently squeezed hers.

"She should be good for the ride. Here is her medication and chart." She handed Tyquan a small white bag of medication. "These are all the things she had in her room." She handed him Kisha's overnight bag.

"Thank you." He took the contents into his hand then laid them on the back seat, before returning to Kisha's side.

"Kisha, I will miss you," she announced as she hugged her neck.

Kisha nodded her head while staring off blankly.

The nurse locked the wheels and began assisting Kisha out of the chair. As she planted her feet, her legs wobbled under the pressure.

"I got her." Tyquan saw the pain on Kisha's face and swooped her up into his arms. "I got you, Ma." He held her close as he carried her to the car and placed her in the front seat. Tyquan fastened her in, then closed the door.

"Again, thank you beautiful." He turned his attention back to the nurse. "What's your name again?"

"Lynn," she responded quickly impressed by his kindness to her patience.

"Lynn, huh?" he repeated.

"Yes, sir, that's my name." Lynn giggled a little as his sexy, hazel eyes peered down at her.

Tyquan then reached into his pocket and pulled out a card and a stack of bills. "You never met me, and she was discharged and left with a female friend." He slid the money and card into her hand.

"If you have any questions or you think of anything you need. Day or late at night, I want you to call me first." He slightly curled the side of his mouth. Lynn looked down at the card and the small band of money and joy-filled her belly. "Just like you told Kisha I got you."

She smiled back, then spun on her heels and headed inside tickled about the whole experience. "Tyquan Wells...Investor," she mumbled the words from his business card as she tucked the money in her bra. "We will see," she said as she hit the elevator up button.

Tyquan dropped the smile from his face as soon as she was out of his view. He jumped in the driver's seat and looked over at his injured friend. "I got you, Key," Tyquan confirmed as he pulled away from the curb.

"I don't even have myself," she confessed, tucking her legs into the seat, and resting her head on the door. She pulled her jacket up over her face and tried to rest her weary mind.

Tyquan wanted to reassure her that shit was going to be alright but at the moment he could not convince himself. He turned on the radio and pushed onto the highway. The first part of his promise was almost fulfilled all he had to do now was plot carefully enough to make sure he collected the whole bank as his enemies were forced to regret their greed.

Tyquan admired the sea of huge trees and vast areas of neatly manicured grass. He went over his plans a million times as he drove. He never worried about the what-ifs. It was the what-if nots, he had to nip in the bud before they had time to sprout. Tyquan made one stop to fill his tank and was back on the road. He glanced over at Kisha between his thoughts as she slept peacefully with only an occasional incoherent mumble or two between her light snores. He thought about the stories Malik had shared with him about her loyalty and dedication. Malik had made it very clear that she was to be respected and taken care of just like his wife.

Tyquan eased past the big iron gates and drove up to the main house. He pulled into a parking spot then turned off the engine. "I'll be right back, Ma," he announced as he hopped out and pressed the alarm locking her in safe.

When he returned, behind him was two tall black men dressed in hospital whites. One pushed a wheelchair and the other held her chart and other paperwork. They walked over to the car, helped Kisha to her feet, and into the chair. Tyquan grabbed her bags then followed close behind.

Kisha's eyes darted over the huge campus as she was pushed along the bricked walkway to a small cottage a short distance from the main house. An unexpected surge of peace crept into her soul as she eyed the lake and gazebos in the distance. When they entered the neatly kept room, Kisha inhaled the sweet scent of lavender. She glanced over at the assortment of red and black roses and the depression she was fighting to contain surfaced forcing tears down her pretty brown cheeks. Kisha wiped her face with the back of her hand as she was rolled to the middle of the room, she watched closely as the staff began to put her things in place.

"We will be right out of your way," one of the orderlies assured as they hurried back and forth.

Kisha eyed the small cottage with a huge king-sized bed decorated with an assortment of fluffy pillows placed neatly on top of an all-white comforter. She gazed over to the far corner by the window at a high-backed lounge chair which was placed nicely between the end table and mahogany dresser. Kisha investigated the huge bathroom and walk-in closet as the last of her things were put in place. She took a deep breath folded her hands then just stared down at her feet.

"I got it from here," Tyquan asserted as he tipped the two orderlies and escorted them to the door.

"The intake nurse will be over here momentarily to get her situated."

"Thank you," Tyquan responded as he closed the door behind them.

Kisha ran her hands over her face then looked up at Tyquan. "Please help me see that this shit will be okay," she pleaded for just a small glimpse of hope.

"I swear to you, everything will be okay," again, he tried to convince them both.

"Can I see my daughter?"

"Not yet, I need you to stay here and let me finish getting things in order."

"I'm so broken," she mumbled.

"I know, Ma, we are all fucked up over this whole situation." Tyquan bent down directly in front of her.

"Did they take care of him? Did he look like himself?" she asked as the reality again cut deep into her stomach.

Kisha searched Tyquan's face for answers but she knew no matter what he said nothing would turn back the evil hands of time. Tears streamed hot down her cheeks as his silence confirmed her worse fears.

Tyquan pulled her from the chair and into his arms. Kisha cried against his chest as he tightened his grip. Tyquan didn't say a word. He just held her against him and allowed her to release all she had left. Kisha cried until she could barely produce air and Tyquan just held her until she could no longer hold herself.

Kisha had so many questions. She forced her heavy lids to open as she prepared her mouth to ask just a few more. "Tyke, I nee..."

Knock! Knock!

"Hello, I'm Holly and this is your personal staff. We are going to get you situated real quick." She pushed the door open, walked right in, and started moving through the room.

"I really just want to rest," Kisha stated as she watched these strangers began invading her personal space.

"No worries, Kisha, we will be in and out of here in no time." She smiled big and kept on moving, ignoring Kisha's request.

Kisha looked up at Tyquan who shot her a comforting smile.

"If you don't mind, Mr. Wells. Can you step outside for a minute? We will call you back in as soon as we can."

"Absolutely."

"Tyke." Kisha gripped his arm as he moved to the door.

"I'm right outside the door." He comforted her as he headed to the exit.

Tyquan stepped right outside the door and played his plan over and over in his head while he waited.

The nurses worked quickly drawing her a bath and laying her clothes out on the bed. As the bathroom door closed, Kisha sank into the hot suds and closed her eyes in an attempt to enjoy a long-awaited moment alone. But there would be no such luck the woman entered the bathroom and assisted her step by step until she was clean and fresh.

By the time Kisha was bathed and dressed, nurse Holly had ordered her food and had it placed on a TV tray in front of the chair. Kisha walked over to the table and eyed the bowl of vegetable soup, a salad, soft sourdough bread, and a glass of water with lemon on the side. She moved slowly to her seat then eased into the comfort of the suede.

The nurse came to her side and poured several pills into her palm.

Kisha tossed them into her mouth then put her head back taking a sigh of relief.

"You can come back in, Mr. Wells," one of the nurses announced as she pulled back the cover and fluffed the big white pillows.

When he walked back into the room, he took a deep breath then stood right beside her relieved to see a slight glow to her appearance.

"Someone will be around in an hour to collect her dinner tray," the head nurse announced as she straightened the bathroom and collected Kisha's dirty clothes.

"Thank you." Tyquan again pulled out a stack of money and placed it in the woman's hands. "She is very special to me. I want her treated like you would treat your own mother." He gave the woman a look that caused chill bumps to cover her skin.

"Whatever she needs or wants. You better make it happen." He handed her his infamous calling card. "Call me every Wednesday and Sunday with a full report. And we never met, and you don't know her," he stated without blinking an eye.

The nurse looked at the money then back up at him. "Yes, sir," she agreed terrified not to.

"Have a good night," he dismissed her then returned to Kisha's side. Once the door was closed, he began talking to his friend. "You a'ight, Key?"

"I'll never be alright." She looked up at Tyquan.

"I just need you to ride this shit out. Then we can get the family back to normal."

"Back to normal." She chuckled. "Who you trying to fool?" Kisha leaned forward in the chair. "Ain't nothing normal about burying the innocent and praising the guilty. We fucked up out here," she slurred as the medication took hold. "This shit ain't never gonna be normal."

Tyquan felt every bit of the pain and utter disgust in her words. He wanted to say more, but his mouth could not open to speak another lie.

Kisha picked up on the hesitation in his silence and spoke instead, "You can leave now I need to get some rest. Thank you for everything." She sat back in the chair like she had not a fuck left to give.

"I'll be right here whenever you need me, Key," Tyquan assured her.

"Just remember this, I'm putting my daughter's life in your hands. Don't fail Malik again." She turned and stared out the window.

Tyquan became sick to his stomach as her words cut deep into his gut. He swallowed what little spit he had left, walked over, and grabbed the small blanket from the bottom of the bed, and placed it over her.

"I promise, Kisha, I will not rest until we are all good." He leaned in and kissed her on the forehead. "I will see you in a week," he stated then turned towards the door.

Kisha didn't part her lips. As the door closed, she eased into the tall suede chair and pulled the knitted blanket up to her chin. Her eyes danced around the room at what had become of her life. There she was a young woman now forced to live as if she was dead and buried all to hide the next man's secrets. Kisha had spent her whole life chasing destiny to only find out that hers' would end without the man she loved by her side or the child they had created. Tears rolled steadily down her cheeks as she began to playback all of Malik's promises only to have to live with the fact that they would never come true. Kisha did know one thing for sure. Malik's last words to her would be the ones she'd hold dear. Those same words would make her enemies bleed.

Kisha closed her eyes, took a deep breath, then fixed her gaze back out to the tops of the tall oak trees and watched the birds who seemed to laugh and play without a care to another man's suffering. Kisha enjoyed the glare of the sun as it separated from the sky, she thought about the day Malik picked her up from her small stent in Clinton Correctional Facility and the look in his eyes was the one she would hold onto, and never let go.

Kisha looked through the silver iron fences and barbwire to see her right hand standing exactly where he said he would be. As the gate slid open a smile widened on both of their faces. Kisha nervously fidgeted with the knot on the bag in her hand as she waited to be given the signal to pass through the gate.

Malik licked his lips as the sight of her thick thighs in those tight jeans took his imagination into overdrive with the possibilities. His dick slightly hardened as she got closer to the exit. It was his baby girl, his rider. The one person he knew he could take a shit, and nap around and never have to worry about his neck.

"Look at you scared of them, niggas. I'm the one you need to be scared of," he teased moving closer.

"Ain't nobody scared of you," she strengthened her tone and put some pep in her step as the last fence began to open.

"Stay outta trouble!" one of the female officers yelled out as the gates closed shut behind her.

"And you stay out these streets." Kisha dropped the smile from her face as she turned her head to give a threat of her own.

She turned back to face Malik as the echo of 'fuck that bitch' slid through her mind. She let that weak shit hit the back of her ear lobe as she had no more energy for the trolls.

"Baby, I missed you so much," she confessed, jumping up into Malik's arms and wrapping her legs arms around him.

"I missed you too, baby," Malik responded gripping her ass with both hands.

They stood void of time as the moment they'd been waiting for seemed to play in slow motion as they enjoyed each other's touch. Kisha placed her lips on his, then slipped her tongue in his mouth and damn near to the back of his throat. Malik returned the passion wrapping his tongue around hers. She pulled back and planted sensual peeks and soft nibbles on his lips.

"Mmmm...damn, baby," she whined as the heat between them became almost unbearable.

"Thank you for all your sacrifices," Malik mumbled between the soft kisses he placed on her lips.

"Always."

Kisha placed her forehead on his and inhaled his cologne, which caused her pussy to tingle followed by a slight flood in her panties. *"I don't want to let you go,"* she whispered then ran her tongue along his lips.

"You ain't talking about shit. You gonna have to beg me to climb outta this pussy," he threatened as he felt his dick stiffen. *"Come on before we get locked up for fucking in the middle of the prison parking lot."* He chuckled sliding her down his pole and onto her feet. He took her hand and opened the door with the other.

Kisha laughed at the thought. *"You ain't gotta tell my black ass twice."* She joked hopping into the passenger seat.

Malik went around the other side, hopped in, and peeled out leaving them suckas where they belonged, in their dust. As they pulled onto the freeway, he pumped up the volume and opened the roof.

"Where we going, baby?" Kisha said as her ponytail blew in the wind.

"Somewhere, that will give me all uninterrupted access to you," he shot back taking her hand into his.

"Awww…baby, I love the shit outta you," she cooed placing a single kiss on the back of his hand.

"I love you, more!"

Kisha was on fire, her pussy pulsated against the seam of her jeans causing her to twitch in her seat. She reached over and let her hand roam between his legs. She released him from his enclosure and played up and down his length.

"I have been dreaming about tasting him," she said as she lowered herself to his waist.

Malik threw the Beamer in cruise control and moved his chair back to enjoy. Kisha devoured every inch of him until she felt his hand on the back of her head and heard a hiss leave his lips. She eased further down and massaged the head with her throat while enjoying the melody of pleasure slipping from his lips.

"Ssss…damn, Ma," he mumbled as she sloppily played with the head. She jerked and sucked getting him wetter with every grip. He rose out of his seat as she took no mercy in serving herself a full plate. Kisha drooled and devoured him inch by inch until his grip tightened on her ponytail.

"Mmmm…" she moaned as he pulled harder.

"Hold on, baby," he pleaded as he felt his nut ready to release.

"Shut the fuck up and get this work." Kisha combined hand and jaw action that had Malik struggling to stay between the lines.

Malik wanted to stop her, but she was about to make him bust, she was sucking like she wanted it all down her throat.

"Give me that work then." He pushed her head down on him and pumped up slowly.

Kisha gagged and moaned with every stroke, she stiffened her jaws, then rotated and prepared to taste his essence as it slid into her mouth.

"Get that shit," he growled feeling the sensation to release grip his belly.

The sound and her wet lips wrapping firmly around his dick put him right on the edge. Malik pushed her up and down on him faster as he tried to stay focused on the road.

Kisha held his pants leg for balance and did what she was told as she called for Daddy's nectar.

"I'm about to cum, baby," he mumbled as he began to coat the back of her throat.

Kisha sped up her pleasure and swallowed all he had to offer. She slurped and drank every drop, then spit out a little on the head and played in it with the tip of her tongue. "I miss sucking your dick, baby," she purred lapping at his swollen tip.

"I'ma fuck the shit outta you."

"Good, a bitch pussy been depressed," she said as she came up from his throne.

"Conversation done, I got you ma. I wanted you to have your pleasure," he slurred in a relaxed tone.

"I know," she confirmed. "You taste so good, I couldn't wait."

"You so bad! Reach over in the glove box and grab those wipes."

Kisha wiped him down and tucked her favorite toy back in the box then attended to herself. She leaned over and kissed his lips before sitting back and fastening her seatbelt.

"Thank you for everything." She grabbed his hand into hers and settled in her seat.

"No, thank you, I know your sacrifice. I promise you, not one day you spent behind that wall will go unrewarded." He looked over at her pretty face that was now getting wet with tears.

"I just did what I know you would have done for me." She allowed their eyes to connect.

"I know." He kissed her hand. "I know." Malik wanted to say more but he too was becoming overwhelmed with emotion. He could never explain what it was they had. He just knew that shit was powerful, and there was no way he was ever going to let that go.

They drove on and laughter filled the car as Kisha sung terribly to every song. Malik was back in his heaven. He looked over at her dancing in her seat and flashing that pretty white smile. His heart skipped at the perfect loyalty she had for him. Malik pulled off the exit and drove through the suburbs of Jackson County, New Jersey. He pulled slowly in front of a two-story home that sat on the end plot.

Kisha's eyes were all over the place. "Where are we?" she asked stretching her long legs.

"You tell me," Malik said as he reached in the glove box, pulled the folded documents out, and placed them in her hands.

"What is this?" Her brow wrinkled as she flipped to the first page. Tears filled her eyes when she read her name on what she now knew to be a deed.

"Really, Malik?" she asked as tears filled her lids.

"Just the beginning." He reached in the back seat, grabbed a small gift bag and passed it to her, then sat back.

Kisha's eyes lit up as she snatched the tissue paper from its place and tossed it to the floor. She reached inside and pulled out a small red box. She unsnapped it and her eyes lit up when she saw the ring Malik gave her right before she went in. He had upgraded the shit out of it for her. She admired the added platinum band and new yellow diamonds he added to the original design.

"Oh my, God, Maliiiikk..." she pouted.

"You're welcome, baby."

Malik reached over, pulled the rings from the box, and placed them back on her finger where they belong. Kisha turned her hand back and forth watching the sunlight dance off her finger.

"This shit fiyah," she said as she bobbed her shoulders up and down. She kissed his lips then put her attention back on her ring.

"There's more," he announced then sat back in his chair.

83

Kisha dug a little deeper and pulled out a matching diamond bracelet, earrings, and a necklace. Malik fastened each piece in place and watched as she snatched down the mirror and admired her new jewelry.

"Thank you so much, baby."

"I told you I got you, get that last box."

Kisha eagerly searched the bottom of the bag and pulled out the last box. She pulled the ribbon and popped it open. "Oh shit." She did a jig.

Malik hit the button on the visor and the garage slid open revealing her new baby. There she sat identical to his, a sexy ass candy apple red BMW right off the factory only 50 miles on the meter. He pulled in next to it and closed the garage.

"I love it." She jumped out, hit the locks, and hopped inside.

Kisha ran her hands over the leather then touched every button like a kid at Sesame Place. She giggled and eased the windows up and down as the reality of freedom had just set in. Kisha flexed with her hands on the steering wheel displaying her ice. She posed and primped in the mirror with her lips twisted bopping to the music.

"You crazy as hell." His heart was filled with excitement as he watched her enjoy her gifts.

"I'm about to shit on these bitches," she announced as she pretended to holla at fake haters.

"Come on crazy." He grabbed her hand and proceeded to pull her from the seat.

"Oh, shoot hold on!" she yelled as Mary J. blared through the speakers. She turned up the volume and sang along. "Baby, there's no need to tell ya. As far as I can clearly recall. My love has been here for you. So, you don't have to worry at all. I'll sacrifice my time; I'll make sure you're satisfied. And it's no hard thing to the joy I bring, I want to give you all my love."

Malik smiled as she sang and popped that pussy in his direction. "You need to bring my pussy in this house. I got something special planned for you," he tried to order over the music.

"Nah, baby, I want my dick, right here." She unbuttoned her jeans, lifted her ass, then slid them along with her panties down, and off her feet. She spread her legs wide and showed him her glistening pink center.

Kisha pulled at his waistband until his rock-hard dick was released. Malik ducked inside and pulled her ass to the edge of the seat. Kisha gripped his neck and he took no hesitation at pushing that steel all the way to the bottom. He fucked her hard and fast just the way her pussy begged for it. Kisha moaned in sync with the music as she pushed into him with every strong deep stroke. She dug her nails into his back as he lifted her with each pussy widening dig.

"Fuck me," she chanted as he showed her tight walls no mercy.

Malik remained silent as he hit her spot fucking to the rhythm of her moans.

"Come on this dick, Ma," he repeated as he watched his dick get wetter with every stroke.

Kisha wrapped her legs around his waist and tightened them at the ankle, she wanted him deep as he pumped widely inside of her.

"Baby, I'm cumming!" Kisha came and screamed for mercy but Malik didn't have any.

Her tight wet pussy had his dick charged all the way up and her pussy was about to submit all those months of wanting and waiting.

"Turn around," he ordered, then flipped her over, opened her legs with his feet, gripped her hips, and got between those slippery lips enjoying her ass cheeks against his thighs.

Kisha held on to the center console as Malik pulled her into him. She rotated her hips and bounced as he entered with speed and precision.

"Fuck me," she moaned as her body rocked to his pleasure.

Malik answered the call holding her in place and banging that spot until he felt her juices flood and hit his shaft. In between the music the sounds of her pussy juices fueled his passion. He grabbed the back of her shirt and twisted it into his fists as he did just what she asked. He fucked her from the back until her knees gave in, then he opened the back door pushed her onto her back, threw her legs over his shoulders, and drilled.

Kisha pressed her hands against the door as she tried to take all that deep dick. She had played with what she wanted him to do with that pussy for months. Teasing and talking shit every chance she got and today he was making sure she was pleased.

Malik's mind was working overtime as he put in well-deserved work, he had to make sure she knew nothing had changed, he was still that nigga.

"Baby, you in my spot," she cried as her soul began to quake.

Malik ignored her tears for mercy and bounced against her slippery walls until her body went limp beneath him. He still showed no mercy. He needed her to be back in the game 100%. He had to make sure she knew and understood all of her belonged to him. He rocked from side to side until he felt her pussy tighten around him.

"Where you want Daddy to cum?" he taunted, dipping in and out of her throbbing opening.

"Wherever you want," she moaned as she felt her body gearing up for another release.

"Mmmm… I can come in this pussy?"

"Yesssss!"

"Where can Daddy cum? Can I cum in this pussy?" he teased as he stood up inside her pressing her knees back towards her head.

"Yesssss… Daddy, yes! Come in your pussy, baby!" she screamed as her pussy juices squirted up on his stomach.

"Fuck," he mumbled, pumping faster and faster. He pushed in as deep as he could and filled her womb. "Shit!" He removed her legs from his shoulders and kissed her lips as he reached down and played with her swollen clit.

Kisha's body jerked as she allowed him to do whatever he wanted to do. Malik lifted her shirt and sucked her erect nipples then eased his face between her legs and began a feast of his own.

Kisha squirmed and yelled out in pleasure as he sucked her clit like only, he could. He teased her pussy to the point of no return. He licked slowly savoring her sweet chocolate on his tongue.

"I've been waiting to taste you," he confessed between soft sucks on her clit and lips.

"I love you, baby," she whined as she rotated her hips pushing her pussy into his face.

Malik followed her lead and let her ride his face until she squirted all over his lips. When she could take no more, he pulled her to her feet then quickly got her into the house where he could cater to her every need.

After Malik walked her from one room to the next watching her admire her new life, he ran Kisha a hot bath, undressed her slowly, and helped her into the hot Jacuzzi, then left her to enjoy her first bath in months. Kisha closed her eyes and enjoyed the afterglow and euphoria he had just put her in mind, body, and soul.

When Malik returned to the bathroom, he handed her a tall glass of red wine, sat on the edge of the tub, and rubbed chocolate covered strawberries on her lips as she enjoyed the force of the water jets against her back.

"I love you, baby!" she confessed as she nibbled the fruit.

"I love you, too!" He leaned over, kissed, and sucked her sweet lips.

Malik washed every inch of her body, rinsed her off then wrapped her in a huge fluffy towel taking time to play in that pussy, then led her to the bedroom.

"Awww... baby, what is all of this?" Kisha became intrigued when she saw what he had planned for little old her.

There were at least twenty dozen red roses that adorned each corner of the room. At the base of each vase were several bags reading Gucci, and Fendi. There were little boxes with big ribbons and big boxes with little ribbons.

"Baby," she looked over at him and her eyes filled with tears.

"I owe you so much more," he vowed. "Go open your things."

Kisha smiled as she tore into the many boxes of clothes, shoes, purses, and jewelry. When she got to the last envelope. She ripped it open and poured out its contents. Checkbooks and safety deposit keys fell into her lap. She looked up at him with concern.

"I want to always make sure you are good. Our thing is set up a certain way. But no matter what, you and our daughter will always be a'ight."

Kisha got to her feet and went right into his arms. "All we will ever need is you," she stated as the thoughts of not having him sunk into her gut.

"You will always have me," he vowed, lifting her to his waist, and sliding back into his favorite place.

"And I will love you forever," she too vowed, wrapping her legs firmly around him as he pulled her all the way back in.

Malik carried her to the bed, tossed the pillows to the floor, climbed all in his pussy, and became lost as he stroked nice and slow. He wanted her to remember every curve and revel in all the love he had for her. That night they strengthened their bond one orgasm filled position at a time. When Malik dozed off Kisha just laid there next to him watching him sleep and listening to him breathe. She moved a little closer and held on as if it was her first and last time.

Malik clutched her waist and snuggled against her breasts. To him, this was the only place he could feel safe, and at peace. "Always remember, Ma, there is nothing in this world that can challenge our love, but us. We got that forever shit," he mumbled.

"Forever, and always," she confirmed as she closed her eyes and drifted to sleep.

"Forever and always," Kisha mumbled as she opened her eyes, darkness had taken the light from the sky.

Tears rolled effortlessly down her face, as she forced her weary body over to the bed and climbed between the sheets. Tonight, she just needed to sleep, because tomorrow she was going to use all the energy, she had left to help shit on all their enemies.

Chapter 9

If It's Yours...Take it

Tyquan entered the hotel room eyeing the beautiful redbone woman to his left dressed in a red, lace bodysuit as she slipped into a side bedroom. He held eye contact with security as they unbuttoned his jacket and removed the leather pouch from his inside pocket.

They handed the pouch back to him after a small inspection allowing him to also keep his gun. He was then escorted to where the Don sat awaiting his visit.

"Please have a seat," Don Anibello offered as he brought the white porcelain cup to his lips.

Tyquan took a seat in the chair across from him and slid the leather pouch across the table.

"You promised us this shit would be wrapped up in a week." Don Anibello blew the steam from his cup as he sipped slowly on his Espresso.

"I got it, trust me." Tyquan tried to ease the Don's mind.

"Trust you?" He chuckled. "You want me to trust you after you handed me your family?" He paused again taking a sip of the dark brew.

Tyquan looked at the aging man, dressed in an all-white suit thinking carefully before he spoke his next words. The last thing he wanted to do was jeopardize everything he had in place with a slip of the tongue.

"I handed you only what I was willing to sacrifice." He crossed his legs. "In return, you handed me the people you were willing to sacrifice. I think we both owe each other at least a glimmer of trust."

Don Anibello looked over to the far corner at his brother then back at Tyquan and a smile crept at the corner of his mouth. "I work with you because you have always delivered." He sat forward resting his cup on the saucer. "But these days people like you I can buy and sell for less than half the trouble I pay for waiting for you." He sat back and let silence take control of the room.

"Is that right?" Tyquan asked, then let silence again take its place.

The Don held a strong gaze before speaking his peace. "I will play your game. Today that is…tomorrow, a whole different feeling may take over. Then…maybe people who are safe now, won't be." He shrugged his shoulders.

"Don, I'm insulted." Tyquan put his hands up to his chest. "I have always kept my word and my money has always been a comfort to your pocket."

"Sometimes it's not about the money." He grabbed a cigar from a small marble box. "It's about blood." He looked Tyquan right in the eyes not allowing even a blink to disturb his point.

Tyquan held eye contact as he gave Anibello his word. "Then Blood it is," he stated smoothly as he rose to his feet.

Tyquan buttoned his jacket and straightened his tie. He headed to the door without saying another word.

As the door slammed closed Don Anibello turned to his brother and made an oath, "When the money changes hands, kill him and his team, then his son. We must snuff out even the evil, in his seed."

"Done." His brother Cheech stood fastening the single button on his blazer.

"Have someone bring the car around. Tonight all debts will be paid," Don Anibello ordered as he put fire to the end of his fine Cuban.

He dutted the thick ash into the glass tray, grabbed the thick leather pouch, tucked it in his inside jacket pocket, and with an evil smirk he uttered. "Blood it is."

****

Monique hurried from one destination to the next passing out final instructions and checking every trap. She made her last stop at the bank to sign over several accounts and transfer money to others. It was time for the transition, and she needed to make sure every piece was in place. She crept along the winding road until she saw the two lights at the dead end.

Monique eased up to the side of the vehicle, turned off her lights, and eased down the window.

"Is everything in place?"

"Do you have my money?"

"Only thing short about me is my fucking patience," she spat back as the exchange seemed to heighten.

"You on my time. Watch your mouth!"

"And you on borrowed time so watch your fucking mouth." Monique clenched her teeth then her gun releasing the safety.

"You know what, fuck you!" The man hurled back then grabbed his gear shift. "When you dick-suckers learn how to talk to a nigga holla at me. Until then stay the fuck away from me," he growled then spat at Monique's car.

With one swift move, Monique pulled her hand to the window and put a single shot between his eyes. She watched his head fall to the side and his lips tremble with bloody regretful moans before she took her foot off the breaks and pulled around his vehicle. Monique eyed him take his last breath then sped off back in the direction she came.

"Every time a nigga puts his dick in the game. He will always come up short," she mumbled as she crept along the dark road. "One down…three to go."

Chapter 10

Scattered Pieces

"You ready to take me to Paradise?" Cheech asked grabbing his treat for the night by the hand.

"Whatever you want, Daddy," she responded in a thick Cuban accent.

She followed closely behind him as he walked over to the large picture windows and pulled open the curtains. He placed her right in front of him and pressed his stiffened dick against her soft cheeks as he looked over the city.

"This is about to be all mine now. I want you to share it with me."

"I want to share it with you, baby," she purred as his hands slid over her ass and down between her legs. "You deserve it, Cheech. You deserve it," she cooed as she felt him spread her cheeks and slide in her slippery opening.

"And you deserve this," he grunted pushing back and forth inside her."

She palmed the glass as his stroke quickened. "Cum for me, Cheech," she moaned feeling his hands tighten on her waist.

Cheech mumbled incoherently as he felt his knees weaken. He pushed her down slightly changing the angle of his stroke.

"Yes, Cheech right there, baby," she cried out as his dick spoke directly to her spot.

Cheech stroked deep until he released all he had to offer inside her. He pulled back allowing his now semi-hard dick to ease out of her wetness.

"Thank you, baby," she cooed as she turned to face her lover.

Cheech leaned in and hungrily kissed her lips, as he pulled back slowly his brow creased with fear as he watched Lauren's eyes widen. He looked up at the window for a reflection but was blocked by a plastic bag that was now over his face. Cheech pulled at the bag in an attempt to be freed, but it only tightened with his every movement.

Lauren crouched down and watched the thick plastic cling to his lips as Cheech fought for air and life. She screeched and covered her mouth as he dropped to his knees taking his final gasps before surrendering to his fate. Before Cheech's soul could settle his murderer pulled out a 9mm and put two bullets in the back of his head. Lauren grabbed her chest as she watched the bag fill with blood and brain. When his lifeless body hit the ground the strength in Lauren's knees forced her to drop to the marble below.

"Get up," the voice boomed in her direction.

Lauren slowly rose to her feet and panic set in when she saw the gun aimed in her direction.

"Mo, please, I did everything you said," she cried as urine began to run down the inside of her legs puddling at her feet.

"Every war has its casualties…today bitch, you are it." Monique put one in her chest and one in her head before she hit the floor.

Mo tucked the gun in the small of her back and faded into the darkness.

****

"To the Bride and Groom, may they have much wealth, health, and many children. Salute!" Don Anibello held his glass high in the air as he admired his beautiful daughter's smile. Her tear-filled eyes glistened back at him melting his heart into a million pieces.

The crowd rang out in cheer as the music started for the father-daughter dance. He placed his glass on the table and prepared to meet his Princess. Together they moved to the center of the dance floor then took their spot right below the Crystal chandelier and began to move gracefully in front of their family and cherished friends.

"I have waited for this moment all my life," the Don confessed looking at his perfect angel in all white.

"I love you, Daddy," she said looking up into her heroes' eyes. She placed her head on his shoulder and enjoyed the beat of his heart as they eased across the dance floor.

As the song came to an end the guests erupted in cheer. He walked his daughter back to the center of the dance floor, placed a single kiss on the back of her hand then waived over at the staff to begin the money ceremony.

Don Anibello headed back to his table as his guests formed several lines in preparation to adorn his daughter with riches. Before he could reach his seat, his trusted security rushed over to him and whispered into his ear. He divided his attention between his daughter smiling occasionally as he listened to the time-shifting news that was being presented to him.

"Did you find my brother?"

"Not yet."

"Find my brother." He looked coldly into his eyes.

"Yes, sir," he answered then took off towards the exit.

He struggled with the information he received along with the discomfort he felt as the realization set in that his brother may have caught up with time.

"Oh, nooo!" a screeching voice rang out snapping him back to the here and now.

Don Anibello turned toward his daughter to see thick red blood pouring from her nose and mouth down onto her dress.

"Daddy!" she screamed when their eyes connected.

The Don ran to her, pushing his guests to the side as he made a path to his angel. Catalina grabbed her stomach dropping the bag of money to the floor. The Don grabbed her in his arms as he yelled for security to get help. He pulled a white handkerchief from his pocket and wiped at her mouth as she screamed out in pain.

"God, no…please no!" he cried out clutching his daughter to his chest.

Don Anibello screamed at the top of his lungs as he heard his Princess gurgle on the thick crimson that was pouring from her mouth.

"Daddy, I love you," she uttered with her last breath.

"Hold on, Princess…hold on," he spoke the words as her body went limp in his arms.

Don Anibello's ears lost the ability to hear all sound as he looked at the fear in his guest's faces. He looked over to the bridal table and his arms buckled as he watched each person hunch over in pain with blood oozing from their nose and mouth, their heads hit the table and bodies slumped in their chairs causing an uproar in the ballroom.

The guests screamed and scattered as close family fell to their knees around Catalina and the Don as he held his Princess in his arms. The Don looked at her blood-soaked dress pinned with the very money made from the blood he had shed. He closed Catalina's eyes, brought her to his chest, and made his final promise.

"I will not close my eyes, until your enemies and each one of their children closes theirs."

Chapter 11

Decisions

Tyquan sped along the winding road as thoughts roamed through his mind about what he needed to talk to his boy about. The ink on the deals was almost dry, he just needed to tie up a few loose ends. As he approached the dead end, he saw flashing lights in the distance. He drove up a short distance from the black and yellow tape and dead his engine.

"What the fuck?" he mumbled as he realized Bison was the person being loaded onto a gurney.

Tyquan put his car in reverse and slowly eased backward until he saw a small grass path to turn around in. He drove about a half-mile up before turning on his lights. Once he pulled onto the expressway, he hit the speed of over 90 mph.

"What the fuck is going on?" he yelled pounding on the steering wheel.

Tyquan pushed on until he got back to his office. He pulled into the parking garage, right into his spot. He jumped out and slammed the door rushing to the elevator.

"Good evening, Mr. Wells," the doorman announced pulling the door open as Tyquan approached.

Tyquan didn't respond as he passed through the open space. He jumped on the elevator impatiently waiting for his stop as rage filled his belly. Tyquan hurried off the elevator as soon as the doors cracked and moved swiftly to his office. He moved right to his safe, pushed in the code, popped it open, and grabbed a few envelopes inside. He quickly read over the documents and his heart almost collapsed in his chest when he got to the signature on the last page.

"Fuck," he uttered then crumbled the papers and threw them back into the safe slamming it shut.

One of his men had been touched which threatened the new foundation he was putting in place. Tyquan needed to make sure the deal with Don Anibello and the Cubans went through. He didn't want to end up on the side of the coin that didn't win the flip. He picked up the phone and confirmed his meeting before heading to the door.

****

Don Anibello sat in his hotel lounge chair staring down at his white suit stained with the blood of his beloved. His trusted men moved back and forth making calls and plotting plans that he only grasped bits and pieces of. Flashes of his daughter filled his head and clouded his thoughts as he wiped an occasional tear.

"I just need one name!" he yelled over the chaos stopping everyone in their places.

"No worries, Don. You will be able to hear many. And rest in peace will follow each one," Bruno affirmed in his thick Italian accent.

"Action…I need action don't make me no fucking promises," he ordered then cleared the table with one arm knocking everything to the floor. Glass scattered across the square tiles sending eerie chills up everyone's spines.

His team jumped to clean up the mess as they turned every rock, they knew to get the answers they needed. This was not business. It was not personal. It was immediate. He wanted immediate execution of anyone involved. That was the only solution he was willing to accept.

"Hello?" Bruno answered then listened intently.

The room fell silent as they awaited the verdict from the other end of the phone.

"Are you certain?" Bruno asked forcing the words from his mouth. "Okay, thank you," he continued then ended the call.

Bruno placed the phone on the receiver then moved over to where the Don sat, leaned down to his side, and whispered their worse fear.

Don Anibello didn't have enough energy to speak. They had taken his brother. He just dropped his head and closed his eyes. Each man in attendance stood staring at their leader broken and torn, knowing that the only remedy would end in puddles of blood. The seconds seemed like hours as they awaited the parting of his lips, issuing their enemies' fate. The Don took a deep breath, lifted his head, and spoke his orders through closed lids and a dark heart.

"I need you to make sure every hand that has touched my cradle feels the weight of five they love. And I need them to watch."

100

Chapter 12

Seal All Deals

"Thank you so much for meeting with me on such short notice." Tyquan stood to welcome his guest.

"No thanks needed I am here only a short time. I needed to make sure my money was about to be well spent." He extended his hand.

Tyquan gave him a firm shake as they took their seats. He waved over the waitress who quickly took their drink orders and returned with something dark and smooth.

"So, Tyquan, are you sure you are the right man for my money?" Miguel spoke soft but firm.

"When I secure your first million ask me again," he spoke with pure confidence.

"Millions I can get myself I am looking for a type of loyalty that will keep my millions safe and my family safer." He reached for his drink then sat back awaiting Tyquan's response.

"That's why I'm here." Tyquan sat back prepared to engage in his mental tug of war."

Both men sat silent feeling the other out. Miguel had the whole hand preparing to only lose a few cards, whereas Tyquan stood to lose the whole deck. Tyquan had one mission and taking no for an answer just wasn't what he was going to accept. After sitting in an eye embrace Tyquan decided to put his balls on the table first.

"We are both here only to connect the dots. My family took a loss. That debt will be paid in blood. But while that's spilling ain't nobody making no fuckin' money." He sat forward folding his hands on the table.

"I dealt with your father for years. I put the men in the room that need to be there and then I walk away.

****

Monique glared through her shades out of the window into the distance as her driver pulled along her mother's Connecticut estate. She set her eyes on the three black horses grazing the property and her mind flooded with warm childhood memories. She quickly shut them down as the car pulled up to the Ranch. Monique took a deep breath and prepared her soul for what it was about to endure. When the door opened, she stepped out of the car, straightened her pants and blouse, then headed to the front porch. Monique took one last breath then opened and walked through the doors she had not passed through in years.

"Momo!" A screeching voice bellowed out as she walked down the foyer.

"Ms. Lois." She smiled as she hurried towards her.

"Seeing your beautiful face brings my old heart so much joy." Tears left her eyes as she took Monique's face into her hands holding their gaze firmly.

"I missed you so much," Monique uttered as she too lost the battle with the water threatening to leave her eyes.

"Welcome home, my love." She released her face and pulled her in her arms and hugged her until her arms became weak around Monique's body.

Monique hugged her even tighter as a surge of emotions flooded her body. The woman stood in their embrace until they were jolted back to the here and now by the sound of ringing chimes. They both looked up at the top of the banister as all the joy they had just experienced drained from their bodies.

"Lois…" the heavy voice rang out followed by gags and gasps.

"Coming, Miss!" she yelled back then turned to Monique. "Go and see your son, he's in the study. I will tell her you are here." She once again touched Monique's face, smiled then headed up the staircase.

Monique choked back her emotions, steadied her breathing, then walked down the hall toward the study. When she reached the solid oak door, she pushed it lightly then dashed her sights around the room until they settled on the back of Kayson's head as he watched the movie playing on the television. A smile took control of her lips and again her heart beat with happiness.

"King," she said softly.

Kayson's little head spun around, and he jumped up from his seat and ran in her direction. "Mommy," he squealed as he jumped into her arms. "I missed you," he said holding her firm in his grip.

"How much?" she asked as she tickled his side.

"Soooooo…much!" He giggled and twitched as she poked all his little silly spots.

"How was your day?" she picked him up and carried him to the couch then placed him on her lap.

"I had so much fun. I rode horses and a four-wheeler and ate cheesecake," he rattled off his day detail by detail.

Monique held him close to her and listened as he filled her ears with all his little adventures. He laughed and chattered a mile a minute and Monique just bathed in his innocence. She sat getting an earful until he ran out of words. When he was done, he sat back in her arms and just laid silently as he rotated his hearing from her heartbeat to the movie that was playing only feet away from them.

"I love you, mommy," he said as he closed his eyes and just enjoyed her warmth and sweet perfume.

"I love you more," she uttered as she took his little hand into hers.

Kayson settled into the calmness and his eyes became heavy as Monique had begun to slightly sway. Monique held Kayson in her arms until his body went limp. She kissed him softly on his forehead, then laid him down and coved him with the cashmere throw, then placed a pillow under his little head. She stared at his beautiful face, then again placed a single kiss on his forehead. Monique grabbed the remote and turned down the volume then tipped out of the room. When she reached the end of the hall, she was met by Ms. Lois.

"She is ready to see you," she spoke gently as the severity of the situation pained her heart.

Monique nodded her head then headed up the stairs. Miss. Lois scurried to the kitchen to prepare lunch. Monique's feet became weighted as she got closer to her mother's bedroom door. Her breathing quickened as she stood frozen in the doorway. She stared at her mother's frail defeated body and her throat tightened to see this once strong beautiful woman now weak and pale.

"Don't just stand there looking at me. Come here," her raspy voice bellowed followed by an uncontrollable cough.

"Yes, mother." Monique moved to her mother's bed grabbing the glass of water from the nightstand.

Monique put her hand behind her mother's head and brought the glass to her mouth. She watched her mother struggle to both drink and breath as she fought back her feelings the things her mother called weakness. Monique set the glass back on the nightstand then eased her mother back to the pillow. She pulled the chair next to the bed right up to the edge. She took her mother's ice-cold hand into hers then brought it to her mouth and placed a kiss on the backside.

"Bath and dress me," her mother ordered again coughing with every word barely able to maintain steady breath.

"Yes, mother," Monique answered then quickly stood, grabbed the big porcelain bowl from the side of the bed, then gathered all the things needed to handle the task. She walked into the bathroom and began filling the bowl with hot water. She stared at her reflection in the mirror and the image staring back at her caused vomit to rise to the back of her throat. As the steam rose from the bowl and settled on the mirror her mood worsened as the distortion she viewed brought her to even more feelings of disgust. Monique turned off the water then hurried to her mother's side and began to strip her down and clean her skin. Once she had her nice and fresh, she rolled her from one side of the bed to the other, changed the sheets, dressed her in one of her finest dresses, and then finished the task by putting on her pearls and diamond earrings.

Monique propped her mom up on the many goose feathered pillows, adjusted her oxygen tube, and pulled the silk comforter up to her waist then sat back down next to the bed. She watched as her mother labored to breathe then struggled to talk.

"Did you do everything I told you to do?" She coughed and gagged with each word.

"Yes, mother. All of your affairs are in order," Monique answered quickly.

Mother rolled her eyes at her daughter as her chest filled with disgust. She then searched for the next words she wanted to say to her daughter. "They took your father and sister and left me with you," she forced the words from her mouth as each breath took her wind. Tears filled her eyes as the arms of death wrapped themselves around her.

"I'm sorry, mother," Monique confessed as she grabbed the water from her bedside and brought it to her lips.

Mother struggled to drink then with the little strength she had left she pushed Monique's hand from her face. "Yes, you are. Very sorry." She gasped for her next piece of air. "Just make...sure my grandson..." she paused. "...is not as sorry as you." She coughed back the phlegm in her throat then laid her head back into the pillows.

"Yes, mother," Monique vowed as she watched the very life drain from her mother's veins.

Mother closed her eyes and tried to rest as her body fought for its right to live. Monique watched her mother struggle and the fight she was having with the water behind her eyes pushed its way down her cheeks.

"Momo," Ms. Lois spoke softly from the doorway.

Monique wiped at her eyes then turned in her direction. She wanted to speak but the pain in her heart stole her words as it dug deeper into her chest.

Ms. Lois walked over to her and pulled her head into her chest. "No worries little face. She does truly love you," she spoke a little over a whisper as she too realized the severity of the hour.

Monique placed her hand on her mother's leg as the flood gates broke pouring tears steadily. "All I ever wanted was her love," she uttered as she watched her mother hang onto the last bit of life she had.

"Take comfort in knowing Kayson will be better than us all. She gave him all the love she had left." She held her close as they both wept. "I'll go prepare a bath for you." Ms. Lois kissed Monique on the top of her head then released her from her grip.

"I won't leave her side," Monique's broken words eased from her lips. "Leave us."

"Yes, my love," she replied as she eased out the same way she had entered.

Monique took her mother's hand back into hers then brought it to her face. She placed several kisses on the backside then laid her head on her mother's leg. "I will make you proud, Mother. I promise." She vowed closing her eyes and enjoying the last moments they would have together.

Monique drifted off and when the light of day touched her face her eyes fluttered in place as she gripped her mother's hand. She sat straight up as the coldness settled against her palm. She pulled her mother's hand to her face and cried from the depths of her soul. It was final, God had broken the hold, but the scars would always remain. Monique sat with her mother until the ambulance arrived and arranged her dead body in the back of the cold truck. She stared through the window and watched them cover her face, it was over. She turned back to the house headed right to Kayson's room. Monique climbed into bed next to him and held him close. He was all she had left that was pure and she vowed to make sure she did not ruin him. Monique closed her eyes and filled her soul with the warmth and love from the only person who would matter from this day until her last day.

****

"Baby, are you done with your plate?" Zibra yelled from the bottom of the steps.

"Yeah, I'm done!" Smoke yelled back as he pulled the T-shirt over little man's head. He lotioned his face and hair, then swooped him into his arms and headed back downstairs.

"Aww look at my little chocolate man," Zibra cooed as his bright, brown eyes lit up with excitement.

"This little nigga needs to get a job shittin' like that." Smoke busted out laughing.

"Well, welcome to my world. This is all day, every day at daycare Zibra." She too busted out laughing.

"Well, I'ma have to get you something real special when we get back in motion. I had no idea my son was breaking your nose ten times a day." He walked over and kissed her lips.

"Aww...you are so amazing. But you and him, are all the gifts I need," she confessed as little J.T. rubbed her face and hair.

"I love you, baby girl." He kissed her again.

"I love you, too! Now grab that bottle and get him milk wasted so I can ride that dick," she teased. Then rubbed her hand up and down his semi-hard dick.

"You gonna give him somebody to play with you keep being fresh," he mumbled as he reached for the warm bottle.

"I'ma play with something in a minute right in my mouth," she continued her wordplay.

"I'm about to give him a shot of Hennessey. Oh, he going to sleep."

"You better not drug my baby, crazy." She giggled shaking her head at the thought. "I'll meet you upstairs, baby," she announced.

She placed the last dish in the dishwasher. Then headed upstairs to wash away her day. Smoke sat in the recliner and

107

rocked his prince to sleep, then placed him nice and snug in his crib. He stood silently over him watching his little tummy rise with each breath. His chest filled with pride as he watched his greatest creation only inches from him sleeping with no worry, yet the threat of danger and death was all around them. He rubbed over J.T.'s tight curls then headed to his and Zibra's bedroom.

"Baby, you okay?" she asked noticing his whole mood change.

"Just wanting the best for you and my son," he responded pulling his T-shirt over his head.

"It will be okay, baby. Come lay with me." She patted the empty spot next to her.

Smoke sat on the bed and rubbed his hands over his face as he tried to empty his mind of the rushing bad thoughts that were now clouding his judgment. "I don't want to put you in danger," he uttered with a heaviness in his heart that he knew would not be settled with a few kind words.

"It's going to be okay, baby, I promise." She crawled over to where he sat and wrapped her arms around him. "Everything will be okay," she spoke a little over a whisper. She squeezed him tighter with the hopes of erasing all his pain.

Smoke turned to face Zibra and held her tightly in his grip. He placed kisses along her neck and face savoring every sweet spot he tasted. Zibra wrapped her legs around his waist and prepared to feel those long deep strokes. Smoke went into overdrive as he slipped into her wet, tight spot. They were in a full tug of war as he fed her thick, dick and she pushed his wet pussy right back at him.

"Damn, baby, you feel so good," he mumbled as he bit into her right breast then sucked the nipple slow while fucking her the way she liked it.

"Smoke, I love you," she whined as he showed her spot no mercy.

"I love you, too," he chanted as he felt her wetness saturate his thighs. "Fuck," he growled as she rotated her hips positioning him deeper and deeper with every push.

Smoke got firm in a pushup position with her legs draped over his arms so he could watch his dick get wetter with every slide. He looked back up and into her pretty, brown face as he filled her body with all the pleasure it could handle.

Zibra closed her eyes and held on tight as she felt waves of heated passion take over her body and her mind.

"Ahhhhh!" Smoke yelled as immense pain shot through his body.

When Zibra looked up she screamed to the top of her lungs at the sight of the sharp end of the blade sticking out of his stomach. She scrambled to be free as blood began to pour from his mouth and nose onto her chest. When she looked up and saw who was at the other end of that unforgiving blade her heart almost stopped.

Smoke fell over to the side shaking and gargling as his lungs begin to drown in their own blood. Zibra scrambled to a corner, tucked her head against her knees, and prayed as the events of the night boomed in her head.

"Don't cry, Ma, it was his time," Skully spoke in his husky voice.

"Why?" she screamed from the top of her lungs while looking over at Smoke's lifeless body.

Smoke's empty eyes stared back at her. She cried from her soul as she realized she would never have him actually look at her again.

"Make this easy for me, Ma," he said as if she would just run into his arms for her fate.

Zibra pissed right where she sat as she watched him walk towards her with the knife firm in his grip. He moved closer and closer ready to seal her deal with the devil. As he stepped over her ready to strike, Zibra heard two light sounds then watched Skully's white T-shirt fill with thick crimson as he fell to his knees. She looked up into the doorway with squinted eyes trying to make out the figure that had just saved her life.

Pashion moved slowly toward her with her silenced nine tucked against her palm. "I came here for two reasons. One of them is already gone, then there's you." Pashion stood over a traumatized Zibra praying she didn't make her change her mind.

"I don't know nothing, I don't want to die," she mumbled through tears and pain.

Pashion stared down at her and a small piece of the heart she had left jumped slightly as she thought about her own daughter's pain.

"They took my life. But today I'ma spare yours and the life of your son…" She paused as a flood of emotion-filled her chest. "Today he lives, and you live, too. Don't make me regret it," she spoke softly then eased out the same way she entered.

When Zibra heard the tires peel down the driveway she jumped up, ran into her son's room, and pulled him into her arms. She let out all her confusion and anger in one scream causing him to yell out with her. Zibra quickly jumped into action, placed him back into the crib, and began running through the cabin packing everything she could. She threw everything in the back of the truck then headed back inside. Zibra grabbed a towel, wiped herself down, and threw on a pair of sweatpants and a T-shirt, then retrieved J.T. and his bags. She stopped in the bedroom and kneeled next to Smoke.

"Baby, I'm sorry," she whispered as she closed his eyes shut. "I will always protect your son." She kissed him on his forehead one last time. "See you soon." She promised as she quickly jumped to her feet and headed to the truck.

Once inside she made a vow. She was now going to take the mercy that woman gave her and use it for revenge. One thing she knew for sure and two things for certain, in this game never leave an enemy breathing.

****

Tyquan sped through the streets of New York headed to Don Anibello's Queens restaurant. Within days everything had gone from bad to half-past deadly in one blink. This was his last chance to get ahead in this dirty game they played. Tyquan pulled up to the curb and watched as the Dons' family and friends poured into the venue. He turned off his engine and hopped out to pay his respect. When he walked through the doors his eyes settled on the women in hats and veils and men in their crisp black suits. He looked over to where the Don sat and watched him try to interact with his guests through the hurt in his chest. Tyquan moved around the room waiting for his chance to get close to the Don for a quick conversation.

When Tyquan got to the point where he could finally have his say. He looked up and saw Miguel walking into the restaurant. He stopped at a few tables then headed right over to where the Don sat. Tyquan watched the two men have a very intense conversation then a white envelope was pulled out and placed on the table. Don Anibello confirmed their conversation with a nod. Just as Tyquan thought to make his way over to where the two men sat, he looked up and saw Monique walking through the door. She moved through the room shaking hands and kissing babies until she reached the Bosses.

"So, sorry for your loss, Don Anibello," she spoke softly as she leaned in and kissed him on both cheeks.

"You are a true treasure. Thank you for coming," the Don added as the severity of his current situation tugged at his heart.

"As are you, Don." Monique sat in the chair next to him and spoke quick and direct. She too went into her purse, pulled out an envelope, and slid it across the table. She followed it with a small piece of paper that the Don picked up. She watched while he read it intensely then he closed it and placed it in his front pocket.

"Thank you," Don Anibello mumbled as the information sank into his spirit. "It is settled we will move forward," he confirmed.

Miguel nodded his understanding then rose to his feet leaving the venue without even a small acknowledgment of Tyquan's presence. Monique stood as well settling their meeting with a kiss on the Don's pinky ring. She walked away not even looking in Tyquan's direction.

"What the fuck is going on here?" Tyquan mumbled to himself. He then headed in Don Anibellos' direction. Before he could get to the table the Don was rising from his seat.

"My condolences, Don Anibello," Tyquan said as he approached.

"We will talk another time," Don Anibello said leaving Tyquan standing in place as he stood abruptly.

Tyquan watched the Don and his team moved to the door. He stood there for a few more seconds before he put a slight smile on his face then turned to leave the venue. When he got outside none of the culprits were present. He scanned the block then jumped into his car and sped off. Answers were needed and he knew where he needed to get them from.

****

Monique exited the bathroom in her white fluffy robe with a towel wrapped tightly around her hair. She walked into the kitchen with a slight victory smile on her face. The torch had been passed and now she needed to make sure the heads she put in place didn't roll before she got everything that was promised to her. She walked into her living room, moved over to the wine station, and poured herself a tall glass of red, sweet wine. As she brought the glass to her mouth to take the first very needed sip, she heard the intercom ring from the foyer. Monique sashayed over to the wall unit and pressed her finger to the answer.

"Yes," she bellowed into the speaker.

"Mrs. Wells, your husband is here," the caller announced then waited silently for her response.

After a brief pause, Monique spoke, "You can send him up."

Monique removed the towel from her head and walked into the kitchen, then stood on the other side of the island and waited for the fallout.

"What the fuck is going on, Mo?" Tyquan stormed into her apartment slamming the door closed behind him. The vibration rocked the picture frames against the wall as he pushed his way through her apartment.

"Don't come in here with all that energy, Tyke," Monique said calmly as she rubbed the towel over her damp hair.

"Don't fucking play with me, Mo. All this shit going on ain't no fucking coincidence."

Monique laid the towel on the counter, tightened the belt on her robe, then began, "Has anything been a coincidence, Tyke?"

"What the fuck are you talking about?" he growled as his temperature began to rise.

"Malik, his family, his children. What part did you play? Why are you untouched? Why is it that you always skate by?" She rested her arms on her chest.

"I ain't have shit to do with Malik or his family. He chose to put snakes around him and he got bit. I warned him just like, I'm warning you. Stay the fuck outta my way."

"*Warn?*" She chuckled as the words left her lips. "You don't have the power to warn me about shit."

Tyquan forced himself to calm down as the invitation to choke the shit out of her tightened his fists. "Mo, I promise you if anything I have set into motion is jeopardized, you will wake up every day in regret."

"I don't sleep, that's why I'm ahead of your dumb ass. So, trust me I have no regret," she spat with gritted teeth."

"You are a grimy bitch."

"And so is your mother," she spat back.

"Please don't make me kill you over this kingdom."

"This is Malik's kingdom. You don't own shit, muthafucka!" She raised her voice with every word. "I promised to protect it and his children."

"His dick must have been sweet on your tongue," Tyquan spat with disgust rising in his belly.

"I gotta protect our son no matter what. And if a dick is involved, I'ma ride that shit right into victory." Monique chuckled. "See that's the difference between a real man and a sucka ass nigga." She looked him square in his eyes. "He kept my pussy wet

113

and never even touched it." She gripped the tassels on her robe then placed her hands on the cold granite countertop.

"You are an evil bitch. And now you in this muthafucka ass deep. Enjoy your reign."

"You brought me into this shit. You made it possible for me to have all this pow...."

"Worst mistake of my fucking life. But *you* will be the one to regret it," he cut in, then turned toward the door. "You wanted to be a Well's, let's see if your walls are tight enough to hold your position."

"Tighten up, Tyquan. Your panties are showing." She chuckled as she watched him walk off in defeat.

"Remember you said that when all this power you want chokes the shit outta you." He snatched the door open slamming it against the wall as he sped through the opening unable to stay in her presence another second.

"And you remember to stay the fuck outta my way as I claim my throne!" she yelled as the door slammed closed.

Monique rushed over and put the locks back in place then ran and grabbed her gun. She hopped in the bed placing it on the pillow she stared at the steel, knowing that from this day forward it was the only bitch she was going to bow to.

Chapter 13

It's Their Turn

Sixteen Years Later

Kayson walked into the pool hall, hoodie over his head and jeans laying perfectly over his black Timberlands. He placed his finger to his lips as he moved past the red velvet tables. The loud slick talk and downtime antics wasn't something he was interested in. Voices lowered as they watched Kayson's tall dominant frame move through the room without making eye contact with a soul present. He looked past the tables of card and pool tournaments and spotted Aldeen and Wise playing cards and headed right in their direction.

"Reports?" he asked as he walked over to the table where they sat. He picked up the daily receipts and checked the figures as he waited for the information.

Aldeen spoke first, "We got weight moving through the city real nice. I dropped prices just below the Queens connect rate and every borough been getting at me."

"Good, I need them niggas to get in line," Kayson spat.

"I can't get a handle on who is in charge in Harlem. They got a crazy-ass connect, and that shit is raw. The ship is run ass cheek tight, and all them niggas are quiet, state your business and get the fuck on type niggas."

Kayson stood in silence tossing around what moves he wanted to make next. "Just put somebody on watch. I might have to stir some shit up in order to bring the boss out."

"On it."

"What else?" Kayson began to scan his mind.

"Fred wants a sit-down. I'll chop that up with you later," Aldeen said then looked down at his cards.

"Indeed." Kayson nodded at Al's sign of privacy and closed the conversation.

"What you got, Wise?" He turned his attention to his other right arm.

"I ain't got shit my whole team is on point. I'm just watching the clock and counting the dough. And if a bitch nigga fold, I damn sure won't buckle."

"Is that right?" Kayson had to chuckle.

"Hell, yeah, like a fat bitch poots greasy air."

"What the fuck, nigga? You a muthafuckin' fool." Kayson busted out laughing causing them all to erupt.

"Shiiieeettt! Just stating the facts." Wise said shrugging his shoulders.

"You see what the fuck we gotta deal with? This nigga retarded." Aldeen shook his head.

"I'll be right back, y'all niggas crazy," Kayson said as he left the table.

Kayson went to the bar first and checked the register then spoke to security. When his soldiers got a little more comfortable with his presence, he made his rounds around the room collecting information and passing out instructions. A few guys passed him rolls of money then continued their games. Kayson tucked the money in his hoodie pocket then took a seat at the bar and just watched the movement and the money as he sat for a minute reflecting on everything they had been through and all they had lost. The faces of friends and family flashed through his mind, then the pain behind the murder and betrayal filled his heart with blackness.

"You need anything, Boss?" a squeaky voice rang out from behind the bar.

"Nah, I'm good," he responded keeping his eyes set on the room.

Kayson rose to his feet then headed to a booth in the far corner of the room and took a seat. As he settled his body into the soft leather, Kayson looked at his soldiers and thought back to the day all the decisions about the family would be on him, lives were in his hands and it was that time when take over meant blood and tears and when it was a time of war, all a nigga could do was strap up and knock off the strongest heads. He watched as his men laughed and joked enjoying their downtime. He tried to settle his mind, but his uncle's words always took over when he was faced with a difficult victory. He pulled his hood down to his eyes then put his head back and drifted deep into his past.

"Kayson, come here," Rabb called out from the back office. He had sat back for years watching and learning from his nephew. Then watched him become great.

Kayson walked in and closed the door behind him. "What's up, Unc?" He walked over, took his uncle's hand, and bumped shoulders with him then headed to the seat right across from the desk.

"You good, Nephew?" He looked at the stress beginning to form on his nephew's face.

"Yeah, Unc, I'm good. I just gotta keep moving my hand so these niggas can keep coming up short."

"I know, and that's why I lose sleep at night," he confessed.

"No need to, you know if nothing else, I'ma make it home at night. And if I don't, I'ma burn half of New York to the ground on my way out.

"Shit don't feel right, Nephew. These niggas are on your ass. We got the best shit in town. The price is cut and when niggas get hungry as you put it. They tend to act the fuck up."

"Good, I want them to act up. That's the shit I pray for."

"War...is that what you are asking for?"

"Not asking for it...welcoming it! I don't want to rule no fucking throne I stumbled upon. I know I gotta make these niggas bleed." He sat forward asserting his authority. "Your only job is to make sure I know what I need to know."

Rabb nodded his head slowly as he processed his nephew's words. "You know what you want, right? However, I'm not exactly sure what these niggas are doing yet. So, I need you to chill. I have people in the streets just waiting on confirmation. In the meantime, just chill and be careful." He sat up and lit his cigarette then tossed the lighter on the desk.

"How the fuck you gonna be a killah and be scared?" Kayson joked at his uncles' statements. He was the man he learned everything from and here he was afraid.

"You see, that's the shit that worries me. You have no fear."

"Have, fear for what, Unc? You think them other niggas gonna be scared if they get a chance to peel my shit back?"

"Nephew, fear keeps you alert…fear keeps you alive."

"Well, then good, cause I'm afraid to die so fear is keeping me alive. But the niggas gunning for me better stay scared, too."

"You are your father's son." He chuckled.

"What the fuck is that supposed to mean?" Kayson's blood started to stir.

"Exactly what the fuck I said. You are a fucking, Wells… hardheaded…fearless and fuckin' power-driven. And that shit ain't healthy."

Kayson took a minute to go over his next lines. He loved and respected his uncle and all facts on the table, he was the only father he ever had or cared to know. "Unc, I respect your guidance. Thank you." He got up from his seat. "Unc, I need you to remember this. Fear is one thing but being afraid is a whole other animal. If you scared get out now. Because that shit definitely ain't healthy." He turned to the door.

"I love you, nephew. Just want the best for you," he said as he watched him leave the room.

Kayson grabbed the knob and before closing the door he yelled out. "I love you, too, Unc. Please do me that favor. If you scared get out. The shit I'm about to do is gonna bring these niggas to their knees. I'm forcing all opposition to bow." He left closing the door behind him.

"Boss, you ready?" Aldeen asked as he walked over to where Kayson sat.

"Always," Kayson snapped back to the present as he rose from his seat.

When he approached the exit, he waved at Wise. Wise jumped up, ending his conversation with one of the waitresses, and moved toward the door.

"Where to?" Aldeen asked as they approached Kayson's truck.

"I'll tell you on the way." He tossed the keys to him and walked to the passenger seat.

The three men headed to Aldeen's truck plotting and planning on how they were going to push evil through the streets.

"This the time of year that a nigga's gun gets nostalgia. I think it's time to bust some ass," Kayson stated firmly slamming the door behind him.

"These nigga's mamas better get their black dresses and sad talk ready, cause it's nightmare season," Wise slurred as Aldeen pulled off into the night.

Chapter 14

Reasons

The Celebration

"I have had the opportunity to watch this brilliant young lady grow from a college intern full of ambition and drive to one of the top earners keeping this company in the black for the past year. Also, the first woman to hold the title of VP in the history of this firm. Please raise your glasses," he instructed as he looked over at Lisa's smiling face. "To Lisa!" John Kline closed his speech, glasses were raised, and cheers rang out.

Lisa smiled widely as she basked in the applause and well wishes that echoed throughout the room. It had been two years since she stepped out of college and through the doors of Krovitz Sherman and Klein, now she was taking the lead as Vice President over sales and marketing for both New York, Connecticut, and California.

"Thank you so much," she announced as the applause lightened. "I am so blessed and grateful to have such an amazing team and support system." Lisa looked over at her fiancé James and her heart filled with joy. She mouthed, "Thank you," then gave him a wink.

As Lisa continued, she gazed into the smiling faces of her guests and became emotional as she thought about all the sacrifices it took to stand where she now stood. It had not been an easy road and the things and people she'd lost almost changed her mood from happy to sad in one blink of her tear-filled eyes.

"Again, thank you all for coming out and celebrating with me. Cheers to another successful year," she concluded and raised her glass high.

Applause again rang out and the cheers and well wishes filled the huge hall from floor to each crystal chandelier. James stood and pulled her into his arms. Lisa enjoyed their embrace then gently pulled away to greet her family and friends.

"I'll be right back." She smiled as her hand slipped from his.

"I'll be right here." He smiled back as he watched her ass wiggle against the soft form-fitting fabric.

The music started as she moved through the crowd receiving the love, cards, and gifts. She passed handfuls of envelopes and designer gift bags to her assistant as she hugged and thanked her guests. Flashing cameras and frozen smiles filled the room as the party kicked up into high speed. Lisa stopped at her parents' table and hugged her mom and dad.

"I'm so proud of you." Her mom squeezed her cheeks as if she was still five years old.

"I love you, Mommy." She took her mom by the face and kissed her gently on her forehead.

"I love you more. Please enjoy this moment. Nothing else matters, right now," she reminded her as she noticed a small glimmer of false cheer shining through her eyes.

"Yes, ma'am," she answered and forced the biggest smile she could muster.

Just as Lisa was about to continue through the room, her assistant tapped her shoulder and alerted her to a phone call at the front desk.

"Excuse me, I'll be right back," she announced before walking off toward the exit.

Lisa scanned the area then headed to the front desk. "Hi, I'm Lisa, I was alerted that I have a call on hold," she told the red-headed woman as she searched her mind for who could be calling her.

"I'm sorry, Ms. I don't see any calls for you," she answered.

"I was just told to come to the lobby," Lisa asserted.

"There are no calls on hold ma'am. Let me check my messages." She grabbed a stack of pink post-it notes and thumbed through them carefully.

Lisa stood patiently waiting as the woman also searched the area to see if she had missed anything.

"No, ma'am, I'm sorry there have not been any calls for you. But if anything changes, I will see to it myself that you get the messages." She smiled.

"Thank you." Lisa hesitantly smiled back. "Is there a bathroom close by?"

"Yes, ma'am, just around the corner to your left." She pointed Lisa in the right direction.

"Thank you." Lisa walked off with a big question at the front of her mind.

Lisa walked into the bathroom, placed her hands on the sink, and just stared in the mirror and questions again flooded her mind. She finally had everything she wanted, a man who loved her, the money, and a position she busted her ass for. But, inside there was an emptiness she could not fill no matter how happy she pretended to be. Lisa turned on the water, washed and dried her hands, fingered through her hair then headed to the door.

When she snatched it open, she could have pissed right where she stood.

"Did you forget our secret code?" Kayson asked looking down at her with that knee-weakening gaze.

"What the fuck?" she mumbled as her heart began to beat rapidly in her chest. "Why are you here?" she asked trying to look over his shoulder.

"It's your special night. I never miss anything that's special to you," he stated calmly as he held out a black medium-sized gift bag.

"You never missed anything special except protecting my heart," she said as she fought back the million emotions that flooded her body and mind.

Lisa looked up into his eyes and tears filled hers. "Excuse me, I have to get back to my guests." She tried to push past him.

Kayson knew no words could heal what he had broken, so he didn't try to search for any. Instead, he did what he knew always soothed her savage. Kayson grabbed her face and slipped his tongue into her mouth. Lisa gripped his wrist in an effort to loosen the pull he had on her soul. The bag hit the floor as his hands began to explore what was hiding under her skirt.

Lisa enjoyed the taste of his lips as five hundred thoughts crowded her mind. Kayson backed her further into the bathroom as he sucked soft then hard on her tongue and lips.

"Kayson, no, we are not doing this." She pulled back and gave them enough space for her thoughts to get back on track. "You made your choices. You need to live with them. I'm good with the ones I made," she tried to convince them both.

"Is that right?" he asked as he closed the gap between them.

"Yes, it's very right." Lisa stepped back a few more steps then put her hand on his chest attempting to keep the distance she needed to stay strong.

"I don't believe you," he stated as he grabbed her hand and pulled her closer to him.

"Kay, please don't do this," she pleaded with her mouth, but her heart wanted something different.

"Don't do what?" he asked as he hugged her tightly.

"Kay, please," she whispered while his hands began to arouse her every pleasure.

Lisa struggled to resist him but the force of his hands and the scent that rose off his skin paralyzed her rational thoughts.

Kayson placed her on the counter and stood firmly between her thighs. He slipped his fingers deep inside her wetness and kissed her lips and neck with the passion her body had been missing.

Lisa felt his dick stiffen as he worked his fingers inside her. She wiggled in sync with his finger foreplay until he was right in the spot that made her pussy scream. Lisa unzipped his pants and slid her hand along the length of his dick.

"The Enforcer," she whispered as the memories of his precise stroke caused her clit to throb and nipples to harden.

Kayson heard her body cry out for more and he gave her what she needed. He slipped the thin strap of her dress off her shoulder then placed his warm mouth over her erect nipples.

"I'm about to cum," she moaned as he tickled her spit.

Lisa licked her finger then wrapped them around him and stroked faster as her body began to shiver. As soon as she released her sticky juices all over his fingers, he pulled her to the edge of the counter, tilted her back, and began loosening that tight spot.

Lisa moaned loudly as the force of every inch pushed through the tightness of her walls. It had been months since she had cum and having Kayson's thickness fill her up caused tears to flow from the corners of her eyes. She held his arms and held on as he took full advantage of her pussy grip.

Kayson traced his tongue along her neck as he lifted her ass off the counter with every push. The pussy was warm and soaking wet just the way he loved it. He slid back and forth hitting all sides until she came again. Kayson pulled her down to her feet and bent her over. Lisa placed her hands on the sink and braced herself. He pushed her down onto the counter causing her nipples to rest on the cold marble as he slid in fast and stroked her pussy just right. He reached around and played with her clit as she whined and moaned as he did to her what no other man could.

"You giving that nigga all this good pussy and he don't know how to fuck you?" He teased as he moved to each spot paying it the perfect amount of attention.

Lisa rested her weight on her elbows and lowered her head against the cold stone. "Kayson," she whispered as he pulled out and slid back in slow.

"This your dick, baby girl. Throw that ass back and let me feel this pussy."

Lisa did as she was told. She pushed back into those thick inches moving her waist to his rhythm until she heard a slight hiss leave his lips.

"Come on baby get this dick right," he moaned in that deep hypnotic tone.

"You gonna make me cum," she cried out as the heat between them took over time and space.

"Wet this shit up and stop playing." He grabbed her waist and sped up his push. "Look at me," he commanded as he fucked her faster and harder.

Lisa looked up into the mirror barely able to keep focus as she pushed that wet pussy back into his every thrust. Her eyes rotated open to close as she prepared herself for a body-rocking experience. It was like they were teenagers all over again sneaking in their parents' bedroom.

"Look at me," he demanded as he placed his hand around her throat bringing her gaze up to match his.

Kayson stared into the mirror connecting with her soul as he fucked away all her anger and regret. He stroked and stroked until her legs shook and her body went limp, then he played in her wetness until he was ready to let go.

Kayson pushed himself deep inside her, wrapped his arms around her waist, and released. Lisa inhaled as she felt him fill her womb.

He leaned forward and whispered in her ear. "You belong to me. Don't ever forget that," he taunted then placed a few kisses on the back of her neck.

Kayson eased himself out of what felt like heaven and pulled her to face him. He looked down into her eyes and told her what she always knew.

"You are the only woman I will ever love with my whole heart," he confessed staring at her with his warm hazel gaze.

"I know." Lisa held back her tears as she pushed herself up on her tippy toes and gently kissed his lips.

"Oh, it's like that?" He chuckled.

"You know whose dick this is. And don't you forget," she joked as the warmest smile eased across her face.

Kayson just chuckled at her cockiness. He knew what they had. He also knew the sacrifice he had to make to let her go.

"I'm always here for you. No matter where I am in the world. You call me and I'm coming."

126

"Same here." She squeezed his hands in hers. "But…we can definitely not have this situation again. I'll admit, I needed you, but he doesn't deserve to get hurt behind what I need."

"Shiiieeettt…you think that show up outta nowhere is free."

"Shut up you get on my nerves." She slapped his arm.

Kayson grabbed her in his arms and kissed her deeply before letting her go. He then adjusted his clothes. Kayson touched and tickled her as she pulled her wardrobe back in place.

"Stooppp…hurry up, I have been gone a long ass time," she said trying not to panic. Lisa quickly cleaned up then began pushing him towards the door.

"I'll be back in a week. Can I see you when I get back in town?"

"No, now go. This was a one-time thing." She continued to push him.

"Well, damn, don't forget to leave me the money on the nightstand." He stopped next to the gift bag that had crashed to the floor.

"You so crazy." She giggled.

Kayson picked up the bag and handed it to her. "Please enjoy your gift and the rest of the night." He kissed her lips one last time savoring all her sweetness.

"Thank you so much," she stated as she looked up into those sexy hazel eyes.

"I'm always here for you." He placed a kiss on her forehead then left out as smooth as he entered.

Lisa turned and sat the black gift bag on the counter, grabbed a stack of napkins, saturated them in water and soap. She then pulled her dress up to her waist and scrubbed over her skin then washed between her legs once more wanting to make sure to erase all traces of his scent on her skin. She turned the water as hot as it would go as guilt began to fill her chest. She wet and soaped up some more paper towels and cleaned herself up carefully scrubbing her neck and face. Lisa grabbed another stack, dried off, then pulled her dress down over her ass.

Lisa stared at herself in the mirror and became tickled at the thought of having her fiancé and family only feet away while she was getting fucked proper in the bathroom. She dapped at her bloodshot face and tugged at her dress trying to straighten the wrinkles. Lisa looked around for her panties but there was no need she knew where they were. She smiled at the thought of her thongs in his pocket as she picked up her package.

Just as she opened the bathroom door there stood James. She almost jumped out of her shoes.

"You okay?" he asked with a wrinkled brow.

"Yes, I'm…fine," she confirmed looking past him praying he had not passed Kayson.

"I was getting worried. Who was on the phone?"

"It was just a little business and a pick-up." She held out the bag. "Someone I used to work with had this package delivered," she stated as she proceeded out the door.

"You have so many people who love you." He took her hand as they headed back to the ballroom.

"Yes, I do. Yes, I do," she said as she took a deep breath and prepared to walk back into the crowded room.

Chapter 15

Bitch Move

"Let me get a Philly, Papi." KoKo threw her money on the counter.

"You know your money is no good here. I want to put a ring on your finger," Papi joked sliding the Philly and money in her direction.

"Man, fuck you, Papi. Keep talking, I'ma put a ring around your fucking eye," KoKo spat as she snatched the blunt off the counter leaving the money and Papi behind the counter smiling and mumbling in Spanish.

KoKo stepped out of the store strolling her eyes up and down the block. It was the percent midnight shift change, and everything would be dangerously quiet for the next hour. She cracked the blunt open and began filling it with the sticky green as she walked to the alley beside the Bodega. KoKo slid into the shadows and pulled the thick sweet-tasting smoke deep into her lungs. KoKo ran a few figures through her mind as she prepared for the night pickups and drop-offs.

KoKo paged the team then prepared to head to her first destination. Just as she was about to step back into the light, she saw several cars pull up and doors slam shut one by one. She eased along the wall, pulled back her hoodie, and peeked slightly past the brick wall. All she could see was the back of the last man that entered the store with what appeared to be something shiny.

KoKo reached behind her back, pulled out her heat, and gripped it firmly against her palm. She pulled the strings to her hoodie tight to her face revealing nothing but the whites of her unforgiving eyes.

Just as she started to step out of the darkness the men came rushing back to the waiting vehicle. KoKo ducked back also and clung close to the wall.

"Hurry the fuck up. They said Fred is there now!" She heard one of the men yell as the car doors slammed closed and the tires screeched against the blacktop.

KoKo took off running through the alleys, hopping fences, and jumping over porches until she was a block over from Feather Fred's drop house. She crouched low moving alongside the parked cars. As she reached the top of the block the dark green Cadillac, she saw in front of the store was pulling a few feet away from her. She moved back and stayed low behind a minivan.

"Them niggas are in there. Keep it clean get in and out. Don't play with them niggas," the driver instructed as the three other men quickly jumped out with guns tucked in their grip and pulling black masks over their faces.

The men moved fast toward the front door of the house peeking in the windows and watching the block as they approached the porch and prepared to enter. As the men got up on the door the driver pulled off and KoKo sprang to her feet.

Boom!

"Get the fuck down!"

KoKo heard the thunder of the front door as the men entered the house.

"Niggas, do you know who the fuck I am?"

"Muthafucka, do I look like I know who the fuck you are?" the front guy yelled pointing his gun right at Fred's head. "Give me the fucking money!" He yelled tossing two black bags at Fred's feet.

"Muthafucka you gonna have to kill me," Fred said as smooth as if he was ordering coffee.

"This Nigga think we playin', bust that nigga's knees," he ordered.

As the man pulled one in the chamber, the blast of KoKo's whistle took off the back of the man's head and the side of the other man's next to him. She kicked what was left of the door

130

closed and walked up behind the so-called ringleader and pressed her heat to his spine.

"This is how this shit is going to go." She snatched the gun from his hand.

Fred walked over and grabbed the dead man's gun from the floor and put it to the last man's head. "Move back, KoKo," he ordered.

KoKo eased back slightly with both guns firm and ready.

"On your way outta this bitch, you remember this." His finger began tightening on the trigger. "A dead man can't spend money," he spat then put two in his head.

Chapter 16

Gone

Kayson led the way as he, Aldeen, Wise, and Baseem pushed through Miami International Airport headed to baggage claim in all black from hat to boots. They snatched up their duffle bags and headed to the curb, within seconds a limo pulled to the curb and out jumped the driver popping the trunk along the way. They jumped inside and ordered the driver to the hotel.

"We gotta get in these niggas faces and make them see what we see," Kayson asserted to his trusted men.

"If they are ready for the change, then we won't have any problems getting them to meet up halfway," Aldeen responded.

"Good, get them, niggas, comfortable."

"On it," Aldeen confirmed as they exited the elevator.

Baseem pushed the key card in the door slot and opened the suite wide. Wise began doing a sweep of the area moving from one room to the next checking the closets and under the beds.

Wise propped his bag on the couch and pulled back the zipper. He reached inside and pulled out a black wand and got ready to do his sweep.

"I love this shit. Got a nigga feeling like, MacGyver." He laughed as he powered up the device.

"Who the fuck let this nigga out?" Baseem joked as he watched Wise wave the wand over the furniture, curtains, and lamps.

Aldeen took down the fire detectors and removed the batteries. Kay kept a straight face as he pulled stacks of money out of his and Baseem's duffle and tucked it in the wall safe.

"I need this shit to be clean," Kayson ordered.

"Yes sir, Boss," Baseem added as he left the room to call the connects for the girls.

Aldeen hit his boy for the other naughty party favors then prepared the rooms for the evening's event.

"I'ma hit this shower, so I can make this run. Y'all keep them niggas fucking, sucking, and high as a muthafucka until I walk through that door."

"I'ma have them niggas more than comfortable," Aldeen confirmed as they continued to get ready.

Kayson entered the bathroom, sat his bag on the counter, and turned on the shower. As the water ran filling the bathroom with hot steam, he stripped down and walked around the room going over his plan a million times in his head. He stepped into the steamy water and adjusted it to his comfort.

Kayson lathered his chest as he thought about what his uncle had said. He started to fall into his uncles' feelings then he realized why he sat him down in the first place. Kayson tucked his emotions and instead filled his heart with the hate he needed to accomplish his mission.

****

Pashion sat quietly in her car as she prepared her mind to exit and face the moment she had been dreading. She grabbed a diamond flask from her purse, put it to her lips, then drank until it was empty. She dabbed the rim on her tongue assuring she had every drop then tossed it into the seat next to her. Pashion breathed deeply then popped the locks and stepped out onto the gravel. Her black stiletto boots clicked against the pavement until she reached the flat stone walkway. Pashion clutched one hand in the other as her chest became heavy with every step. She walked right up to the glass door and pulled them open and headed inside.

Pashion adjusted her vision from the sunlight as she looked along the marble wall for her daughter's name. When she saw Sabrina Barnes, her throat seemed to close as the tears began to roll down her face. Pashion began to shake as the pressure of the moment tugged at her soul. She stumbled over to a hard stone bench and sat down just before her legs gave way beneath her.

"Why did they take my baby?" she cried out as a bone-chilling scream followed her words echoing through the mausoleum.

Pashion hugged herself and rocked as she pictured her beautiful child locked in a dark box rotting day by day.

"You should be here. *You should be here*," she repeated as she stared at the dates and inscription on her tomb.

Loving Daughter Mother and Friend Sabrina Barnes ~ Our Butterfly. She read silently only causing her grief to grow thick inside her.

"I'm so sorry, baby," she whispered between the tears.

It had been five years since her body would allow her to sit in that room and between the guilt and blame, she had begun to crumble. "Whyyyy!" Again, she cried out searching for the answers only God could give but she had severed all ties with him years ago as she pledged what soul she had left to the devil. "They will pay for every tear I shed, and I will match them with their blood," she confirmed as she struggled to rise to her feet.

Pashion walked over to the face of the tomb and placed her hands right on the words. She rubbed her fingers back and forth over the inscription longing to touch her daughter just one more time. She stood still and Sabrina's voice played loudly in her mind. She pictured that pretty smile and for the first time, one almost eased across her lips but was instantly stolen by the visions of blood and torn skin she was forced to witness as she had to identify her only child's body.

"With everything that is left in me, I will kill every joy they dream to have until all they feel is pain and death," she promised as she put her lips right on the marble which only iced over the last bit of heart she had left.

Chapter 17

Home

Kayson pulled into his carport, drove past his treasured fleet, then right into his spot next to the elevator. He turned off his radio, silenced the engine, then hopped out of his truck. He popped the trunk, grabbed the small black duffle, then headed to the elevator, typed in the code, and hit the basement button. When the doors opened, he moved through the room and tucked the bag safely away before heading upstairs. Kayson hopped back on the elevator removing items of clothing along the way. He walked out of the silver sliding doors tossing his clothes on the chair across from the fireplace. He walked over to his king-sized bed and stared down at her curves through the thin sheets.

Kayson's dick hardened in his boxers as he imagined the many positions, he was about to fold her into. "You gonna let a man get wet by himself."

Her eyes fluttered open and closed as she tried to keep focus. "Hey, baby, you been home long?" She gave him that sexy low eyed gaze and bright white smile.

"Long enough to wake both of us up." He pulled the Enforcer from his encloser.

"Well, let me holla at ya boy real quick." She sat up, threw back the comforter then crawled over to take her position at his waist.

She pulled at his boxers until they touched the floor, then took her favorite toy in her hand, then her mouth. Kayson looked down at her taking a few inches at a time in and out of her mouth as she caressed him with her tongue and hand.

"You acting like you missed me," he mumbled gripping a handful of hair to hold her perfectly in place.

She sucked and moaned drenching his length with every lick. She circled her tongue gently around the tip then pulled back easing him from between her lips. "I only missed him. Not you." She looked up into his intense hazel gaze and her pussy got wetter by the second.

"Is that right? Come show him." He pulled her up from her kneeling position.

Kayson lifted her into his strong grip and stared into her eyes and she wasted no time wrapping her legs and arms tightly around him. She winded her waist against him as she felt the Enforcer pushing against her wet pulsating opening.

"Baby, I wanna feel you deep," she purred between biting into that knee-weakening spot on his neck.

Kayson answered the call entering her pussy in one strong stroke and brought her all the way down on his length.

"Mmm..." she cooed as she whined into his stroke.

"That's what the fuck I'm talking about get that shit." He pinned her to the wall next to the nightstand, gripped her ass cheeks and assaulted her G-spot as he rotated deep just as she requested.

"Kayyy..." she moaned as she felt his thickness fill her insides.

"Come on this dick," he grunted as her pussy muscles tightened and the warm wetness made his slide even slipperier.

"Baby, I'm cumming," she panted as her body began to quake beneath him.

"Let that shit go," he commanded showing no mercy.

Kayson put his mouth over her hardened nipple, held it between his teeth, and flipped his tongue back and forth while trying to keep her in place. She gripped his shoulders and pressed her head against the wall as she felt her pussy release.

"Baby! Baby! Baby..." she moaned then took his face into her hands and sucked his lips and tongue as he continued to grind.

Kayson stroked faster until he felt his knees weaken. He pushed in deeper and let go of all his heat inside her womb.

"Damn, baby," he whispered as he collected his breath. "You be trying to break a boss."

"Nope just trying to make sure my dick is satisfied." She giggled as she placed a few kisses on his soft warm lips.

"The Enforcer said you don't play fair." He nibbled her collar bone then slid from between her swollen pussy lips.

Kayson got up from the bed then pulled her to her feet. "Come bathe the Boss," he requested ready to take her on another wild ride.

"Damn, Boss, I thought you was all broken." She grabbed onto Kayson's shoulder as her legs regained their strength.

"That's why you shouldn't talk shit," he teased as they headed to the shower.

"Whatever." She popped his arm as they entered the bathroom.

Kayson grabbed her around her waist and walked her into the shower prepared for his next round of terror. She was in her personal heaven anticipating his next move. They stepped into the steam-filled enclosure and the warm water covered their bodies. Kayson wrapped her in his arms and held her close enjoying the beat of her heart against his. He relaxed his mind and let go of the day.

"Let me wash the Boss up." She broke his trance as she reached over for the sponge and honey body wash.

Kayson turned toward the water, placed his hands on the wall allowing the hot drops to ease his tension while enjoying her handwork as she lathered his skin. As the suds eased down his legs, he turned and took the sponge from her hands and place a single kiss on her lips. Her heart fluttered as she looked up into his loving stare while he circled the sponge on her breasts.

"You so fucking sexy," he mouthed in a love drunken haze.

Kayson slid his wet fingers between her legs and got all his favorite spots ready to be consumed. They touched, tasted, and enjoyed every inch of each other while rinsing their skin thoroughly, and as the last bubble left their heated flesh the Enforcer was ready to finish his work.

"Bend over," he ordered as he pushed her forward.

"Take it, Daddy," she moaned as she looked back over her shoulder watching him get into place.

"Remember you said that," he said as his throbbing dick connected with her pussy lips.

"Sssss…baby," she purred.

Kayson slid in slow then found a rhythm that caressed him just right. She threw her ass back at him gyrating with every push. When he hit that special spot, she moved to avoid his deepness.

"Mmmm…baby," she moaned biting into her bottom lip.

"Cum on this dick for, Daddy!" Kayson held her in place and made her do what he told her to do, take it. He slid in hard pounding against her sweet spot until she begged to be free.

"I'm cumming, baby! I'm cumming. Don't stop!" she screamed out in ecstasy as her body began to quiver.

When Kayson saw her body surrender, he slid the Enforcer from his wet enclosure and pulled her to her feet, then walked their dripping wet bodies to the bed. He gripped her legs and placed his face between her thighs, first tasting her nectar before he pushed her legs back to her ears and rested her feet on his shoulders.

Kayson fucked her fast and hard showing no mercy as he filled his cup. Their bodies played between the sheets until the sun crept along the tree line then he laid on top of her defeated frame and dipped in and out slow.

"I love you, Kayson," she confessed as her pussy rewarded him one more time. Tears slipped from the corners of her eyes as her breath quickened.

"I love you too, baby," he returned her love the same way she was giving it.

"Baby, I can't cum no more," she incoherently mumbled as he talked shit in her ear while executing his deadly slow stroke game.

"One more time." He gripped under her shoulders and pushed in until their pelvises touched.

"Ahhhh…" she cried out as her pussy made him wet and sticky.

"I'm about to cum, baby." He picked up his speed fucking her fast and close.

When the last of his seed flowed free inside her, he slid in and out until the Enforcer said stop, then he rested his head on her breasts and closed his eyes.

"Thank you for loving me," she mumbled totally drained of all struggle and fight she laid beneath him and peacefully dozed off.

Chapter 18

Set The Pace

KoKo sat quietly on the passenger side of a dark-colored Chevy Cavalier. She listened to the engine hum as she waited for Miguel's street crew to arrive. Ha'Roo sat just across the parking lot in a separate vehicle awaiting the same verdict. When the headlights appeared at the entrance, they all ducked lower in their vehicles.

Mateo and Pablo eased along the parking lot looking for their meeting spot. They pulled into an empty parking space and turned off the headlights.

KoKo pulled her hood down to her eyes then nodded at her anxious driver. She pulled one into the chamber then lit her blunt as a signal. On cue, both vehicles pulled up boxing Mateo and Pablo in.

There were loud incoherent screams from inside the vehicle as the two men tried to free themselves from the vehicle. KoKo hopped out, ran up to the hood, then jumped up on the rooftop. She pointed her gun into the sunroof as she pulled hard on her blunt.

Ha'Roo jumped out and walked over to the driver's side window. He tapped on the glass with the tip of his gun then motioned for Mateo to roll it down. Mateo reluctantly eased the tinted glass down as his heart raced heavy in his chest.

"Where the fuck is the money?" Ha'Roo barked pointing his gun right in Mateo's face.

"It's in the trunk," Mateo wasted no time telling him exactly what they wanted to hear as his eyes shifted up at KoKo straddling the roof's opening locked and loaded.

"Pop that muthafucka then," Ha'Roo ordered smacking Mateo across the front of his head.

Mateo reached down and popped the trunk then placed his hands on the steering wheel. One of Ha'Roo's boys hurried to the trunk, grabbed the two duffle bags, and threw them over his shoulder, then slammed the trunk closed. He handed Ha'Roo a bottle as he headed back to the driver's side of their vehicle.

"Yay tho' I walk through the valley of the shadow of death, I shall fear no evil," Ha'Roo mumbled as he squirted the liquid all over Mateo and Pablo.

"What the fuck man? I gave you what you asked for!" Mateo yelled his voice cracking with each word.

"I am the evil," KoKo spat releasing the blunt from her lips and a cloud of smoke followed. She jumped down and let off her gun sending several shots through the doors into Mateo's legs and the others hit Pablo in the chest.

The two men winced in pain as they began to go up in flames. KoKo hit each of them with a final shot to the head then jumped into the Chevy.

Ha'Roo hopped into the passenger seat of the car he was in, then both vehicles sped off in reverse as they watched the flames rise off Mateo's car.

KoKo's blood sped through her veins as her driver sped into the night through those tight New York streets. She sat thinking they had just set the pace, and the other side needed to catch up.

****

Kayson and Wise stepped into the building's front entrance then up to the small panel of doorbells and pressed 1C. He looked up into the camera, and after two flashes Kayson lifted his shirt and turned prompting Wise to do the same. Once they were cleared a buzzer released the locks and they pushed through the doors and down the hallway. They stopped in front of the apartment door and stood waiting for it to open. After a few seconds, the door eased open and Kayson and Wise walked in toward the living room. Kayson led the way, stopping at the entrance to the living room. He stared over at Miguel in his lounge chair then walked right over to him.

"Are we at this point again?" Miguel spoke with his heartbreaking right where he sat.

Wise stood behind Kayson with an evil grimace on his face.

"How is your wife?" Kayson asked as he took a seat on the couch.

"They took our only child. She will never be okay," he responded resting his chin on his hands.

"Do you have any information on the contract?"

"Nothing." He smacked his hand against his leg as he agonized about his son's burnt body lying on that cold slab.

"I got you." Kayson rose to his feet.

Miguel flagged at a member on his team who then brought over a small leather pouch. He passed it to Kayson then walked off. Kayson unzipped the pouch and nodded his understanding of the mission at hand. He tucked the pouch under his hoodie then headed to the door.

"Make them hurt!" Miguel yelled out as Kayson reached the front door.

"No fucking doubt," Kayson spoke firm as he moved out of the apartment and back to his truck.

Miguel sat up and grabbed the shot glass in front of him, then the whole bottle of brown liquor and filled his glass to the top. "Make them hurt," he mumbled taking the entire shot down his throat.

****

KoKo stepped into the living room and locked eyes with the dealer at each table giving them a slight nod of approval as she took note of the players and movement in the room. She listened to the chatter of shit talk emitting from a few men in the room as she moved strategically around the perimeter watching hands and money. KoKo checked the food and drinks, whispered in the servers' ears, then posted up in a far corner and just observed all movement as the cards smacked the table.

"Nah, fuck that nigga pay me!" Chinkz yelled out slapping his cards against the table as he began reaching for the stacks.

"Fuck you, nigga!" Tron yelled back as he slid another stack in his direction.

"Nah, I'ma fuck ya bitch, and from the looks of it…" He held the money to his eyes. "You gonna pay for it."

Laughter rang out as they watched Tron's face tighten. The next hand was dealt and the money was placed on the table as the men continued to take their turns with lady luck. KoKo's mood didn't change she just watched her money stack as the hands of fortune laid heavier on a few bitter players in the room. Just as KoKo was ready to collect and bounce to her next pick up, she looked up to see her man from Jersey Butchie and his crew. He shook hands with a few in attendance then noticed KoKo. He made his way through the room headed in her direction.

"Fam." Butchie walked up with his hand extended.

"What it do, playa?" KoKo extended her fist.

"This your world, I'm just chilling among the squirrels." He closed his hand to a tight fist and bumped KoKo's sealing their greeting.

"What you doin' on this side of the world?" KoKo asked without waiver.

"They only run these games with heavy hitters a few times a year and I don't miss em'."

"Heavy hittas. These niggas?" She chuckled.

Butchie shook his head at KoKo's ignorance. She was always on top of shit, however, she was sitting right in the hornets' nest and didn't even see the sting.

"That nigga right there." He nodded at the table with Chinkz and Tron. "That little nigga is one of the old boss's sons, Bisson. He only comes to the big games, him being here is strange. His team must be close, and that shit means changes are in place."

"How he movin'?" KoKo held her gaze at their table.

"He's one of those I take whatever the fuck I want hood type niggas." He out here on game.

"Thanks for the heads up." KoKo rose to her feet again extending her fist. "Keep your eyes open."

"Anytime, Boss Lady. Anytime," he returned hitting her fist as she walked off. "Let me get some of this money." He smacked his hands together as he took a seat at the table.

KoKo pulled her hoodie over her head and walked toward the door. She met the money man just before her exit. KoKo grabbed the backpack from him, tossed it over her shoulder spoke a few words of instruction then headed out the door.

Butchie's eyes stayed on the interaction until the door closed then he turned his attention back to the table just in time to see Bisson taking note of KoKo's activity. Butchie also took note then made the rest of the night's focus purely on Bisson.

Chapter 19

The Exchange

Pinky hurried back and forth from the safes to the Louie bags. She carefully counted each stack of hundreds until they were filled with Kayson's order. Just as she zipped each one closed, Kayson and Baseem came walking through the wooden sliding basement doors.

"Everything ready?" Kayson asked as he approached her.

"Have I ever been late?" she shot back looking up into his hazel eyes.

"Watch your mouth," he gently warned pulling her into his arms. "Is Dee Dee, ready?" he asked looking at her thick frame and tiny waist in that hot pink bodysuit.

"Always thinking about the next bitch when I'm right here in your arms," she spoke direct as she pushed him back. "It's a hundred thousand in each of the four bags and the guns are in that smaller bag with the ammo." She pointed at each bag.

Kayson just smiled at her cockiness. She was right she was always on time and always handled business. "Come here, stop being mean," he spat then signaled for Baseem to grab the bags.

"I'm good for, right now. I don't want your little leftovers. Come to me when you can spend some time." She smiled big crossing her arms over her chest.

Kayson looked at her pretty red face, pouty lips, and perky breasts. "Do I have to come get you or are you gonna come here?" he spoke firm.

Pinky's kitty got wet as she stared at all that sexy standing before her. She sucked her teeth then adhered to his command.

"You know I got you. I need you to only worry about yourself. As long as you are good that's all that matters, remember that." He pulled her into his embrace and squeezed her tightly.

"I'm never worried. You know I'm always going to be here for you, Kay," she confessed gripping him in her arms.

"I know and thank you." He closed his eyes, nuzzled his nose in her neck, and enjoyed the few moments of peace.

The sound of the horn blaring broke their trance placing them right back into reality.

"Be safe," she spoke softly as she pulled back from him.

"Always," he spat with a slight smile. "That ass getting fat, I gotta get back over here."

"Yeah, right I know the Boss got options. Go ahead before Baseem comes in here with his eyebrows all raised." She giggled shewing him toward the door.

"Ya mouth slick, I'ma find out how slick it is." He smacked her fatty. "Tell Dee to come on, then lock up and set the alarm. Be safe," he ordered as he slid out the same way he came in.

"Always," she uttered as she slid the door closed and locked and chained them. She headed upstairs gave Dee Dee her orders, then saw her out the front entrance.

Dee Dee sped down the steps with her overnight bag, hopped into the back seat of Kayson's truck and they peeled out with Wise trailing them in his truck. They pushed on until they hit the turnpike headed South. They settled into their seats with plots brewing in their spirits. Shit was about to get real different.

****

"Good Evening, Miss Ce'Asia." The man spoke from behind the large marble desk as he rose from his seated position. "Your laundry went out it will be back in the morning." He tipped his hat as she moved past his station.

KoKo glanced in his direction, nodded, then headed to the stairway. She climbed the fifteen flights of stairs, then slid her key in the door, opened it wide, then slammed it closed behind her.

KoKo hit the alarm, then the lights. Her eyes dashed around the room connecting with every corner. She tossed the black backpack on the couch as she headed to her bedroom.

KoKo punched in a separate code and her room door swung open, when her eyes settled on the huge king-sized bed, fluffy white comforter, and pillows her soul gained a small amount of calm. KoKo placed her gun on the dresser, stripped down to her bra and panties then headed to the bathroom. She turned on the shower then stared in the full-length mirror as the steam filled the room. She looked deep into her darkly set eyes wanting to reject the evil image gazing back at her, but her destination was sealed the day she was born all she could do was live with it. KoKo walked over to her vanity, opened a red leather box, pulled out a freshly rolled blunt and a lighter, and lit the end then pulled deep. She blew the smoke high into the air as she enjoyed the heat on her skin as sweat formed on her brow, she continued the chief then placed the other half of the blunt in a marble ashtray then headed over to the CD player and popped in her favorite tunes. She stood there haunted by the souls of the bodies she claimed as the soothing sounds of Tyrese belting out *Sweet Lady* allowed her soul to feel.

KoKo blinked back the lonely tears as she placed another layer of ice over her heart because caring had gotten the best of them killed so a fuck was one thing she could not afford to give. She stepped into the steamy hot water allowing the streams of heat to wash away her guilty sins. She closed her eyes and let the water wash over her face and down over her breasts. In those moments she was free, she was safe the only place she could sit alone with her thoughts. It was her prayer that each shower would cleanse her of her guilt and her grief. But there was no escaping reality, even though she justified every dirty deed that bitch Karma was always one step away from her. In KoKo's mind if she had her nine anywhere around her that bitch had better be careful and watch her muthafuckin' step.

KoKo reached out and pressed track 6 on the CD player she needed to change the mood from beauty to beast. Ice Cube, *Today was a Good Day* began knocking through the speakers. She inhaled deeply as she planned her stick and her moves. She was a bad bitch caught up in a so-called man's world and the one thing she was not going to let happen was have the shit she worked to maintain taken from her hand. When Snoop and Dre's *Nothing but G thang* CD came on, she was rocking to the beat as she moved the soapy sponge over her chocolate skin as she plotted each stage of her plan. She was determined to get back everything they took from her even if it meant sacrificing those closest to her. She turned her back to the water and let the heated beads massage her neck and shoulders as she took the last few moments of solitude into her spirit. KoKo said a little prayer then rinsed her skin and turned off the water.

As she stepped onto the thick bath rug, she knew the fate of her enemies was sealed. KoKo oiled her skin, slipped into her uniform, a pair of black jeans, a white T-shirt, a black hoodie, and black boots. KoKo brushed her teeth then combed her hair into a long, neat ponytail and tucked it under a baseball cap, applied a little gloss to her lips then hit the lights cleaning up along the way.

KoKo turned off the music, grabbed the other half of the blunt from the ashtray and tucked it behind her ear, placed her guns in her waist then walked through the living room and into the kitchen snatching up a bottle of water along the way. She grabbed the black bag from the couch, set the alarm leaving the apartment like she had never entered it.

"I hope you muthafuckas are ready? Cause here I come," she spat pushing open the exit door.

★★★★

"So, how were the games?" Nino asked his godson as he poured Espresso into his favorite porcelain cup.

"Shit was smooth." He threw a few thick, yellow envelopes on the table.

"Smooth indeed." He nodded up and down as he stirred the spoon in the thick caffeine.

"They had everything on deck, very secure and all the players came ready to play and pay." He took the seat next to his father's chair then grabbed an orange and began to peel it open.

"Very good. Were there any other bosses in the room?"

"From what I can tell, they send either their second in command or street-level workers each playing their Boss's hand." He popped a slice in his mouth and waited for his father's next question.

"Did you see anything out of sorts?"

"Nah, everything surprisingly went very well..." He paused and ate a few more slices. "But one thing did catch my attention."

"What was that?" he asked bringing the cup to his lips.

"It was this broad. She was collecting the money."

"Why is that different. You know we always send in a lady to keep them at ease."

"Nah, this chic had authority. She wasn't dressed like no baddy. She was dressed like a nigga and all them niggas came to attention when she got there and didn't relax until she was gone."

"Humm...what did she look like?"

"I couldn't really see her face. She sat in the corner then pulled her hoodie on when she moved out. And she was short as hell."

"Why the fuck would they have a bitch making those types of pickups and with power?" Nino asked puzzled by the information.

"If you want my guess." Chinkz rose to his feet wiping his hands as he chewed the last of the sweet fruit. "The same reason you take information and orders from that badass older lady that creeps through here. Somebody got pussy trapping these niggas." He chuckled at the thought as he pushed the chair under the table.

"Well, don't guess. Know," his godfather ordered unmoved by his son's humor.

"On it." Chinkz put his right hand to his forehead and saluted his dad then left the area before he pushed the envelope a little too far.

"Be safe!" Nino shouted out as he began to put together what play was on the board and who had sat that piece right in the

153

middle. He took a few more sips then got up and headed to his study. Bisson walked inside, locked the door behind him, then walked over to his safe. After punching in his digital code, he opened the door and retrieved a small black book, then headed to his desk and picked up the receiver. Bisson punched in the numbers then waited for someone to pick up on the other end.

"Hello," a soft Jamaican accent eased from the woman's lips.

"Yes, can I speak to Scarie?"

"May I ask who is calling?" the woman asked as she turned over and looked Scarie in the eyes.

"Bisson's brother Nino," he stated firmly.

The woman's eyes widened as she realized who was on the other end of the line, she didn't even repeat the name she just put the phone to Scarie's ear and let him see for himself.

"Speak," his thick accent rang through the receiver.

"We need a sit-down," Nino quickly got to the point.

"Me a been waiting for dis call so. Tomorrow at noon me a see ya at the riverside," Scarie spat then disconnected the call and laid back in the pillow.

"Everything okay?" the woman asked laying her hand on his chest.

"The day me pray to never come has just put its head pon de sword."

Chapter 20

The Deal With The Devil

Kayson extended his arms as he was patted down. He eyed the lustrous paintings dressing the walls and crystal chandeliers hanging from the ceiling.

"This way." Security directed him down a long hallway.

Kayson was in awe as his eyes explored the high taste and quality of the furniture and décor.

"You can have a seat. He will be right with you." He was led into a library, then onto a patio, and offered a seat.

Kayson sat on the edge of his chair and folded his hands in anticipation. The soft sounds of chirping birds calmed his spirit as he waited to step into the next chapter of his life.

"Welcome to my home, Mr. Wells," a short Asian man announced as he bowed slightly then walked toward where Kayson was seated.

"I thank you for meeting with me on such short notice." Kayson rose to his feet and bowed as well returning the greeting.

"Oh, I'm an old man. What else do I have to do but take up a meeting or two?" he asked as he took a seat. "Please make yourself at home," Mr. Li offered as he sat back with his hands on his chest and crossed his legs ready to pass his verdict.

"Can I offer you something to drink?" he asked as he poured himself a hot cup of tea.

"No disrespect, but I know we are both on valuable time and we can't afford to lose a minute or a dollar," Kayson went straight to the point.

"Well, a man after my own heart." Mr. Li sipped his tea then placed it back on the saucer. He crossed his arms over his chest and prepared to lend a good ear. "Please proceed."

"Again, I appreciate you seeing me. As I stated, I want to get right to the point."

"That's the best way always for me." He gave Kayson a reassuring smile.

"If you put a million dollars in my hand. I can triple your money in less than six months." Kayson threw his ball in the middle of the table.

"You speak with great confidence."

"I just speak what I know."

"I have been working with a certain amount of people for a particular number of years. Why should I take my loyalty from them and give it to you?" he asked then waited.

"I didn't ask for your loyalty," Kayson returned locking eyes with Mr. Li. "I'm asking you to let me make you the money a boss deserves to sit on…" He paused and sat forward in his chair. "…but if you give me your loyalty and it is tested during our business. You have my word I will kill the traders whole fuckin' family to save mine."

"Hmmm…" Mr. Li uttered. He rubbed his hand back and forth over his chin then leaned in, grabbed a bell from the table, and rang it twice.

Kayson looked over his shoulder as he heard footsteps approaching quickly.

"Yes sir, Mr. Li?" His secretary appeared ready to serve him. The woman walked over, leaned down, and placed her ear near his mouth, then trotted off in the same direction she came from.

"I like you. You have a rare type of passion in your heart. The kind that lets a man kill by day and sleep by night," Mr. Li analyzed.

"I am who I am, Mr. Li, I make no excuses for it."

"And I respect it," Mr. Li agreed as he looked up to see Lucy returning.

"Here you go, Mr. Li." She set two golden plaques on the table. "Will there be anything else?" she asked.

"No, that will be all for now. Leave us and close the study door."

"Yes, sir." She bowed in submission and disappeared.

"Do you know what these are, Mr. Wells?" He slid them in his direction.

Kayson picked them up and turned them over checking out the design. "These look like the shit you make money with," he assessed.

"Very good, Mr. Wells. You see, Mr. Wells it's like this. What I do with a few so-called associates is not what I want to do with you." He reached out and passed Kayson the gold plates.

"How much do you need?"

"A million," Kayson said without wavering.

"A million dollars…yes? I could surrender that but then you would spend all your time paying me back. But if you can take on what I want to give you. We will both be very wealthy men in less than six months."

"You have my ear." Kayson moved his chair a bit closer and listened like his life depended on it.

Mr. Li laid out his whole plan. He gave Kayson some names and contacts then booked him a few flights to meet some very influential men. Kayson's head was heavy when he got up from his seat.

"I will see you in a week." Kayson shook Mr. Li's hand then picked up a bag from his feet.

"That you will, be safe," Mr. Li confirmed.

Kayson walked out of Mr. Li's office with a whole new program. He thought he was coming in there to cop a few keys and get permission to move freely in a certain territory. As circumstances would have it, Kayson was just given the vault, the armored truck, and the keys to the fucking Pentagon all in one sitting.

Kayson rode back on a high. He grabbed the bag of money, hopped out of the cab, and moved swiftly through the lobby, then jumped on the elevator. As soon as the doors opened, he stepped hard down the hallway anxious to see how them Florida niggas was going to accept new rules.

Kayson knocked on the hotel door then walked into the room with his eyes darting from one side of the room to the other. There were wall to wall dudes with money and jewelry out in the open and frisky hand hoes gawking like vultures ready to pick their dumb ass bones clean, he was amazed at how these niggas could be all loose and off-guard during business. His sights settled on Wise who had them on the card table, then on Aldeen who had the strippers passing out pussy and blowjobs like communion crackers on first Sunday. He recognized the so-called leader in the room and got security to have him brought to a back room along with Aldeen and Wise.

Kayson walked over to the wet bar and poured himself a drink, then swallowed it down while waiting for them to enter the room.

"You good, Boss?" Baseem asked from a recliner by the window.

"Always. Just gotta make sure these niggas understand this shit can be nice or it can be nasty. I'm prepared for both," Kayson responded then headed over to the seating area and took a seat next to the coffee table.

Gotti walked into the room full of confidence with his head held high. Aldeen and Wise were tight behind him with a firm plan to rule by give or by take. They positioned themselves strategically around the room. Gotti took a seat on the couch across from Kayson and made his introduction.

"I'm Gotti, thank you for taking the meeting."

"Indeed," Kayson said as he took a seat in front of him.

"How may I assist another, Boss?" the cocky, young gentleman asked.

"You can't assist me. You can assist yourself, though," Kayson returned.

"Is this nigga serious?" Gotti looked back directing his question at Aldeen and Wise.

"What is it about this man that makes you think he's fuckin' playin'?" Aldeen asked pulling his heat out of his waist.

"Wait, hold the fuck up. Y'all niggas said we was good. What the fuck is this?" His pitch got higher with each word.

"Calm the fuck down. Niggas don't know when I'm gonna' kill them, they just end up dead," Kayson reassured him.

Gotti tried to calm his breathing as he realized he was at their mercy.

Kayson lowered his gaze and sat forward in his chair as he began to school the rookie, "Every man has to ask himself when he wakes up in the morning. Is he going to make money or keep jerking his dick in the cereal? Which man are you?" He looked him hard in his eyes.

Gotti sat forward and looked into the blackness of Kayson's soul through his intense glare then responded, "Shiiieeettt…folk, I just came up outta some pussy you gifted to me. So, it's safe to say, I'm ready to get money," he slurred in his thick country accent.

"Good then, let's fuckin' get it," Kayson spat as he sat his thrown in the middle of this niggas palace. "I met a foreign friend of yours today the money ain't right. Instead of taking heads, we decided that I'm now going to oversee the movement."

Gotti's brow closed together as his mind wandered off to his connect. He knew that his connect was greasy, but he thought he had earned himself enough loyalty to not have a stranger enter his space and set up camp.

"Look I can understand you being here out of invite. I need to speak to the higher-ups. We got our own system and men we trust. I will take advice, though," his voice slightly elevated as he rubbed one hand in the other.

"I don't fucking advise. I order," Kayson spoke firmly rubbing his hands together in the same fashion.

Baseem and Wise pulled the heat from their waist and rested it at their side.

"Your team has already been briefed. Close your fucking mouth and open your ears. This ain't no fucking open floor discussion," Baseem barked ready to exclude this nigga perinatally from the process.

"Look I don't want no trouble with you man." Gotti put his hands up in surrender. "Just tell me what needs to be done," his voice lowered as he realized the takeover had already been made.

"The Floor is yours, Boss," Baseem asserted then moved behind Gotti with his gat tight in his grip.

"This is how this shit is going to go from here on out," Kayson stated then ran down the pick-ups and drops that would take place and where they would take place. He had to set Florida in motion then move on to the next. Once, Gotti calmed down and listened to the new moves and prices he had to nod in agreement. He was ready for everything Kayson was offering he had spent a lot of money trying to get his team to move right and was still coming up short. It was time to get what he felt he deserved. They tossed a few ideas back and forth and Gotti began to feel like a new man. He brought Kayson up to speed on how shit was ran around there and who was an enemy and who was a friend along with their friends on the good side of the law just in case. The money was there for the taking and they were about to fill both pockets.

"Is everything clear?" Wise asked as he walked over to the door.

"Crystal clear. Please excuse the slight disrespect earlier. You have my full cooperation." Gotti vowed his alliance to Kayson as he rose to his feet. He shook his hand firmly sealing their fate.

"We will see," Kayson uttered nodding his head toward the door excusing Gotti from the room.

"All I can do is show you," Gotti spat as he headed to the exit.

Baseem followed him back to where the team was still being entertained by Kayson's special treats.

When Gotti joined his boys, he ran the night through his mind as he watched them laugh and play and the money that must have been slipping right through his fingers at the hands of fools. He had to admit he now had nothing but respect for Kayson. He

160

thought he was about to get fucked but as luck would have it, he was about to be the biggest muthafucka in Dade county. The shit was now set in stone. The only thing that could fuck it up, was greed.

"So, how do you feel about ol' boy?" Wise asked as he walked over to take a seat across from Kayson.

"Like I told him. We will see," Kayson responded then gave Wise specific orders before he headed to the main room of the suite to dismiss the team and get them on the money, playtime was over.

"I'm just waiting to see which one of these niggas gonna sign up to an example." Aldeen chuckled.

"You know at least one of them dumb ass niggas gonna make us put a boot in they ass."

"Y'all niggas stay on ready," Kayson chimed in. "Come on we got a flight to catch," he ordered as he headed to the door.

Kayson let Gotti and his crew go in thirty-minute increments and put a man on each one of their movements. He had the girls get the room back in check, when the room was cleaned thoroughly, he paid the team and let them go for the night. The men put security in place, then moved to the backroom to pack the counterfeit money into one bag and the legit money in another. Kayson passed out his final instructions to Aldeen and Wise, then prepared the trip for him and Baseem. They packed Kayson's truck then rolled off to the Airport. Wise pulled into the airport parking, they jumped out, grabbed both bags then headed to departures.

"Y'all get back safely," Kayson ordered, then he and Baseem headed to International, and Wise and Aldeen headed to Domestic. Their whole lives had just changed with a bag of fake ass money. Kayson had to chuckle. He was the King and with his new armies in different locations, he felt like his throne was eternal.

****

KoKo walked up on the porch and just stood there thinking about the direction things were going in. She had a connect's son down and from what she'd heard there was a contract on the nigga's head responsible and that nigga would happen to be Ha'Roo. She debated with her inner voice that said, *'tell'* and the other one that said, *'KoKo just handle it'*. She pulled her hood back and headed inside. She hopped the steps a few at a time until she got to the second floor.

KoKo stopped in the living room and just shook her head at their team comfortably playing video games and smoking when they were in the middle of a full-fledged war.

"Y'all niggas make my ass itch."

"What's up, KoK. Why you trippin'?"

"Y'all some dumb muthafuckas," she spat then headed to her third-floor duck off spot.

She unlocked the door, moved inside then secured herself safely behind it. She had to start moving different. She had to make sure every move made was for her come up alone. Niggas were moving sloppy and she wasn't about to get caught up over another nigga's failure to rule. She emptied her safe and removed all her guns except one. She changed her sheets then swept and mopped her floors. When she was done straightening up, she hopped in the shower, then into a fresh pair of black jeans and a thick hoodie. She threw a vest on and brushed her hair into a neat ponytail.

KoKo tucked a gun in her waist then strapped a .22 to her ankle and tucked her blade in her bra. She counted the stack then zipped her backpack closed. KoKo tossed it over her shoulder then headed out the door locking the place down on her way out.

"Where the fuck you goin'?"

"Talk to ya bitch like that," KoKo shot back as she headed to the door.

"Let me holla at you for a minute," Ha'Roo said as he tried to calculate where this new attitude was coming from.

KoKo stopped and stood in place as she contemplated whether to entertain him or just walk out. She wrestled for a few moments then turned and headed into his bedroom.

Ha'Roo let her pass then closed the door behind her. "You got some shit you need to get off your chest?"

"Do you?" she shot back.

"This the shit I don't have time for." He bucked up at her.

KoKo just stood in place. "You need to make the team tighten the fuck up. You out here making powerful moves against some very powerful people. I need you to put that at the front of your mind at all times," she rattled out her feelings in one long breath.

"Trust me, I got this. I ain't letting nothing happen to you or me." He tried to comfort her weary mind.

"I only trust my gun. That's the only one on your team that won't bitch up," she stated smoothly. "I'll see you in a couple of days. I need to make a run. Instructions have been passed out. You should be straight until I get back." She turned to the door.

"Where the fuck you going?"

"A bitch work hard, I'm taking a vacation," she hurled back then kept on moving,

"You need a fucking hug." He chuckled as he closed the door behind him. The smile dropped from his face the moment he was hidden behind the wooden panel.

"I gotta keep her close to me," he mumbled as he tried to gauge what type of moves, she was making."

KoKo stepped onto the stoop, lit the end of her blunt then blew the smoke over her head as she waited for her cab. When she saw the yellow and black Ford pull around the corner, she ran down the stairs and hopped inside.

"LaGuardia," she said then slid a small stack in the plastic hole.

"Yes, Miss," the driver said as he pushed into traffic headed to the airport.

****

It's Morning...

Kayson laid back on the huge fluffy pillows watching Lady run back and forth trying to get ready for work.

"You gonna fuck around and break your neck." He chuckled.

"If you would come home before four o'clock in the morning. I could fuck you and still get some sleep and not have to rush in the morning," she said leaning in to kiss his lips.

"I'm the boss I get my pussy when I want it."

"Whatever just don't forget to go by the other house and let the insurance adjuster in and we have that appointment with your mother's doctor tomorrow. So, please don't be late," she reminded him then walked back into the closet.

"Shit, I forgot about that." Kayson tossed the comforter off and headed in her direction.

"I know and the last time I had to make up a thousand excuses while your mother looked at me like dirt," she said putting in her diamond earrings.

"What you mean? My mother adores you," he said then pulled her into his arms.

"Kayson, your mother hates me. She just tolerates me." She pulled away from his grip.

"She doesn't hate you she just loves her son. What can I say?" He flashed her that sexy smile.

"Whatever, she loves her son with his ex," she mumbled as she tucked a few things in her briefcase.

"You jelly?" he asked coming over to where she stood.

Lady dropped her smile and looked him in his eyes. "Never jelly, I know what we have. I just know she will always wish you were with her."

"Don't worry about my mother. She knows you are not Lisa. What you need to worry about is making it out this door."

"Why is your dick the cure-all?"

164

"You see this nigga? He needs what he needs," he said as he tried to lift her skirt.

"Nope, I have meetings." She kissed his lips. "And you have a whole world to run."

Just as Kayson was about to make another move the gate alarm went off. "See." Lady stepped back grabbing her purse and laptop bag. "We both have work to do."

"You lucky as hell. You were about to get this damage." He smacked her ass.

"Whatever!" Lady shot her usual statement his way. "Tell everyone I said hello. Oh, and the deposits are in the safe."

"Bye, spoiled ass."

"Bye, sexy face." She blew him a kiss as she headed out of the bedroom.

Kayson buzzed Aldeen and Wise through the gate then headed to the shower. It was time to punch the clock.

****

Wise and Aldeen walked into a back room of the pool hall admiring how the crew was stripping and cleaning weapons. They closed the door and locked it then moved from one table to the next thumbing their hands through the currency stacked neatly from one corner to the other.

The final shuffles of the cash machine rang in their ears as the finished loads were placed in bags. Flights and hotels had been booked and the cars were on the way. Kayson didn't play with his money and Aldeen and Wise made sure he never had to. They'd been on this end of war before, this time Kayson wanted to make sure everyone was covered and there were no interruptions in the flow of the money's movement.

"I need to make sure each Borough gets their drop-offs before we make these next moves. It might put some shit outta commission for a minute," Aldeen ordered as they stepped into the back office.

"I have a drop going out at midnight and every hour after up to five o'clock in the morning to each head," Wise confirmed as he pulled a small sack of weed and a Dutch from his back pocket and placed them on the desk, and began cracking the Dutch down the middle.

"We really need an inside track. I heard it's a bitch that be running them Harlem niggas." Aldeen chuckled taking a seat at the desk."

"A bitch? Get the fuck outta here." Wise busted out laughing.

"I said the same thing when I heard about it," Aldeen confirmed as he laced the leaf with the sticky green.

"Who she with?" Wise's brow creased as he ran a few names through his mind.

"She a loner. She pulls that gun, and they respect that shit. The count ain't never fucked up and they upped the delivery," he said as he put fire to the end of the blunt.

"What you mean?"

"I made three drops to them niggas this week." Aldeen pulled the smoke into his lungs then blew it over his head.

"Three?" Wise asked nodding his head and counting the figures.

"Yeah, I think we need to pull her a little closer." He reached out and passed the heat to his boy.

"What's her name?" Wise sucked the thick exotic smoke into his chest then pushed it into the air.

"I gotta get that shit. Them niggas lips be glued like a muthafucka. Haven't caught one slipping yet." Aldeen got up from his seat and walked over to the safe and began spinning the dial.

"Then push one," Wise spoke direct.

"When we get back from Cali we need to set up a meeting," Aldeen confirmed as he thumbed through the contents of the safe.

"Word. Can't have as much as a rat moving in the city and the Boss ain't aware and benefitting off that nigga's cheese." Wise chuckled as he again inhaled deeply.

"We on it." Aldeen nodded his understanding. "Yo, on another note what the fuck happened with them broads from the club last week?" Aldeen gathered a gun and three stacks of crisp hundreds then moved over to Wise and reached for the blunt.

"Mannn...wifey fucked that up." Wise laughed at the thought.

"What the fuck happened?" Aldeen took a seat, placed the gun on the table, and then tucked the money in his hoodie pocket.

"Not a muthafuckin' thing. She blocked the shit outta me. Had a nigga running all over the fuckin' place. Set up some family shit, had me skipping rope and coloring in the lines all fucking day." He shook his head.

"Married ass, nigga. Fuck that I need my pick of pussy uninterrupted," Aldeen joked as he reached out for the heated blaze.

"Nah, I'ma stay in the married lane. You and Boss Man got too many pussy problems. Bitches all in their fucking feels and shit. Fuck that," Wise said sitting back in his chair.

"Yeah, but you keep swerving over here nigga," Aldeen spat back causing them both to laugh hard.

"Fuck you, nigga." Wise rose to his feet. "Just remember when your dick be over there tingling."

"Oh, shit, not the tingle. Fuck that get me a bitch to wife." Aldeen grabbed his dick and shook at the thought. "Shit, it's short notice but fuck it. Find me something nice I need this nigga healthy."

Wise held his stomach as he watched his friend quiver at the idea of having his dick in a sling. He knew that nigga was joking and low key serious at the same time. They passed the blunt until it was gone, locked up, then headed back to the main room to assign the final orders to the crew then smoothed off just as nice as they entered. They headed to Queens with a mission in place. They needed to get a few more allies under their thumb and the mystery chick was at the top of their corrupted list.

Chapter 21

A Mother's Love

"Did she eat?" Kayson walked in with two bags full of designer items and a few bags of groceries.

"She ate a little bit, but you know on her chemo day she gets very testy," Lady said as she took the bags from Kayson's hands.

"Yeah, I know. Thank you, baby, for being here for her." He kissed her on her forehead.

"You know I got you, baby," she confirmed.

"Let me run back to the car and grab the rest of the bags." Kayson went back to his truck.

When Kayson returned, he set the bags full of fresh fruit and vegetables on the counter then placed the fresh Salmon in the refrigerator.

"You got this, baby?" he asked as he picked up the gifts he had for his mother.

"Yes, baby, go see your mother I got this," she said then leaned up on her tiptoes and kissed his juicy lips.

"Mmmm..." he responded to the heat rising off her puckered smile. "I owe you." He looked hard into her gaze.

"You only owe me your heart," she said a little above a whisper.

Kayson winked at her and she winked back. It was one of their silent *I love yous'* that they could share in a room full of people just as they could as if they were alone.

Lady turned to the sink and began unwrapping the vegetables and rinsing them thoroughly. She moved around the kitchen meal prepping for Monique's week.

Kayson walked up to the second floor and was immediately filled with peace. He had remodeled his mother's brownstone and opened the bedrooms to make one huge space which Monique turned into her personal resort. Large indoor palm trees and tall vases with long-steam red and yellow roses accented each corner of the room leading up to her Caribbean style patio with ceiling to floor white and platinum sheer curtains which allowed the sun to peek in slightly. The scent of Hawaiian mango and lavender and a cool breeze flowed through the open space accompanied by the soothing sounds of waterfalls and birds chirping as if in a rainforest played lightly as a backdrop to the beautiful space.

"Come to me, my son." Monique put her hand out from her Chaise lounge.

Kayson moved to where she sat and placed the bags next to her. "How is my favorite girl?" he asked leaning in and kissing her cheek.

"Your only girl," Monique said sitting up and tightening her robe.

"I spoil you too much." He shook his head.

"As you should. Now, what do you have for momma?" Her smile widened as she rubbed her hands together.

"Just a little something…something," he responded filled with pride that he could give her that smile she needed to heal if only for a few seconds a day.

Monique began going carefully through the bags pulling the contents from inside. She started with the medium-sized bags. There were several Gucci shirts, dress pants, and tracksuits with sneakers or slide-on shoes to match. The smaller bags had three boxes of perfume, lotions, scented candles, and a few designer head and neck scarfs. The last was the medium-sized bags which contained two Gucci wallets with a diamond Cuban link bracelet and necklace to match inside one and a few stacks in the other.

"My son." Monique smiled from ear to ear.

"Only the best for you." He smiled back feeling good that his queen was now smiling.

"Come put these on me please." She turned in her seat as she passed him the two jewelry boxes.

Kayson stood and began placing the diamonds on his mother as he thought about the fact that at any moment, he could be doing this for the last time.

"Are you going to spoil me like this every time I go for a treatment?" she asked rubbing her hands over the cold ice.

"As long as there is breath in my body, your soul will never see worry," he responded as he fastened the bracelet.

"Thank you, my love." She put out her arms and Kayson leaned down into his mother's embrace.

"Love you, Ma!"

"Love you more, forever, and always!"

Monique and Kayson embraced for a few seconds then he moved back to his seat. As usual, Monique needed to get the statistics of the family business. They shared information, ideas, and a few laughs as they enjoyed the afternoon.

"Knock...knock," Lady said as she entered the room holding a silver tray full of Monique's favorite items.

"Come on, Child," Monique said waving her over.

The side of Kayson's mouth turned up as he watched her sexy frame sashay over to where they sat.

"Thank you, sit it right there," Monique responded looking down at the wheat toast with fresh avocado and tomato on top, a bowl of fruit with honey, and fresh Salmon with asparagus on the side.

"You did good," Monique said as she noticed the glass teapot filled with hot water, lemon, and mint.

"It's my pleasure. I have also prepared your dinner and three days of breakfast and lunch. The maid and chef will handle your dinner and anything you may need after hours," she said then stepped back by Kayson's side.

"Thank you, baby." Kayson took her hand and kissed the back of it lightly.

Monique's smile dropped as she tried to accept the woman standing next to her son. In her eyes, no one was good enough

171

and it was only a matter of time before she realized it was something she was not going to be able to handle.

"I need a minute more with my son if you don't mind. Thank you very much."

"You are more than welcome. I'm going to leave any way I have a few things to do. See you next Tuesday," Lady replied then prepared to leave the room "I'll see you at the house I'm going to run a few errands," she said to Kayson.

"Let me walk her down," Kayson said as he rose to his feet.

Monique put a fake smile on her face until they were out of the room then she reached for her phone and slid off to the restroom. Kayson helped Lady gather her things then walked her to the car.

"Thank you for everything. I know she is a handful, but I thank you from the bottom of my heart," he confessed as he closed the trunk.

"Baby, I love you so no thanks *is* ever needed."

Kayson pulled her into his arms and hugged her tightly. He owed her a lot, and he was going to make sure she had everything she wanted.

"Thank you for loving me," she spoke softly.

"You make it easy. Go ahead, so you can be in my bed when I get home." He brought her chin up and kissed her lips then walked her to the other side of the car and secured her inside.

"See you tonight," she said as she pulled off.

Kayson jogged up the steps, locked the door then rejoined his mother upstairs.

"Ma!" he yelled out as he reached the top of the stairs.

"I'm out here!" she yelled back.

Kayson looked in the direction of her sunroom then headed that way.

"You okay?" he asked as he looked over her face to make sure.

"Yes, I am fine. That damn woman you hired for the night shift will be here soon. I wanted to have a minute to talk to you alone." She reached over, grabbed a bottle of sparkling water, and opened it up.

"What's up, you straight?" he asked now feeling like she may have been uneasy.

"What's going on with business?" she got right to the point.

"What do you mean?" Kayson took a seat and laid his head back.

"I'm sick, not dumb, I know there is a war brewing. I have been down this road a million times," she spoke firm.

"Everything will be fine. I just have to stay one step ahead," Kayson said looking at his mother's thin but beautiful face."

Monique sat thinking for a minute. "Don't get blinded by love," she spat then locked her brown eyes with his hazel ones.

"Ma, you ain't gotta worry about me getting caught on pussy. I'm good!"

"Hump." Monique sighed with a slight grin on her face. "You are so much like your father." She rose to her feet then headed to the deck table to pour herself some tea.

"I know you ain't feeling, Lady. But trust she is a good girl. I need you to be a team player." He tried to handle things as gingerly as he could.

Monique turned and looked at her son then busted into laughter. "You think I am concerned with that girl." She walked back to her seat. "I don't know her and don't give a fuck about her. I only care about you," she stated firmly as she sat comfortably with her drink tight in her grip.

"Understood," Kayson said with a slight crease in his brow.

Monique took a deep breath and released the air from her lungs as she prepared to school her young bull. "Son, you must learn to listen..." She paused. "...I said you need to control what you love. The love I speak of is love of friends, love of money, love of power, and love of things." Monique sat forward then continued, "People will always be able to compromise your plan in accordance with what you love. You gotta have balance for the shit, you need and the shit you gotta have and love ain't one of them."

173

Kayson nodded as his mother spoke power into him.

"Love life...love your children. Trust only your gun and bust that bitch without prejudice," she said with her teeth clenched tight. "You are at war, ain't no fuckin' love."

Kayson nodded his understanding. He thought about everyone around him. He thought about who he trusted and who he loved. Flashes of conversations and oaths played in his mind. He quickly put a value on each relationship and vowed not to mix them.

"I love you, son, but there are people who do not," she spoke a little above a whisper. "I have always prepared you for these days. Minimize your distractions they will get you killed," she said then sat back and put her feet up on the ottoman.

"I understand."

"Good, don't be foolish like your father. His greed and lack of loyalty has clouded his judgment in every situation."

Kayson stood then moved to his mother's side. "Thank you for everything, Ma. I love you!" He leaned in and kissed her cheek. "No worries, Ma. You're right, I'm a Wells. We kill what we hate and destroy what we love. I'm ready for both," he spat in her ear with intensity.

Monique looked at her son as his body stretched to his full six-three frame. He was a man no doubt, but it would be aching pain of losing something he can't replace that would make him a true boss.

"Just remember, my son. The only true General is one that plans his own funeral before the battle. Fear of the cold grave motivates more than the end of a cold gun."

"You are always and forever my favorite lady." He leaned in and kissed her again. "See you in a couple of days." He turned to walk away.

"You are my life. Always remember that," her voice trembled as the words left her lips. She looked toward the window in an attempt to gain her composure. "Oh, and feed that little girl, dick ain't enough!" She yelled out as he descended the steps.

"Bye, mommy, get some rest." He chuckled as he headed past her assistant. "Make sure she stays on her medication and call me if anything goes wrong."

"Yes, mister." She bowed her head then walked over to retrieve the teapot and cup.

Kayson moved out the door and headed to the truck, he knew his mother was right about everything she shared. The thing now was to let these niggas show him who they were so he could remove all opposition. He drove through the streets putting each piece in place, there were moves to make and he was only interested in the ones that would end up being fatal.

****

KoKo's black and yellow pulled in front of the Parrow Street projects then she checked her surroundings. She turned off her engine, grabbed the paper bag from the passenger seat then hopped out of the car. She stepped hard up to concrete steps then through the double metal doors. KoKo hit the steps jogging up to the second floor skipping every other step as she ascended. She walked up to the first apartment and grabbed the door knocker taping it lightly on the door.

"Who?" the shaky voice from the other side rang out as she watched the lid of the peek hole slide to the right.

"It's KoKo, Mrs. Lee!" she yelled through the steel that separated them.

The locks clicked and the chain clanked against the door as she removed it from its place. As the opening widened KoKo put her face to the crack easing Mrs. Lee's anxiety. Once she caught firm eye contact with KoKo, Mrs. Lee pulled the knob allowing KoKo enough space to enter.

"Why do we have to do this every time? You are worse than airport security," KoKo said shaking her head as she headed to the kitchen.

"Well, you never know," Mrs. Lee said as she locked the door and put the chain in place, then checked the peak hole to make sure the hallway was clear.

"Let me find out you owe the bookies some money," KoKo said as she began removing the items from the paper bag.

"Go on child." Mrs. Lee waved her hand as she chuckled at the thought. "In all my years, I ain't never owed nobody except the bill man and I make sure he gets his on the first. I don't want no trouble." She smiled widely.

"I know that's right." KoKo joined in her joy as she removed the last items and folded the bag then tucked it in a draw behind her.

"Did you get everything I had on the list?" Mrs. Lee asked as she eyed the items on the table.

"Yes, ma'am, and Mr. Johnson has the grocery order, and he should arrive shortly." KoKo looked up at the fruit-shaped clock confirming the time in her mind. Her heart skipped as she realized that was the same clock that had been hanging there since she was five.

"That's my girl." She reached out, grabbed KoKo by the arm, and squeezed her then took a seat at the table. "Thank you for always looking out for an old lady." She removed her hand then reached for her ticket and list of numbers.

"I'm always one phone call away," KoKo said as she turned to put the three cases of cigarettes in the cabinet and the beer in the refrigerator KoKo grabbed the tissue and paper towels headed to the hallway closet and put them in their place.

"Did you check the numbers to make sure they were correct?" Mrs. Lee yelled out from her seated position.

"Yes, ma'am, I don't want no problems," KoKo repeated her statement.

"I know that's right." She chuckled as she compared the list to the tickets.

"Did you eat?" KoKo asked as she opened the refrigerator and looked around.

"I had a little toast with my coffee. You know I don't eat much." She sat the tickets on the table. "Pass me a pack of those cigarettes," she ordered as she fidgeted in her chair.

"Do I need to come over here every day to make sure you are getting what you need?" She closed the refrigerator door then turned to look Mrs. Lee in the eyes.

Mrs. Lee took a deep breath as she realized she needed a little assistance. KoKo had been offering for years to get her a home care professional but she had turned down her offer each time. But today her soul was tired. "I do need help," she confessed with tears slowly rising to the corner of her eyes.

"No worries. I got you." KoKo kneeled at her feet and took her hand into hers. "I got you," she confirmed squeezing her this time offering whatever comfort she could.

"Thank you." She forced a smile through her tears.

"No thanks needed." KoKo squeezed her hand again then stood and moved to the cabinets to gather what she needed to fix her a decent breakfast.

KoKo grabbed a few pots, put some water on the boil then filled the frying pan with several pieces of bacon. Mrs. Lee took her seat by the window and stared out at the activity in front of the building as KoKo got her meal together. KoKo stirred thick oats in the hot water as she simultaneously placed the crispy bacon on a paper towel. She rinsed the pan then scrambled a few eggs with cheddar cheese. Once each item was done, she placed them on a plate and sat it on the table, and poured her a glass of orange juice.

"Come on beautiful let's get this meal in you. You gotta keep your pimp hand strong," KoKo joked as she helped her back to the table.

"Pimp hand?" She chuckled. "Not these old thangs. The only thing I'm raising is this fork to my mouth. This smells so good." She inhaled the aroma rising from the plate.

"Well, show that bacon who's in charge." KoKo smiled as her mind flooded with memories of her grandmother.

"Yes, ma'am cause he don't know who he's fooling with." Mrs. Lee picked up a piece from the plate and took a bite. She then grabbed her fork and got started.

KoKo placed the teapot on the stove and turned it up high as she filled a coffee mug with Mrs. Lee's favorite brew and sugar replacement. When the whistle began to blow, she retrieved the steamy water and filled the cup. She placed it in front of Mrs. Lee who was tickled with joy to watch KoKo moving around her kitchen.

"You need anything else?" KoKo asked as she grabbed the creamer from the refrigerator and a spoon from the dishrack, sitting them down beside her plate.

"No, this is fine. Thank you, my sweet angel," she responded as she continued to dig in.

"Okay, I'm going to get the bathroom situated for you."

"Okay," Mrs. Lee said as she lifted the fork to her mouth.

KoKo headed to the hallway closet grabbed a pair of gloves and the cleaning supplies and washed the bathroom down from top to bottom. Then ran her a tub of hot water. She poured in Epsom salt then headed to the bedroom. When KoKo entered the room, she damned near choked at the heated, smokey, dry air that settled in her nostrils. She quickly lifted the shade and opened the window, then began stripping the bed and wiping down the dressers and nightstands. She retrieved a fresh housecoat, undergarments and slippers then placed them in the bathroom.

"You still good?" she asked as she got the house in order.

"Yes, ma'am, just finishing my coffee!" Mrs. Lee yelled back as she had now moved back to the window seat and was enjoying the early morning eye hustle as the dealers and buyers moved back and forth with evil words and bad intent.

KoKo turned on the 12:00 news then headed back to the kitchen. "You ready, my dear?" KoKo held her hand out.

"Well, guess I am." Mrs. Lee surrendered her power allowing KoKo to take care of her.

KoKo walked her to the bathroom then cracked the door until she heard that she was in safely. "You got it from here?" she asked listening intently.

"Yes, ma'am," she answered as she settled her weary frame into the heated water. She put her head back and closed her eyes.

KoKo closed the door then headed to the kitchen and cleaned it from top to bottom and removed all old food from the refrigerator. By the time she dried and put away the dishes, she saw Mr. Johnson pulling up in his truck. KoKo looked back and forth then whistled at two boys playing in the D-circle.

They looked up then ran toward the sound. "Y'all want to make some money?"

"Heck yeah," the boldest one spoke first.

"Go get those bags from Mr. Johnson and bring them to me." KoKo chuckled at Little Man's take-charge character.

"A'ight!" Little Man grabbed his friend and pulled him to where Mr. Johnson was unloading the trunk.

"The lady up there told us to bring her these bags and for you to stay here for a tip." He pointed at the window then grabbed two bags and his friend grabbed the other two.

"Go straight there," Mr. Johnson ordered as he slammed the trunk closed.

"Yes, sir." They ran up the steps and knocked on the door panting and smiling ready to get their come up.

KoKo opened the door gave them both a fifty-dollar bill and sent them back with a hundred for Mr. Johnson.

"Thanks, Little Man. What's your name?"

"Jamal." He poked his chest out slightly.

"That's what's up. If you stop by every so often and see if she needs anything. And when you are out here make sure she gets back and forth safely, I'll have you fresh all summer." She looked right into his eyes.

"How much?" he got right to the point.

"Seventy-five a week." She put the offer on the table.

"What about my boy." He pointed his thumb toward his friend.

"That's your boy. You gotta make sure he eats." KoKo began to teach Little Man how shit was supposed to go.

"But we both brought you the bags." He applied the first amount of pressure.

"Nah, you responded then made him come with you. He operated on your word. I trust you."

Jamal nodded his head as he processed what KoKo was feeding his young hustle mindset. "Cool. Then I want one hundred and fifty."

"Nah, I'll do a hundred, but then you gotta run out her trash and go to the store."

"Bet." He put his hand out to seal the deal.

KoKo gripped his little hand admiring his little gangsta. "See you next week."

"A'ight." He turned back to the steps. "You know that price is to start?" He smiled flashing his one dimple resting deep in his chocolate cheeks.

"To start? Let me find out you trying to put the squeeze on a sister."

"Nah, you just never know what else you may need." He put an offer of his own on the table." Then headed down the steps.

"Indeed," KoKo shot back as she watched him jump from one step to the next.

She closed the door and went back to the window to assure the transaction was successful. She whistled again and Little Man threw up his thumb as he held his money up to the sun, checking to see if it was real.

She filled the refrigerator and cabinets with the items from the bag then headed to put fresh bedding on the mattress and help her out of the bathroom. Once Mrs. Lee was dressed, she returned to the living room just as her favorite soap *All My Children* came on.

"Just in time," she announced as she took her seat on the couch. "Where's my ashtrays woman?" she joked as she looked around at everything neat and tidy.

"I thought you was quitting woman?" KoKo joked back as she retrieved the ashtray from the kitchen.

"Well, until I do. I gotta put these ashes somewhere." She chuckled as she turned to the television to catch the opening credits.

KoKo grabbed her a half glass of soda and some crackers then took her place next to her on the couch. She sat the items on the coffee table then laid her head back for the show. They sat staring intensely at the screen at the drama from Erica Kane and her counterparts. By the time, the third commercial aired Mrs. Lee was ready to get a few things off her chest.

"So, did you ever have a chance to follow up on the things your grandmother told you about?" she asked keeping her gaze on the screen.

"What things?" KoKo's brow creased as she waited to see where this conversation was about to go.

"The things about your father…" She paused to let it sink in.

KoKo turned in her direction. "What about my father?" Mrs. Lee now had her whole attention.

She took a deep breath then began what she thought of as making her peace. "There was a lot of things surrounding the death of your father. One of those things was a very powerful woman…" She again paused as she chose her words wisely.

"Say what's on your mind." KoKo sat slightly forward holding firm eye contact.

"Your dad was tied into some very powerful things and people. Things outside of all this we see every day. When he learned how to move money different, he became a target."

"Are you telling me you know who killed my father?"

"You need to go see your Godfather." She turned her gaze back to the television.

"My Godfather?" KoKo's brow creased as the words left her mouth.

Ms. Lee chuckled. "I told your grandmother these secrets would eventually fall from the cracks." She reached forward and grabbed the remote control and turned off the television, then prepared her mind to release what she was willing to render.

"You have a Godfather, a man your mother trusted. She loved him different. She told him things she didn't even tell your father."

"What kind of things?" KoKo continued to prob.

"Even though your mother loved your father with all that she was. A crazy kind of love if you ask me." She shook her head. "But anyway, she made sure to put some information with him sort of like an insurance policy."

"What is his name?"

"Money." She spilled without hesitation.

"Money?" she said remembering her grandmother having a conversation with a church friend, but she did not know what it meant at the time.

"So, the whole rearranging of my life and all that I have endured was all for money? KoKo's brow creased as she thought about each step of her life.

"Yes. But you never heard it from me. I'm an old woman I don't need that element sniffing around my stoop." She again took the remote control into her hand and turned the television back on to catch the last half of *One Life to Live.*

"Where can I find him?"

"He's not too far. Just look around and ask the right questions. You'll find him." She held her gaze at the floor model.

Just as KoKo was about to ask another question she decided against it as her pager again vibrated against her hip confirming her decision.

"I'll see you next week." She rose to her feet, kissed Mrs. Lee on the forehead then headed to the door.

"Remember. Never go to the center of the circle. Skate just along the edges that will force the traitor to the middle and then you can see them better. And never let people know you know let them tell you."

"Indeed." KoKo headed to the door. "Lockup," she reminded her as she reached for the knob.

Mrs. Lee rose to her feet and walked over and locked the door. She took a deep sigh of relief as her soul made peace with her part in all the lies and secrets.

KoKo ran down the steps and then walked over to the phone booth that stood a few feet from the entrance. She picked up the receiver and called a cab then called the coded message back and typed in her coded response. She placed the phone back on the receiver then reached in her pocket and pulled out a blunt and lit the end. As she stood waiting for her ride, she watched the two youngins who helped her out playing around with a football.

KoKo whistled and waved them over. She whispered into her partner's ear then slid him a fifty-dollar bill then sent him on his way. She needed to start her hunt, and she needed to distinguish everyone who was her prey. It was time she made her enemies pay their dues.

Chapter 22

Paid Heat

Kayson sat straight up in the bed as he placed the phone on the receiver. He rubbed his hands over his face as he processed what Wise had just told him.

"Baby, you okay?" Lady asked sliding over close to where he sat.

"Yeah, get some rest. I'll see you in a few days I gotta run outta town," he responded as he got up, grabbed his pants and shirt, and put them on while gearing up to make a trip.

"Kay you know we have a doctor's appointment tomorrow." She folded her arms over her chest.

"Damn, I forgot baby." He turned towards her. "I'ma have my mom go with you." He headed to the bathroom.

"Your mother?" She cocked her head to the side. "She does not care for me. I'll take Octavia." She got up off the bed and followed him into the bathroom.

Kayson chuckled. "Look at you." He stared down at her swollen belly. "She got you. My mother is all about family. You have her legacy in your belly." He reached down and ran his hand over her stomach.

"Kay, I don't want to do this by myself." She spoke softly as she fought back the flood of emotion.

"You won't, I got you," he said taking her into his arms.

"You promise?" she uttered as his lips touched hers.

"I promise," he vowed as he lifted her, placed her heated body on the counter and stepped between her legs, then released the beast and slid deep into her tightness. "I promise."

"Don't let me down." She shuttered as she began to push against her walls.

"I got you." He responded as he rained kisses all over her face and neck. Kayson nibbled and stroked as Lady gripped him tighter with every push.

Lady held onto what she felt she had left of him knowing she would never have all of him. The little she did poses was seeming to slip right between her fingers. She dug deep into his back as his stroke touched spots inside that quaked her soul. Lady moaned as her body lifted with every headed thrust.

"I got you." She heard his whisper as she squeezed her eyes tight and released sticky passion over every inch of him.

Kayson allowed her to catch her breath then placed her on her feet. Lady's wobbled in place causing them both to giggle as they headed towards to shower.

"Your dick is medicine." She mumbled as she reached into the shower adjusting the water.

"Well step in that water and let me inject something from the back so we can both be healed." He stroked his dick as she assisted her into the shower.

"You are soooo... nasty," she said as she placed her hands in the wall.

"And you love it." Kayson stepped into place then slid slowly back inside her and pumped nice and slow.

Lady erased all her fears and allowed herself to just enjoy her man. Tomorrow was only promised to the sunlight, it owed her nothing she just wanted to enjoy whatever he had to give her.

****

"Well, damn! I thought you weren't coming?" Octavia said placing her fork down on her salad plate. She smiled as she looked at her friend, glowing in a yellow strapless sundress and red Fendi slides with her tiny little bump leading the way.

"Girl you know how it is." Lady slid in her seat swinging her beveled inches on her way down.

"Uh, no bitch, I don't." She twisted her lips to the side.

"Had to, girl gotta get it in when it fits in." She wiggled in her chair. "I know you ride a good dick from time to time."

"You're the one with all that good dick lying next to you. Strolling in here on cloud fifty-five with hickies, not ever shamed." She shook her head. "Whore," she said in a British accent.

"Whatever." Lady busted out laughing.

Octavia joined in as she looked at the happy sadness in her friends' eyes. "I ordered you some wings and fries."

"Thank you, best friend you be knowing." She did a little dance in her chair.

Octavia waved over the waiter and Lady gave her drink order.

"Bitch, you cut your hair?" Lady asked looking at the juicy brandy-colored layers swooped to the front and tapered on the sides and back.

"You know cuffing season is on the horizon. A bitch gotta cast the net," she said smoothly rubbing her hand over the back of her head.

"Bitch, you know what? I will not do this with you." She chuckled bringing the glass of ice-cold water to her lips.

"Yes, you will…and you will love it." She flashed a big cheesy smile.

Lady just shook her head as the two of them begin their usual banter which always led with Octavia's 'niggas ain't shit' rants. Lady sat listening and laughing as she waited for her food.

"Here you go, please let me know if you need anything else." The waitress announced as she placed the seafood appetizer on the table.

"I'm so in love, right now." Lady's eyes lit up when she saw that piping hot plate of Teriyaki wings coming her way. When the hot platter hit the table, she grabbed one of the small plates and quickly filled it with the steamy wings.

"Yessss… it's about to go down." She wiggled in her seat as she picked up a piece of the crispy meat dripping in sweet Teriyaki sauce.

"Greedy ass." Octavia giggled.

"Sticks and stones bitch…sticks and stones." Lady did a little neck roll as she continued to chow down.

The waitress returned with Octavia's lobster eggrolls and white wine and sat them right in front of her as a server following her sat a basket of fried shrimp, seasoned fries, and cheese sticks on Lady's side of the table.

"I'ma have to roll your ass outta here."

"Well, get your weight up cause I'm about to be a ton of fun." Lady wasted no time collecting something from each plate and adding it to her saucer.

Octavia looked on as she brought the tall glass of wine to her lips. While also battling with her words trying to formulate the conversation she needed to have with her friend.

"Sooooo…when are you going to tell your father about this pregnancy?"

Lady dropped the wing from her hand to the plate below and took a deep breath as she was not trying to have this conversation. "Look, Tay, I know you get worried about me and Kayson, but trust me I got it." She tried to convince them both.

"If you're happy why are you hiding it?" She took another sip.

"Tay please not now," she asserted herself.

"Then when?" She leaned in lowering her voice. "You are in love with the devil. Nothing good can come of that."

"Devil? What is wrong with you? Are you trying to hurt me?" she asked looking at her longtime friend.

Octavia bit into her lip again trying not to say too much. "Lady, I love you, real love. I don't want anything to happen to my friend." She looked directly into her eyes as she reached for her hand.

Lady placed her hand on Octavia's as she internalized her words. "I'm so scared, Tay," she confessed.

"I know," Octavia said as she wiped the tears she was struggling to hold back. "I'm scared for you."

"He loves me, Tay." She was now also wiping her eyes.

"Love yourself! Love that baby! Always prepare for the worse, and just know, I am here for you." She squeezed her hand tightly affirming her promise.

"I am in so over my head, right now. I didn't know who he was when I met him. I just knew he was so loving and attentive. I just wanted every day to be like the first.

"He's not hitting you, is he?"

"Hell no, Kayson is not like that…" She paused. "His pain comes from his absence and them fucking females. That shit kills me."

"You letting that nigga cheat?" Octavia's eyes widened as she pulled her hand back and reached for her glass.

"No, I don't let him cheat." Lady looked over at the table of women who had caught that last question. "I just know he's fucking them, thirsty ass bitches, he deals with." She lowered her voice.

Octavia sipped and sipped until her glass was empty, then held it in the air as she waved the waitress over for another. "Sooo…let me get this straight." She slid her glass to the edge of the table to be refilled. "You love him, he's a good man. Buttt…you let him sling your dick around with other bitches. Explain?"

"First of all, what we not gonna do is act like I haven't comforted you through twenty-five breakups and ten 'I thought that nigga was the one'." She sat forward tightening her lips as the last word eased past her teeth. "I never judge you and I never will. So, please do us both a favor by not speaking on my man's back."

"How the fuck am I speaking on his back? You are sitting here pregnant by the fucking plug, scared to tell your dad, scared for you and your baby's life! And you want me to just mind my business? Cool, fuck it." She rose to her feet and grabbed her purse.

"Tay don't." She grabbed her arm as she tried to pass the table.

"I am your friend. I love you, but I have learned that you can't get between a woman and her dick. I'ma step aside I don't

189

want to say anything that we both will regret." She reached in her purse and sat a few neatly folded hundreds on the table then leaned in and kissed Lady on her cheek. "Here if you need me." She walked out of the restaurant leaving Lady sitting at a well-prepared table of food and guilt.

Lady choked back her tears then slid her chair back and headed to the bathroom. She rushed into the stall, closed and locked the door. She rested her back against the cold steel and cried. She needed today to help strengthen her fight but instead, she shut down on her friend. She struggled to stop the tears but was so overwhelmed by their interaction she just let it all go. Lady stood in that stall crying until she felt dizzy. She grabbed some tissue from the roll, blew her nose, then wiped her face. After taking a few short breaths she unlocked the door then headed to the sink quickly turning on the cold water and dowsing her face and neck. She dried off took a few more breaths then headed back into the restaurant. When she got to the table the waitress had bagged her food and was waiting with her change.

"I thought you may have gotten sick, so I packed your food and added a little chocolate treat." She winked at her then reached out and gave her a hug.

Lady settled into the stranger's embrace needing to have a moment of comfort with all the emotion that was rushing through her body. "Thank you," she whispered then pulled back from her and grabbed the bag from the table.

"Your change." She reached her hand out filled with the two hundred and ten dollars.

"You keep that," Lady said with a slight smile as she pushed on to the front doors.

The woman stepped aside and just smiled as she watched Lady exit the restaurant. The smile left her face as she felt a heaviness in her heart for this woman, she didn't know but knew she was in misery. She tucked the handsome tip in her apron. "Thank you, God," she said a little prayer and moved on about her job.

Chapter 23

The Foundation

KoKo walked up to the basement door, gave the knock then stepped back and waited to hear the locks. When the door opened, she nodded her head then moved past Big Rob.

"What's up, KoKo?"

"Ain't shit," she said as she kept it moving towards the steps.

KoKo's eyes bounced around the room to see the team enjoying pussy popping Fridays. The crease in her forehead deepened as she witnessed heads bobbing and pussy popping. KoKo's lips twisted with disgust as the fumes of weed, ass and desperation rose in her nostrils. She kicked a few heels and red plastic cups as she moved through the room.

"Why you always hating when you come through here on a Friday?" Rome asked as he pulled the Spanish chick's ponytail and fucked her mouth.

"These bitches in here passing out Chlamydia and halitosis and y'all niggas celebrating. Well fuck it, enjoy," she said as she ascended the staircase.

"I am clea…"

"Shut the fuck up she ain't talkin' to you," Rome cut the woman's response by pushing all nine inches into her throat. She gagged and her eyes watered as she tried to pull back.

Rome smiled as he punished her for attempting to get in a grown man's conversation.

"That's, right bitch, eat a dick up until you hiccup." She snickered as she reached the top of the steps. "Nasty muthafuckas." She locked the door behind her.

KoKo walked through the kitchen and looked around the dimly lit room trying to focus her vision.

"Why you always come that way if that shit fucks with you?" Ha'Roo's voice echoed from the far corner by the window.

KoKo turned towards the sound of his voice. "You know I don't fuck with the front entrance…" She paused taking a few steps closer to the third level where she had a room.

"You have access to all of this, I told you that." He got up and headed towards her.

KoKo watched his 6'2 muscular, chocolate frame, move in and out of the shadows. Her heart fluttered the closer he got but her ice-cold demeanor stayed the same.

"Count good?" he asked looking down into her slanted eyes.

"Did you get a causality report?" she asked tossing the duffle bag at his feet.

"Your little ass ain't hard." He chuckled. "I got something hard for you thou." He looked down at all that hot KoKo wrapped in baggy jeans, a hoodie, and Timberland boots.

KoKo looked down at the bulge in his sweatpants then back up into his light brown eyes. "Mannn…fuck outta here." She turned to the flight of stairs. "Save that hard dick for that dirty fish y'all be boning." She ran up the steps two at a time.

"Punk ass." He snickered as he picked up the bag.

"Suck my punk-ass dick," she hurled back as she clicked the locks and moved into the room.

"Pull your pants down." Ha'Roo laughed as he heard KoKo locking herself safe behind the door. "Scary ass," he mumbled as he headed back to his seat to check the count.

****

"Here you go, baby. I'll see you next week same time." He placed a folded wad of money in Tiny's hand while holding the phone to his chest with the other.

"Okay, Papi." She leaned in and kissed his cheek then turned to her clothes which were skillfully placed near the bed.

The Don turned his attention back to his caller taking a seat in the chair near his bed. Tiny slipped into her bra and thong then eased her skintight dress over her body. She forced her ear to hustle the conversation trying to catch what she could through the receiver. When the Don's voice began to escalate, she knew this was a conversation she needed to be privy to. She turned towards Don Anibello and gave him a sexy smile then walked over to him and opened the towel and put her mouth right on his dick. She sucked slow and sloppy causing him to pause and listing to the caller allowing her to hear a piece or two as well.

Anibello tried to focus on his comrade's words but his attention was snatched back but the tightening of Tiny's jaws. She sucked and twisted her hand around the base of his stiffness until she felt his hand rest on her head. Tiny took him to the back of her throat and continued to listen trying to catch the voice or a name. She gripped the head of his dick with her tonsils then let her mouth lubricate the up and down slide. Tiny picked up the speed until he did what she needed him to do, and that was run his mouth.

"Edwin, I'll call you right back something came up." He hung up not waiting for the man's response.

Don Anibello gripped her hair between his fingers and pumped up wildly until he released all that he had to offer.

Tiny played in his sticky white causing chills to cover his body. She stood up wiping her mouth with the back of her hand then headed to the bathroom switching her butt as she walked off. The don tucked himself away and put his head back as he tried to catch his breath. He grabbed the phone and dialed Edwin's number. When he answered he picked up right where they left off.

Tiny walked out of the bathroom picked up her money and purse then headed to the door. She turned and waved then blew a kiss, one she knew would soon end in death. The Don waved and smiled as he watched his afternoon snack slip from his grip.

Tiny hurried to the car and hopped in the back and as the Don's driver pulled away from the driveway, she texted a message to Dee Dee to call a meeting. It was time to turn shit all the way up.

Chapter 24

In The Light

"Yes, Mrs. Mo, I picked up your cleaning and the chief will be dropping off your meals in an hour." She looked at the time on her watch as she zipped through traffic.

"Okay, great, please make sure you get Kayson to sign those documents then get them over to the realtor by noon Friday."

"No problem. Is there anything else we may have missed?" she asked not really wanting an answer.

"If it is, I will call you back." Monique struggled to hold her tongue.

"Okay, I'm here if you need me," Lady responded then heard the call disconnect without the last greeting made.

"Fucking bitch! Oh, Lord please forgive me. This woman brings out all my demons." She sucked her teeth as she thought about having to see her.

Lady pulled into her office parking lot, then into her designated space. She looked up at the seventeen-story building that she'd built with all her pain, mistakes, and fear. She had everything she wanted and a man she loved but still with all her power and success. Lady knew something was just wanting and waiting to pounce from the shadows and destroy her peace. Her mind then drifted to the best thing in her life. The only person who gave her pure bliss. She put her head back on the headrest and just zoned out and thought about the first time she saw those deep dimples and smooth caramel skin.

Lady had walked over to the bar and leaned in to order herself a drink. She gripped the thick glass and brought it to her mouth. Lady scanned the area to see what type of money was in the room. Her eyes rested on a few sections but when she saw Kayson and his people her clit started to tingle. Lady had been looking for a way in and it looked as if the opportunity had fallen at her feet. She turned her back, downed her drink, took a deep breath, then headed in Kayson's direction.

Kayson's attention was divided between Dee who always made it known she was his and this new energy that was heading in his direction.

"So, can I warm your bed tonight, Boss?" Dee requested, nuzzling her nose against his ear as her hand explored his lap.

"Why you always trying to get in my bed?" Kayson asked easing her hand away from the Enforcer.

"I'm at my best when you are between these thighs," she confessed trying to close the deal.

"Is that right?" he asked holding eye contact with the woman whose body was swaying in a way that read 'fuck me'. "Sit up, I need to take care of some business real quick," he stated smoothly as he rose to his feet.

The smile on Lady's face almost dropped to the floor when she saw him get up.

"Damn," Dee mumbled as her opportunity seemed to be about to walk off.

Just as Lady had decided she was going to just pretend she was going in another direction Kayson moved towards her then reached out and grabbed her hand.

"Bitch, be cool," she told herself as she looked up at all that man. "Is this what you do, grab people up?" she shyly asked while bating her pretty light brown eyes.

"Why you always following me?"

"I ain't gonna front I was trying to get an opportunity to see what all the talk is about." She put her offer on the table.

"The talk? You can't believe what you hear. You should always check for yourself."

"You can't handle what I would check yo' ass with." She twisted her lips to the side.

"Why light-skinned women always got an attitude and shit to pop?" he shot back.

"Excuse me?" Lady responded with a wrinkled brow.

Kayson shot her that sexy smile. "You heard me. You don't want none of this grown man work," he threatened.

"I do, I really need that for something," her mouth watered as the words left her lips.

"We gonna see," he uttered as his eyes roamed over the plumpness of her breasts through the black sheer material.

Lady exchanged a few more slick remarks and subtle laughs with Kayson then gave him her number. Lady excused herself to rejoin her friends with a smile plastered on her face.

"Don't wet your seat!" Kayson yelled out as she walked away. He had just sent her wet pussy into a frenzy; it was now only a matter of time before he was deep stroking.

The sound of a car alarm blaring snapped Lady back to reality. She looked around the parking lot then turned on her engine. She pulled off thinking was that night at the club her luck, or her curse.

****

Ha'Roo pressed his back against the wall a few inches from door 7A. He signaled to the crew who were waiting just an eyeshot away for their signal to move. Everyone positioned themselves strategically along the musty, dimly lit corridor and at each exit and waited for the green light. Ha'Roo pulled the black mesh over his face and everyone followed suit. Ha'Roo locked eyes with KoKo who stood only feet away, a pretty bitch but dressed like a killer. KoKo winked her left eye then covered her beauty because for this the only thing them niggas was going to see was a beast.

Ha'Roo looked down at his watch and watched the hands tick by slowly. In his mind, he did the countdown to his come up.

"Five…four…three…two…one," he mumbled then looked down at the knob.

"Nah, fuck you, nigga. I'll be right back!" The stocky gentleman yelled out and chuckled as he pulled the door open.

197

Ha'Roo swung around, grabbed Little John by the collar with one hand, and shoved his gun in his mouth with the other. He held him in front of him as they moved to the living room. Magnum followed close behind Ha'Roo with both guns drawn. KoKo moved in and headed to the kitchen for the stash. While Linkz held the door praying a nigga would give him the reason to squeeze. He motioned at the men on exit duty then eased the door closed.

"What the fuck is going on?" Murph yelled out throwing his hands in the air.

"Shut the fuck up!" Ha'Roo yelled out as he positioned himself right in front of Murph.

"Where the fuck is the shit and don't play with my fucking dick...let go!" Ha'Roo yelled out waving his gun around the room.

The other three men in the room froze when they saw the horror standing at the other end of two very big guns.

"Do you know who the fuck runs this spot?" Murph yelled out as he watched KoKo walk in with a double-barrel ready to go.

Ha'Roo looked over at KoKo and she shook her head no with a frown etched deep in her brow. Ha'Roo turned back to Murph then squeezed the trigga causing Little John's brains, skull, and blood to paint Murph's face as the body hit the floor.

Ha'Roo rushed up on Murph and slapped him across the head with the gun then placed it right under his chin. "Where...the fuck...is the stash," he growled as Murph's fear fueled his beast.

"Y'all ain't gotta do this," one of the young soldiers spoke from his seated position on the couch.

"Shut the fuck up before I make you this nigga's roommate."

"Nigga, fuck you, I ain't dying on my muthafuckin' knees," he barked then grabbed the handle of his gun from under the cushion.

Boom! Boom!

The bullets from KoKo's gun tore through the young boy's stomach forcing him back and over the couch. KoKo ran over and pumped up on the cushions and put two more in his chest.

She then smacked the shit out of the guy who was sitting next to him just to send a message. She braced her feet and placed the trigger at the back of his skull, then looked over at Murph.

"I'm not asking you again." Ha'Roo's bloodshot eyes peered through the mesh and into Murph's soul.

"Fuck that, tell that nigga. What the fuck are you protecting another nigga's money for?" Q yelled out with his shaking hands held high in the air.

Just as Ha'Roo was about to start beating Murph with his gun they heard a noise coming from the back. He looked up at KoKo who shrugged her shoulders. She had gotten the headcount from her informant and there were only four on the list. She nodded at Linkz who pointed his heat at Q and the other terrified guy sitting in the love seat and motioned for KoKo to walk down the hall. Ha'Roo eased his gun into Murph's mouth as he watched KoKo approach the closed door at the end of the hall.

KoKo put her back against the wall, counted to three, then ran and kicked the door open blasting her gun on the way in.

"Oh, God please," a woman cried out as she crouched down to the floor with a baby clutched tightly in her grip.

KoKo moved to the woman's side, grabbed her ponytail, and pulled her to her feet. The woman screamed and cried as she struggled to keep a grip on her newborn son.

"Please…please…please," she pleaded as her son's cries began to overshadow hers.

Murph's eyes widened as he saw Tomeka being pulled towards him with her robe disheveled trying to keep a firm grip on her son.

"Tell them!" she screamed as it felt as if KoKo would rip her head from her scalp.

KoKo put the gun to the infant's head and looked at Murph.

"Okay…" he mumbled with the end of the gun still resting on his tongue.

Ha'Roo eased the steel back and allowed the man to speak. "You were saying."

"It's in the trunk of the black Lexus," he blurted as he watched KoKo's hand gripped the butt of the gun.

"Where the fuck is the keys?" Ha'Roo barked growing tired of the whole scene since they should have been in and out.

Murph pointed at the keys sitting on the glass table. Magnum snatched the keys off the table and moved to the door. He waved Roman over, then gave him the keys and instructions. Roman trotted up the hall and down the stairs, he popped the trunk, grabbed the bag, and tossed it in the back of their van.

//: *Got it!* The text came through to Magnum.

//: *Stay downstairs!* He texted back.

Roman read it, tucked his phone, and jumped inside. He started the engine, put his gun on his lap and neck on a swivel.

Magnum nodded at Ha'Roo who was anxious to let his gun speak a deadly conversation. "Being loyal only pays if what you are loyal to is worth dying for." He turned and gave KoKo the eye.

KoKo moved the gun back and forth from the woman's head to the child's.

"Please you got the shit you came for," Murph pleaded as he watched his baby's mother at the mercy of his enemy. "Please, I ain't' gonna be no trouble." He cringed as the sounds of the baby crying and Tomeka pleading broke whatever part of a man, he thought he had left.

Ha'Roo looked down at him, then back up at KoKo and gave her the signal. KoKo smiled under her mask as she pulled the trigger.

"Noooooooooo…" Murph yelled out at the horror before him.

Tomeka's body slumped over to the side with her baby tightly wrapped in her arms. Her blood and brains filled the floor under her as her eyes fluttered in pain. KoKo reached down, grabbed the baby, and placed him on the couch closes to Murph.

Murph looked over at his whaling baby and all life slipped from his helpless body.

"Now give me the money." Ha'Roo grimaced.

Tears flowed from the corners of his eyes as he gathered enough air to answer. "In the backroom in the closet."

Magnum moved to the back, fumbled through the closet and grabbed the two bags, unzipped them, smiled then headed back to the front and posted up by the door.

Ha'Roo turned his attention back to Murph who had broken down into a million pieces.

"I'ma let your future live, but your present is gone." Ha'Roo pulled the trigger making Little Man an official orphan.

Murph's body shook as he took his last breaths. As his lids lowered the blurred image of his son would be the last thing, he would ever take in.

Ha'Roo, KoKo, and Magnum eased out the door and down the hallway with the baby's screams echoing in the background. They hurried to the van, as a black Tahoe pulled past their vehicle. They quickly hopped inside and slammed the door. The Tahoe busted a U-turn and headed back in their direction. Before they could get the car in drive, bullets started flying through the window.

"Fuck!" Magnum threw the van in reverse and speed down the street.

Ha'Roo busted out the front window and Roman busted from the back. They sped down Harrison and turned quick on Central Avenue.

KoKo opened the back window and pumped one into their front windshield. The truck swerved, hitting two parked cars the man quickly gained control and kept on towards them. She pumped two more in their direction hitting the driver in the forehead sending him into a light pole at Central and Evergreen.

"Yeah, nigga, you see that shit!" Link yelled out as they turned on Munn Avenue headed to 280. They sped down the block and jumped on the highway.

KoKo sat in her seat breathing heavily as the adrenaline rushed through her veins. Flashes of her night placed another layer of darkness over her soul. Ha'Roo looked at her in the rearview mirror and his heart skipped at the sight of the woman he knew had his back, front, and both sides. He exited at the Kearny ramp thinking, the war had started, and he knew he didn't have a chance without her right there by his side and anything that threatened that he would destroy.

****

"Put all that shit on the muthafuckin' line bitch ass nigga," Wise sang out as he threw the dice against the wall. He went into an uproar when he rolled his tenth seven. "Play with this hot shit if you want to. Pay a nigga his money." He swooped down and gathered the game room's standard form of currency, stacks of hundred-dollar bills.

"And hand me them, two bitches." He pointed at the dice. "About to make these hoes suck my dick. Come on bitches' daddy need to bust one more time." He shook the black and white squares in his fist as the crowd threw their money down for the bet.

"This nigga is a fuckin' nut yo'!" Choppa their head of operations in Yonkers yelled out as he placed a few more hundred on the floor.

Wise bent down and smacked the corner of the wall with the dice and again the crowd screamed and talked shit as he hit the eleventh roll.

"Man, fuck y'all niggas. Y'all trying to get a man emotional and I ain't gon' do it." He pretended to cry as he again swooped up his earnings. "Bring me a drink, I'ma let these niggas get some of their money back," he said pulling up a chair as he organized his cash.

The dice went to the next man's hand and the bets were placed. Wise threw down his bet, lit a blunt, and sat back sipping his favorite dark liquor.

Aldeen sat close to the door watching everything moving and the shit that was sitting still. He thought about the moves they needed to make and what it was going to take to pull it off then began plotting their next strike. Aldeen was about to wave over one of the bar girls when he saw security patting Dee Dee down. He gave them the nod and she headed to his booth.

Dee walked right over to him, leaned down by his ear, and filled him with that street heat. She stood up, folded her arms across her chest, and waited for her instructions.

"Grab your girls, transportation will meet you at the spot. Walk low a few weeks."

"Say no more." She turned and headed back to the exit.

Security handed her a wallet filled with crisp bills. She tucked it in her Celene and was out.

"Wise!" Aldeen's voice boomed through the pool hall.

The men came to attention as Wise hopped up from his seat walking right through the game stomping on dice, money, and feelings as he moved to his comrades' side.

"What's up?" Wise asked with a ruffled brow.

"Call a meeting."

****

"Kayson please come in," Edwin said with a huge smile as he watched Kayson enter the room tall and strong.

"What you up to old man?" Kayson asked as he embraced Edwin.

"Trying to stay young. What I would not give to rewind the clock twenty years. Come sit, they have prepared lunch," Edwin said as he walked to the head of the dining room table and took a seat.

Kayson followed behind and took the chair to the left of Edwin. "I appreciate you taking the time to sit down with me."

"Appreciate?" Edwin chuckled. "You are like a son to me. Closer than my own seed. What is, this appreciate?" Edwin's thick Spanish accent rang out.

"No disrespect, I just know you have a whole legacy you are preparing for your family. Just humble to be at your table."

"You belong at my table. Your seat has been paid for in blood."

"Indeed," Kayson responded then silence fell over the room as the servers began to place the dishes on the table.

Hot steam rose off each platter as his wife walked over and began serving each man a healthy helping of Spanish chicken, rice, and beans, with a basket of her freshly baked rolls.

"Ohhh...my son." She held Kayson's face and kissed him on the forehead.

"You are one of my favorite people. Thanks for this amazing meal, Mama Cruz," Kayson said taking her hand into his and placing a single kiss on the backside.

"Always my son." Her face lit up with joy. "Now eat up I know you don't eat," she said as she prepared to exit the area.

"Papi, is that all?"

"Yes, thank you," Edwin responded as he picked up his fork.

When the dining room doors slid close Kayson got right to the point. "So, what can I expect from the Cubans?"

"He always offers you a single hand. That is his way of testing your loyalty to me."

Kayson looked at the strong man he once admired as a mentor now aged and troubled by what would be. His mind turned as he thought of what now needed to be done.

"My loyalty is solid."

"This I know. And he will use that against us both." He placed a fork full of the tender meat in his mouth. "Let him see your other side."

Kayson nodded his understanding. "Don't worry when the smoke clears the only thing you will have to do is read about the casualties."

"My son." Edwin smiled looking over at Kayson once a young bull, now a full-grown savage.

****

Baseem pulled up to Pinky and Red's townhouse and hoped out his truck. He popped the trunk grabbed a few bags then headed to the front door. He placed the bags at his feet and tapped on the door then rang the bell like he was serving an active warrant. Beseem looked at the windows then back at the door as he rand and knocked a little harder with every waiting second.

"Who the fuck is it?" a female voice based through the hardwood.

"Open the fucking door." Baseem based back.

The locks clicked and the door opened wide. When Baseem set his eyes on Red's curvy frame with a Gat tucked closely to her hip and his dick jumped against his zipper.

"Why you out here acting a fucking fool at nine in the morning?" Red asked with sliding the safety back in place.

"Don't take so long next time," Baseem said pushing past her. "Stop staring at me and lock the door." He ordered tossing the bags next to the love seat.

"These muthafuckas," she mumbled as she closed and latched all locks back in place.

"Where's your sister?" he asked as he looked around the house like he lived there.

"Pinky is sleeping like I want to be," she responded dryly wanting to crawl back into her nice warm spot.

Baseem walked into the kitchen pulled off his hoodie and tossed it on the chair then moved to the sink and washed his hands and face. He grabbed a few paper towels, dried off, then headed back into the living room. He tossed them on the coffee table, then pulled his nine out of his waist and an ounce of purple haze from his front pants pocket.

"Why the fuck y'all ain't up?" he asked walking up right behind her.

"Bas we just went to sleep. Why the fuck you outside banging on doors and disturbing the peace?" she leaned forward placing her gun on the end table.

"Checking these traps." He softened his tone grabbing at her long ponytail which was all hers adding to a niggas fantasy.

"You ain't ready for the traps I set." She teased then turned to look up into his light brown eyes.

"Tag me in coach. I'm ready to dunk some shit."

205

"You so fucking nasty." Red folded her arms over her nipples as they hardened against her tank top.

"You about to be nasty too. Roll up." He gripped her ass then walked over to the black suede high-back chair and settled into its comfort.

Red turned to watch him walk away. His thug had her kitty purring she was definitely ready to be tamed. She walked over to where he sat and looked down her stomach flipped seeing that he too was ready to be tamed, nothing a deep suck couldn't handle, and her sweet tooth had just kicked in.

Baseem wanted to keep up the tough guy charade but her pussy print was sitting fat in those white see-through booty shorts causing the corner of his mouth to curl at the corner.

"Can you roll that up for me, please?"

"Got you begging already. You don't want this work." She teased reaching for the razor blade and pack of Philly blunts. She sat on the table in front of him, split two Phillies then filled them with the sticky purple and licked them closed.

"Here you go, sir." She put her hand out passing him the two fat blunts.

Baseem sat watching all that pussy staring back at him and his morning wood grew slightly down his thigh.

"Come sit on my lap and smoke with me." He patted his leg.

"Really, Bas?" she said with her lips twisted to the side.

"Don't make me ask you twice." He looked up into her eyes and pouty pink lips then waited for her movement.

Red reluctantly stood up then straddled his lap placing her feet behind him. Baseem looked down at that fat mound pressing against him then rubbed his hand up and down her swollen lips.

"That's what the fuck I'm talking about, this what a man needs after the hustle." He said as he moved the shorts to the side to see the pretty pink peach waiting for him to devour. "Yeah, I got something real thorough for Miss peach." He teased then put her shorts back in place.

"I bet you do." She looked down at his growing bulge.

"How did last night go." He quickly checked the reports.

"Everything went well, we bagged and tagged and made all drop-offs. We just got in the bed at six o'clock," she responded as she enjoyed all that muscle and power between her legs.

"I thought we was smoking?" She tried to bring him back to focus.

"Light up," he ordered as he ran his finger over her nipples.

Red clicked the lighter putting fire to the end of the blunt then inhaled deeply. She sucked in the smoke deep then blew it out heavy into the air. Baseem watched her play with the purple as he played with her clit through the thin cotton of her shorts.

Red turned the blunt and placed it in her mouth then brought his face to hers. Baseem opened his mouth and sucked in the smoke as she blew it into his lungs. They exchanged playful emotion and thick smoke as their bodies heated up by the second. They finished the first blunt and lit the second with Baseem's dick rock hard between her throbbing lips she leaned in and sucked his lips then whispered in his ear as he pulled heavily on the haze.

"I need to suck your dick." She panted as she felt his finger slid between her wetness.

"What else you need." He asked as his finger slide in and out causing her hips to gyrate against his waist.

"I need you to fuck me from the back hard until my pussy moans." She purred taking the blunt from his hand.

"Ewwww... what the fuck is y'all doing?" Pinky came from the back of the house with her face all scrunched up as she realized what was going on.

"Why yo ass ain't sleep, its grown folks' hour." Baseem chuckled as he pulled his hand from between Red's legs.

"What the fuck ever. You got something for me?" she asked walking over to the bags by the loveseat.

"Put that money in the safe and those Nordstrom's bags are for you from Kayson." He said keeping his eyes on Red as she mouthed nasty shit setting the path towards him fucking her good.

"Awww... He is so sweet." Pinky said as she looked through the bags. "Tell the Boss I said thank you." She cooed then grabbed all the bags and headed to the basement.

Pinky counted the stacks then tucked them away. She clicked the lights, grabbed her gifts, and headed back upstairs.

"Did Tiny handle that business?" Baseem asked as he took the blunt from Red's hand.

"Yes. She got that nigga real comfortable; we will have the information we need by the end of the week."

"A'ight. I'll get with you later about that Harlem move."

"A'ight. I'ma get some more sleep a bitch ain't beautiful yet." She laughed as she walked back to her bedroom.

"Turn your music on when you get to the back. I don't want to scare you for life." He joked as he stood up keeping Red attached tightly to his waist.

"That's nasty," she twisted her lips and walked off not wanting the mental picture.

"Now tell me what it is that you need." He bit her nipple through her shirt.

"Only this." She reached down and squeezed his thickness.

"Put him where you need him to be," he spoke firm as he pulled on the sweet purple.

Red rose on the tip of her feet, then unzipped Baseem's jeans and released the demon. She pulled her shorts to the side then bounced on the head until she had him inside her. Slowly she rocked and rolled her hips as his dick filled every crease.

"Damn, Bas," she moaned gripping the back of the chair.

"Don't play wit' it. Ride this muthafucka," he grunted as he watched her pop that pussy just the way he needed it.

Red and Baseem locked gazes as he began to match her rhythm with a few up strokes knocking against her G spot causing a flood between them. Baseem placed his hand on her ass pulling her in with each downward motion. Red picked up the pace until she felt her pussy locking around his throbbing inches. When her body began to shiver, she rocked and grinded against him applying pressure to her clit as he slid in and out playing in her juices.

"Is there anything else you need?" He asked kissing her lips ever so gently.

"I need you to put these bowlegs on your shoulders and drill."

Baseem stood up keeping her attached to his waist. He walked down the hall, into her bedroom and slammed the door shut. He crawled onto the bed with her right beneath him, pulled off his A T-shirt, then his jeans. He pulled off her shorts and tank top, then put her legs right where they both needed them to be. Baseem pushed her legs all the way back to the headboard and dove in and drilled.

Chapter 25

Bitch Nigga

Aldeen pulled up in front of the tall, brick buildings and idled his engine. Kayson eyed their surroundings, then eased his hood up halfway on his head, he checked his two silver friends and hopped out.

"Stay put," Kayson ordered as he gently closed the door behind him.

Aldeen reached into his console, pulled out his Glock, and placed it in his lap locked and ready to talk nasty. He looked up at the small flock of white birds flying from one building to the next led by a sequence of claps and whistles. "I hate this fucking side of town," he mumbled as he watched everything moving.

Kayson walked up to the crowd of men and eased next to Blue. He spoke a few short words close to his ear, then moved past him toward the door.

Blue nodded and the door opened. Kayson stepped inside and headed straight to the elevator. As the doors closed, he thought over the offer he was putting on the table. He watched the numbers rise as he ascended floor by floor.

Ding! The elevator came to a stop and he stepped off, then to the left.

Kayson positioned himself just off to the left, knocked, then waited.

"Who?" a woman's voice pierced the iron door.

"Boss," he bellowed back, then heard the locks and chains being released.

"He's in the back." The short, chocolate woman dressed in only a black lace bra and G-string pointed toward the long hallway. She held her gaze to the floor as she tried to block the heat that was heading her way through Kayson's eyes.

Kayson looked at the oil covering her toned bowlegs and flat stomach and immediately thought about what else he wanted before he left.

"Bossman, last room on the left!" Fred yelled out as he heard Kayson approaching.

Kayson followed the call and headed to the open door. He pushed it open to see an old friend sitting at the far end of the immaculate room, in his favorite chair, sipping his favorite brown.

"You called I came," Kayson got right to the point as he closed the door behind him.

"That you did, please have a seat," Fred offered as he crossed his legs at the knee.

Kayson walked over and sat on the edge of the leather chair directly across from Fred and waited for him to make the next move.

"First of all, thank you. I know you are a busy man, and your time is costly." He brought his drink to his lips.

"You have always used my time wisely. So, I'm here to see how this unscheduled meeting is going to benefit us both." Kayson stared right into Feather Fred's bloodshot eyes.

"There is some movement that will cripple us both and I figured we needed to put a hand on its throat before the small chirps turn into big howls," he spoke straight to the code he knew Kayson stood by.

"Why do you think anything another nigga do can affect anything I got going on?" Kayson sat waiting to see a few more of Fred's cards.

Fred slowly nodded his head up and down, then got to business. "I believe the Italians been fishing, and a few snakes been biting."

"Is that right?" Kayson asked as his brow creased.

212

"I believe if a nigga gets his hook in, then I gotta worry. And you gotta worry." Fred laid down his hand.

"What's in all of this for you?" Kayson folded one fist in the other.

"Nothing." Fred took another sip. "I like what I have. I like the structure, but I'm an old man. I'd rather give up some power to a friend than have to worry about my life in the hands of my enemy," he spoke his offer as clear as he could.

Kayson tossed around what the wise man was saying. The Russians were making a small move and he needed to make a bigger one.

"What are you willing to give a friend?"

"Two buildings off the top and no cut raw at twelve a key. And if we can get a handle on security an old man could sleep easier at night." He took a deep breath, then sat silent and confident in his offer.

"Deal," Kayson answered without hesitation as he rose to his feet. "Oh, and sexy that opened the door. I need that, too." He extended his hand to seal the deal.

"That's a fresh fish, untouched and new to the stable." Fred's heart dropped as he put out his hand.

"Good, have her gift-wrapped and delivered to me untouched and fresh out the stable," Kayson ordered as he gripped Fred's frail hand.

"Deal," he said with his mouth, but a piece of his soul had just leaped from his gut.

Kayson put his hood over his head and moved to the door.

"What am I looking for?" Kayson asked with his hand on the knob.

"I believe his favorite color is Blue," Fred answered as he reached forward and grabbed his hash filled pipe.

Kayson didn't turn around he just walked out of Fred's room ready to pluck the thorn from both of their sides. He moved to the door, eyeing his new toy as he got closer.

Her gaze again dropped to the floor as she reached for the locks to let Kayson out.

213

"You belong to the Boss now. Let me see you." He stood right in front of her then placed his finger under her chin.

She looked up into his hazel eyes and heat moved through her whole body.

"What's your name, Ma?" he asked exchanging surges of energy with her near-naked frame.

She swallowed her spit hard, then forced the words from her lips, "Brielle," she said a little over a whisper.

"You gonna be my tiny treat. Get your shit together a car will pick you up in an hour. Stay put until I come to you," he instructed as he held his gaze with hers.

"Yes," she confirmed as she struggled with the feeling to piss right where she stood.

"Be good." He winked, then reached for the knob and exited the apartment.

Brielle closed the door, then clicked the locks and chains back in place. She looked out the peephole at all that man that had just literally changed her whole world. "The Boss," she said aloud, not knowing if he was ending it or saving it. But she damn sure was about to ride this muthafucka with no hands and no breaks.

****

Dirty Hands...

Aldeen was eyeing the movement and lack of discipline and his face formed a scowl. He took note of each infraction wanting to jump out and smack a few niggas on his way out. He looked up in his rearview mirror and saw a short figure bopping up the block with a hard ass rock to their step.

KoKo had walked a little down from Feather Fred's apartment building with her hood down to her eyes as she stepped through the jets. She put her hands in her hoodie pocket, released the safety on her gun, and tucked her finger tightly against the trigger.

214

When she approached a crowd of men, she met eyes with each one as they came to attention. Her brows met in the middle as she sized up each man.

"Can we help you, Shorty?" Blue spoke out as she got closer.

"I don't know, can you?" she hurled back holding a firm eye lock.

"Fuck you mean, can I?" he quickly responded then threw his Black and Mild down to the concrete.

"Hold up," D'Low said, putting his arm out stopping Blue's movement.

"Nah, Low, let that nigga get buck," she huffed as she walked right up on them.

Blue looked over at D'Low, then back at KoKo whose heart didn't skip or jump.

"That's Fred's people," D'Low slightly warned Blue.

"Fuck that bitch," Blue spat wanting to slap some respect into KoKo's slick ass mouth.

"Slap a bitch when you see one then." KoKo eased her hand from her pocket with Midnight gripped firmly in her grasp.

Blue's eyes rested at her waist, then he looked back at the coldness in her gaze.

"Yeah, okay." He chuckled and sucked his teeth as he stepped back two steps.

"Thought so, bitch boy." She turned her attention to D'Low. "He ready?"

D'Low chuckled realizing his boy almost lost his crown fucking with KoKo. "You need to chill, Ma. Yeah, go on up," he responded wanting KoKo to put some distance between her and Blue.

"Talk to ya girl, he mad," she joked as she headed to the door.

"KoK, be nice," D' Low said as she entered the building.

"Indeed!" she shouted back as the door slammed.

"Fuck that bitch," Blue hurled as he spat on the ground.

"That bitch is official. We fucks with her," D' Low reminded his misinformed friend.

"I'm not fucking with no niggas that got a bitch calling shots and putting niggas on they ass." He reached in his pocket, pulled out a blunt, and put fire to it.

"Don't worry things gonna change," D' Low said then moved to the side to watch the action.

KoKo walked up to the door and was let in by Big Sam.

"What's good, Ma?" he asked as he closed the door behind her. He walked her to the elevator, then pressed the up button.

"Ain't shit, just keeping these niggas one step behind," she said as she slapped hands with him.

"I hear that. Just make sure that step don't cause a nigga to trip into your shit," he spoke firm as he looked up to see the numbers lowering.

"I'm always sure," KoKo said as the elevator doors were about to open. "I'ma hit these steps." She snatched the door to the staircase open and hit the beat two steps at a time.

★★★★

Bing! The doors slid open and Kayson locked eyes with Big Sam as he exited the small box.

"Lock this shit down. Don't release the doors until my team comes through here. Understood?" he barked through clenched teeth.

"Understood." Big Sam's left knee jerked when he saw that small glimpse of death seeping from Kayson's eyes. He stepped to the side, grabbed his walkie, and gave the orders.

Kayson walked out of the doors, along the cement path, and right up to the crowd of men gathered off to the right. He sized up each man as he approached, then tuned his ear to hear the sound he needed to hear, and within seconds his investigation was over. It was him, Blue the loudest, dumbest, and cockiest one in the circle.

D' Low's eyes dipped to the side to where Blue stood as he felt the energy change. "Y'all niggas crazy," he said, then turned to face Kayson. His heart raced as he watched the silver tip of his

216

gun rested tight at his side. He nodded in submission as he stepped out of the way.

"Man, fuck y'all niggas. No pussy getting ass niggas!" Blue yelled, then turned to see what had caught D' Low's attention.

Bloom! Bloom! Bloom!

Kayson sent off three shots hitting Blue in the stomach, chest, and smack dead in the middle of his forehead. Blue hit the ground with blood gurgling from his mouth and running out of the gaping holes in his torso. His hands seized over his chest as he shook in agonizing pain.

Kayson looked each man in the eyes, then walked up to D' Low and spoke his peace, "I don't want to have to come down here under no circumstance. The next nigga gets loud or outta place and you don't kill him..." He stared hard into his eyes. "...I'ma kill you." He tucked his gun back in the pocket of his hoodie and walked to the truck not taking a second look as a canopy of cries and confusion played against his back.

The crew looked at D' Low with confusion as they watched Blue fade into his destiny.

"What the fuck, man?" Little Rob asked as he walked over to where D' Low was standing.

"Change of hands, my nigga. Change of hands," he answered then circled his finger in the air.

Aldeen pulled off into traffic as he heard the faint sound of sirens in the distance.

****

KoKo walked down the short hallway and up to Feather Fred's bedroom door.

"Knock. Knock," KoKo said as she pushed the door open.

"KoKoooo..." Fred said as a smile eased across his face.

"Ain't shit, just trying to stay on this side of the table," she spat as she sat back and pulled her hood from her head.

"You look tired, KoKo," Fred spoke his mind, he could see the stress in her eyes.

217

"Nah, I'm wide awake. Just gotta keep these niggas on their toes," she spoke firm as she pulled a blunt from her pocket.

"I've been having the same concern."

"*Concern?* You need me to take care of something for you?" Her brow creased as she now saw the worry on Fred's face.

"No need, it's taken care of." He waved his hand. "But enough about me. What brings you to an old man's door?" he asked, folding his hands on his stomach.

"Is there anything I need to know?" she asked searching his face for deception.

"There is never anything you need to know. Is there something you want to know?" He threw the ball back in her court.

KoKo thought hard about her next round of words. She needed to get into Fred's head up to this point she never had anything he needed but today would be different.

"What do you know about, Pashion?" she asked, then watched his chest as it rose quickly and slowed its pace.

"Every man should have a little in his life at least once." He smiled and reached for his drink.

"Don't fucking play with me," she spat, not in the mood for Fred's coded messages.

Fred dropped the smile and took a sip from his glass, then sat it on the end table.

"What you want to know is a very dangerous road to travel down. I tucked those demons away years ago. Don't dig up that grave, KoKo."

"Nah, you gonna dig that muthafucka," she insisted, sitting forward.

Fred nodded his head as he thought about what she was asking of him.

KoKo took a deep pull of her blunt and looked her trusted friend in the face. This was a conversation he was going to have with her by will or by force.

Fred took a deep breath and walked a small way into history, giving her only what he was instructed to. The rest she would have

218

to get herself. KoKo sat listening to Fred with half belief and half disbelief. She unfolded a few things in her life and for the first-time shit made sense.

By the time Fred finished talking, her head was on tilt. She stood up, reached into her hoodie pocket, and laid an envelope of money on the table, then turned for the door.

"You good, my friend?" he asked, now concerned with where her head was.

"Always," she answered as she opened the door.

"Here if you need me, Ce'Asia," he said her name for the first time, confirming he did indeed know who she really was.

"Tuck that shit. I'm just, KoKo, baby." She smiled at him in an effort to hide her pain and confusion.

"You ain't gotta be the toughest bitch in the room, KoKo. Even iron bends under extreme heat or pressure."

"Whatever doesn't bend or break…folds. And trust me, I ain't doing none of the three." She threw her hoodie on and moved out, closing the door behind her.

KoKo hit the stairwell and trotted down the steps. She had a newfound purpose. She had a hunt she needed to attend, and she was about to put herself in a position to get everything she ever deserved.

As KoKo got to the last flight of steps she heard what sounded like D'Low and his crew. She busted out the back door and there they stood.

"What's good?" KoKo asked approaching D'Low.

"Same old shit, that nigga Blue got spoken to."

"Damn," KoKo said as she looked over at the area covered with police and black and yellow tape.

"A lot of shit about to change, Kok." He looked over at her cold glare.

"Just make sure you don't," KoKo said, then put her hand out.

D'Low grabbed her hand and she pulled him into an embrace.

"You never have to question my loyalty. You have my word," he whispered in her ear.

"Your life is the only thing you have to protect. Don't let your word put it in jeopardy." She pulled back her hood and looked him square in the eyes.

"Indeed," he responded, then nodded his understanding.

"Catch y'all niggas next time." She moved back and threw her hoodie over her head.

"Not if we catch you first."

"Nigga, I'm too slippery. You'll catch your dick in a bad bitch before you catch me," KoKo spat as she exited the area.

"Crazy as a muthafucka." D'Low chuckled as he watched her move swiftly toward the end of the block. Shit was about to be knee-deep and he was going to be the first one ass high in it.

****

"Damn, I feel like a new person," Malika said as she rubbed the soft, whipped, mango cream into her hands.

"Yes, I needed this shit right here," Pashion agreed as she put her legs up on the long furry couch. She placed the ice mask over her eyes and laid her head back against the pillows and inhaled deeply.

"So, what is our next move?" Malika asked as she too placed a mask on her eyes and laid back in what felt like clouds in heaven.

Pashion laid enjoying the soft jazz and inhaling the lavender steam as she thought of her next words. "First, we need to continue our moves with the Don and Miguel. Then we need to continue to sow the seeds in our beloved granddaughter, so we can put an end to all these secrets we have been holding."

"It has been too many years, I'm tired."

"It's almost over. Just a few more steps and we are going to bust the muthafuckin' door open." Pashion sat up and removed her mask. She stood up and headed over to the wet bar, then poured two glasses of the sweet red wine.

220

Malika sat up and removed her mask as she fought back the heaviness in her heart.

Pashion walked over, handed her a glass, and continued her point, "We have to have patience. This may take a little longer but trust when it's over we will be the only ones standing with our grandchildren in their rightful places." She sat back on the couch and crossed her legs as she sipped.

"I know Malik would have never wanted us to have to fight for what belongs to him. But trust me, I am going to do whatever it takes and cross whoever we have to in order to get what is due to us." She brought the glass to her lips.

"Once KoKo realizes what is going on. She will take the justice her father deserves."

"I hope so. Because Star is not built for this and my grandson is not ready yet."

"I saw him the other day. He is getting stronger. He will be strong enough when the time comes."

"Malik would love that he is so strong and carries all of his features."

"Malik would have made that boy a beast." Pashion chuckled as she reached for her vanity bag.

"I guess we are blessed that he isn't around to do that." Malika got up, walked over to the CD player, and shuffled the music until she hit *Sade*. "If we could just get Mo to go the fuck away, we could move a lot easier." She sat back in her comfy spot.

"Mannnn…fuck that bitch. She is a convenient distraction."

"What you mean by that?" Malika put the glass back to her lips.

"Tyquan should have never brought that bitch to our circle. She got into that so-called friendship with Malik and weaved her way right into his pocket." She looked over at Malika for her response.

"I don't know what type of hold she had on my son. I know that he loved his wife and he loved Kisha. But I do not know what he shared with Mo." Again, she took a swig of the red bubbly, embracing the euphoria that took over her body.

"Let me drop game. She is fuckin' every player in the locker room and has to keep up with these niggas and their lies all while watching her own back as she tries to manipulate each of them."

"I see that." Malika nodded in agreement.

"We are all the way out of the way. We have each one of them thinking we are not involved meanwhile pulling all the strings. Let that dumb bitch gamble with her pussy. We will just sit back and place our bets."

"I know that's right. Cheers." Malika held her glass in the air.

Pashion pulled a joint from her wallet and a liter, then got up and locked the door.

"What the fuck is that?" Malika asked looking past her at the locked door.

"Look, for the money, we are paying for these hos to rub us down, shiiieett...I'ma smoke this joint." She poured a little more lavender and lemongrass oil on the hot rocks, plopped back down, and lit the end.

Malika got up and grabbed the bottle, filled their glasses then raised hers high into the air. "To the end."

"To the end." Pashion put her glass out and they clinked. She passed Malika the joint and released the smoke from her lungs.

Malika sat back, inhaled deeply closing her eyes to enjoy the high.

Chapter 26

Setting The Tone

Baseem stepped out of the limo and waited for Aldeen and Wise to step out of the other side. When their boots hit the curb, they were ready for action. "We about to act a fucking fool," Wise said as he put his fist out toward Baseem.

Baseem connected his fist to Wise's. "I might need a medic after this shit is over. One to carry my ego and one to carry my dick." He chuckled as the words left his lips.

"I heard that shit." Wise burst into laughter.

"Let's go, nigga." Aldeen waved them toward the doors.

The three of them walked up the concrete steps past the line of people waiting to get in and up to the big red doors. As they approached the last step, the door popped open allowing them to enter what was called, *Paradise For The Night*. This was the third annual event and from what they could already see it was going to be the best.

Wise led the way looking over the area at the array of half-naked women and niggas spending that bag. He quickly identified who was in the VIP sections as he moved toward the back of the building. Baseem nodded at a few dudes as they passed and Aldeen did none of the above. He kept one eyebrow lifted and a scowl on his face as he pinpointed the suckas in the room. They continued through the sea of glistening bodies and drunken dances until they reached a glass-enclosed area. Wise snatched the door open and the men moved inside.

"Surprissseeee...." the room rang out in cheer.

Wise froze in place as he looked around the room to see who was in attendance.

"Yeah, nigga. We snuck one in on your ass," Aldeen taunted shaking Wise by the shoulders.

"Fuck y'all, nigga," Wise said putting his hand on his chest.

"We love your punk ass, though. Happy Birthday, nigga. We made it," Aldeen said, then waved over one of the bottle girls.

One of the scantily dressed women came over to them with a golden tray filled with tall, black crystal wine flutes. Baseem took a glass for him, then passed one to Wise. Aldeen took one into his hand, then patted little mama on the ass. She giggled, as she scurried with her booty bouncing leaving each man with a slight watering mouth.

"Congratulations, compadre, cheers to another year of life, wealth, and one foot ahead of a dead dog's grave." Kayson stepped from behind a few guests with his glass raised high.

"Thanks, Boss, and may your rule be successful with my gun strong by your side." Wise raised his glass in Kayson's direction.

"Salute." Kayson brought his glass to his lips.

The crowd repeated after him, then sealed the toast with a sip of the finest bubbly. Wise, Aldeen, and Baseem began moving through the crowd toward where Kayson was seated. When they reached the velvet-roped area Wise's eyes lit up when he saw the arrangement of gifts and bottles spread across the glass table.

"A feast set up for a king," Kayson announced, then summoned a few of his teammates over to the area.

Several women entered the section taking Wise by the hand as they sashayed in their two-piece, red, lace thong sets. "For you." Kayson rose to his feet allowing Wise to be seated.

Aldeen and Baseem were seated right next to him, then the entertainment began. Two of the ladies helped him open his gifts while the others danced and clapped those luscious ass cheeks all around him. They eased his Presidential Rolex onto his wrist and adorned him in the matching diamond necklace and bracelet. He smiled wide as he turned the bracelet back and forth catching the strobe lighting on his expensive gems.

Kayson looked at his partner enjoying his gifts and his chest filled with slight pride as he thought about Wise's loyalty. Security pulled the curtains and dimmed the lights even more. The ladies dropped to their knees and began the first round of fun.

"Y'all niggas enjoy," Kayson said over the music, then turned to the door.

"We sure will," Wise said taking a shot as he watched his dick disappear down this Spanish mami's throat.

Kayson turned to the door, dropping the slight curl to the corner of his mouth, ready to make his rounds. He stepped into the loud music and flashing lights and inhaled deep as he searched the crowd for his gems. The first to catch that intense glare was Dee Dee. She wasted no time sashaying in his direction wearing an all-black, leather catsuit. Kayson's eyes settled on her legs at that sexy gap and fat V-shape that rested right between it.

Dee Dee smiled wide as she walked over to Kayson staring hard into his hazel eyes. Kayson motioned with his finger directing her to him and she willingly accepted the challenge, walking right up to him putting her 38Ds against his chest.

"Good evening, Boss," she mouthed looking up into his intense gaze.

"All this sexy needs to sit on a man's tongue," he mouthed back.

"Anytime you want it," she responded as she felt her pussy get wetter by the second.

"Be a good girl and make sure these niggas spend money and these hos stay in line and the Boss might have a special treat for you."

"Say no more," she replied easing her hand down his chest and over the Enforcer. "I hope it's real special." She ran her tongue over her lips, then turned to carry out the Boss's orders.

Kayson rubbed her ass as she sauntered away back to her duties. The next face he saw was Tiny's. She sat off to the side watching the room and learning the game. Kayson hadn't really seen her over the last few weeks. She was strictly assigned to the girls and she was in his stable and his bed but had not yet been broken.

He figured he needed to let her get her mind strong on the business before he spun her head around with all that good dick. He spoke to a few dudes in attendance as he made his way to where she sat. He sat down next to her and gripped her thigh, then leaned over and whispered in her ear. Tiny giggled and wiggled in her seat as he said things that caused her to cross her legs and squeeze her thighs.

"Are you behaving yourself?" He pulled back looking right in her eyes.

"I've been a very good girl. Doing exactly what the Boss told me."

"Good and make sure you keep the Boss's pussy tight," he gently warned.

"I got you, Boss," she confirmed.

Kayson leaned in and shared a few slick words putting her kitty on marinate mode, then got up leaving her wet and wanting him even more. She stared hard as her body filled with heatwave after wave, she was starting to understand who he was and what the whole organization stood for and she wanted every part of it.

As soon as he looked up his eyes met Pinky's. She was positioned at the bar and turned around on the bar stool as if she had not seen him staring in her direction.

Kayson eased through the crowd and stepped behind Pinky who wore an all-white, see-through dress with the small piece of material from her thong giving him a peep show through the material. The Enforcer jumped against his zipper as he focused on all that ass perched up high on that stool.

"You turned your back on me?" Kayson spoke closely to her ear sending chills from her neck to the tips of her toes.

"Never. I know the boss loves the view of these back shots," she purred as the heat in his body transferred from him to her.

Kayson placed his hands on her waist and bit lightly into the back of her neck. Pinky closed her eyes as she felt the beat of his heart competing with the blare of the music.

"You talkin' slick to the Boss," he mumbled in her ear pressing his soft lips against her lobe.

"I don't want no trouble, sir."

"I want some, though."

"Is that right?" she repeated his favorite phrase.

"Yes, it's very right," he teased as he nuzzled in her neck and talked his shit.

Pinky just closed her eyes and enjoyed all that slick shit falling off his tongue.

Dee Dee rotated her attention from Kayson and Pinky and the traffic at the door. She wanted to get in her feelings but when she looked past security, she noticed Wise's wife in a full argument with the head of security and pointing at the clipboard at the cash register. She hopped up and headed toward the commotion. As she neared the door, she looked over at Kayson who just gave her the nod as he continued to tease and play with Pinky. Dee Dee nodded back and approached to calm and defuse the situation.

"What's going on?" She forced a smile looking back and forth between Lashay and the officers.

"I'm tryin' to tell the help that I should be on that list and if not my face and name card should have me inside and not over here fuckin' explaining." She shifted her weight from one leg to the other.

"No worries just step back and let me take care of it," Dee Dee stated calmly, then turned to the hostess and whispered a few words. She escorted Lashay and her friends out the doors.

"Really, Dee? You walking me out?" her voice raised as the disrespect settled in the pit of her stomach.

"Look it's nothing just let me holla at you real quick," Dee Dee said moving a little further away from the line.

"I know you ain't just leaving," one of her friends said trying to escalate the situation.

"Watch your fucking mouth," Dee Dee said holding a firm glare. She smiled again as she turned to Lashay. "Are these your keys?" She took the key fob from her hand and passed it to her

227

loudmouth friend. "Y'all wait in the car she will be right with you." She tossed them, then turned her attention back to Lashay.

"Y'all go ahead!" she yelled to her friends causing them to stomp off and mumble slick shit as they headed to her Benz.

"Look, Ma, you know what this is. It's not wife night," Dee Dee stated smoothly holding her stare.

"*Wife night?* It's his fucking birthday. How am I excluded from that?" she spat as her eyes lowered into a squint.

"You know what it is. Tonight, ain't your night." Dee Dee reached into her bra, pulled out a roll of hundreds, and passed them to Lashay. "Look take your little friends over to the other side of town and enjoy. I'ma try to get him home early enough so he can give you the dick you deserve," she spat, then pulled her forward.

"*Dick I deserve?* Really, Dee Dee?"

"Don't cause a scene, bring it in." She pulled her close to her and whispered in her ear. "You enjoy all this that you have, right? Then don't get that nigga mad. Be a good girl, enjoy the night. Hug me back," she said wrapping her arms tightly around Lashay.

"All this shit is fucked up," Lashay responded as she battled with the water that insisted on leaving her eyes.

"It is what it is." Dee Dee pulled back then turned to head back inside. "Have fun!" she yelled as she switched that fat ass past the crowd and through the doors.

Security let her right by the check spot, and she gave them a few words before heading back to the party. "No wives under any circumstances," she asserted.

Security gave her a nod of understanding before heading back to the line. Dee Dee gave the hostess the same instructions, then moved back into the party. Her eyes darted around the room then landed on the spot she had last seen Kayson and Pinky. The empty space told the tale of what the Boss ended up having a taste for. She quickly checked her emotions, took a deep breath, then worked the room.

She knew one thing for sure if she couldn't have Kayson tonight, she was definitely going to make sure his business was straight, and his guests were well entertained, assuring a very special reward to come. Dee Dee filled her chest with pride as she made sure each VIP section had the proper entertainment and was spending the right money.

"You a muthafuckin' beast yo'!" Aldeen yelled past the sexy woman that had taken a permanent spot on his lap.

"Just doing my small part!" she yelled back as she tossed a few cups and bottles in the trash and ordered them a few more and an assortment of wings and fries.

"Salute," Bassem said from a far corner.

"Salute," she returned the love raising a bottle in the air. She then put it to her lips and tilted her head taking the last of the Hennessey down her throat.

"Enjoy the rest of the night, let me know if you need anything. As she reached the doors in walked the next round of entertainment.

Smiles crept across the men's faces. She smiled as well knowing she had accomplished the perfect night for the team. She said a few words to the girls, then security, and moved out just as smoothly as she entered.

****

"Yup take all that shit off," Kayson said from his seated position in a private suite in the back just for the Boss.

"All of it, Boss?" she asked standing only a few feet away from him as she slid the zipper to her jumpsuit down to the top of her throbbing pussy.

"All of it," he responded bringing his glass of brown to his lips.

His eyes feasted on her thick legs and thighs traveling up over that small waist ending on her perky C-cups. His mouth watered as he thought about how sweet she tasted.

Pinky eased the all-white, whole piece off her shoulders and down to her waist, then shimmed it past her ass.

"Mmmm…" he replied, looking at her pretty, pink, suckable nipples and fat pussy in that G-string. "Come here," he spoke calmly locking gazes with hers.

Pinky stepped out of her clothes, then strutted all that sexy in his direction, caressing her tittles as she rolled her tongue across her top lip. She stepped between his legs putting her pussy lips leveled with his. Kayson eased his finger along the thin strap of her G-string, then slowly rubbed up and down the thin piece of white sheer material standing between her clit and his tongue.

"You brought the Boss something sweet."

"Whatever you want," she panted as his soft lips connected with her skin.

"Whatever I want," he said a little above a whisper as he nibbled and sucked right above her kitty and prepared to put something pink and pretty in his mouth. He pulled at the strings until they slid down her legs meeting her heels at the floor, then sucked gently on her clit.

"Ssss…no, baby. Tonight, I just want to please the Boss," she moaned, placing her hands on the side of his face bringing his eyes to hers.

She kissed his glistening lips tasting her sweet nectar, then placed her hands on his knees, squatting down in front of him, giving him a view of her pretty pussy.

"Is that right?" He took another sip as the Enforcer stiffened and slid down his thigh.

She eased up his thigh and onto the Enforcer. Pinky tugged at his jeans until they were below his knees. When the Enforcer stood tall, she gripped him with both hands and lowered her other pink lips all the way down on his greatness. She played with him in her mouth sucking and stroking until wetness covered every inch of him. Pinky released him from her jaw grip and watched as his dick saluted to her Queendom.

"I want to play with him," she whined as she stood, then once again turned her back to him.

Kayson grabbed the beast at the base, holding it right in place for her coochie assault. Pinky positioned her pussy right on the head of his dick and began to bounce that ass slowly playing with just the tip.

"Get that shit." Kayson placed one hand on the small of her back bringing her down a little further as she rotated to his pleasure.

"Like this, Boss?" She rode his inches until he was comfortable inside her.

"Yup, pay a nigga good money." He laid his head back and watched the show as her ass cheeks smacked his thighs, she squeezed her muscles with every up and down motion.

"Make me cum, Kay. Make me cum," she moaned, leaning slightly forward and speeding up the action.

Kayson took the last few sips of his drink, then set the glass on the end table beside them. He gripped her hips and dug deep, fucking to the pleasure that left her lips. Pinky zoned out while Kayson zoned in reaching around her waist. He gripped one of her nipples between his fingers and with the other hand, he pressed on her clit, then began applying small circles. Pinky continued to bounce until she felt waves of heat take over her body. She leaned back into Kayson's chest and rode the wave as he took over the ride.

"You feel good as shit." Kayson bit hard into the back of her neck as he applied more pressure and speed to his clit play.

"You feel good inside me, baby," she panted as the Enforcer dug deep and purposeful.

"Thank you, baby, for making sure a nigga is always good."

"Kay, wait," she cried as he showed no mercy pushing every inch inside her with each upward thrust.

"Nah, keep playing with it," he taunted as her juices flowed.

"Okay, baby, I'ma play with it." She turned and looked in his eyes, then leaned all the way forward placing her hands on his legs just above his boots.

"Ride that shit." He smacked her ass leaving his prints behind.

Pinky bounced her butt and rotated her hips to the rhythm playing right outside the door. She blocked out all thoughts except to please him. Kayson helped control her movements with one hand and while the other continued giving her clit a fit. She gripped his legs tighter as she felt her kitty flood his lap.

"Kayyyy…" she called out while rocking and swaying her hips to the rhythm of his stroke.

"Let that shit go, Ma. Gimmie what's mine," he teased leaning forward, sinking his teeth into her neck and back.

"Yes…yess…yesssss…" she mumbled repeatedly as he once again made her pussy purr.

Kayson sped up his push and pull as he enjoyed her soft skin against his. He watched her move freely as he felt his stomach tingle wanting to release inside her womb but tonight that was something he could not do. He held her in place and pumped wildly until he could not hold on any longer. When his seed was threatening to be free, he pushed her slightly forward.

She jumped off him, turned and dropped to her knees, then took the Enforcer into her mouth and tightened her jaws back and forth on his thickness until she drunk all his sweet essences. Kayson grabbed a handful of her long, red hair as she eased her lips and tongue over his swollen tip causing him to release light moans from his lips.

"You a whole fucking problem," he grunted while trying to control his breathing.

"Only for the Boss." She looked up at him through a glossy gaze and smiled at the pleasure she had just given him then rose up and just stared at the Enforcer.

"That's what the fuck I'm talking about." He smacked her ass as she turned to retrieve her clothes. He then stood up and grabbed a towel from the bar and headed to the private bathroom.

Pinky reached in her small, leather purse and bodysuit and tossed it over her arm. She looked around to make sure she had all her things. When Kayson came out of the bathroom, she headed in his direction to get herself together.

"What time should I be ready for the drop-off tomorrow?" she asked as she stood in the doorway.

"Two o'clock," he stated firmly as he headed to fix himself one last drink.

"I'll be ready." Pinky walked into the bathroom and closed the door behind her, then turned on the water in the sink and began to get her kitty fresh and clean.

She washed and rinsed, then dried herself off and slipped back into her bodysuit. She retrieved a comb and lip gloss from her purse and a small bottle of Listerine and put the finishing touches on her hair and face and gargled away her sins.

"Damn, you a bad bitch." She twirled back and forth then put everything back in her purse along with her G-string that she wrapped in a paper towel. Pinky scented her skin and hair, then headed back to where Kayson was waiting.

"You good, Boss?" she asked as she walked over to the bar.

"Always," he spoke between gulps of the smooth Bourbon.

"If you don't mind, I would like to be excused for the rest of the night."

"Excused," he sat his glass down and walked around the bar, and stood directly in front of her.

"Yes, Boss a bitch needs a bath and a nap." She looked up at his sexy ass face.

Kayson pulled her into his arms and held her closely then kissed her softly on her lips. "Yes, go get some rest. Behave yourself and keep daddy's pussy tight."

"Always," she confirmed as she felt his lips touch her's one again.

"Leave your car, I'll have it brought to you. Tell security I said to get you home and safe inside."

"Yes sir," she confirmed as she felt his hands wandering and his dick harden.

"Damn you feel good." He gripped her hair as he slipped his tongue into her mouth.

Pinky struggled to catch her breath as Kayson backed her up to the bar pressing his body against hers. She pulled back and looked down afraid to feel the energy that was taking over her soul.

"Thank you, Boss. I'ma go get some rest."

"Yeah, you do that and open the door when I get there."

"*Get there!* Are you asking me or telling me?" She reluctantly looked up.

"Telling you. I need to pin these knees to the mattress and make you talk to me nice." He palmed her ass in both hands positioning her pussy right on his dick.

"Yes, sir! I'll have everything you like fresh and clean and ready."

"Be naked," he instructed, then stepped back releasing her from his grip.

"You so nasty." She giggled.

"Make sure your people are good and happy and go say happy birthday to Wise on your way out."

"I got you, Boss." She slipped past him afraid that he wouldn't wait until he got to her house and she wanted to feel all the Boss had to offer.

Again, Kayson smacked her ass and watched it jiggle as she moved toward the door. Pinky unlocked the door and as she stepped back into the light, she inhaled the smoke, music, and dirty dancing in full turn-up mode. She headed straight to VIP.

"You enjoying yourself, Wise?" she asked as she leaned in and hugged his neck.

"Hell yeah. Y'all did this shit."

"That's what's up. Well, you earned this night. Happy birthday, enjoy yourself."

"Damn you leaving already. I was just about to get some fresh fish in the line." He smacked the dancer's ass while enjoying the shake and bounce.

"Yeah, a bitch ain't just beautiful. All this ass in this dress gotta rest," she joked, then turned back to the door.

"Talk yo shit, Ma. See you on the other side." He put his attention on the hottie riding his lap.

Pinky eased through the crowd and straight to the bar. She spoke to the team, then moved around the room until she hit security. Pinky handed out Kayson's orders and waited for her escort. When the car pulled up in front of the club the doors swung open and she was led to her chariot.

Kayson finished his drink, locked up his office, and headed back to the party. He stopped at the bar and passed out the next stages of the night. By the time he reached the area where his brothers were partying there were seven bottle girls headed in his direction behind them were two girls carrying a cake. They entered the room, and the doors were locked behind them. The next few hours were going to be filled with pure what happens in Vegas stays in Vegas type deviance.

"Fellas let's enjoy the night," Kayson announced as he took the seat between Baseem and Aldeen.

Wise was led to a chair all by itself ready for the pleasure and entertainment of a king.

Chapter 27

Call Of The Wild

Tyquan placed a bottle of Bourbon in a bucket of ice, then put two glasses on the table next to it. He walked over to his music player and turned it on low. He moved around his LA apartment waiting for his archenemy to arrive. When he heard the buzzer, he headed to the door and prepared himself for the fight he knew was on the other side.

"Who?" he called out as he adjusted the peephole. He reached for the chain, loosened it, and clicked the locks. When he cracked the oakwood from its frame his eyes roamed from the tip of her toes to the crown of her head.

"If you're going to have your eyes all over me at least invite me in." She pushed the door and walked through the space.

"Sounds like you missed me?" he spat as his eyes settled on her phat ass in those tight jeans.

"This is cute," she stated looking around the plush layout.

"You know I keep my shit on point." He closed the door and locked it.

"It's been a long time." She sauntered into the kitchen and took a spot next to the counter beside the tall brown bottle and short crystal glasses.

"Yes, it has." He walked to the counter and poured them a drink, then headed to his black, suede, high-backed chair.

Monique gripped the glass in her hand as she followed him into the living room and took a seat on the couch.

"I heard you are about to be somebody's grandma," he joked bringing his drink to his lips.

"Shittin' me! You see all this? Ain't nothing grandma about all of this." She chuckled.

"How did you let that happen?" he asked dropping the smile from his face.

"*Let?* I don't keep that little nigga's dick in my pocket. He is grown, Tyke," she returned, then took some of the smooth brown liquor into her mouth.

Tyquan stared at her as he prepared his next sentence. "You know that is very risky?"

Monique took a deep breath, then set her glass on the coffee table. "Let me worry about the risks."

"Cool, but if I began to worry you won't have to," he gently warned.

"So, what is it that you need to see me about?" she asked placing her drink on the coffee table.

"It's that time, Mo. That boat ride was not a game." He sat back and crossed his legs.

"Yes, the days we prayed would never come." She flashed back to the many promises she had made and now it was time to make good on them.

"Our son is strong. But he needs to get in line," Tyquan reminded her.

"There is no need to worry about Kayson. He will do what needs to be done."

"Will he?" he asked bringing his drink to his lips.

"What is that supposed to mean?" Monique's voice slightly elevated.

"Mo, you know like I do. When it's time for shit to change the bosses have a way of making sure that it happens."

"Tyke, you don't need to tell me the rules of the game. I have lived and sacrificed my life by these fucking rules for over twenty years." She sat forward locking gaze with his.

"I know and you still think this shit is a game. But you got to know that all your mercy will be paid for with lives you may not want to lose."

"Trust me, nobody wants that type of trouble with me."

"Ha." Tyquan laughed.

Monique's blood began to boil. She was ready to reach into her waist and remove the skin from his scalp. "I only came here to remind you to stay the fuck away from my son." She stood up slamming her drink on the table as she prepared to leave his evil palace.

"Your son?" he repeated with a sly grimace on his face.

"Don't reach out to me anymore. The next invite will end with my son's gun in your face." She stormed off toward the door.

"Pop that titty out of his mouth. Ain't no breast milk on the battlefield!" He yelled as the door crashed against the frame.

Tyquan chuckled from his reclined position taking another sip. "Silly bitch," he spat as he thought about what had to be done.

****

Monique stepped out of the car and closed the door behind her. "I won't be long," she announced, then turned toward the entrance of the building.

She walked up the steps, then right inside. The nurse at the desk looked up from her computer and nodded at Monique as she passed her. Monique pressed on down the hall and through the double doors at the end which led to an outside walkway. Her heels clicked along the cobblestone as her eyes focused on the little cottage out by the lake. Monique walked along, taking deep breaths of the crisp air while feasting her eyes on the assortment of yellow flowers and orange leaves as they slipped easily off the branches. When Monique arrived at the door to the cabin, she took another deep breath, then gripped the knobbed and knocked as she entered.

"Kisha? You up, Ma?" she asked as she pushed the door a little more,

"Yes, I'm over here," Kisha responded from her seated position in front of the window.

Monique pushed open the door, walked inside, then closed it behind her. "It's been a long time," she spoke softly as she held back many emotions flowing through her body.

"Too long." Kisha stared into Monique's eyes.

"You look good." Monique attempted to lighten the mood.

"I guess I have been well preserved," Kisha spat with slight tension in her tone.

"All of the family has always been very grateful for your sacrifices and the strength you display in holding us down."

"I have always been loyal to this family, and I always will be. There is no thanks needed," Kisha replied holding her gaze with Monique's.

Monique just remained silent as she chose her next words wisely. "I don't want to fight with you, Kisha. I am just here doing my part."

"Your part." She chuckled. "Yes, I guess that is what you call it. And what is your part here for today?"

"It's time," Monique spoke few words not wanting to escalate the situation.

Kisha turned and looked out the window, crossing her hands over her stomach. She stared out at the ripples in the water as she processed what Monique was there for.

After a few more seconds she offered her demands, "I want assurance that my daughter is going to be good." She turned back in Monique's direction.

"Of course, this is all for them. You know I am doing all of this for his children."

"Not without getting you something off the top, though, huh?"

"Let me explain something to you." Monique walked over to where she sat and stood only inches away from her. "I have risked more than you know while they got you all tucked the fuck away.

240

Everything I have sacrificed has been for the promise I made to Malik. I have not betrayed our friendship from day one." She held back the tears as the words slid from her lips.

"Just give me the papers. I took enough disrespect while he was here. I am definitely not going to have wordplay with another bitch he loved," she spoke with clenched teeth.

Monique started to say some hot shit but pulled it back. There would be enough time to make her pay for her disrespect. As for now, it was too much money on the table to tongue wrestle with Malik's side bitch.

"After today you won't see me again. Your money will come to you as usual and the large amount will be deposited into Star's account once everything goes through." Monique pulled a folded contract from her purse and placed it on the end table next to where Kisha sat.

Kisha looked down at the paper with disgust, then took it into her hand. She read over the pages and extended her arm. Monique handed her a pen and stood waiting for her to sign and initial each page.

"I want to see my daughter," Kisha said, passing Monique the pen and papers.

"I don't have control over that, Kisha. I know that she is good, but we have no contact, and you know exactly why," Monique reminded her.

"Make it possible," Kisha asserted looking back out of the window. "You can let yourself out," she spoke with a slight tremble in her voice.

Monique did not respond. She had what she came for. Now it was time to tuck Kisha away a little further. She folded the contract and pushed it back into her purse with the pen, then headed toward the door. She grabbed the knob, pulling the door open in one swift motion. As she stepped past the threshold, she smiled knowing she was one step closer to the power.

"Before you go, let me ask you something. If your love and sacrifices are so strong for Malik. Why didn't he tell you who his son is?" she taunted.

241

The smile moved from her face and settled as a knot in the pit of her stomach. "I know what I need to know," she spat keeping her back to Kisha.

"Just as I thought. A pawn." She again chuckled. "You're right, I don't need to see you again." She kept her gaze on the glistening water, a smile now gracing her face.

Monique exited, then stepped quickly back to the main building. She walked through the doors and over to the receptionist desk.

"Everything okay, Mrs. Wells?"

"Yes, it was, thank you." Monique reached into her purse, pulled out a stack of hundreds, and passed them to her. "Please keep up the good work. Oh, and she seemed a little anxious. You may want to increase a thing or two."

"Yes, ma'am." The woman took the money, nodding her head as she received her orders.

Monique walked away from the desk, right out the front doors with one more task crossed off her list. She hopped into the back of the limo and just like that was gone with the bag tucked tightly in her grasp.

****

Pat slid down in her seat as she watched Monique climb into the back of the black four-door Mercedez and pull away from the entrance. She stayed low until the car was down the driveway and turning at the stop sign. She grabbed her purse and a few bags from the back seat, then hopped out of her car and headed inside.

"Good afternoon. Is my sister in her cottage?"

"Yes, she is." The woman peeled off half the stack and slid it to Pat, then looked back down at her computer.

"Thank you," Pat said as she tucked the money into her bra.

Pat damn near jogged down the trail heading to Kisha's door. When she opened it, she frantically looked around the room until she had her niece in her sights.

"Girl, I almost had a heart attack," she said grabbing at her chest.

"It's all good. And it's time to play the last cards in the deck," Kisha announced.

"It's on then," Pat said pledging her allegiance.

Monique was deep in the game but there were players she knew nothing about and that was the deadly hand Kisha was about to deal on a cold dish.

244

Chapter 28

Cali Love

KoKo stepped out of the airport into the beaming summer heat and took in that crisp Cali air. She pulled her sweatshirt over her head, then tied it around her waist. She walked to the curb and looked around for her boy. As she began to feel the heat on her back, she heard a horn honk and an S-Class Mercedes Benz pulled up to the curb.

"What's up, KoKo?" Wadoo asked rolling the window down.

"Hollywood ass nigga," KoKo said snatching the door handle.

"That hate is ugly on you," Wadoo joked pulling out into the far lane and onto the expressway.

"I need some shit to smoke and some shit to wear."

"I see you, big money." He looked over at her. "Open the glove box," he instructed.

KoKo opened the box which revealed a gun and a stack of cash. She retrieved both, then smiled big as she opened the small box of already rolled blunts.

"Welcome to Cali," Wadoo said with pride as KoKo put fire to the end.

"Indeed." She put her fist out and bumped his as she settled in her seat and puffed that good old Cali bud.

Wadoo ran KoKo to a few stores, then dropped her off at her downtown hotel. They had a long night ahead of them, restructure was happening whether they wanted it or not. The only thing they could do was strap the fuck up and have the best plan.

"See you around ten," Wadoo said handing her the room cards.

"A'ight." She jumped out and headed inside.

KoKo moved through the lobby with two fists full of bags. She hopped on the elevator, rest and strategy were all KoKo had on her mind. She slid her key card into the slot and entered her room. KoKo took a deep breath as she threw her bags on the bed. She walked over to the window, pulled the curtains open, and just stared over the city. She was taking every risk for what she wanted.

KoKo turned on the water in the Jacuzzi, then took the items from the bags and laid them out on the bed, and began to undress. She added a floral liquid to the water and slipped into the hot steamy bubbles. KoKo turned on the tub jets and let the hard blast hit her back as she lit one of her exotic gifts and pulled deep. She thought about her team and the sacrifices she would have to make.

KoKo soaked her body for over an hour, then showered off. As she headed to the bedroom to lotion her skin and comb her hair, she filled her stomach with the beast she needed to lay niggas down. She slipped into the white fluffy hotel robe and fell onto the bed. She crawled up to the pillows, flipped the comforter over her weary body, and pushed her head into the pillows. KoKo knew this was the last rest she was going to get before she sealed someone's fate with flashing lights and yellow tape.

****

Miguel shook hands with Don Anibello sealing their deal. They had put in the work to be on top and wasn't gonna let a bitch with apron strings tightly tied to her son's waist stand in the way.

"Are you sure nothing will trace back to me or my family?" Miguel asked as he brought his drink to his lips.

"Once you make a request never question if it will get fulfilled. My word is clade," The Don spoke straight with his new alliance.

"I am not questioning you. I just want to make sure I don't lose anyone else in this battle for the throne," he asserted.

"Loss is a part of who we are. If you are not willing to sacrifice even the queen to be on top, then retire. On this level no one is safe," he reminded him of the oath they all chose.

Miguel nodded in agreement. He knew things were about to be deadly and the only way to take anyone's power was with blood, either spilling it or pouring it. There was no other way to be on top.

****

It's Your Turn...

Wadoo eased through the hotel lobby, walked right over to the elevators, and pressed the button then waited patiently for the doors to open.

Ding!

The doors popped open and he walked inside. He pressed the penthouse level, then stood in the corner plotting the evil of the night.

Bing! Bong!

The elevator came to a stop and the doors opened to the plush hallway. He eyed the paintings and floral arrangements along the way as he pushed to her room. Wadoo knocked a few times then posted himself in front of the peep hole.

KoKo glanced through the hole, then popped the locks allowing Wadoo to enter.

"Damn, why is it so dark in here?" he asked placing his backpack on the table.

"Did you get everything I asked for?" KoKo got right to the point.

247

"You fucking know it," he responded taking a seat next to the table.

KoKo opened the backpack and eyed the content, then placed it under the table. She continued to get into her mode. She turned up *California Love* by *Dr. Dre* and *Tupac* and rocked to the beat.

"You done?" she asked Wadoo not even looking in his direction.

Wadoo tilted his head to the side and questioned, "You trying to go at these niggas alone?" His brow creased as her request settled in his spirit.

"I'll see you when I get back." She turned, grabbed the bag, and set it on the bed.

"KoKo, I can't let you go out there unprotected. Fuck that." He bucked up.

KoKo began unloading the contents in the bag onto the bed. She loaded the clip, then clapped it into the chamber. "Just be where I told you to be." She walked over and turned the music up a little louder.

She turned the gun back and forth in her hands switching it from one to the other. She picked up the Glock and pumped the little iron pellets into the chamber.

Wadoo watched this young killer get into her mode and a small amount of admiration swelled his chest. He took in some air, then headed to the door.

"Ashes to ashes," he said as he turned the knob and moved through the open space.

"Dust to dust," she responded, closed her eyes, and squeezed the rubber handles against her palms.

She kept her eyes closed and said a small prayer, then laid the guns on the bed and geared up. KoKo slipped on a pair of black jeans and put a pair of black sweats on top. She tightened a bulletproof vest around her chest, slipped on a T-shirt, and a long sleeve, black hoodie. KoKo slipped her feet into a pair of crisp, black hard, leather Timbs. She brushed her hair straight back into a ponytail, then tucked it all under a fitted cap.

KoKo grabbed the backpack, positioned her guns and ammunition inside, then tossed it on her back and headed to the door. Each step she took filled her heart with darkness. She erased all feelings of love and respect cause tonight there was no love, only greed, and payback. She rode down on the elevator avoiding eye contact with the few people already on as she eased to the far corner. When the doors slid open, she slipped through the lobby, out the hotel doors, and into the brisk LA night. It was hunting season and the only thing to quench her thirst was fresh blood and her hollow points were ready to claim her taste.

****

Baseem and Aldeen hopped out of The Don's truck extending their arms as his security began patting them down. Baseem scanned the area taking note of each man and their big-ass guns in attendance. Aldeen looked over at Baseem as he dropped his hands to his sides. He could tell he was ready to let these niggas know what was on his mind. The two of them followed close behind The Don's security anxious to see what this so-called emergency meeting was about. Once they entered the warehouse, they were searched one more time as if the first assault was not enough.

"They already checked my balls, so unless you got a bitch on the other side ready to suck em' move your fuckin' hands," Baseem spat with venom in his tone.

He looked coldly into Baseem's dark eyes and continued his pat-down disregarding the slick shit dripping from his lips.

"Go through those doors," the man ordered as he tightened his grip on the automatic weapon that rested a little from Baseem's chest.

Baseem spat on the floor as he passed him, then entered the door with even more hate in his heart.

"You gotta chill, yo'," Aldeen tried to soothe the beast that was growing within his comrade.

"Do your part, I'ma do mine," Baseem reminded Aldeen who he was.

Aldeen didn't respond he just kept walking not wanting to open the flood gates to disaster.

Don Anibello waited eagerly for the arrival of his East Coast partners, then prepared his young comrades for what may lay ahead. If he didn't know anything else, he knew how this life they lived could turn tragic at any moment. The last thing he wanted was to lose his best during the fallout. He watched as they loaded the back of several vans from the docks and a few fast boats.

Once he saw the last door close, he walked back into the warehouse and took a seat at the small wooden table. He picked up his cup of Espresso and put it to his lips. He organized his orders in his head as he realized what he was setting in motion. He placed the cup on the saucer, crossed his leg at the knee, and watched his men move the work as he waited for his special guests.

Baseem trailed a little behind Aldeen taking note of all the action that was going on at the back gates of the warehouse. When he saw The Don sitting at the table in the far-left corner, heat began to move through his veins.

"We just going to listen and report that's it," Aldeen reminded Baseem.

Baseem just stared at the back of Aldeen's head, he kept his lips pressed tightly together trying hard not to cuss Aldeen the fuck out. They continued toward The Don each with a different intent in their heart.

"Welcome my friends." The Don rose to his feet.

"Thanks for the invite, Don Anibello," Aldeen returned the greetings.

"Thanks for the invite," Baseem repeated Aldeen's jester.

"How was your trip? I hope all the accommodations is to your satisfaction," The Don replied perching back in his seat.

"Yes, everything was on point. We appreciate the hospitality."

"Great, have a seat, let's get to business."

Baseem and Aldeen sat in the two empty chairs and prepared themselves for the outcome of the meeting.

"Did you get the delivery and did everything meet your approval?" Aldeen asked looking over at The Don.

"Yes, we received the package…" He paused and took a sip from his cup, then set it back on the saucer. "Please thank your boss. We are overly impressed by his delivery time. However, there will be a few changes. We will be changing the money drop off time and place," he stated and folded his hands on the tabletop.

"*Changes?* Is there a reason why you are changing things in the middle of our understanding?" Aldeen's brow creased as the words left his mouth.

"There has been no problem. I just want to make sure we don't have one."

"Why the fuck would we have one?" Baseem sat forward frustrated with the ordeal.

"I see your partner is uncomfortable with my ways of practice," The Don spat looking directly into Baseem's eyes.

"No disrespect. He just doesn't move unless the boss says move. I'm sure a man in your position can understand that, right?" Aldeen tried to calm the situation.

Don Anibello took in some air, then sat back in his chair. Baseem didn't budge he sat firm in his seat awaiting the next words to leave Don Anibello's lips.

"Understood. Do me a favor. Take my offer back to your boss and let him conflict with me if there is going to be one," he offered.

"Indeed." Baseem rose to his feet.

"Thank you for your time." Aldeen stood up next to Baseem.

"You can leave out that way. The car is ready to take you back to the airport. Have a safe trip." The Don dismissed them, then picked his cup up from the table and brought it to his lips.

Two of The Don's men headed in their direction ready to escort their once welcomed guests to the door.

251

Baseem turned first and Aldeen followed. As the two men stepped quickly to the exit Baseem fought every killer instinct inside him to grab up one of them niggas and choke the shit out of them. When they got to the back entrance, they stepped even harder, the doors opened, and they jumped in the back seat and slammed them as they settled into their seats.

"I don't like none of this shit," Bassem mumbled as the truck began slowly rolling to the guarded exit. As they moved past the door, Baseem's antenna went up when he saw a little nigga in a hood being patted down in the same fashion they were. "None of this shit," he repeated.

****

KoKo stepped quick with the security leading the way, she glanced a little ahead and noticed out the corner of her eye, a red Tahoe rolling slowly past her. She kept her head down and moved through the tight space provided, then headed to the next group of security. As she stood watching the gates close tight, she was frisked and relieved of her weapons. She placed her hands in her hoodie pocket and followed closely behind two of Don Anibello's trusted men.

"Stay right here," one of the men ordered while the other one stood staring down at her with squinted eyes and tight lips.

KoKo stared back into his eyes not moved or shaken.

"Let's go," one of the guards bellowed as he approached breaking the standoff. He pointed at an iron door, then stepped to the side.

KoKo shot him a glare, then moved in the direction that he pointed at. She pulled open the door and headed to the figure off in the distance. The iron door slammed closed forcing her to realize she was totally at his mercy. She mapped out an exit as she did a headcount of each person moving in the space just in case she had to act a fool.

"Glad you could make it on such short notice." The Don rose to his feet to greet KoKo.

252

"You called, I came," she spoke direct as she approached his table.

"For that I am grateful. Please take a seat," he offered, waving his hand at the empty chair beside him.

"Thank you," KoKo said as she sat down.

"How are your accommodations. Is my team treating you alright?" he asked crossing his legs.

"Everything is good. However, ol' boy upfront needs a little more customer service training. Ain't shit a little ass whipping won't cure, though," she spat, looking over at Don Anibello.

Don Anibello chuckled as he processed what had just left KoKo's lips. "It is confirmed, I made the right choice. What is your fee?"

"What is your offer?" she returned.

"My offer is that we can build a friendship from this and have a long-running relationship," he stated looking for her response.

KoKo sat for a minute, then put her cards on the table. "A million."

Don Anibello nodded his head, then waved his hand at one of the men packing a load into a van. The man jogged over to where they sat and placed his ear near The Don's mouth. When he was done speaking, the man jogged off back to the van, grabbed a backpack, and hurried it back to the table.

"This is five hundred thousand. The rest will be forwarded to the account of your choice once you are done."

The man unzipped the bag and placed it on the table so KoKo could view its contents. She peeked inside, then thumbed through the cash. After assuring it was all there, she zipped the bag closed and pushed it back in The Don's direction.

The Don opened the bag and pushed it in front of KoKo. She looked inside, then slide it back to him.

"Is there something wrong?"

"No. Hold onto that. Slide me the list," she said looking him square in his dark eyes.

"So, you want to work for free?" he asked with slight confusion as he slid her the instructions.

"Nothing is free." She opened the small piece of paper, read it from top to bottom, then tucked it in her hoodie pocket. She rose to her feet and extended her hand.

"How will I pay you?" He put his hand in hers and gripped it tightly.

"I want an open pass for movement. And the next jobs from here on out will be double. Other than that, this never happened, and your enemies are now my enemies." She squeezed his hand confirming her words, then pulled her hand from his and turned back for the exit.

"Done," he agreed as he watched her eagerly head out to fulfill her end of their newfound relationship. "You are a very different type of person!" Don Anibello yelled as she approached the iron door.

"Indeed," KoKo spat as she exited the way she came.

She retrieved her weapons, then headed to the car waiting for her right outside the door. She rode back to the hotel running the names and places on her list through her mind. When the car came to a stop in the hotel valet, she grabbed the handle and jumped out. As the door closed, she heard the window going down, she turned with her hand tightly wrapped around the butt of her gun, then slipped her finger on the trigger.

"We will see you around midnight," the driver instructed.

"No need, I move all by my loneliness," she spoke direct and turned to head inside.

The driver rolled up the window, eased down the driveway, and into traffic. Her orders meant nothing to him. He was still going to be in place.

"No bitch should have that much power."

****

Lady turned over and looked at the empty spot on their bed and her stomach became sick.

"Where are you?" she said aloud. *In another woman's bed,* her thoughts screamed back at her.

She jumped up and ran to the bathroom just in time as everything she had eaten did a total reverse. She heaved and coughed as she released what she had left. She flushed the toilet then moved her weary frame over to the sink and cut on the water. As the steam rose from the porcelain bowl, she stared at the heat forming in her eyes.

Lady washed her hands, brushed her teeth, and gargled. As she turned the knobs off, she questioned her motives. What was she doing living in the shadow of a man whose days were probably numbered? Guilt filled her spirit as she realized she had contributed to the monster she felt Kayson had become. Regret took over her mind as she thought back to the times she should have run as fast as she could, but instead stood still. Lady placed her hand on her belly trying to snap out of the funk she was in. A flutter pushed back at her and a huge smile took over her face. Lady slowly walked back to bed and laid back in the cool sheets pulling the thick goose down comforter to her chin.

She put her hand back on her stomach and made a vow to her unborn child, "All of this is for you. You will have everything I didn't." She rubbed back and forth trying to stimulate a little more movement. The baby confirmed its bond by giving her a few more comforting movements putting her heart slightly at ease. "Even when daddy no longer loves me. I know he will love you," she uttered as tears left her eyes creating a small stain on her pillow. She cried herself into a slumber.

256

Chapter 29

Suspicion

Kayson pulled into the valet portion of the county club and turned over his keys. He stepped through the doors, eyed the west patio entrance, then headed in that direction as he approached the exit doors, a waitress approached him for his order.

"Would you like something before you take to the green?" the vibrant young woman asked as she extended the silver platter before him.

"Thank you, beautiful." He gave her a smile, took a short glass of brown, and continued through the doors. As he approached the awaiting golf cart, he pulled a cigar from his pants pocket and lit the end as he stood patiently waiting for his ride.

"Welcome, Mr. Wells. Your party awaits your arrival," the man spoke firm in his thick Asian accent.

Kayson nodded his head and took a seat. As the man pulled away from the curb, he organized his thoughts and deals he was ready to put on the table. They rode along the pretty blanket of grass, passing tall, beautiful, oak and willow trees as they cruised along. When they eased up on the small gathering, came to a stop and stepped off the cart with a drink and cigar in hand. Kayson took that last swig down his throat, then placed the glass in the cupholder. After the smooth Bourbon eased down his throat, he pulled hard on the Cuban, released the thick smoke from his mouth, and dutted it out on the side of the cart.

"Gentlemen allow me to introduce my business partner, Mr. Wells," Mr. Lu announced looking at his other business partners.

The men in attendance bowed in his direction. Kayson bowed back in respect, then gathered his thoughts before he spoke.

"I appreciate you coming together to meet with me. I trust Mr. Lu spoke of the asset my organization can be to yours…" He paused gaging their moods. "I just want to make this money and put us all where we want to be…" He paused again giving them an opportunity to speak.

"We look forward to the same things then, Mr. Wells," one of the men spoke.

"Then you have my word that I will eliminate any obstacles in the way of our arrangement," he assured them.

"Very good, Mr. Wells. Very good." Mr. Lu extended his hand to Kayson.

Kayson extended his hand and shook it with the full intent of taking the power they were giving and the power they weren't. They began hitting hole after hole as they put together the next five moves involving their investments, their earnings. When they got to the last few holes Mr. Lu stopped to speak to Kayson in private.

"So, do you believe you will be able to pull off this money movement?" Mr. Lu asked as he got in position to hit the ball.

"It's already done. Just waiting on the word," Kayson assured him as he pulled a club from the leather bag.

"Just make sure there is no trail," he warned as he struck the ball.

Kayson placed his ball on the tee, then positioned his club for the hit. "Just remember." He stopped to line up his club. "Whoever doesn't get down. I will lay down." He swung hard at the ball sending it out into the field.

Mr. Lu formed a slight crease to the side of his lips as he watched the ball head off into the distance. A tingle formed in his belly as he thought about how much money this young bull was about to make him, all while wiping out the very seed of his enemies.

"Let's get richer," Mr. Lu said patting Kayson on the back.

"Indeed." Kayson nodded and headed to the next spot on the green.

****

Pat grabbed the door handle, then passed through the huge glass doors. She flashed a pretty smile at the security desk as she walked to the checkpoint. Pat stretched her arms allowing the woman to wave the metal wand over her body. Once cleared, she walked to the elevators, pressed the up button, and waited for her turn.

When the door opened, she walked inside, pressed the top floor then moved past the few men and women inside and rested against the wall. She watched as the numbers went up until she was at her stop. Pat exited the elevator, marching quickly to the end of the hall. She pulled open the door announcing herself as she walked up to the receptionist.

"Pat for Mr. Lu." She rested her hands on the marble counter.

The young Asian woman looked her up and down then coldly answered, "Please be seated." She picked up the phone announcing Pat's presence. "You can go in," she instructed with a hard stare.

"Gee thanks." Pat formed a semi smile, then rolled her eyes as she rose to her feet.

The young woman's eyes lowered to a squint as she watched Pat walk away. She mumbled incoherently under her breath causing Pat to turn her head, right before reaching for the knob to Mr. Lu's office. Pat puckered her lips and blew a kiss as she opened the door leaving all that negative energy on the other side.

"Thank you for coming down here. Please be seated." Mr. Lu stood up and waved her to the chair in front of his desk. He walked over to the mini-refrigerator.

Pat sat down, then pulled a folded piece of paper from her bra and slid it across the desk. Mr. Lu reached forward and took it from her fingertips then opened it to read the contents. His eyes rotated from one word to the next, then up at Pat. She sat anxiously in her seat afraid to breathe until he rendered his verdict.

"Is this all he is asking?"

"I assume so. I never ask, I am only the messenger." Pat put her hands out to the side.

Mr. Lu placed the paper in his drawer then got up from his seat. He walked over to a long marble counter, opened a gold box, and pulled out a cigar, clipped the end and lit it, then pulled gently on the other end. He slowly walked back to his seat looking out at the view of the city. He thought about the offer and all the risks and wondered was this a welcomed hand or a knife to the back. He turned to Pat and began his verdict.

"You know, when Kisha used to come here these deals were so much easier to digest," he said piercing Pat's heart. "I guess you will do," he stated with disdain.

Muthafucka! Pat screamed in her head as she clenched her teeth together fighting the urge to let her lips flap all over his ass. She slowed her breathing, then forced a slight smile. "I guess I will." She gripped one hand in the other and squeezed tight using every piece of restraint she had to not fuck up the deal.

"Tell Tyquan I will consider his order." He sat forward. "However, I will meet with him directly," he stated firmly in his thick Asian accent. "I trust his ears only please have a great day." He rose to his feet for her exit.

Pat stood up and just turned to the door not uttering a word as she did not trust her lips to part.

"My assistant will compensate you for your travel," he said coldly as he sat back down.

Pat again said not a word as she snatched at the knob leaving his office as fast as her feet would carry her. She picked up the pace as she approached the desk. The tiny Asian woman slid an envelope to the edge of her desk with a cynical smirk on her face.

"Be safe," she gently warned as Pat grabbed the envelope in mid-stride continuing to the elevator.

Pat gripped the envelope in her fist as she vigorously pressed the down button on the panel. She stared back at her reflection in the elevator door, a sinking feeling settled in her belly. The doors opened and she rushed inside not looking back. When the doors closed, she rested her head against the walls fighting back the tears as she heard Malik's words play loudly in her head. *"You will always be a pawn because you are too scared to be a Queen."*

She tried to steady her heart, it felt as if it would beat out of her chest. The doors opened and she bolted from the enclosure into the lobby, then rushed out of the entrance, right up to the car awaiting her arrival. Once inside, she slammed the door shut, put her face in her hands, and cried. Even in his death, his haunting words would bear fruit, planting more hate and disdain in her heart. She road on, staring out the window, vowing to make sure she put the wrench in his program that needed to be put into place very carefully.

Malik was right about the pawn, but he missed an important component. The pawn if it stayed out of the way it could move across the board and be a Queen.

****

Kayson walked into the upper East side apartment and locked the door behind him. He looked around the huge loft-style living room and made a note to add some color to all that white. He enjoyed the aroma of sweet vanilla and lavender along with the light Jazz he heard playing from the back of the apartment as he eased through the room. He tossed his keys on the circular glass coffee table, then proceeded into the kitchen.

When he got to the entrance of the hallway, Tiny as he now called her was walking on her tiptoes over to him in a silk button-up that rested right at her kitty. She had left the first three buttons open allowing her perky C-cup breasts to peek through the slit.

"Hi, I'm sorry, I didn't know you were coming. I was in the shower," she spoke loudly, avoiding eye contact as music serenaded the room.

261

"What you know about Jazz?" he asked with a slight smile.

"My grandmother used to listen to it on Sunday mornings while she read and prayed." She shyly smiled back. "I can change it if you want me to." She moved over to the sound system.

"Nah, you're good," he spoke firmly stopping her in her tracks.

"Did you eat?"

"I need to." He looked at her from head to toe.

"Well, I cooked, and you can also have whatever else you want to put your mouth on." She looked up at his muscular frame and her pussy began to moisten.

Kayson didn't respond, he just walked in her direction allowing his eyes to roam over her soft, caramel skin. Tiny stared back at him with a hazy gaze while trying to control the feelings rising in her stomach as his energy took over her space.

"Did you handle that business with Baseem?" he broke the silence.

"Yes, everything went well, and we picked up the money. We took care of what you said, then he dropped me off here. Aldeen brought over a bag for you it's in the closet."

"You good? You got everything you need?" he asked sitting two duffle bags on the hardwood beneath his feet.

"Yes, I'm good. And I wanted to tell you personally." She took a deep breath. "You saved my life." She choked back tears as they rose to the corners of her eyes.

"No thanks needed, but can a boss feel how much he is appreciated?" Kayson walked over to where she stood, then moved around her frame inhaling the sweet mango that rose off her skin.

"What...ever...you want," she agreed, closing her eyes, and enjoying the heat that pushed from his body to hers.

Kayson's eyes peered down at her erect nipples hardening through the thin material and his dick began to swell.

"Can I taste you?" he asked as he stopped right in front of her.

"I'm all yours," she responded softly feeling his hand ease between her thighs.

Kayson walked back in front of her and lifted her head so her eyes could meet his. He stared down into her soul. "You never have to be afraid when you are with me," he spoke softly then placed his soft lips on hers.

Tiny gripped his hand and tried to control her breathing as every emotion she could muster rushed heavily through her body. Kayson eased his tongue into her mouth taking her breath with every swirl. He then tested Fred's theory by sliding his middle finger inside her one inch at a time.

"Ahhh..." she moaned as he began to move inside her. Tiny's pussy began to flood his finger as his other hand caressed her breasts.

Kayson walked her back into the wall and pressed her against it as he continued to open her tightness. He released her lips from his and stared down at her pretty face as he continued to play with his brand-new toy.

"Cum for me," he whispered opening her shirt, then placed his mouth over her nipple. He sucked gently as he now moved two fingers back and forth inside of her increasing her moans as she held on tight to his arms. "Cum for me," he commanded as he moved to the other nipple and showed it the same pleasure.

Tiny's body was filled with heat and confusion as she embraced the contractions moving back and forth from her stomach to her clit while he played just right with her G-spot.

"Kayyyy...wait," she cried as her body jerked beneath his merciless push.

"Let that shit go," he growled picking up a little speed.

Tiny's body released what felt like waves of heated energy, her pussy squirted sweet juices all over his hand, then down between her thighs. Kayson ran his fingers back and forth between her swollen wet lips enjoying the innocence that rained onto his fingers.

"I need all your loyalty. I need all of you to belong to only me," he whispered again placing his hand under her chin bringing her eyes to his.

Tiny slowly lifted her lids, then looked up into his gaze melting in his hand as he continued to play between her legs. "Ssss…yes. Whatever you want," she replied biting her bottom lip as she felt him enter her again.

"Let me train my pussy," he said looking at her breasts standing up waiting to be devoured.

"Whatever you want," she confirmed, embracing stage one of the Boss's training.

Kayson leaned in and bit her neck as he spread her legs with his feet. His finger stroked her to climax over and over until her legs could no longer support her body. Tiny laid limp against his chest trying to catch her breath. Kayson scooped her up into his arms and walked her to the bed. He placed her in the thick, soft comforter, then pulled the other side over her exhausted body.

"You been keeping daddy's pussy tight?" he spoke firm causing her kitty to tingle.

"Yes, Daddy," she agreed, looking at him through a glossy vision.

"This pussy feels like it wants to surrender to the boss," he spoke smooth as he eased his fingers from between her legs.

"I'm ready." She looked up at him with a firm glare confirming all acceptance to his request.

Kayson walked her heated frame to the bed, lifted her under her arms and placed her on the bed, then climbed up between her legs, rock hard and ready to force all his will and power into every stroke. Tiny closed her eyes gripping his shoulders as she felt his swollen head meet her wet heated entrance.

"Be good while daddy is gone. I'll see you in a couple of days." Kayson sat up stretching his long frame.

"I will be good," she cooed surrendering to all his power.

Kayson kissed her forehead, stepped back, and headed to the bathroom.

Tiny shivered in place and stood replaying that moment in her head. Sticky juices eased down her thighs tickling her heated flesh as she struggled to gain composure.

Kayson turned on the water, then undressed placing his clothes on the edge of the vanity, he eased his body into the warm water letting the Enforcer lead the way. Kayson lathered his skin as he thought about the meeting he had coming up and the men he would have to lay down in order to maintain a strong hand. He closed his eyes and took in the steam as he prepared his mind to train Tiny to be exactly what he needed, a strong force on his team who could move without guilt or regret. His only question was always were they ready. He inhaled the scent of mist as he soaped each muscle, soothing his spirit. He embraced the peace as he rehearsed his mental checklist.

Tiny sat anxiously on the bed shaking her legs, debating with the idea of being forward or being submissive. She had heard all the rumors and she wanted to see for herself, but the fear that played devil's advocate in her gut formed a battle she was now determined to win with her pussy. She headed to the living room to retrieve his bags and quickly tucked them in the walk-in closet in the spare bedroom, then hurried back to the bedroom. She lit a few scented candles, shut down the front of the apartment, and set the alarm. She dimmed the bedroom lights and lit a few more candles. Her heart raced with hot surges as the realization that she was about to give Kayson what she had never given another man.

He had come over a few times over the past couple of weeks, talking mostly business but tonight she wanted to seal her loyalty to him. She jumped up on the bed, rearranged the pillows and comforter then laid in different positions and played with her hair trying to feel her sexiest. Tiny could no longer take the heat, she listened to the sound of the water and Jazz playing as a backdrop to the porn show that was taking place in her head. She hopped off the bed and moved for what she wanted.

When she got to the entrance of the bathroom, she froze in place watching his silhouette through the shower curtain. She quickly again battled with the thoughts of being too forward with the boss versus just waiting for him to take what he claimed as his. She turned around and came back a few times before she took a deep breath and walked over to the shower. Slowly she pulled at the curtain until his magnificent body was exposed. Tiny's eyes danced with delight along the thick inches before her mouth watered as she imagined the possibilities.

Kayson put his head under the shower nozzle and let the water rain over his face, then opened his eyes to a very pleasant surprise.

Tiny slowly unfastened the remaining buttons on her nightshirt while trying to control the saliva from leaving her mouth as she watched him take his dick into his hand and began stroking it to full strength. Her eyes roamed over his perfectly chiseled frame, steeled tool, and the urge to drop to her knees took over her soul.

"Can I join you, Boss?" she asked avoiding eye contact.

"You sure you want to be this close to a beast?" he asked caressing his thickness.

"Make me ready," she purred stepping into the steamy water, dropping her shirt as she entered.

"You ready to make this pussy obedient to the boss?" he asked as he pulled her body to his.

Tiny nodded her head unable to speak another word.

"Let me ask your pussy if she's ready." He grabbed her waist, lifted her to his face, and positioned her against the shower wall with her pretty puff within tongue and mouth distance.

Tiny rested her legs on his shoulders as the heat from his lips got closer to hers, she arched her back as he made the first connection with her clit.

"Awww...." she moaned placing her hands around the back of his head.

Kayson didn't plan on giving her all the smoke tonight but after he made that kitty wet, she wanted to feel how deep he could get. That pussy was ready and responding to every lick and passionate tongue kiss just right, and Kayson was ready to answer her pussy calls.

Tiny began rotating her hips to the rhythm of his tongue as she felt what she could only describe as heaven. Her legs fluttered back and forth as her pussy surrendered sticky heat all over his lips.

"Oh...my...God! What are you doing?" she uttered between labored breaths.

"Mmmm...I'm letting you feed me." He gripped her ass and rotated his suck from her clit to her pussy lips until her hot kitty jerked against his mouth.

Tiny again lost control of her juices as he lapped at her throbbing clit. She put her head back against the cool marble and rode his face allowing him to have her soul.

"That's right, baby. Feed me," he repeated as he pleasured her opening with his tongue, he placed his mouth over her clit sucking firm, then slow, showing no mercy as her body surrendered to his taste and touch.

Tiny slipped into another world as he took her body and mind from one crazy feeling and emotion to another. By the time they stepped out of the shower she could barely hold on to reality. Kayson slid her down to his waist, walked her to the bed, and climbed between her legs positioning the Enforcer right at her hot opening.

Kayson began easing into her tightness one inch at a time giving her only a few inches at first. He slowly stroked trying to make her comfortable with all he was packing but the grip of her walls sucked him deeper with every push. The loud moans from her lips and the grip of her hands forced him to quicken his stroke as her flower opened and received him.

"Fuck," he mumbled as he looked down at her biting her bottom lip trying to take the pressure but losing the battle with every thrust.

"Daddy," she cried as she felt her pussy lips spreading with each side-to-side stroke.

"Ssss...shit," he mumbled as her virgin pussy strangled him.

Tiny gripped his shoulders as she scooted back slightly trying to avoid the pain while welcoming the pleasure.

"Awwww...Kayson...please," she said as his push deepened.

"Just relax...and feed me my pussy," he whispered in her ear as he proceeded to open her up.

"You're too deep," she called out as his stroke switched back and forth from slow to quick playing inside her.

"I thought you said you were ready?" He showed no mercy.

"Ahhh...Kay..." she chanted while trying to comprehend what he was doing to her body as his slip got more slippery.

"Feed this beast, baby. He's hungry." He sunk his teeth into her neck, placed her legs in the crook of his arms, and punched the clock. He wanted it all and she was giving it to him and whatever she didn't give he was gonna take. He needed her entire body to be his mind, body, and soul.

When Kayson was finished with phase one, he pulled out of her wetness and stared down at her weary body covered in sweat, stomach heaving, and pussy glistening with sweet nectar. He placed two fingers on her clit and circled slow watching her body jerk with every motion. He woke the Enforcer up with a few strong strokes then placed his next request.

"Come let daddy show you how to ride for him." He pulled her to her feet and walked her over to a chair in the far corner of the room. He took his place on the throne, then placed her hot pussy right on the ruler.

Tiny's wobbly legs shook beneath her as he put her in place. She moaned as he eased her down on his throbbing rod. Tiny pushed back up each time he pulled her close trying to avoid all that dick from violating her ribcage.

Kayson placed her nipple in his mouth and sucked as he pulled her all the way down on him.

"Ain't no running, Ma," he teased as he pulled her legs up from the side of his waist and placed them on his shoulders, then tilted her back a little so he could fill that pussy just the way he needed to.

"Kayyyyyyy…" she cried as he swiftly pulled her back and forth along his length.

"Make it mine, baby. Make it mine," he chanted as he bounced her on his lap making sure to snap her head back with each upward push.

"Kay, I can't!" she moaned, as pressure filled her gut.

"Give me my pussy. Don't play with all this good dick. Ride this muthafucka," he ordered through clenched teeth.

Tiny closed her eyes, slowed her breathing, and held on tight as she began to rock and rotate to his pleasure. Low-toned moans left her lips as she felt him in her tender place. Kayson let the head of his dick play with her G-spot until the moans filled the room loud and uncontrolled.

"I'm about to cummm!" she yelled digging her nails into his arm as he forced her kitty to tangle with the beast.

"That's what the fuck I'm talking about. Let that shit go." He quickened his thrust taking all of her with each push.

Tiny bounced and bounced as her pussy contracted around him. Her hips took over with each connection circling in his thickness until she felt her body quiver and kitty rain down on him. Kayson didn't let her get a second of rest, when he saw how that pussy responded he took her through the motions over and over again until she was unable to speak.

Tiny laid her tear-stained cheek against his as she held tightly around his neck. She cried and shook as he slowly played in her wetness.

"Is it mine now?"

"Yesss…" she said between sniffles.

Kayson released her legs from his shoulders and held her tight around her back continuing to poke at her spot. He placed a finger on her clit and rotated as he stiffened inside her.

"Make daddy cum," he whispered in her ear as he bit tenderly into her neck and shoulders.

Tiny used what little strength she had left to push up on her toes and ease up and down. Kayson enjoyed the feel of her soft breasts on his chest as her pussy swallowed him whole. She was learning to take the dick just the way he needed her to. Tiny listened closely to each sound that left his throat adjusting her glide to enhance the pleasure in his tone.

"Ride that shit, Ma." He popped her ass sending chills up her spine. He rotated faster and faster as she hopped up and down riding to her pleasure.

Tiny put her head back and followed every instruction until she could take no more. "Kayyyy... wait!" she screamed as her pussy contracted, sending a flood of liquid heat all over him.

Kayson gripped her ass with both hands and spread her cheeks, then pulled her back and forth until her vibrations rocked the walls. Tiny wiggled in place as her body twitched surrendering entirely to his will. Kayson rose to his feet rushing over to the bed, he flipped her over on all fours and dogged walked her pussy from one end of the bed to the other. Tiny scrambled and struggled to be free but all effort was lost as the boss took all her innocence and replaced it with grown-ass woman pussy.

Tiny came, cried, and surrendered from every position. He was right she was not ready for the beast, but she was damned sure going to let him make her ready. Kayson's hunger woke up in force as he opened his gift, there was no turning back now. She was his from head to toe.

Kayson sat up and stretched his long frame releasing the tension from his muscles. He looked over at Tiny and smiled, he had to admit little mama was a trooper. He looked down at the Enforcer and shook his head. That nigga had struck again and all he could think about was how she was going to secure him that money.

Tiny opened her eyes, then eased up next to him placing soft kisses on his back. "I just want to help you." She pledged her allegiance.

Kayson enjoyed her tender touch taking in her gentle spirit something he needed while out there being an animal. He turned to face her, then grabbed her by the back of her head, gripped her hair in his hands, and damned near swallowed her tongue as he

270

kissed her deeply. Tiny placed her hand on his arm as she struggled to catch her breath.

"Mmmm…" he moaned as he snatched her soul right from her chest.

Tiny road the wave as her body weakened with every motion. Kayson pulled back kissing her lips a final time.

"Come wash up the boss." He stood up and walked into the bathroom.

Tiny barely able to move her tattered frame forced herself to her feet and followed him to the bathroom. She didn't know what was going to happen next in her life and really, she didn't care. She was all about Kayson and she was ready to endure all that came with all that man.

Chapter 30

Money and Envy

KoKo crept along the pier in the darkness then positioned herself on the dock next to a speed boat and laid on her stomach. She arranged her gun on its stand and fastened the silencer in its place. KoKo watched the movements of several silver containers move from truck to boat. She kept each man's movement in her scoop waiting for her moment to strike. She patiently stalked her prey until the last case was loaded. After the load was secure the men chatted a little, shook hands, then half of them hopped back in the trucks while the others organized the boats take off. KoKo laid and waited for her targets to create an opportunity to let her whistles speak.

The men covered the cases with tarps then headed inside leaving just one-armed man to secure the boats.

"Mistake number one," she whispered as she pressed her body against the hardwood and crawled slowly into position.

The man pulled out a cigarette and lit it, then pulled deep. As the smoke left his lungs, KoKo filled them with hollow points. She released the heat until his body fell against one of the boats shaking violently until no life was left. Quickly she moved close to him and checked for movement. When none was there, she crept up to the doors, then slipped inside.

Four men sat laughing, toasting their victory right there in their assassin's hairbow. KoKo flipped her scope, took a deep breath, then hit three of the men with headshots, and the last one she hit once in the arm and once in the knee.

273

"Ahhhh! What the fuck?" he yelled in a thick, Italian accent grabbing at his bloody wounds.

KoKo ran up on the grieving man snatching her gat from her waist. She shoved it under his chin, slid her hoodie back slightly, and matched evil gazes with his.

"Don Anibello said your services are no longer needed."

"Tell Don Anibello...Vaffanculo," he gruffed with red crimson painting his lips.

"Dall'inferno. Muthafucka," she spat back then blew his skull out the back of his head.

KoKo snatched the speedboat keys from the soiled table, pulled down her hoodie, and hurried to the exit. She snatched the door open as the black Escalade eased up slowly. The doors popped open and two huge frames emerged rushing in her direction. KoKo met eyes with the men, then tossed them the keys, they slammed the doors closed, and headed to the boats.

"Don't fuck up," she ordered, shooting her gaze at the driver.

Wadoo gave her the nod, then pulled off leaving his smoke in the wind.

KoKo took off in the opposite direction she had come dismantling her weapon as she moved in the shadows. When she got to the end of the pier, she snatched a bag with weights in it from under a nearby car, tucked a few pieces of the gun inside, zipped it closed, and tossed it into the water. She trotted a few yards down, then tossed the last pieces one by one a foot away from each other. Once her hands were empty, she tucked them into her hoodie pockets then double-timed it until she was far from the scene. When she reached the main street, she slowed her pace, pulled out a blunt, and lit the end. She walked a few more yards until she saw a cab. KoKo hailed it down and hopped inside.

"Where to?" he asked pressing his finger on the meter.

"Just drive straight. I'll tell you as we go," she mumbled then took more smoke into her lungs.

"There is no smoking in here, Ma'am," he asserted as he eased away from the curb.

"Shut the fuck up and drive," she shot back then tucked a few hundred in the slot.

The man looked back at her in the rearview mirror and the reflection that she returned confirmed his cooperation.

"No problem." He turned his attention back to the road avoiding looking back in her direction.

KoKo slouched down in her seat, stared out the window, and enjoyed her tasty treat, secretly celebrating her victory.

Chapter 31

What Goes Up Must Come Down...

"You made me promises. Why am I getting ready to fucking bury people!" The Don yelled into the phone.

"Let me get on this shit," Kayson said calmly.

"Yes, get on it," he responded, then ended the call.

Kayson tossed the cordless on his desk and rubbed his fingertips against his temples. He took a deep breath, then headed to an adjoining room. Kayson moved around his gym trying to make sense of the turn of events that had taken place in the last 48 hours. There weren't too many men that had the power to call the hits that were taking place and those that did must also have big ass balls to put him right in the middle of a full-fledged war.

He grabbed two weights from the rack and began curling his arms. He pumped the iron until sweat began to form on his skin. He did several reps, then moved on to his bench. Kayson laid back, gripped the steel pole, and pressed the two hundred pounds back and forth above his chest.

"Kay!" Wise yelled as they searched the first few rooms for Kayson.

"Back here!" Kayson yelled back as he placed the weights back in place.

"What the fuck is going on?" Wise said as he walked over to Kayson.

"That's what you need to be finding out," Kayson said trying to remain calm.

"I'm on it," Wise said nodding his head.

"What are we going to do about the West connects order?" Aldeen chimed in.

"I gotta take a trip over there. I'ma take Baseem. In the meantime, y'all lift every square inch of bitch ass nigga and find out who the fuck has their hand in my pocket." Kayson rose to his feet driven by the rage in his heart. "Who else knew about the Cali trip?"

"That shit was on the hush. It had to come from over there?" Aldeen responded.

"Make sure." Kayson looked right into his eyes. "Make sure," he repeated, then returned to the weight bench. He sat down and got back into position. He removed the barbell again pushing the iron back and forth this time with more speed.

"What the fuck y'all waiting for a tip?" Kayson spat not breaking his stride.

"Nah, we on it." Wise turned to the door and Alden followed.

He started to share something with Kayson but decided to hold it until he had news he really wanted to hear. They half stepped back to the truck and hopped inside ready to peel the streets for the rat.

"I don't trust Aldeen's movement," Baseem spoke clear words.

Kayson pushed the weights above his head a few more times, then put them back in place. He sat up and grabbed the towel hanging from the bench.

"Report."

Chapter 32

The Pawn

Monique extended her hand and was assisted out of the car. She stood still in her all-white, custom-made, two-piece suit looking at the beautiful array of flowers. Red, yellow, and white adorned the freshly manicured lawn. She took a deep breath and prepared her mind for the conversation she was about to have. A few seconds passed and her escort came to greet her curbside.

"Welcome, Mrs. Wells," the tall, olive-toned gentleman spoke with a smile as he approached her.

"Good afternoon. Pleases to meet you," she responded extending her hand.

"Your beauty is a welcomed presence to our home…" He paused and took her hand, placing a single kiss on the back. "Please come this way." He took her hand and placed it on his forearm and led her inside.

"Thank you so much for your hospitality," she softly stated as they entered the huge wooden doors.

Monique was escorted into the back-patio area where Don Anibello sat awaiting her arrival. She looked out over the lake and took in the crisp Cali mountain air as she approached his table.

"Moooo…" The Don called out as he looked her over. He had heard about her health and this would be the first time he laid eyes on her in over ten years.

"Anibello," she called out with her arms extended.

Monique walked right into his arms. Don Anibello gripped her tightly enjoying the sweet fragrance that rose off her skin.

"It's been far too long, Mo," he spoke softly as he pulled back from their embrace.

"Yes, it has." She looked into his eyes, then over the features of his face. Age had also been kind to him and seeing him just put her back into her youth.

"Come be seated. Join me, my chief has prepared a special menu just for you," he offered, leading her to the empty chair next to his.

"Thank you, I can't wait." Monique sat down placing her clutch beside her. She unrolled her silverware and placed the silk napkin on her lap. She adored the crisp linen tablecloth and the porcelain and gold plate settings, each piece sitting perfectly in its place.

Don Anibello began speaking plans for expansion and the many investments he made for the advancement of the family. Monique's input was always welcomed. She spoke when she needed to and was quiet when she didn't want to. Between his banter, she sat gracefully in her all-white, tasting each course of tender chicken and vegetables, yellow rice, fresh fruit, and decant desserts, all while enjoying the conversation with her old friend. He was more than wise. He was the one directing each instrument in the orchestra and she was just taking in all the tunes.

"The main thing you must always remember…" She paused as she set her teacup on the small saucer. "There is always one that is waiting to be king. Rule with mercy, so he will at least allow you to eat." She folded her hands on the table.

Don Anibello folded his hands over his chest as he allowed her words to settle. "I had one man prepared for my throne and somebody took that from me, along with my wife, my daughter, nieces, nephews, and a host of my daughters' friends. The blood that I sacrificed for this seat has already been shed. I have no fear of anyone coming for this throne. I have nothing else to lose."

"I understand that all too well. I too have sacrificed. I lost a lot and I have gained a lot. Either way, I have never been angry at the game, it is the same. But those players, they can always surprise you with some sort of disappointment," she humbly stated with a smile.

"Come walk with me," he offered as he rose to his feet.

Monique stood as well placing her napkin over her teacup. She moved around the table and took his hand. Don Anibello placed her hand on his shoulder and led her off the deck and down the stone stairwell to the sand below.

"Monique, I don't want to go on this next part of the journey without the support of New York. I need you to make sure I am always at the front of their minds and that crossing me is a war no man wants to bear," he requested as he stared out into the horizon.

Monique stared in the same direction as him admiring the hues of orange and gold as the sun threatened to leave the sky.

"You will always have my loyalty," she vowed taking his hand into hers. She placed her lips on the diamonds of his pinky ring as she held his hand in hers. They gazed out at the water for a few more seconds before continuing the walk.

Don Anibello also made vows assuring her safety and the safety of the ones she held dear. Monique listened but she knew better. She knew that if the lion needed a meal, he would trip her ass and push her friends just to make sure he was not the meat. What the Don seemed to forget, is the lioness protects the cubs, his lioness had failed but Monique would not.

Don Anibello walked Monique back to the house and out to her waiting limo. He kissed both of her cheeks, then assisted her into the back seat.

"There is a nice gift for you in the trunk. Please enjoy it." He smiled, then lightly tapped the roof of the car.

Monique smiled back and settled in her seat.

****

KoKo and Ha'Roo pulled up in front of the Tropicana, in Atlantic City New Jersey, grabbed their bags, and hopped out of the rental. As Ha'Roo tossed the parking attendant the keys, he took in the night air as they moved inside. He scanned the room for the desk then headed in that direction.

"I need to pick up my room keys," Ha'Roo asserted as he walked up to the front desk and checked them in.

KoKo looked around the lobby at all the different types of people coming and going all sharing that American dream of hitting it big. "Suckas," she mumbled under her breath thinking about how much money they were fucking up on a bet.

"You ready?" he asked coming up behind her.

"Don't get all up on me, yo'," she spoke firm pushing her hand in his chest.

Ha'Roo didn't budge. He stood tall looking down into her pretty brown eyes. He shot her that pearly white smile then ran his tongue over his lips.

"I'ma make yo' ass calm down this weekend," he warned locking gazes with hers.

"You gonna get fucked up this weekend you mean," she popped her shit, then turned to the elevator.

"Sexy ass," Ha'Roo spat and popped KoKo on her left butt cheek.

"Touch me again and you're gonna have to count with your toes."

"Oh shit, it's like that." Ha'Roo laughed at the thought.

"Indeed," KoKo confirmed without waiver.

The elevator doors opened, and they stepped inside. Ha'Roo walked right up on KoKo almost pinning her to the wall.

"All this space and you up in my cipher. Can you give a bitch ten feet?" she asked putting both hands on his chest.

"Feel that shit, that's a grown-ass man little girl."

"Why niggas think everything hard on them makes them a grown-ass man?" She looked down at his semi-hard dick then up into his cold, black eyes.

"It may not make me a man, but it will damn sure make you a woman." He looked down at her with wicked intent.

"Dick ain't shit if it's swinging between the legs of a disloyal ass nigga." She put her hand on his chest.

"I ain't never made you question my loyalty. So, it must be my dick you question."

"Nah, I don't question shit. Your dick ain't got nothing to do with me. So, pipe the fuck down and back up." KoKo pushed him back a little further trying to assert power.

Ha'Roo snatched her hand off his chest and slid it up and down the length of his dick. "All that tough shit is foreplay for me, baby. You just sweetening my tooth," he said as the doors opened wide and a couple stepped on.

"This is us." Ha'Roo turned and put his arm out to block the doors.

KoKo's mouth became dry as she choked back the feelings that were causing her pussy to throb. She walked out of the elevator and stood still until he led the way. Ha'Roo put on a serious scroll as he bopped hard to a beat of his own. He eyed the numbers until they came to the last suite on the end. He slid the card in the slot and popped open the door.

KoKo's eyes danced from one thing to the next as she tried to hide her excitement. The side of her mouth creased when she looked out the window and over the ocean, something she had told Ha'Roo she wanted to experience for a very long time.

"Damn, your money long," KoKo joked as she headed over to the window. She placed her palms on the glass and looked out over the water.

"I have a lot of long things," he joked grabbing at his steel.

"Save it for ya hos, I'm good." She chuckled.

"Y'all always putting hos on a nigga."

"Whatever," KoKo shot back, then put her attention back to the view.

"Let me ask you something," Ha'Roo stated moving a little closer to where she stood.

"What you need to know?"

"Why do you always disappear?" he questioned moving up right behind her.

"I be having shit to do," she answered.

"You are the only one I can trust. I just want to make sure my trust is safe," he softened his tone.

"Always," she confirmed.

"Always." Ha'Roo walked up behind KoKo and put his hands on hers.

"Ha'Roo, I already told you," she asserted but was cut off by his soft lips on the back of her neck and stiff dick between her ass cheeks.

"I don't fuck with nobody like I fuck with you, KoKo," he spoke softly against her ear. "I'm ready to give you that other shit we need to be on to take this whole fuckin' city," he continued, then kissed and nibbled her neck and shoulders from one side to the other.

KoKo's eyes rotated from open to shut as she felt his energy penetrating her body. "We can do all of that as friends. I don't want to fuck up what we got," she replied softly caught up in a cologne filled haze.

"I want all of you, KoKo," Ha'Roo confessed pressing his body against hers.

"I can't give you all of me," she mumbled then eased out of his grip.

Ha'Roo put his hands on her hips and pulled her into his chest. "What are you afraid of?"

"Everything...and nothing," she spoke firm.

"Let me take some of that fear. I need you on my side and in my bed." He wrapped his arms around her bringing her even closer.

KoKo stood silent listening to his heartbeat against his chest. She had toyed with the idea a time or two but dismissed it not wanting to mix work with play. She had managed to make it to eighteen with all her morals intact. There had been many niggas who were calling, but the kitty would not answer. However, being next to Ha'Roo had her pussy ready to purr. Her first time hitting that pole she could eventually handle but it was her heart she knew needed the protection.

"Let's just get through the night. Then we can talk about it. Fair enough?" She stared off at the moon touching the water while enjoying the warmth of his embrace.

"Fair enough."

Chapter 33

Love? War?

Kayson walked up the steps to his mother's brownstone eager to find out why he had not heard from her in a few days. He put his key in the lock and turned it with reluctance in his steps. He moved down the short hall and into the dining room where he saw his mother sitting at the long, cherry wood table with an arrangement of photos in front of her. She had a glass next to it and tears in her eyes as she stared down rubbing her fingers over one picture in particular.

"I was calling you. You okay?" he asked approaching the table.

"They took my brother, and I didn't do shit," she mumbled looking at the pictures of Rabb.

"That was handled I told you that," he responded kneeling at her feet.

"But who gave the order?" she asked with pain in her soul.

"I told you I took care of it," he assured her.

Monique sniffled as she ran the back of her hand over her eyes. "It should have been by my hand. I promised my mother to watch out for him and I failed," she cried harder as she thought about the agony he suffered and the fact that she still had to sleep not knowing where the order came from.

"You don't need to worry about all that. I told you I will settle all debts owed. Just let me put the rest of this plan into action." He took her hand into his.

"I need this to come to an end. They don't get to win, Kay. They don't get to win," her voice cracked with every word.

"You have my word. None of them will escape this revenge. I want them comfortable. I want them sleeping peacefully. And then I want their life and their empire," he confirmed his mission praying to comfort her weary mind.

"Promise me I'll get to watch at least one of their demise," she requested.

"I promise," he vowed then kissed her hand and brought it to his heart. "It's just me and you. Nothing or no one else matters," he confirmed. "Come lay down you need to rest."

"Yes, son." She surrendered feeling exhausted from reliving years of tainted emotion.

Kayson stood, then helped her to her feet. He walked her down the hall, into her bedroom and tucked her tightly in her bed. He placed a call to her nurse, got her a hot cup of tea, and sat by her bed just waiting for his relief.

When help arrived, he sent her to help Monique with a nice hot bath, then into some fresh clothes. She changed her bedding and cleaned her room from top to bottom. Kayson heated his mom a nice bowl of soup and made her a strawberry and spinach salad. He removed the teapot from the stove and filled her mug with several herbs, a mint leaf, and honey, then placed each item on the tray. Kayson smiled big as he walked through the bedroom doors and over to her bed placing the meal on the tray over her lap.

"I need you to stay strong," he said tucking a napkin in the top of her silk robe.

"I will. Thank you, son. You are my everything," she uttered as she brought the teacup to her mouth.

"Well, now you will have more." He took in a little air. "I wanted to tell you when we were together, but you know I be running…" He paused smiling big. "I'm about to have to pick you up a *Proud Grandma* t-shirt." He chuckled as the words left his mouth.

"Is that right?" she asked forcing a smile to take over her lips.

"Yeah, Lady is four and a half months," he stated with pride.

"So, we are keeping secrets now?" she asked placing the cup back on the tray.

"Nah, never that. I wanted to make sure everything was progressing well before we told you."

"Congratulations. I pray for the best." She again forced a smile.

"Don't worry, Ma. You will always be my number one," he assured, then leaned in and kissed her forehead. "Eat and get some rest. I love you." He stood and prepared to leave.

"I will be fine. You be careful. I love you more than life, my son."

"You have my word," he responded then turned to exit. "Get some rest, woman," he asserted and stepped toward the staircase.

When Kayson was out of her view, her smile turned into a full-length frown. She pushed the food to the side and swung her feet over the edge of the bed. Her blood boiled as she thought about her seed being fertilized in unauthorized grounds.

"Tracey!" she yelled out as she stood by the window watching Kayson pull off.

"Yes, Miss Mo." She came to the doorway.

"Prepare my bag. I need to make a trip," she requested as she moved to her closet to pick out the perfect traveling outfit. Black was what she needed to wear to go along with what her heart was feeling. It was mourning season and she was planning on making sure she wasn't the only one in pain.

****

KoKo and Ha'Roo had been to five states in seven days. KoKo was worn out. From car to plane to car again, she really just wanted to climb in the bed and let the pillow bust her brains out. She slid the key card in the slot and stumbled inside.

KoKo tossed her bag in the corner, set her guns on the nightstand, and stripped naked leaving her clothes on the floor.

She adjusted the water using whatever strength she had left to scrub her chocolate skin thoroughly.

KoKo stepped out, wrapped her body with the thick white towel, stumbled along to the fluffy king-sized bed, then plopped dead in the center, and closed her eyes. As she felt her mind drifting to what felt like heaven, she was jolted to reality by a rapid knock on the door.

"Whyyyyy…" she grumbled as she forced her body from its rested position, grabbed her gun, then headed to the door. She peeked through the hole provided then rested her head against the door.

Knock! Knock! Knock!

He pounded his knuckles against the door, then posted up and waited for her to appear. KoKo cracked the door, peeking through the small space between the door and the bar lock.

"What's up?" she asked with her eyes squinted low.

"Let me in. Why you talking to a nigga through the fucking chain lock?"

"What do you need, Ha'Roo?" she slurred ready to shut the door in his face and dive back in the bed.

"Open the fucking door. Got me in the hallway."

KoKo huffed, then shut the door and removed the lock. She opened the door and stepped back.

"You mean as fuck when you sleepy. Close the door and put your little punk ass lock on it," he said pulling his shirt over his head.

"Why the fuck you strippin'?" she asked walking over to her bed ready to slide back between the sheets.

"I need to crash in here. I got the team counting money in the other two rooms." He stepped out of his boots then unfastened his jeans and tossed them on the chair.

"You need to go get another room. I gotta get some sleep, I don't feel like playing," she said with a full attitude.

"I'm about to lay right here. Put that piece of shit gun down and lay yo ass down." He laughed at the sight of KoKo standing there with a full attitude, holding heat. "Miss I'm so fucking sleepy." He laid across the bottom of the bed ignoring her request.

"Fuck you. And stay on your side." She walked over and placed her gun under her pillow then crawled back between the soft cotton sheets. "You touch me, I'ma make sure this is the longest nap you take," she spat as she pulled the comforter up over her head.

"What?" Ha'Roo chuckled as he pulled the blanket from the bottom and grabbed her feet.

"Stop, Ha'Roo." KoKo squirmed and jerked as she tried to be free.

"Nah, you tough." He squeezed her thigh causing her to scream out in laughter.

"Stooopppp…" She wiggled and yelled as he continued to find every ticklish spot she had.

Ha'Roo ran his fingers along her frame taking time to caress her smooth skin. He laughed and taunted her while they enjoyed a well-needed pause. He continued until she became exhausted from laughter.

"Stop, boy," KoKo uttered out of breath, then pushed Ha'Roo off her with her foot. "You play too much," she hissed as she laid still in the disheveled sheets and blanket.

"Like I said, take your punk ass to sleep," he asserted pulling the comforter up to his chin.

"You get on my nerves." KoKo grabbed the other half of the blanket and pulled it to her chin.

Ha'Roo didn't respond, he just smiled and plotted as he dozed off. Within seconds he was stretched out and knocked out. KoKo peeked her head from under the covers when she heard a light snore.

"What the fuck?" she mumbled then pulled the cover back over her head and tried to slip back off to sleep.

When KoKo finally drifted off, the sun was creeping through the darkness. She relaxed against the coolness of her pillow and let the sandman do her duty. By the time they settled into a small slumber a knock rapped on the door.

Ha'Roo jumped up and grabbed his gun from his hoodie pocket. He moved to the door, stood slightly to the side, and peeked through the hole. Relief settled in his chest when he realized it was his boy. He cracked the door to see what he needed.

"It's time to move, Roo," he stated smoothly, then turned back to the other room.

Ha'Roo closed the door shut, then went to wake KoKo. To his surprise she was already in her sweats, waiting for his orders. "It's on," he confirmed as he began to grab his clothes.

Chapter 34

Pay Attention

"Hello!" Lady yelled into the speakerphone as she rushed around the room trying to get ready.

"Hey, baby girl," Kayson's voice played smoothly through the speaker.

"Hey, baby." Excitement filled her body as she placed her diamonds in her ears.

"You sound like you miss the boss?" Kayson asked with a cocky undertone.

"I miss Kayson. I do not miss the boss."

"Just make sure you are on time," Kayson ordered as he put on his suit jacket.

"You are still in the doghouse, sir. You are lucky I am coming." She scented her skin then slid into a strapless all-white dress.

"Oh, trust me, you cumming," he spat back with a wicked smile on the other end of the phone.

"Can I finish getting ready, Boss?" she asked voice dripping in sexy sarcasm.

"Yeah, get daddy's pussy ready for me. I have a taste for you. See you at nine." He hung up not waiting for a response.

"Asshole." She giggled as her kitty tingled with every step.

She then headed to add the finishing touches. Lady struggled to control her anxiety and the smile that had taken over her mouth as she applied a shiny red matte' gloss to her lips. She retrieved a red snakeskin Chanel clutch and slipped on ankle strap open toe shoes to match. Lady stopped at the full-length mirror giving herself a once-over.

"Bitch you bad," she said aloud as she admired the silky material hugging her caramel skin, she ran her hands over her frame, then caressed her slightly plump belly and smiled big.

Lady grabbed her floor-length, pearl white, mink coat, slipped it over her shoulders then moved to the door. She punched in the alarm and headed to the Mercedes limo awaiting her arrival.

"Good evening, Madam." The man extended his hand assisting her into the back seat.

"Good evening. Thank you." Lady sat back and relaxed as she tried to imagine the evening Kayson had planned.

The driver got into the front seat and eased down the driveway headed to his destination. Lady enjoyed the light as he weaved through traffic, then onto the tunnel. When they arrived on Broadway, her eyes danced from one building to the next enjoying the colorful billboards and excited crowds of people snapping pictures and living life. There was nothing like the unique movement of the city that never sleeps.

When they pulled in front of the theater, the driver rushed around to her door and popped it open. Lady stepped out of the limo, onto the pavement with her eyes shifting around the area in search of Kayson. She gazed at a few crowds of well-dressed men looking for what she knew would be the sexiest man in the room. What would not be a total surprise there he was in the shadows ready to prove her right.

Kayson stood a little off to the side watching her gaze from one spot to the next. His eyes moved over her body settling on each of his favorite parts. The tiny, white, off the shoulder dress, laid perfectly against her soft skin accentuating her perfect breasts line. His eyes traveled up her legs which were competing with the spotlight shapely and shining.

Lady started to slightly panic, then she turned to her right to see Kayson coming right at her. Her smile widened as she watched all that man approaching her, wearing an all-black, three-piece suit,

Ferragamo's on his feet, and a red tie to pop the whole scene into motion.

"You're late." He took her hand and brought it to his lips.

"Beauty can't be rushed, sir." She blushed and giggled as he pulled her into his arms.

Kayson squeezed her tightly as he inhaled her scent then placed a few sweet kisses on her shoulder. "I'ma show you things tonight that you will never forget."

"I can't wait," she said a little over a whisper.

"Nasty ass, let's go." He laughed then released her and led her to their seats.

Lady smiled the whole way to their section. As Kayson moved through the lobby, he spoke and nodded at what she knew connected men. She could not contain the joy that was rising in her belly. There was money, power, and unexplainable amounts of respect oozing from every corner of the building, and she wanted some of it all.

"I love you!" She looked at Kayson with her baby doll eyes.

"I love you, more!" He confessed as the doors opened. They stepped into the VIP elevator and she squeezed Kayson's hand with childlike excitement.

"You are so spoiled." He shook his head at how amped up she was.

"Yup and don't you forget it." Lady did a little shimmy with her shoulders.

The doors opened, and they were handed two programs and two pair of glasses then guided to their seats. Lady was in heaven. She had finally gotten Kayson to come enjoy what she loved, and he was delivering more and more joy by the second.

Lady's eyes filled with water when she walked onto the balcony and was greeted by three bundles of skillfully placed roses and a short stand with two bottles and two glasses.

"Please enjoy," the young man said as he closed the curtains.

"After you." Kayson put out his hand for her to take a seat.

"Thank you. Baby, you are amazing," she responded as she eased into the soft leather.

295

"You deserve the best."

Kayson sat down next to her then reached over and opened the bottle of champagne and poured him a glass then poured a glass of sparkling cider for her. They mouthed I love you, clanged their glasses together, and prepared for the show.

Lady wiggled in her plush red velvet chair as she looked over the program. She put the glasses up to her eyes and looked around the room then focused in on the stage as the lights began to dim. She took another sip of her champagne then got comfortable.

Kayson took her hand into his and pulled her close. He had specific plans for Miss Lady. He was just waiting for the right time to execute each one. The lights began to dim, and the actors and actresses took to the stage one by one. High pitched melodies escaped their lips as the stage came to life with music and emotion. Kayson watched Lady's chest rise and fall with each intense sound and motion as they acted out the theme of the night.

Lady put her hand up to her chest as she watched the leading male as his voice bellowed out confessing his love to his bride. She eased her hand down on her stomach and cradled the bottom of her belly as tears rose to the corners of her eyes.

Kayson looked over at Lady sharing this special moment with their child and his heart slightly skipped in his chest. He reached over and placed his hand on her leg and squeezed it filling her body with even more emotion. He slid along her thigh until he had her legs slightly spread enough for him to play. Lady looked over at him then put her hand on top of his.

"Pay attention," Kayson mouthed and pointed at the stage.

Lady bit into her bottom lip, then slowly turned back to the show. Kayson rotated her clit to the beat of the music in the room taking her from one intense feeling to the next. Lady squirmed in her seat as she felt his fingers enter her opening. As a light hiss left her lips, he tickled her spot just right. He picked up a little speed as the instruments increased in volume.

"Ssss…" Lady sighed as she felt her juices began to flow. She pushed her pussy to the edge of her seat forcing his fingers deeper inside her.

Kayson rode her wave tickling her spot just right causing her body to tremble with every push. Just as she was about to cum again, he reached over and grabbed her by her face and put his tongue deep into her mouth. Lady lost her breath as he poured his soul into hers. Kayson placed his thumb on her clit and pressed as he pulled his finger in and out of her wetness.

"Mmmm…" Lady tried to muffle her moans as Kayson showed no mercy.

The music peaked and so did she. Lady's breathing labored as Kayson's lips eased away from hers. Lady's eyes remained closed as he slid his fingers from between her throbbing lips.

He grabbed the handkerchief from his inside pocket and wiped his hands then sat back in his seat. Lady opened her eyes to catch a woman across the theater staring right at them. She looked down as Lady tried to focus her vision.

Lady looked over at Kayson with low eyes and just shook her head.

"Pay attention," Kayson mouthed as he gave her that pearly white smile.

Lady giggled, picked up her glasses, and crossed her legs at the knee feeling the slippery heat between her thighs and doing exactly what the boss said. Paying attention.

Chapter 35

Dirty Pool

Baseem pulled up in front of the diner and walked inside. He scanned the area until he spotted Kayson at a booth in the back then headed that way and tried to control his stomach as the heavy scent of pancakes, syrup, and sausage took over his nostrils.

"Basss…" Kayson's voice rang out as he placed a piece of tender beef into his mouth. "What's good?"

"Sheeiiittt…that steak from the looks of it." Baseem rubbed his hands together as he eyed the T-bone, thick-cut seasoned fries, and cheese omelet.

"I ordered you one, sit down," he ordered then waved at the waitress who quickly moved to the back to retrieve Baseem's meal.

"Let me wash my hands." Baseem spotted the bathroom then slid off. When he returned his plate was perfectly placed at his spot with a side of grits and a tall glass of Welch's grape juice.

"The next best thing to pussy," Kayson joked as Baseem fell into the booth with his hand on his chest.

"If pussy arrives on a plate I'ma eat that shit like Hannibal Lecter. Have a nigga out here cannibal," Baseem slurred as he picked up his knife and fork.

"You crazy as hell." Kayson chuckled as he continued to dig in.

Baseem cut into his steak as he organized the information, he needed to share with the Boss and.

"I believe the orders given for all this extra movement is closer to home than we think." He looked intensely in Kayson's direction.

"Reports." Kayson rested his folk on his plate.

"Shit getting real interesting."

"Really, how so?" He reached for his glass bringing it to his lips.

"You remember Fred told us about the old transition and one of the bosses?" He put the glass to his lips and took a swig before continuing. "One of them niggas name was Bisson, right?" He stopped and scooped up a piece of egg and meat.

"Yeah, the original twelve," Kayson confirmed.

"Yup. And that nigga's son is snooping around. He was at the game in the Bronx a few weeks back and was seen at a few spots in Harlem. The big game we are hosting, my people said he is set to be there. But that nigga ain't on our list." He cut into the juicy meat, took a bite, then just stared at Kayson waiting for instructions.

"Is that right?" Kayson's head tilted to the side. "What you think is going on?"

"I can't call it yet. But I do know all of a sudden bosses' sons are dying, and chaos is seeping deeper than they are prepared for."

"Make sure that game is heavily secured. Get everybody on war mode don't leave shit to chance if it barks, bite it." He looked intensely at Baseem not waving an inch. "And, in the meantime, put some pussy on that nigga."

"Done," Baseem confirmed as he finished filling Kayson in on the team's movement.

Kayson was listening but his mind shifted as he thought about the stories he heard from his uncle. Some heavy plays were being made in the background and he needed to get a better view before he became the dead son of a boss.

Chapter 36

Watch What You Ask For

"Are you sure you don't want to meet these people with me?" Ha'Roo asked as he prepared his mind to meet with Miguel.

"Yeah, I'm sure. Them niggas don't need to know me until they need to know me," she smoothly stated as she flipped a pancake in the frying pan.

"You swear you a fucking tough guy." Ha'Roo shook his head as he stacked the money neatly in the bag.

KoKo just shrugged her shoulders as she began to crack eggs into a bowl.

Ha'Roo watched her booty jiggle in her sweatpants and his mind began to wander.

KoKo picked up on the heat from his stare and spoke slick as usual, "Watch them eyeballs before I use them for dice," she spat not skipping a beat in her cooking rhythm.

"Damn, you gonna take a nigga eyes? How I'ma see all that pretty KoKo skin?" He rose to his feet.

"Don't come over here," she warned as she slid her omelet out of the hot pan and onto the plate.

"If I do?" He proceeded in her direction.

KoKo grabbed a knife from the cutting station and turned quickly placing the blade right under his chin.

"What are you willing to lose over all this KoKo?" she asked looking right into the windows of his soul.

"Everything," he said without waiver matching her stern stare.

KoKo held the sharp tip only an eyelash hair distance from his skin and her body only inches from his. Heated breath moved back and forth between them causing Ha'Roo's dick to harden. KoKo blinked when she felt his steel moving closer than she wanted it to.

"Keep your little beady eyes and hands away from me."

"Let me get up in that rib cage and teach you how to bark and whisper." He moved a little closer so she could feel the pressure.

"You must want me to dig deep." She kept the blade in place.

"Nah, you want me to dig deep." He ran his tongue over his lips."

"You so fucking nasty." KoKo pulled some of the tension in her wrist as she felt the blade connect with his skin.

"Yeah, just as I thought. All talk." He moved back just a bit. "Let me get some of them pancakes, Scary Ass. And I want a lot of syrup." He chuckled going back to his seat.

"That's the only thing sticky you gonna get anyway," she slyly stated turning back to the stove as her heart beat heavy in her chest.

"I hear you," he said as he got situated to accept his plate.

KoKo put three thick pancakes, crispy strips of fried pastrami, and a cheesy omelet onto the glass plate, then began dressing the pancakes. Ha'Roo's mouth watered as he watched her slice fresh strawberries and bananas then added whip cream to the pancakes to top them off. She placed one plate in front of Ha'Roo and the other in the empty space across from him. She grabbed a couple of forks, then sat down. After passing him his silverware she bowed her head and whispered a few words over the food dug in.

"Let me find out thugs pray," he joked while filling his mouth with a fork full of each item on the plate. "Damn," he mumbled chewing slowly to savor the explosion in his mouth.

"Yeah, fuck with it," KoKo talked her shit as she put a folk full of pastrami in her mouth.

"Fuck that. What you got planned for next week? I'm about to marry yo ass," he mumbled as he tried to chew the mouth full he'd just taken in.

"Shittin' me, I'm only married to the gun. Yo' little nigga can't bust and reload quick enough for me."

"Talk your shit." Ha'Roo snickered. "We gonna see." He looked directly at her as he pulled the fork from his mouth.

"Indeed," she shot back as she continued to chew and bob her head to the beat.

Ha'Roo just snickered and plotted, he knew she was going to have him some of that hot KoKo and he was planning on drinking her up one hot sip at a time. The two of them ran a few of the daily tasks making sure all safety was at the top of the conversation. Times were changing and so was the seat of power the last thing they wanted to do was become a *remember when* story.

"Thanks, baby girl, that shit was the bomb." He rubbed his hands over his stomach.

"You I got you." She smiled at his food drunk gaze.

KoKo got up from her seat and gathered the plates and scraped the scraps into the garbage. She washed and rinsed their dishes then did the pots.

"I'ma get fresh real quick before a nigga fall asleep." Ha'Roo got up and headed to the shower to wash away his day.

"Don't use all the hot water." KoKo turned in his direction.

"You just miss me that's why you always talking shit." He walked off to the bathroom and stripped down.

As he stood in the hot steam and reflected on the power exchange at hand, his mind rotated between life and death. Everything he had sacrificed was about to come full circle and he needed his whole head in the game. He stepped out onto the cool tiles and chill aligned his soul with the darkness he was about to rain. Ha'Roo walked over to the closet and snatched his clothes from the hangers, popped the tags, then dressed his frame.

"What you got planned for tonight?" he asked walking back into the kitchen.

"I'ma let the night handle itself." She put the dishtowel over the sink then turned in his direction.

"Why your mouth so slippery?" he asked moving a little closer.

KoKo inhaled his scent causing her kitty to tingle as his body got closer to hers. "Why you always in my ten feet. Back up a little." She put her hand on his chest.

"Let your hand slide down to the left so I can bless you," he teased looking down into her pretty brown eyes.

"Watch out I need to go get wet," she teased back.

"Let me get you wet." He moved in closer pushing her into the sink.

"Damn, what you need a hug?" She held their gaze.

"Yeah, I need a hug." He pressed his body against hers.

"Here let me hook you up." KoKo pushed up on her tiptoes and put her arms around his neck.

Ha'Roo eased his hands down onto KoKo's apple bottom and squeezed as he enjoyed her soft breasts against his chest.

"Mmm..." he moaned in her ear then wrapped his arms around her body.

"Okay, you should be good now." Koko melted into his strong arms.

"Nah, I'm not good. I need a little more." He began placing kisses on her neck.

"Stop, boy." KoKo put her hands on his chest trying to be free.

"Nah, talk your shit." He squeezed a little tighter as he sank his teeth into her collar bone.

"Ha'Roo, stop," she moaned as his hands took control of her frame.

"Let me taste these slick ass lips." He grabbed her by the chin and put her head back, then connected his lips with hers.

KoKo lost her breath as his tongue tangled with hers. She slightly dropped her guard allowing him to have what he wanted. Ha'Roo pulled back and nibbled on her lips and chin.

"You need to stop playing and let me act the fuck up between these sexy ass legs," he mumbled between passionate kisses.

"You got enough legs to crawl between. Try them." She pushed him back licking her lips tasting the essence of the heat he left behind.

Ha'Roo stood back looking down into her hazy eyes. "When you ready to let me change your life, let a nigga know." He grabbed his erect inches holding them firm in his hand.

KoKo looked down at what she could only describe as beautiful. She looked back up into his eyes and the tension in his gaze caused flutters in her stomach.

"Exactly," Ha'Roo uttered as he placed his hand at the back of his head and brought her lips to his.

KoKo tried to pull back but the heat between them had taken over her rational thoughts. Ha'Roo increased the pressure as he pressed his muscular frame against hers. He let his hands roam free reacting to the small moans that escaped KoKo's mouth as he swirled his tongue around hers. KoKo gripped his arms for balance as she felt her legs becoming weak beneath her.

"Let me have you, baby..." he paused briefly, then began biting and nibbling on her neck as he walked her to his bed.

KoKo wanted to respond but the only sounds that would pass her lips were pleasurable whimpers. Her body filled with chills as she felt her clothes being lifted from her body. His hands and lips moved over her hot flesh like they knew exactly what she needed. Soft sounds of *H-Town's Emotions* played as he released her breasts from the lace bra.

Ha'Roo sang lightly along as he sucked and tickled her erect nipples with the tip of his tongue, "Emotions make you glad sometimes. But most of all they make you fall in love."

"This is dangerous, Ha'Roo," she said a little over a whisper.

"Everything is dangerous. Let me worry about that." Ha'Roo pulled KoKo off her feet and just held her tightly in his arms.

He inhaled her scent as he enjoyed her heartbeat against his chest. He squeezed tighter as she nuzzled her face into his neck. KoKo wrapped her legs around his waist as he laid her in the middle of the elevated king-sized bed. Ha'Roo rested between her soft thighs and began his tongue assault.

"Ha'Roo, we can't," KoKo whispered as she felt him tugging the sides of her underwear.

"Let me have it, KoK," he growled in her ear as he eased the head of his dick up and down her lips. His fingers found their way inside her causing a flood between her thighs.

"Ha'Roo..." she moaned quivering beneath him as he teased while finger stroking her pussy deep and slow.

"Let me have it," he repeated as he again rubbed his swollen head in her wetness. He gently tapped her clit causing her body to jump with every movement. He placed his mouth on hers and tasted the sweetness on her tongue.

"Ahhhh..." KoKo moaned as Ha'Roo continued to play between her slippery lips. He rose over her, looking into her pretty chocolate face then down at her perfectly shaved kitty glistening like a juicy peach. He rested the head at her opening placing only an inch inside her.

"You want it?" he asked kissing and nibbling on her lips.

"Rooo...." she panted as she felt her pussy get wetter and wetter with his every movement.

"What you need, baby?" he taunted knowing she was on the edge of no return.

"Let me have it," she purred in his ear as he continued to tease.

"You want it?" he whispered as he placed the head right at her opening.

"Please," she begged as the intensity from his body set her flesh on fire.

Ha'Roo answered her cries. The next morning, he showed no mercy for the lesson he put on her pussy. Instead, he had her riding wood and filling his room with loud moans of pleasure. KoKo rode to his rhythm and push until she felt her body become light. She squeezed her legs against his thighs as he pumped against the grip of her walls.

"I'm about to cum," she cried out increasing her bounce until her pussy let go. She moved up to the tip and up and down until her juices squirted up onto his stomach.

"What the fuck?" he groaned out of breath as he looked at the puddle she'd just rained down on him. Ha'Roo continued to push until he was ready to release. He pulled KoKo all the way down on his stiffness, then filled her womb with little soldiers. He looked up at this tiny, shy woman with the ability to cum on command.

"Yeah, play with it if you want to," KoKo teased, then hopped off the bed, walked to the bathroom naked, and jumped in the shower.

"Shit," he uttered as he laid back onto the pillows, closed his eyes, and savored the moment.

"You better get up and get that dick right, we got shit do," KoKo said walking into the bedroom fully dressed.

"Damn, you made a nigga close his eyes," he said as he realized he had been asleep for over thirty minutes.

KoKo chuckled. "Put that dick in a chokehold." She talked her shit.

"This real nigga pussy, right here." He slid his hands between her legs and leaned in for a few soft kisses.

"That's because I'ma real nigga," KoKo spat as she tucked her guns in her waist.

"That's why you were crying and running," he teased taking his steel into his hand.

"Indeed," she spat, then turned to the door.

"Scary Ass!" he yelled as the door closed.

He chuckled to himself as he replayed the evening's events in his mind. He turned on the shower, then stepped into the steamy water. From this point on things would be different. KoKo was now his and the price of fucking with her had just changed.

****

"Feather Fred," Old Man Charles sang out as Fred entered the Barbershop.

"What it do, old friend?" he returned the greeting as he walked over to his chair.

"I can't call it. Just waiting to be graced with your magnificence," he joked as the two men smacked hands, then embraced.

"You ready to get a brother, right?" Fred asked as he took a seat in the chair."

"Is a wet duck slippery?" Charles replied as he grabbed a smock and snapped it in the air.

"What's on the menu? And let me place my numbers," Fred said as he took his place.

"Ms. Marie is doing fish plates and I'll have Lil' Mike run your numbers, slide them to me," Charles said as he placed the barber smock around Fred's neck.

"Bring me two plates and here are my numbers." Fred handed Charles a small stack of folded bills and a piece of folded paper with his numbers on it.

Charles walked over to Lil' Mike handed him a hundred-dollar bill of Fred's money, then gave him his instructions. Lil' Mike tucked the money then ran out the back door off to handle his mission.

Charles moved back in place, grabbed a small bowl and brush and whipped up Fred's face cream, then set the bowl on the counter, and grabbed a hot towel, placing it on Fred's face. After massaging it against his skin for several minutes he removed it, then lathered his cheeks and under his chin.

"So, how is business?" Charles asked taking the straight razor in his hand. The few men awaiting their turn got up and walked to a room in the back of the shop leaving only Fred's right-hand man and three people on Charles's security team.

"Things may be getting way out of hand," Fred revealed as the blade eased over his face.

"Yeah, I'm hearing some things about that young bull and his team. I don't think Mo is gonna be able to pull his collar."

"Yeah, I was thinking the same thing," Fred confessed as he felt the hair lift from his skin.

"Do you think it was right to send Kayson in the opposite direction?" Charles asked. "I believe it may be time to intercede." Charles looked down into Fred's face.

Fred opened his eyes as he contemplated over Charles's words. "We gotta remember. You can't un-ring a bell. Once we put our hands all the way in the pot all we can do is stir."

"But sometimes if you put your hands in too many pots, it's a chance we could spend the rest of our life an amputee," Charles gently warned his friend.

"I'm willing to risk it, even if the dick I put on the line is connected to my own balls," Fred spoke firm as Charles shaped around Fred's mustache.

"Just make sure it's really worth it cause I don't want to come up an inch or a dollar short," Charles responded then continued to render his services.

Fred didn't respond, he just closed his eyes settled in his seat to receive the rest of his treatment. He vibed to the beat playing in the background as he moved the mental piece from one spot to the next.

Charles changed the subject and went over the numbers and movement of the shop. Lil' Mike came back with the food, placed it on the counter and handed Fred and Charles their numbers, then made himself what the grown folks said seen and not heard. He tucked himself in a little space in the back and laid low.

****

Pat sat gripping the steering wheel as she stared at the tinted glass of the Barbershop. She played over and over in her mind if she was ready to take the risk of cutting right in the middle of the field as Monique and Tyquan played their little game. She toyed with just riding off and letting things take their course and the reality of how Kisha and the people she had been looking out for had been pushed to the side and left for dead so all these snake ass niggas could live rich and famous.

Pat's blood began to boil as she accepted the task at hand. There were already lies on the table, and she was sure that digging a few up and putting some truth to them would make all this shit a little more interesting. She reached over and placed her purse under the seat, slipped a blade into her bra, and prepared to exit the vehicle. She slammed the car door shut, hit the alarm, then moved swiftly to the entrance.

"Can I help you?" Charles came to attention.

"Maybe," Pat responded with a slight smirk gracing her lips.

Fred's eyes darted at the door and widened when he saw who was in attendance.

"Good afternoon, Charles. Always good to see you," she greeted the puzzled man.

"Same," Charles was short with his words as he continued Fred's haircut.

"Don't get up, Fred. I love to see a King on a throne," she said as she walked over to where he sat. "We really need to talk." She sat in the chair next to him.

"How do you always find yourself at my feet?"

"I'm where I need to be when needed." She placed her hand on his knee.

"Why would I need you?" Fred asked giving her a little smile.

"Well, for one I am close to several people. You need information and I know how much you love information."

"I've learned a long time ago to watch where I receive it from."

"You have no reason not to trust me."

"You are Kisha's aunt, right?" He looked down at her.

"You know that already."

"But you fucked Malik knowing how she feels about him." He lowered his gaze and waited for her response.

Pat's eyes widened at his accusation. "What I have or have not done will go to the grave unconfirmed." She sat back and crossed her legs at the knee. "But I will say this, I have only done what we have all done and that's survive, by any means."

"Just as I thought. I gotta be careful where I get information." He again closed his eyes trying to enjoy the last of his haircut.

Charles shook his head as he shaped around Fred's edges.

"If that is all, I want to finish my alone time. *Alone*," he gently dismissed her.

"Is that how you're gonna handle me?" She sat forward staring firmly at the side of his face.

Fred opened his eyes then turned in her direction. "What do you really want?"

"I mean look at us." She waved her hand around the room. "Scraps. You think Tyquan is getting his hair cut in a fucking shit hole in the hood?" She looked him in his eyes. "We were stepped over. I want what the fuck I got coming. And I know you do, too."

"Stepped over? I am right where I want to be. Maybe you were stepped over. And I don't give a fuck what Tyke does or where he does it."

"You think you know everything there is to know. You have no idea of the things they hide from you." She shook her head at his arrogance.

"They?" His brow creases at the thought. "You have no idea what you are talking about."

"Mr. Feather Fred, All-knowing, all involved, but still, you have no idea what is going on." She tossed him a schoolgirl giggle.

"I don't know who sent you in my direction? However, I just lay low and count my dough. I don't need nothing extra in the way of my progress."

"You know where my niece is and the sacrifices she's made for all of us. Her man, her child, her family. Y'all owe her. Y'all owe us," she pleaded.

Fred looked in her eyes and for a brief moment he wanted to just say yes, but there was also greed he felt from her spirit that would not allow his lips to accept her offer.

311

"Let me on the team, Fred. I promise I am the best ass you could have on your shelf."

"All the ass on my shelf sells pussy." He threw his proposition on the table realizing she must have had something he just may need.

"I don't want to sell no pussy. But I would like to interview," she whispered as she reached under the barber cape and tugged at Fred's zipper. "I guess the rumor is true." She released his heat from the slit in his boxers, then moved her hand slowly up and down his length until he rose against her palm.

"Excuse me for a second, Charles," Fred spoke low as Pat's gentle touch pleasured every inch of him.

Charles set the clippers on his station, then brushed the hair from Fred's neck. He threw the towel over his shoulder, then headed to the back waving any lingering eyes or ears into a side office, and closed the door tight. Fred's trusted man turned his back and posted up as Pat lowered her mouth onto him.

Fred rested his hand on the back of her head guiding her suck as he enjoyed the sloppy wet sounds that left her lips. Pat placed her hands on his knees and worked his steel from the tip of her tongue to the back of her throat.

"Just like that," Fred ordered as he pushed himself as deep as he could go.

Pat answered the call by tightening her throat around the tip of his dick as she massaged the shaft with her tongue.

"It's all about the kids." He gripped the arms of the chair as she sucked him deeply.

Fred's stomach filled with pressure as he prepared to release down her throat. His excitement intensified when he realized he'd just got free pleasure for information he already knew. He pumped widely into her up and down motion until he had no choice but to let go.

Pat drank until he had nothing left to give then sucked the head until he shuttered against her. She played with her new friend as she looked up into Fred's eyes.

Fred looked down at the small amount of seed on her bottom lip and as she licked it clean, he placed his final piece on the board. "I already know about his daughters." He applied a crease to the corner of his mouth.

Pat rose to her feet holding a firm gaze. She leaned in and whispered in his ear, "But do you know about his son?" she asked, then pulled back again staring into his eyes. She now creased her lips as she turned to the door. "I'll be in touch," she said as security unlocked the doors.

Fred watched her switch to her car and hop inside. He tucked his dick back in his pants and straightened his shirt before removing the cape and heading to the bathroom.

"Damn, boss that shit was intense. What she say?"

Fred didn't respond he just moved through the dimly lit hallway with a heaviness on his chest. He knew Malik had sacrificed a lot of pieces on the board to protect his queens even himself, but he had no idea he had left a king in reserve to one day come for his throne. Fred locked the door, turned the water on, and just stared in the mirror as he shuffled the deck in his head adjusting to the right card to play.

Chapter 37

Born Ready...

"Yeah, nigga run me my props!" Magnum shouted through the living room holding his hands out for the crew to look at all the amenities in the room.

"Yeah, this shit fire," Link agreed as he walked to the sliding glass door of the patio. "Oh, hell yeah, it's about to be a very ignorant weekend," he continued as he opened the doors heading for the pool.

"Y'all niggas act like you ain't been no fucking where." Ha'Roo chuckled as he watched Magnum open the refrigerator and cabinets.

"Man, this shit don't ever get old. I love this classy ass shit." Magnum pulled a bottle of Cristal, shook it, then popped it open.

Champagne erupted into the air as Magnum hurried to catch some of the bubbly in his mouth.

"Fucking shit up already." Ha'Roo laughed as he watched his boy enjoying some of the fruit from their labor.

"Nah, nigga this is practice. About to put some pussy in my mouth and watch that shit bust." He poured more bubbly into his mouth, then wiped his face with his t-shirt. "Yup just like that."

"You gonna fuck around and leave Miami with your dick on a stretcher."

"Yup and it's going to have a badass Spanish bitch with a fat ass riding that shit to safety. Fuck you thought?"

"Nigga, you stupid." Ha'Roo busted out laughing.

"What the fuck this nigga do now?" Link walked in ready for the bullshit.

"This nigga about to OD. Make sure we got that nigga's PIN and password. I can't let him give away the family jewels," Ha'Roo slurred as he continued to drink the cold ale.

"Sheeiitttt…a bitch ain't getting shit but a nut. She can have it on her forehead or her ass cheeks either way she better not touch my pockets," Link responded rubbing his hands together."

Magnum shot back, "What is this nigga drinking. I need to catch the fuck up."

Link walked to the refrigerator and opened it wide. He grabbed a bottle and began shaking it vigorously. "Hell yeah, let's fuck this lick and take no hostages." Link popped the cork sending champagne exploding against the refrigerator. He watched bubbles ease down the shiny chrome, then put the bottle to his lips.

"Where the cleaning lady? This nigga fucking up already." He took another swig of the bubbly.

"Nah, nigga, we getting everything wet tonight and if she comes through here, she's getting wet, too," Magnum tilted his head back and poured the bubbly into his mouth.

"Keep putting these bitches in your mouth you gonna fuck around and get lockjaw, nigga," Link slurred causing Magnum to spit out the remainder of what was in his mouth.

"Fuck you, nigga." Magnum stuck up his middle finger as he pulled up his t-shirt to dry his mouth.

The three erupted in laughter as they each put a bottle in their hands and held them high in the air. They toasted to the next level, then clinked their bottles together. They took a few more sips as they reveled in the contentment of the moment.

"Y'all know this shit is getting thick," Magnum changed the mood in the room.

"We can't slip not one step on these next moves." Link's smile eased from his lips.

"As long as these niggas paying. We will be laying these niggas down," Ha'Roo weighed in.

"As long as your gun is out, I'ma bust mine," Magnum vowed his loyalty.

"We in this shit from womb to tomb." Link raised his bottle.

Ha'Roo and Magnum brought their bottles to his. "From the womb to the tomb," they sang out.

Just as they sealed the pack the doorbell rang with their special treats awaiting to supply the pleasure of the night. It was time to relax and release the pressure before they applied it.

****

KoKo leaned forward and put two fifty-dollar bills in the slot, then grabbed the bags from the seat next to her. She hopped out of the cab and bopped into the entrance of her building heading straight for the staircase.

"Good morning, Miss KoKo!" the husky security officer yelled out from his station.

"Good morning," she spoke back not breaking her stride.

"Good to see you are well." He moved over to the steel door and opened it wide for her.

"If you wake up everything else is good money," she spat walking past him and into the stairwell.

"Have a great day, Miss KoKo." He closed the door behind her then put himself back in position.

KoKo ascended one level at a time until she reached her floor. She pushed the metal handle and walked down the hallway to her apartment door. She turned her key in the locks, rushed inside, and silenced her alarm. KoKo turned to the door, clicked the locks and security bar on the door, then headed to her bedroom. Once in her room, she threw the bags in her walk-in closet, opened the curtains, and raised the blinds. KoKo stood in the middle of the floor looking around, then stripped the bed and headed to the laundry room.

After loading the washing machine, she filled a bucket with hot water, pine sol, and bleach, strapped on a pair of rubber gloves, and began mopping her house down room by room.

When she was done with the floors, she vacuumed and disinfected both bathrooms, then stripped naked and tossed her dirty clothes into a hamper in the laundry room.

KoKo walked over to the stereo system popped on some Beres Hammond, turned it to the max, then headed to the shower. She adjusted the water just right, then stepped in the hot water and began washing away her night of sin as the heavy reggae beats moved through her body. KoKo stepped out onto the plush bathroom rug, oiled her skin, and headed to the bedroom. She thumbed through her closet grabbed the new black jeans, t-shirt, and hoodie from the bag threw on a pair of boxers and a tank top, then adorned her body with her daily uniform.

KoKo brushed her long hair into a ponytail, then grabbed the bag of money, headed to the living room, and poured it onto the glass coffee table. She stood staring at the stacks and took a deep breath. She headed to the kitchen and fixed herself a huge bowl of Apple Jacks, then headed to the couch and took a seat.

KoKo bopped the music as she neatly stacked the money in five-hundred-dollar piles. When everything was accounted for, she hopped up and walked over to the counter to retrieve a pack of rubber bands. She looked down at a stack of mail she had brought up two weeks ago and quickly thumbed through it stopping at an envelope addressed to her but with no return address. Her brow creased as she tore it open.

She reached inside and pulled out a card that contained a phone number on one side and a note on the other which read, *'When you are ready call me.'*

KoKo walked over to the wall, picked up the phone, and dialed the number.

After a few rings, she was prepared to hang up when a voice answered the line, "Hello."

"Yes, I got your number from a friend."

"KoKo," the voice answered.

"Depends on whose asking," KoKo coldly returned.

"I've been waiting for this day. Can I meet with you? The phone does this conversation no justice?" she asked nervously awaiting KoKo's answer.

"Who am I speaking with?"

"Pashion," she answered without hesitation.

"I'll get back to you," KoKo spat, then hung up the phone.

She stood in the kitchen with her mind turning in a hundred directions. She had only heard that name once before and now with so many years passed it had come to her door.

KoKo picked up the phone and called down to the front desk.

"Good afternoon, Miss Ce'Asia. How may I assist you?"

"Where did you get that letter that you gave me without an address on it?" she asked with heat in her tone.

"Let me check…" He paused, then looked over the mail log. "Ah, yes there was a lady that came by here, older, a little bit of grey hair. She dropped it off, then got back in a car and left."

"Thank you and don't take any more mail from anyone but the fucking mailman. Tell them I moved." She hung up the phone not waiting for his response.

KoKo walked over to the couch and sat down rubbing her hands together trying to figure out who would know who she was and where she lived. She tossed around a million ideas, then settled on the one that made sense.

"Fred," she said aloud, then grabbed a bag and placed each stack inside.

She headed to her bedroom, grabbed her gun and her weed, and blunts placing them in her hoodie pocket. She put the money in the safe, grabbed a few stacks for herself, then moved out headed to the only person with keys to her past.

****

Wise pulled up in front of Monique's Brooklyn Brownstone. He checked all mirrors then hopped out and trotted up to the door. He extended his arm and rang the bell three times then stepped back so she would be able to see him.

Monique grabbed her handbag, checked the area to make sure she had everything, then headed to the door. She paused to look herself over, keyed in her alarm code, and eased out of the door.

"I guess my son was too busy to pick up his mother," she slickly stated looking Wise over. She shook her head at the sight of his jeans, crisp boots, and hoodie, the street uniform as she called it.

"It's always my pleasure to escort the queen." He put out his hand and waited for her to approve his presence.

"We will see," she said resting her hand in his.

Wise led her down the steps and into the back seat of the car. He hopped in the front, turned over the engine, and eased out of the parking spot heading downtown.

"You comfortable, Ma?" he asked looking at her in the rearview mirror.

"That depends," she answered staring back at him.

Wise's eyebrows rose as he tried to see what angle she was coming at him with. He drove on waiting to see what she wanted and at what cost would he give it to her.

"Let me ask you this…." She paused keeping her eyes right on the mirror. "What is troubling, my son?"

Wise looked up and right into her face. He licked his lips then parted them to tell her something satisfying. "You know Kayson just wants to make sure we are all good. He carries a lot on his shoulders, but I know he got it, Ma. No worries," he spoke smooth as he flipped his left blinker merging from one lane to the next.

"Which dick do you think I had to suck to get to the top?" She chuckled, then dropped the slight smile from her face.

"No disrespect, Ma. But you know Kayson is specific about how information is distributed," he spat hoping that would slow her curiosity.

320

"Listen to me, little boy. I am the reason y'all play comfortably in these streets," her voice elevated as her patience began to thin. "Don't make me ask you a second time," she spoke through clenched teeth.

Wise gripped the steering wheel as he processed what he could and could not say. "There are some old players back on the board and they have people on our ass. All I know is Kayson got us all on go. The orders may be coming from out West," he mumbled as his chest tightened with regret.

"Pull over to the right," she ordered.

"Nah, Ma, I got you. Kayson gave me specific orders." He watched her blood rush to her cheeks as she tried to control her breathing.

"Pull over to the right." She tilted her head to the side waiting for him to disobey.

Wise pulled over to the side, parking right next to a row of cars. Monique snatched at the door and got out before Wise could make it to the other side of the car.

"Just let me get you to where you need to go safely, Ma. Please," he pleaded.

"Tell my son I will see him in a few days. Keep him safe," she said as she stepped past him and waved down a taxi.

"Ma, just let me take you where you gotta go," Wise again pleaded while walking beside her as a black and yellow pulled in front of them.

"Look closer to the circle. It is always the greedy, not the hungry," she stated smoothly as she grabbed the handle and hopped in the back seat.

Wise didn't respond he made sure she was safely inside, threw a few yards in the window, and gave the driver the look of death. "Drive like you got some fucking sense, Habibie," Wise warned, then looked at Monique who was now avoiding all eye contact.

"Protect my son," she gave her final order. "Let's go."

Wise stepped back, tapped the roof of the car, and watched them ease into traffic, then hopped back into his car and pulled off conflicted with the decision he had just made, but deep down inside he knew he did not make a mistake. Shit was getting heavy and a big hitter was needed to level these muthafuckas out.

****

Kayson pulled open the huge wooden sliding doors and walked into the dining room forcing his anger to calm. He looked each man in the eyes as he passed them, then looked over at Don Anibello and gave him a nod of confirmation then moved to the head of the table also nodding at each boss in attendance as he took a spot next to the Don.

"Kayson, welcome. Come sit next to me." Don Anibello rose to his feet.

"Thank you. Honored to be at your table," Kayson returned the greeting, extending his hand to The Don.

Don Anibello shook his hand and placed a kiss on each side of his face then waved him to the empty seat next to him. "Please welcome my special friend from the East coast. He will have someone representing New York at the Luxury games tonight," he announced.

"Salute," one of his partners said aloud and the rest of his guests raised their glasses in Kayson's honor.

Kayson bowed slightly accepting the silent friendship. He sat down and slid up to the table. "Thank you for extending your hand. I look forward to the new business ahead. Salute." Kayson now raised his glass and they all followed.

Don Anibello smiled wide as he thought about the money in that room and the power he was about to gain by placing everyone together. Don Anibello leaned over to Kayson as his guests continued to chatter amongst themselves.

"I sincerely thank you for making this happen and putting our roots in New York deeper into the ground."

"Honored to be of assistance," he humbly stated.

"This is one of the most important games in our organization. We need to make sure everything is set in place and our special guests are comfortable."

****

KoKo bopped along the pavement, headed to retrieve some very needed answers. Not only had someone come to her door but their presence shook her reality and was interfering with a fire she had been trying to calm. A fire created by the very ones who forced her to live in this world by herself.

"KoK," she heard coming from her left.

KoKo turned in the direction of the voice connecting eyes with Ha'Roo. "What's up?" she asked slowing her stride.

"I need you to come with me," he responded from the back seat of a red Audi S-class.

"I gotta take care of something real quick," she shot back ready to keep on to her business.

"Nah, come with me. You can do that later," he insisted then opened his door as the car came to a stop.

KoKo stopped and looked at the urgency in his eyes, took a deep breath, then headed to the car and got in climbing over Ha'Roo, into the empty seat next to him.

"This better be good." She looked over at him as she pulled her hood back from her face.

"It's always good, baby," he teased loving her little attitude. "Take me to the spot," he ordered as the car pulled off back into traffic.

KoKo shook her head as she looked out the window again distracted from her mission. Ha'Roo's driver pushed on to a parking garage in Hoboken. He got out, opened the locks on the garage, slid the gate up, then headed inside. Ha'Roo hopped out of the car and popped the trunk then grabbed two Fendi duffle bags and a few brown grocery bags. He waited for his other car to be pulled out of the garage, then headed over to fill the trunk. Once everything was inside, he tapped the window and waved out of the vehicle. KoKo looked through the window then grabbed the handle and pushed the door open.

"What's this about?" she asked looking over at the other car.

"I need you to take a run with me," he answered as he headed to the driver's side of the other car.

KoKo looked at her watch then tucked her hands in her vest pocket and walked over to the passenger's side.

"I'll catch you later. Take that car to Magnum," he ordered before closing the door. He adjusted the seat and mirrors then backed out headed for the highway.

KoKo put the seat all the way back, pulled her cap down over her brow, and closed her eyes.

Ha'Roo looked over at Miss KoKo then turned up the music and pushed on with the beat knocking from his speakers. He weaved through the traffic and toll booths until he crossed the Delaware Water Gap. When he exited tight outside the Poconos he carefully eased around the dark roads until he approached a small road. He turned off and drove past the sea of trees and up to a car pad right outside a beautiful home with floor to ceiling windows. KoKo opened her eyes and sat up, then looked around the isolated area and her mind began to speed playing out different scenarios.

"Where are we?" she asked as she reached for the door handle.

"Just a little getaway," Ha'Roo answered as he exited the vehicle.

"So, you in to kidnapping people now?" She opened the door and stepped out onto the concrete slab.

"We both need a pause," he responded as he began grabbing the bags from the trunk.

"That's cool but I have to be back by Sunday afternoon. I have some business to handle." She turned to look at all the wide-open windows and dimly lit lights. She took a deep breath, then headed to the steps.

Ha'Roo ignored her little time frame as he headed to the porch then opened the front door. He then moved back to the car for the bags. KoKo walked inside to see what he had just gotten her into. Her eyes widened when she saw all the black and red, long stem roses in several glass vases. She walked over to the ones next to the fireplace and put her nose into one of the buds and inhaled. A calmness entered her soul as she embraced the fragrance accompanied by an eerie silence.

Ha'Roo locked them in then carried the bags to the bedroom. When he returned to the living room, he looked over at KoKo enjoying the view as he grabbed the grocery bags and carried them to the kitchen. KoKo took herself on a tour around the dining room, office, and the back deck while Ha'Roo put everything in place. She was impressed with the pristine white walls and floors and glass fixtures throughout the airy rooms. She opened a few books in the office and read a couple of lines then put them back on the shelf.

KoKo gazed over the huge paintings with potted palm trees between them. KoKo took a deep breath allowing her weary soul to relax and enjoy the peace. She walked back into the living room and back over to the window and just stared out into the distance.

"You good?" he asked as he put each item in its place.

"Yeah, I'm good," she responded as she stared down at the lights in the small houses in the valley.

Ha'Roo walked over to where KoKo stood and wrapped his arms around her and cradled her against his body. "I just want you to sit still with me for a few days." He kissed her neck, then squeezed her a little tighter.

"So, you just gonna kidnap a bitch." She closed her eyes and enjoyed his hands as they roamed over her heated frame.

"Shiieettt…if I don't kidnap you, a nigga dick gonna dry the fuck up waiting for his pussy," he joked causing her to chuckle.

"Whatever." She feigned a slight attitude as he leaned in toward her.

Ha'Roo put his mouth on hers, then parted her lips with his tongue and slipped it in her mouth. He gripped her in his arms as he took her breath with every swirl of his tongue. KoKo closed her eyes and enjoyed the heat he was pushing through her body until she felt her knees weaken beneath her. She pulled back detaching his mouth from hers.

"Don't get all scary now. Ain't nowhere to run and nowhere to hide. I'ma test all your gangsta tonight," he teased as he looked at her flushed cheeks and low eyes. "Head upstairs to the bathroom I'ma get this food started I'll be up there in a minute," he offered as he moved into the kitchen. "Sexy ass," he mumbled smacking her ass as he exited.

"You gonna have to kiss that and make it better," she teased as she headed to the master bedroom.

"I'ma kiss everything tonight," he promised as he headed back to the kitchen.

KoKo walked up the open staircase staring at the view through the spaces. She walked down the hallway and into the master bedroom. When she entered the room, she inhaled the floral scents. She walked over to the huge king-sized bed decorated with big square pillows, fell onto it back first, and stretched her arms out as far as they would go. KoKo closed her eyes and settled her soul as the thick comforter seemed to caress her frame.

After taking a few minutes of calm KoKo got up and headed to the bathroom. A smile eased over her lips as she set her gaze on all the shopping bags on the counter. She walked over and looked inside pulling out the tight, sexy, and lacy items, and laid them on the counter next to the bags.

"This nigga," she mumbled shaking her head as she pulled the lotion and perfume set out placing it next to the dress.

The last bag caused her eyes to widen as she pulled out three jewelry boxes placing each of them on the black granite surface. KoKo opened the boxes and diamonds smiled back at her. She put on the necklace then the bracelet and topped it off with the anklet and diamond post.

KoKo began to strip off her layers then stood in the mirror staring at her gems against her smooth cocoa skin. She eased her hands over her body anticipating Ha'Roo's special touch. She walked over to the in-floor tub and turned the water on until it was nice and piping hot. KoKo walked over to the radio and turned the knob until she settled on some Old School R&B. She dropped a few bath balls in the water then turned on the jets causing the tub to fill with scented bubbles.

When the water reached its capacity KoKo stepped into the heated bubbles and sank into the deep water, it was like her whole body took a deep breath. She let the water cradle her neck and shoulders releasing the tension from weeks of chaos and mayhem. KoKo placed her head in one of the paddled craters along the edge and closed her eyes enjoying the relaxation.

Ha'Roo moved from the kitchen to the deck preparing a few T-bone steaks, potatoes wrapped in foil, and corn on the cobb boiling in buttery coconut milk with a touch of O'bay seasonings. He prepared a salad and stir-fried some shrimp and scallops to put on top. Once everything on the stove was done, he put a bottle of red wine and a bottle of Hennessey in the freezer, cut the grill down to simmer, grabbed his travel bag then headed to the downstairs bathroom and hopped in the shower. Ha'Roo lathered his skin as he thought about his special treat only a short distance from where he stood. He washed over his body and hair then rinsed thoroughly. Ha'Roo stepped out onto the plush carpet, oiled his skin then threw on a pair of jogging pants.

Ha'Roo went back to the kitchen gathered a few plates then collected the food off the grill. Once he had all the grilled items, he placed them on the plates, then added the corn and salad. When he had everything laid out on the table he headed upstairs. When Ha'Roo entered the bathroom, his eyes settled on a sleeping KoKo, a smile took over his lips as he enjoyed the view. He leaned against the doorway and just admired her chocolate beauty.

"Let me find out you are a peeper," KoKo said from her reclined position.

"Watch your mouth. You already in trouble," he spoke firm as he moved toward her.

KoKo opened her eyes to see him standing over her with his hand extended. "I thought I was supposed to be relaxing," she responded as she lifted her arm from the water.

Ha'Roo pulled her dripping wet body from the tub and into his arms. "You so fucking pretty," he said inhaling the sweet scent from her skin.

"I missed you," KoKo softened her tone.

"Show me," he spoke softly in her ear as his hands slid over her slippery body.

"I thought we were about to eat," KoKo moaned as his touch heated every inch of her body.

"I'ma eat." He lifted her from her feet. "And you gonna watch." He placed her dripping wet frame on the cold marble counter. Ha'Roo lowered his face to his favorite place and began blessing her with his tongue.

KoKo put her head back and gripped his head as the tip of his tongue slithered along her pussy lips. "Roooooo..." she called out as his lips covered her clit. Her fingers gripped at the counter as the suction and rotation of his tongue set her soul on fire.

KoKo watched through a tear-filled haze as he took great pleasure in her taste. The sound of Silk Freak Me danced between their pleasure as Ha'Roo played with every emotion inside her.

Let me lick you up and down until you say stop. Let play with your body baby make you real hot.

"Baby, I need to feel you," she cried as she released sticky sweet nectar all over his lips.

Ha'Roo rose from his kneeled position and stood rock hard between her thighs. He pulled down his sweats causing his thickness to spring into full potential. Ha'Roo wasted no time answering her calls entering slowly as he pushed against the tension of waiting walls. Ha'Roo pulled her to him with every thrust as all their love and loyalty ignited inside him with every stroke. KoKo wrapped her legs around his waist lifting herself into his power push.

"Ride that shit," he groaned as he watched her slip up and down his thickness.

KoKo worked his pole until he filled her womb with every drop he had been saving. Ha'Roo looked into her eyes as he pulled her into his arms and held her tightly as they breathed each other's air. He pressed his fingers into her skin as he carried her to the high-backed king-size bed that awaited the pressure he was about the apply. His dick rose and pulsated at her opening as the wetness between her thighs ignited his passion. He climbed back between her swollen pussy lips and this time just stroked slow.

"You are the only woman I'll ever love," he confessed as he devoured every bit of her.

KoKo didn't respond in words instead she matched every stroke and sound that left his lips. Ha'Roo picked up the pace as he stared down at his sweat glistening on KoKo's chocolate skin. He dug deeper causing her tight walls to quake around his thickness. KoKo raised her hand and pushed against his chest in an attempt to ease the pressure penetrating her womb.

"You too deep…" she whined as his push quickened.

"Mmmm…let daddy get his." He pulled her legs up to his shoulders. "Let me fuck, baby…sss…let me fuck." He zoned out as he indulged in the slippery grip of every stroke.

KoKo put her hands around his neck and let him have whatever he wanted. Their eyes locked and their souls connected forcing them to let down all guards. They lost themselves by the second as their bodies twisted and tangled in intense sexual tension.

Once they woke from their euphoria they put on the matching robes and headed to the kitchen.

"You trying to make a brother weak?" He slapped her butt as they ascended the steps.

"You already know I'm the hardest nigga in your crew," she spat without missing a beat.

"You tough now. But a nigga brought the punk out yo ass a minute ago," he joked as they walked into the kitchen.

"That's only because you had a deadly weapon." She chuckled as she perched herself on the stool at the end of the island.

"See that's all a nigga wants. Respect." He smiled at her as he leaned in and kissed her lips.

KoKo reached over and cracked open a few Phillies and lined them with that sticky green as she talked shit and watched Ha'Roo fix and heat their plates.

"Go relax, Ma. I'll meet you out there," he said as he put the finishing touches on the meal.

She got up from her seated position and walked over to where he stood and stroked his dick as she pushed up on her tiptoes and stole herself a sweet taste of his lips. KoKo released him from her grip, then headed out to the deck placing the blunts in the ashtray as she prepared for her food. Ha'Roo walked over and placed the plates on the table and went for the drinks. KoKo leaned forward placing her nose right over the steam allowing the aroma to rise in her nostrils. She smiled with glee, then reached over and wrapped her hands around the fork and dug in as if she hadn't eaten in days.

"You gonna fuck around and chip a tooth," he teased taking a seat as he watched her take in one forkful after the other.

"I'ma chip it on something else later." She looked over at him as she slipped the fork from her lips.

"Fuck this food." Ha'Roo put his hand on her plate.

"Stop…" She giggled popping his hand while pulling the plate closer to her.

Ha'Roo laughed as he watched her protect her treasured meal. He took her hand into his as they both filled their mouth with the tender meat and sides.

"Thank you," he said as he brought his drink to his lips.

"For what?" she asked as her heartbeat began to rap against her chest.

"For everything," he confessed as he looked over at his best friend.

"Always," KoKo confirmed her alliance as she struggled to control her emotions.

Ha'Roo nodded to her statement knowing that it was a vow he never had to question. He released her hand, and they continued their meal talking and plotting future moves. When they were finished with their plates, they loaded the dishwasher.

Ha'Roo made himself a stiff drink then they headed back to the deck and settled in the hammock, lit a few blunts, and just laid in each other's arms puffing smoke into the air.

KoKo placed her head on his chest and counted the beats of his heart as they ticked in his chest. Despite all the peace that engulfed them she could not help but be haunted by the secret that was growing between them. She argued with her inner self until she silenced the voice of reason with the excuses, she let take her rational mind. KoKo pulled deeply on the blunt erasing her thoughts and allowing herself to just enjoy the moment. Ha'Roo looked out at the stars sitting perfectly in the darkness and inhaled deeply as he enjoyed the still between the thunder.

For the next twenty-four hours, Ha'Roo took complete advantage of his stolen time. They laughed, ate, and sexed each other until neither of them could stand up straight. When the Sunday morning sun crept through the clouds and settled on the side of Ha'Roo's face forcing the slits of his eyes to open wide, his first sight settled over to where he last saw KoKo laying.

"What the fuck?" he mumbled, and a tickle formed in his stomach.

He sat up in the bed and looked at the empty space where her bag once was and reality set in that she had done it again, the thing she was famous for and that's run. He swung his legs over the edge of the bed and sat still listening to his thoughts briefly feeling as if he had imagined the last few days, but then his dick reminded him as it stiffened against his boxers as the memory of her touch filled his skin with tiny chill bumps. He rose to his feet, headed over to the window, and stared into the distance while accepting the fact the KoKo would always be the ghost in his darkness.

Ha'Roo hopped in the shower got dressed, then packed up and loaded the car. He stood at the rear of his car and took in the last bit of peace, then walked to the driver's side and hopped in. As he pulled away from the house, he flipped the switch back to street mode there was an enemy on his back and from this moment forward he needed to keep his head on a swivel and his chamber full.

Chapter 38

Fate

Lady pulled up to Monique's Brownstone and prepared her mind to deal with the side eyes and slick comments. She turned down the radio and took a few deep breaths, however, once she saw Monique coming down the steps her heart skipped in her chest and her palms began to sweat. It didn't matter how prepared she tried to be Monique had a way of taking her good mood and stomping all over it. She looked at Monique sashay down the stone covered steps in all red everything fitting tight and right. Monique adjusted her vision to the mid-day sun, clutched her Chanelle under her arm then pushed on to the parked vehicle with her stilettoes tapping the concrete with every step.

"Good afternoon," Lady said popping the locks for Monique to get into the car.

Monique pulled the door handle, then eased into her seat. "Good afternoon, I see you are on time today," she slyly stated as she fastened the seatbelt across her chest.

"Well, you know your son gets on me when I'm late. So, I try to be on time at all cost." Lady put a half-smile on her face as she pulled away from the curb.

Monique looked at her from head to toe, then put her gaze back on the road. "You will learn that changing for a man is temporary." She looked over at the side of Lady's uncomfortable profile. "Turn left up there at the light. I want to stop by the Fashion District I have to pick something up," Monique instructed as she slid her shades on.

Lady didn't bother to respond. It was way too early in the day to be tongue wrestling with somebody's disrespectful mother. She just reached over, turned up the music, and drove on lips sealed. When they reached the row of high-end boutiques, Lady found a spot and parked, then prepared to exit the vehicle.

"Nah. Stay here, I'll be right back," Monique ordered hurrying from the vehicle.

Lady looked over with a squinted glare as Monique joined a handsome, very well-dressed, white man. The man kissed Monique on both cheeks then pulled her into his embrace. They exchanged a few words and flirtatious smiles as they began walking to a door with tinted glass. She tried to keep them in her sights but was blocked by the man's security as he and Monique were escorted inside. Lady dead the engine and flipped through the stations until she found a 90s R&B channel. She sat bopping to the beat as she waited for the next stop on her dreaded mission.

Thirty minutes passed, then Monique emerged from the door with the man she had met closely by her side. Monique had a few Louis Vuitton gift bags and a small jewelry bag, again they exchanged a kiss on each cheek, then a prolonged hug which she could see was being enjoyed by them both. Monique pulled away from him then headed back to the vehicle with a look of victory in her eyes.

Lady popped the trunk as Monique reached the curb then popped the locks. Monique placed her bags neatly in the trunk but brought the jewelry with her. She walked to the passengers' side and hopped back into her seat.

"Where to?" Lady asked and pulled away from the curb.

"Take me to Park Avenue," Monique instructed, then sat back in her seat.

"Yes, ma'am," Lady answered as if she was the help.

Monique ignored her sarcasm as she prepared her mind for the next meeting. She opened the bag, then the long velvet box. Her eyes widened slightly as she drooled over the many diamonds smiling back at her. She removed the precious stone bracelet from the case and fastened it to her wrist. She then reached back inside the bag and pulled out two smaller boxes and a card.

Monique popped each box open and her smile took over her face as she eyed the beautiful platinum and diamond pinky ring and earrings to match. She put on the remaining items, pulled down the sun visor, and turned her head back in forth in the mirror. Monique flipped the visor back into place then opened the car and her cheeks became flush as she read the freaky request.

Lady divided her attention between the road and the sparkling treats that Monique was adorning herself with. She started to say something but quickly decided against it. She knew their little time together was mere formality no need to push the relationship. They moved through the busy New York streets ducking through the sea of angry cross walkers, blaring horns, and speeding yellow cabs until they reached the Four Seasons Hotel.

"Pull up to the Valet." Monique pointed at the gentleman in the red vest who was waving them over with his white gloves. "Pop the trunk," Monique ordered as the car eased to a stop.

Lady hit the button as she pulled up to the gentleman, then grabbed her purse from the back seat. Her door opened she took the young man's hand then stepped out of the vehicle. She was escorted to the curb and instructed to wait there.

"Good afternoon, Miss Wells," the young man announced as he came around to assist Monique. He smiled big pulling her door open for her to exit.

"Good afternoon, Conard. Always a pleasure to see you." She extended her hand placing two hundred dollars in his palm as he gently pulled her to her feet.

"The pleasure is all mine. Thank you for your kindness."

Monique walked to the back of the Benz and grabbed one of the gift bags, tossed the empty jewelry bag inside the trunk, closed it, and headed to the curb.

"Please let me know if you need anything." He tipped his hat as he helped her onto leveled ground, then headed back to the car. Monique nodded then moved to where Lady stood. The two ladies walked into the hotel lobby, then into the restaurant.

"We are going to have a little lunch. I want you to start without me. I have some business to handle," Monique instructed Lady as she watched her guest head in their direction.

"That is cool with me. I am sooo...hungry." She did a little shimmy at the thought of chowing down.

Lady looked up at the clean-cut men in expensive suits and leather briefcases and her pockets and her pussy tingled at all the money in attendance.

They ascended the staircase and over to the hostess where they were met by three very tall and mouthwatering sexy men dressed in all black.

"Mo, so good to see you." One of the men took her hand into his placing a single kiss on the backside.

"You know when he calls, I come," Monique responded as she watched all the men bow to her greatness.

"You gentlemen take this beautiful lady to the dining area. Get her whatever she wants while I escort Miss Mo to her meeting."

"Yes, sir," two of her most trusted guards turned toward Lady ready to cater to her every need.

"Follow me," the host instructed as he put his hand out to Monique.

"My pleasure." She put her hand on his forearm and was led out to the elevators.

Monique turned to assure Lady was settled in her seat then stepped confidently with her heels tapping against the marble as she sauntered away with wicked intent swirling through her mind. They rode silently watching the numbers rise one by one until they reached the penthouse level. The doors opened and the gentleman stepped out first then waved her to follow him.

He pulled his heat from his waist rested it at his side, then pointed her to the left. "Last door at the end of the hall."

Monique walked past him in the direction, he pointed rocking her hips to her own little beat. She knocked twice, then once, and stood waiting for the door to open. When she heard the locks click, butterflies filled her stomach, and a lump formed in her throat as she tried to steady her breathing. The door cracked, then opened, she looked up at the mean grimace staring down at her, and her heart raised as the moment became evident. Monique flashed him her sexy smile as she stepped inside.

"He's waiting for you in his bedroom," the deep voice boomed as the door closed behind her.

"Thank you," she spoke softly then moved along the hall headed to his room. Monique pushed open the huge wooden door and adjusted her sight as she searched the room for her chocolate treat.

"Don't act scared now. Bring me all of that sexy," the sultry base caressed her eardrum sending heat down her spine.

"I'm not scared of you, sir," she returned the greeting then walked over to where he stood.

"Mo!" He looked down at her like she was going to be his first and last meal. "I missed the shit outta you," Chinkz stated smoothly looking down at Monique's curves in that body fitted, red dress.

"You're going to have to show me," she cooed looking up into his hungry gaze.

"Can't wait to show you." He stood adoring her beauty with his hands' clasps behind his back.

Monique flashed him her thirty-twos then placed her hands behind her back as well. "Business first, sir. Then I'll let you taste, Mo," she spat giving him that low sultry gaze.

"Nah, you gonna sit on my lap and tell me all your wishes. Then I'ma make them come true," he spoke firmly looking down at her perky breasts sitting up at the opening at the top of her dress.

"Where are your clothes, sir?" she asked as her eyes roamed over his chiseled chest and stomach.

"You about to lose your clothes," he teased, then eased his finger over her breasts.

"Somebody is really confident," she purred inhaling the fragrance rising off his smooth skin.

"Very." Chinkz placed two fingers under her chin, tilted her head all the way back, and placed his lips on hers.

"Mmmm..." Monique moaned between rough and tender kisses.

Chinkz gently kissed her top lip then sucked the bottom until his tongue parted her lips. He kissed her deeply taking her thoughts and her breath with every twirl of his tongue. Monique dropped the gift bag along with her purse to the floor and erased her mind. She slipped comfortably into his trance closing her eyes and enjoying the perfection of his kiss while anticipating his hand play, and the precision of his stroke. Chinkz pulled back and took a deep breath as his dick began to harden against the silk of his boxers.

"Is that my money?"

"Is this my dick?" She reached in the slit of his boxers and released the pressure.

"Every inch," he replied as he pulled at the thin straps of her dress until it fell around her ankles. His eyes feasted on all that vintage wine and he was ready to devour sip by sip.

"Behave yourself, sir." She placed her hands on his chest.

"How much time does a man have? Cause' I need to fuck you long," he asked as he flipped his finger up and down her nipples. Chinkz pulled her close and planted gentle kisses on her breasts continuing to heat her body past the point of return.

Monique pulled back, then delivered her final threat, "Don't play with it, tame my beast."

"Turn around." He took her by the arm and bent her over, placing himself right between those soft red cheeks. He moved the lace of her thong to the side and let the head of his dick play between her plump outer lips.

Monique placed a hand on each ankle as she widened her legs. Then braced herself for all that young power that was about to play wildly in her tightness. She wiggled her ass a little, then looked over her shoulder welcoming his heat, passion, and pain.

Chinkz wasted no time with formalities, he got right to work sliding all the way in without warning. He held her ass cheeks apart as he adjusted his stroke. Monique accommodated his efforts by arching her back and rocking her waist as his speed tickled her spot.

"That's what the fuck I'm talking about. Grown ass woman pussy," he grunted pushing in every inch and fucking deep.

Monique placed her palms on the floor, pushed her legs up to his waist, and wrapped her heels around his back.

Chinkz pulled her back and forth into his heat as her pussy drenched him from head to shaft. Monique pushed into his every pull until she felt her legs shake and weaken.

"Nah, Ma, hold that shit right there," he warned as he continued to pound against her G.

Monique rolled her hips pushing all that good pussy at him as he dug deep.

"Yup, fuck a Boss just like that." He tamed that wild cat she was throwing his way.

Monique did just as she was told until she felt his grip tight and let go. She slid slowly up and down his thickness until he gave her all he had, then eased her legs off his waist and planted her stilettos on the floor.

She rose on wobbly legs as the sticky fluid between her pussy lips began to flood her inner thighs. "I thought you planned on fucking me long?" she spoke a little over a whisper.

Chinkz looked at her glistening body, bra half on and half off, nipples hard and staring back at him, his mouth watered as his dick began to harden along his thigh.

"Talk that same shit when I'm done." He rushed up on her taking her into his arms then walked her to what he could only describe as the terror zone.

He grabbed her up under her arms and tossed her up in the king-sized bed, then took his steel into his hand and stroked it to full ability. Monique's breath quickened as she watched him swell. Chinkz climbed up between her silky thighs, snapped the string of her panties, then tore open her bra releasing her pretty pink nipples stiff and ready for his tongue play. He leaned in placing his mouth right on her sweetness. Monique squirmed beneath him as his finger pushed their way inside her.

"Chinkz," she moaned as her body began to heat up.

Chinkz didn't answer he just moved his mouth from one nipple to the other quickening his fingers between her slippery pussy lips. Monique gripped the back of his smooth bald head and helped as his finger tickled her spot.

"Ahhh…." she cried as she felt her kitty contract. She pressed her head into the pillow as her body began giving him what he was asking for.

Chinkz moved a little faster, pressing his thumb on her clit applying more pressure with every moan. When he had her body on total surrender, he slid that thick heat back between her thighs. Slowly easing in, he covered her mouth with his and inhaled her every moan as the kitty gripped tighter with every push. Chinkz stroked as he stared down into her glossy gaze. Monique caressed his smooth, bald head as he dug deeper with every push. Chinkz wrapped himself in all her sexy and fucked to the pace of her slippery lips.

There was more than heat between them it was the danger and murder that lie waiting in the background that coursed through their veins with every thrust. Chinkz flipped Monique from one pleasurable position to the next and then just as he had promised he ended their tryst with Monique on his lap asking him for a very risky favor and him stroking just right while agreeing to all her terms and conditions.

****

Lady looked down at her watch for the tenth time rotating her gaze between the two men ordered to keep her company and the doors impatiently waiting for Monique to return.

"Wow. Did this bitch leave me here?" she mumbled ready to get really disrespectful.

Just as Lady got ready to request for a driver to escort her home, she looked up to see Monique walking toward her dressed in a totally different outfit.

"You ready?" Monique asked approaching the table with a slightly wicked smile on her face.

"I was ready two hours ago," Lady spat as she slid her chair back.

"Ahhh…you must have missed me." Monique ignored the sarcasm replacing it with a bit of her own. "All of this is part of the territory. Next time read the fine print before you sign up." Monique turned her back and headed back to the door.

Lady just shook her head and bit into her bottom lip. She knew her love for Kayson was endless but having to deal with his mother without chocking the shit out of her was beginning to become the nail in the casket. She rubbed her stomach as she exited the restaurant.

"What kind of world am I bringing you into?" she asked afraid of the answer.

Chapter 39

Fear

Miguel's men loaded the trunks of their Lincoln then shook hands with Wise and Aldeen before getting into the vehicle.

"Tell your Boss we said thank you for the hospitality and we will see you in two weeks," the driver said out the window before pulling out of the parking space.

"Will do," Aldeen replied then headed back inside the pool hall.

The men drove along the streets headed to the highway anxious to get the money safely to the drop-off spot.

Chinkz patiently waited for them to pass, then he pulled away from his parked location following a few cars behind. The two unaware men drove on to their fate anxious to make their Boss proud. Chinkz watched as they turned in the direction of the tunnel and he moved a few cars closer placing himself right behind them when they came out on the other side. He was right on their bumper. Chinkz slid down in his seat behind the tinted windows stalking his victims.

The glossy red Lincoln town car pulled over to the far-right lane and exited in Hoboken. When they came to the first light Chinkz pulled his hood down to his eyes and his red bandana up over his nose. He threw on some shades and readied himself for the kill. When the light turned green, he waited for them to get into the intersection, then pressed his breaks and rammed right into the rear of their vehicle. The passenger jumped out of the vehicle and headed right in his direction cussing and flailing his arms.

Chinkz eased the door open and sprung from his seat, arm extended putting three bullets in the angry man's chest. Before the body could hit the ground, he was moving to the driver's side door.

As he approached the window with his Sig Sauer firm in his grip the door pushed open and the driver hopped out with his own heat ready to let loose. Chinkz smacked the man in the mouth with his gun, then unloaded in his head and chest. He stepped back to watch the body connect with the blacktop, then jogged back to his vehicle with the sounds of blaring horns and loud chants of terrorized drivers and onlookers playing in the background.

Chinkz hopped in his car, pushed the gear in reverse, and backed down the street turning into traffic, then sped off leaving rubber tire marks in his place. He pulled down the bandanna and tossed it in the glovebox then removed the hood from his head. He drove on until he was back through the tunnel headed to the peer. When he got to the docks, he pulled over and parked the car on a side street. Chinkz grabbed a bag from the back seat, pulled off his hoodie, tucked it inside, and put on the fresh one from the bag, then he threw on a black fitted cap.

He grabbed the gun from the glove box tucked it in the bag between the hoodie and zipped it closed. As he hopped out of the car, he eyed the street from one end to the other, closed the door, then removed his gloves and hoofed it to the nearest subway, paid his fee, and headed to the Southside. Stage one had begun, the table wasn't just shook he had just turned that muthafucka over.

Chapter 40

Pause

Kayson and Baseem arrived a few minutes apart on the side of the Hudson river right before entering Jersey and dead their engines then hopped out of their trucks and met at the front of their vehicles.

"I don't know what the fuck is going on, but this shit is getting outta hand," Baseem spat looking over at Kayson.

"This shit is fuckin' with all our plans. Who the fuck has the type of power to hit the drop-offs?" Kayson said losing his patience with the treachery.

"I have had my mind on this shit for the last few days and I can't figure this shit out." Baseem stared out at the water.

"We shook down all them niggas, their teams are getting hit left and right like our shit. It just don't add up."

"We still don't have a handle on Harlem?"

"Only that this nigga named Ha'Roo keeps shit organized. He moves silent as hell but don't touch shit and nobody knows his connect."

"Explain."

"He got men between him and the streets. You never see that nigga on the block ever. And he got a shooter on his team handling any opposition. They say that nigga never misses but don't nobody see that nigga or talk to him either," Baseem reported as his mind boggled with the events at hand.

Kayson looked out over the water staring at the lights on the Brooklyn bridge. He tossed a few ideas around, then looked back at Baseem. "These niggas want my rage. Let's give it to them." He put his fist out.

"I'm always ready." Baseem hit fist with Kayson confirming the terror they were about to rain on anyone involved.

****

Real Don't Fold

Pinky and Red led the way into the basement of their townhouse with Tiny and Dee Dee right on their heels. They moved to the two couches in the middle of the room and placed their shopping bags down then plopped down on the couch.

"Make sure that door is locked!" Pinky yelled laying her head back.

Tiny went over to the door and checked all locks, then headed over to where the other ladies sat.

"Thanks, Ma," Pinky said exhaling the long day at the mall as she sat up grabbing her handbag along the way. "Pass me that ashtray, Dee," she requested as she pulled an ounce of Acapulco Gold and a Ziplock of Fronto leaf from the zipper in her bag.

Red grabbed the ashtray and a bottle of sweet red wine and placed them on the table then moved back to the counter and got four glasses and placed one in front of each one of her girls.

"That fucking massage was everything," she announced as she took a seat.

"Bitch I could do that every other day. And that nail lady is the fucking truth," Dee Dee agreed looking at her shiny, red polish.

"Word, I almost gave that bitch some pussy had my feet feeling like heaven."

"You so wicked." Tiny busted out laughing.

"I'm just saying. That bitch is gifted." She laughed along grabbing the bottle by the neck and popping the cork.

"Bitch, pour me a glass. I don't need that negativity in my life." Pinky poured the weed into the leaf then licked it closed.

"Whatever. Judge all you want. I gets mine by any means necessary." She took the glass then put it out for it to be filled.

"I'ma have to ask that nigga to put his dick in your mouth a few more times cause you're confused," she joked putting fire to the end of the blunt.

"That's why I fucks with you. You keep a bitch grounded," Red said as she put her full glass to her lips. "I almost fucked around and ate some pussy. I'ma have to break up with that bitch," she continued causing them to burst into laughter.

The ladies passed the blunts in a circle and sipped at their glasses as they recalled the day. Tiny was in awe with the openness of her girls. Kayson had kept her tucked away and now she was getting the training she needed to benefit the team. She listened to their words and watched their actions. These were the most thorough bitches she had ever met, and she was beaming with pride that she was on a team where women were the heat in the trigger.

"I'm fucked up," Red slurred as she drank the last of what was in her glass. She got up and retrieved another bottle, popped the cork, and filled each glass again.

"You a fucking alcoholic, yo'."

"The bitch ain't stomp on grapes for nothing," she said unzipping her jeans, then taking another swig.

They busted into laughter, then Pinky responded for them all, "Bitch don't be airing your cat in my ally."

"Shiieeetttt…you know good pussy gotta breath." She popped the string on her thong.

"I'm too high, I don't need this shit in my life," Dee Dee said shaking her head.

Tiny sat among them in awe of their relationship. As she laughed a tear came to the corner of her eye. She was silently celebrating because for the first time she had a family.

"Anyway, what's on the agenda for the night?" Pinky asked rising to her feet.

"Ain't shit. I bagged this nigga who looks like the type the boss wants us to lay down," Red responded. "He wants me to bring a few bad bitches for his boys but y'all don't treat a bitch right," she joked.

"What's that nigga name I need some heavy pockets in my life."

"Chinkz or some shit, I gotta check. You know I only count their money. I really don't care what a nigga name is."

"Set it up. Let's get that paper," Pinky said as she put fire to the end of another blunt. She sat back and blew the smoke high into the air counting the money with every deep inhale she took.

****

Pat hopped out of her car and popped the trunk. She breathed in the fresh afternoon air as the sun kissed her golden skin. She grabbed the Sax Fifth Avenue bags, locked the trunk, and hit the alarm. As she walked along the concrete path, she smiled from ear to ear enjoying the victory which set firmly on her palm.

"Good afternoon, Miss Pat," the young girl bellowed as Pat approached the desk.

"Hey, little face. How are things?" Pat asked while signing the visitor book.

"Shieettt…you know how it is. I'm surrounded by crazy muthafuckas. I'm just trying to stay sane," she shot back as she time-stamped the signed sheet.

"That's a fucked up way to exist." Pat chuckled as she turned to the patio doors.

"Not really, I've learned that a crazy mind speaks a truthful heart. It's the lying lips of those who think they are sane that I worry about. Enjoy your visit, lunch is on the way." The wise young lady sat in her chair turning her attention to the computer screen.

Pat's mind replayed her words causing a little friction in her spirit. She quickly tucked her feelings as she arrived at Kisha's door.

Pat knocked a few times, then entered. "Hello? KeKe," she called out closing the door behind her.

"In here, auntie," she confirmed from the bathroom.

"Girl, it is beautiful outside." She placed the bags in the chair, then walked over to the window. "We might want to have lunch on the lawn." She pulled the curtains open, walked over, and began making Kisha's bed.

Kisha emerged from the bathroom, drying her hands, and shaking her head at Pat's weekly routine. "You are going to do this forever, aren't you?" she asked tossing the paper towel in the trash.

"You know this is my favorite part of the week." She fluffed and stacked the pillows, then headed to the kitchen to retrieve some utensils and glasses.

"You look nice," Kisha complimented Pat on her yellow, strapless, baby doll dress which rested sweetly on her caramel skin.

"They had a sick ass sale at the mall. Look in your bags I got you right as usual."

Kisha walked over to her highbacked chair and began sifting through the bags. She pulled out three strapless sundresses red, purple, and one white. She laid them over the back of the chair, then grabbed the three designer track suites accompanied by two pairs of Gucci sneakers and a pair of Gucci slides.

"Okay, I see you." She tucked the items back in the bag, then pulled from the last two bags. Her eyes widened when she opened the Rolex watch box. "Wow," she mumbled as she released it from the small wooden box.

"This is beautiful." Kisha slipped it on her wrist and turned her arm back and forth in the sunlight catching all the diamonds at their best glow.

"You are more than welcome. I wanted to put a smile on your face. Plus, we had a very, very, good week." She reached in her purse and pulled out two thick stacks of crispy one-hundred-dollar bills and placed them on the counter.

"Thank you." Kisha walked over and hugged Pat tight closing her eyes and taking in all the good vibes in the room. Kisha released her from her grip, grabbed the money, then danced over to her seat, placed it in one of the bags, and placed them on the side of the chair as she admired her new bling.

"Did you tell Fred what I told you?"

"Yes," Pat answered as she set the utensils and glass on the table.

Kisha smiled. "What was the look on his face."

"Between the release of the nut and the shock of the hour. That nigga was stone-faced." She busted out laughing. Taking a seat at the table.

"I guess you can confirm the rumors?" Kisha raised her brow.

"Girrlll...that shit is big as hell. If he was fucking me on a regular, I guess I'd be selling pussy and passing in the proceeds, too."

Kisha screamed out in laughter. "I told you. I was with a trick for a drop off one night and she wanted to test Fred out. She pulled out that monster and he gave her the entire business. Bitch sold her pussy and her mama's." Kisha flashed back in time.

"Bitch I might have to get my jaw looked at," Pat continued her comedic run.

"Gave that nigga a jawbreaker." Kisha jerked her hand back and forth to her mouth.

"Fuck around and have a bitch on shakes for a week." Pat laughed along with Kisha. "One thing for certain they are over there scrambling to find out what the fuck just happened."

"Good. We got all these muthafuckas playing to my tune." Kisha turned to look out the window.

Pat sat, giving Kisha all the juicy details until the staff brought lunch to the cabin. As they swallowed down the tender steak, fried rice, and string beans Kisha laid out the rest of the plan for Pat to execute. Pat hung on every word filling her plate with both meals. She was ready to step into the role she always knew should be hers and she was about to put on Kisha's shoes and march her way right to the top.

"Just remember ain't no cross in our blood. We gotta move together all the way."

"Always." Pat put her hand out to Kisha.

Kisha shook her hand, then got up from the table and walked into the bathroom to brush her teeth. Pat opened her bag and began to redo her lipstick then scented her skin with Marc Jacobs. She popped a piece of gum in her mouth then stood and began clearing the table.

"I'll see you this time next Sunday," Kisha stated as she dried her hands on the towel, then laid it across the chair.

"Sure will," Pat responded as she placed the plates on the tray and set them on a cart outside the door.

Kisha walked over to where Pat stood, gave her another big hug, and walked over to her bed. "I'm about to fuck this pillow up." She chuckled as she dove on the bed.

"I know that's right," Pat returned, grabbing the doorknob. "Sleep well." She eased out the door closing it tightly behind her.

Kisha waved as she settled into the huge down pillows. Her eyes began to close and fuzzy feelings filled her body as she pulled the comforter over her weary body.

Pat walked along the path this time with an evil smirk on her lips. When she reached the receptionist's desk. She reached in her bag, slid a small stack in a white envelope to the slick mouth receptionist, and uttered, "Up the meds," she spoke softly as she headed to the exit.

The young lady quickly tucked the envelope under the desk in her purse, then picked up the phone to make the call. Pat stepped tall along the walkway and hopped in her car cranking the music up high. They had made the biggest mistake in the game, handing a winning hand to a scrub ass player.

****

"Ssss…Aldeen," Mercedez moaned as she wrapped her lips around the head of his dick.

351

"Get this nigga right," he mumbled as he worked her jaw in jerk action.

Aldeen reached down and squeezed her nipples and caressed her breasts. Mercedez looked up from her kneeling position and worked his throbbing pole. It had been her fantasy to be in his bed and tonight she was going to make sure she gave him whatever he wanted.

"I want to feel you, Al," she purred taking him deeply into her throat.

"Do you deserve to feel me?" he asked grabbing a handful of her long, curly hair and pushing his dick deeper into her throat.

Mercedez bobbed along with his motions gagging and choking as she tightened her jaws. She eased him partly from her mouth, she answered, "Yesss..." with him still between her lips.

Aldeen looked on with lust-filled eyes as her spit dribble down his length and onto his balls. "Convince me," he responded in his deep raspy voice.

Mercedez cupped and caressed his sack massaging to his pleasure as she rotated sucking each one gently. She jerked and sucked getting his whole dick soaking wet. She fingered her pussy and rubbed her throbbing clit as she enjoyed the pleasure on his face.

Aldeen hissed and mumbled as she sent a strong surge throughout his body and he was ready to slide between her other wet lips.

"Get up," he ordered pulling her up from her kneeling position.

Mercedez opened her legs wide and grabbed his hand. She rubbed his fingers back and forth in her juices as she leaned in to suck his lips.

Aldeen took over and eased two fingers inside her tight hole and slowly pushed them in and out.

"I'm ready to fuck, Daddy," she whispered staring right into his eyes.

"Turn around," he said as he gripped her waist and turned her to face the wall.

He squeezed her ass cheek with one hand and stroked his dick with the other. When he was ready to bust that ass, he positioned her right at the tip of his dick and played between her pussy lips.

"Ssss...don't tease me, Daddy. Get this pussy," she moaned as his hand held her in place preventing her from sliding down his thick pole.

Buzz! Buzz! The sound of his pager vibrating on the table slightly interrupted his flow.

"Shit," he growled as he reached over and grabbed it. Aldeen looked at the code, then over at the cordless. "Hand me the phone," he ordered pushing her toward it.

"Damn," she uttered sucking her teeth as she retrieved the phone.

Aldeen typed in the number then put the phone to his ear. "Hello," he responded as the line opened.

"What's good?" Wise said back then started his spill.

"Moving product. What's on your mind?" Aldeen looked at Mercedez's hard nipples and pouty lips and his dick jumped right back to attention.

"Well, let me put this shit on your mind," Wise began his coded message.

Aldeen listened intensely as he motioned with his finger for her to get back into position, and without hesitation, she turned her back, grabbed his dick, and sat all the way down on it.

"Mmmm..." she purred as she began to work his thickness against her walls. It had been weeks since he touched her, and she just wanted him to fill up every inch of her insides. She gripped his knees, bounced, and gyrated her hips wetting him up with every motion.

The wet pussy sounds filled the room as she picked up the pace. "Slow that shit down," he commanded as he reached around and played with her clit.

Mercedez did as she was told and eased up slow and bounced on just the head.

"Yeah, I'm listening nigga, go 'head," he barked at Wise as he felt his nut rising in his gut.

"Daddy..." she moaned as she too felt ready to release.

Mercedez quickened her pace and circled her hips as she prepared to wet daddy up.

"A'ight got you. See you in an hour," he responded then disconnected the call.

Aldeen stood up, motioning for her to grab her ankles then placed his hands on her hips, pushed his dick deep inside her womb, and fucked her just the way she liked to be fucked hard and stiff.

"Ahhh...baby, I'm cumming!" she screamed as she threw her pussy back at him matching every long hard stroke.

Aldeen obeyed and hit that spot until she screamed and begged him to stop. Caught up in the sticky pleasure wrapped around his dick, he ignored her cries and pounded until his dick drained and went limp. He fell back into the chair and Mercedez stood and turned toward him. She straddled his lap and took a seat. Still, on fire, she kissed and sucked his lips and tongue anxious to get him back inside her.

"You know you gotta use this pussy to bring Daddy what he wants, right?" He palmed her ass and pulled her closer.

"Yesss...what...ever you want," she agreed as she felt him stiffen between her thighs.

Aldeen lifted her then down onto his steel. Mercedez released a soft moan as she received him.

"Anything you want," she purred as she picked up her pace. "Anything you want..." she repeated as she gave him just what he wanted.

Aldeen closed his eyes and plotted his plan. The pussy was both good and dangerous, and he was glad to test the product before he put it on the line.

Chapter 41

Loose Ends

KoKo sat on the edge of the tub and stared blankly at the white stick and two pink lines that now held her fate. She was filled with mixed emotion as she battled with who Ha'Roo was and what it meant to carry his seed. It had been almost ten years since she first laid eyes on him. She placed the stick on the sink, washed her hands, then stared in the mirror as she realizes there was life growing inside her womb. There was way too much danger haunting her and to bring another person into the toxic world she was forced into would be carrying guilt she wasn't sure she could live with.

Each daunting thought tugged at her heart and emotions causing vomit to rise to the back of her throat she tried swallowing, but it reversed sending her rushing to the toilet. KoKo released her breakfast into the porcelain bowl as she wiped the water that ran from her eyes.

When she could finally stand upright, she flushed and steadied her breathing as she staggered back to the sink. KoKo turned on the cold water then ran it over her face, she slowly took in the air while trying to control her now shaking body. She turned off the water and tipped back to her bed and fell into the cool sheets. KoKo grabbed a pillow and pulled it to her chest hugging it tight, she settled into the calming feelings, she closed her eyes knowing exactly what she needed to do.

****

"Once I sign this, it's all in motion?" Monique asked as she signed both her name and Malik's on the dotted line.

"They must be married, and they must have children. Any outside children from either of them will dissolve the contract. All money will default to Malik's other surviving child."

"I understand," Monique said as she stood and straightened her dress, then extended her hand.

Russo stood also and shook her hand sealing their deal. "I will have some paperwork delivered to your home in a few days."

"Thank you. You have always been loyal to Malik. I know he rests well knowing his business is in good hands." She squeezed his palm before releasing him from her grip.

"Just doing my small part." He rested his hands at his side.

"I'll be in touch." She tipped her hat as she turned to leave his office.

Once the door shut, he hit the automatic lock and grabbed a cell phone from his desk drawer. He moved quickly into the adjoining bathroom and closed the door. Frantically he dialed the number he prayed he'd never have to dial, then waited for the person to answer.

"Hello."

"She came to see me. Her hands are dirty," he spat as the revelation of Monique's intent became clearer by the moment.

"Does she know about all the children?"

"I don't think so. When I laid out the conditions of the contract she didn't buck. If she knows she is hiding it well. I'm sure she would have used that card by now."

"Good. Come see me in a few weeks. Let this shit happen."

"Got you. I will be out of the country until then. The fallout from this is going to be catastrophic."

"As it should. They ruined my whole family. I have not held my child since she was almost two years old. They fuckin' owe me!" Kisha yelled into the receiver. She took a few deep breaths before she continued her point. "I will have everything they took from me. My family will eat well, and I will let them pick the bones."

"I can't wait to watch," he confirmed.

"And watch you shall." Kisha laid the phone on its base, then walked over to her bed and tucked herself in the huge comforter pulling it up to her neck. A smile came over her face as she realized for the first time, she had a valuable piece to the puzzle that only she and Malik shared, and she was about to bust Monique's ass in her own trap. "Greasy bitch," she mumbled, then closed her eyes and rested her spirit. Her day was here, and she just needed to sit back and let shit happen.

Chapter 42

Long Kiss. Good Night.

Kayson slid his key card in the suite door and pushed it wide tapping the wall as he entered. He moved inside bags in both hands with Tiny and Pinky marching close behind. He set the bags on the glass dining room table then moved to the kitchen. Baseem and Wise stepped in last locking the door and securing the bolt before heading to the dining room where they placed their bags next to Kayson's. Pinky and Tiny headed to the living room, looked out the huge windows, then put their bags on the coffee table. Pinky plopped down on the couch, took off her backpack, and placed it at her feet. Tiny took the chair just across from them and laid her head back enjoying the first moment of peace.

"Y'all ready to put in this work?" Kayson asked as he walked over to the coffee table and laid down a tray.

"Yes, sir, let's get it. A bitch needs a shower, a meal, and a nap." Pinky sat up pulling at her sleeves until her jacket was off.

Kayson gave her a smirk as he headed back to the kitchen. When he returned, he headed to the dining room with two cash machines.

"Is everything there?" he asked placing the machines on the table.

"We about to find out," Baseem responded as he placed one stack of cash after the other onto the table.

"Roll some shit up. We about to be up in this bitch for a while." Wise chuckled as he pulled the money from his bag, placing it onto the table.

"Just stay focused," Kayson gently warned as he began running the money through the machines. "Put the clean money in the brown leather duffels and put the dirty money in the black duffels."

Pinky pulled out a Ziplock bag full of purple haze, then cracked open five blunts. She filled each one, then licked and sealed them tight. She pulled the lighter from a side pocket, blazed the end, and inhaled deep.

"That's what the fuck I'm talking about. Now a bitch can focus." She blew the thick smoke into the air, then rose to take three blunts to Wise.

"This is why I fucks with you hard." He took them from her, reached inside his pocket, and pulled out his lighter.

"I do what I can," Pinky responded as she continued to inhale on the way back to her seat.

Baseem and Wise put the heat into rotation as they counted and placed them back in the appropriate bags. Pinky and Tiny began cutting up the bricks and bagging them up in delivery order.

"It's dry as fuck up in here feeling all funeral parlorish and shit." She hopped up, grabbing her bag along the way. Pinky reached inside, pulled out an *MC Lyte* CD, and put it in the player. *"Gotta who? Gotta getta what? Gotta get Ruffneck."* She turned the volume up and hit her favorite song, then the beat dropped, her head started bopping as her body moved in sync with the rhythm.

"You are always where the party is," Tiny said as she sang along and shimmed to the music.

Kayson watched her ass pop in those form-fitting, booty shorts as she made her way back to the couch. His eyes rested between her thighs on that fat cat as she rocked and grinded to the music. He ran his tongue over his lips and shook his head as the taste of that sweet peach watered his mouth. He shook it off, then got right back to work. The hours ticked by as they cut the bricks and counted the cash.

Tiny periodically glanced at Kayson who she noticed was keeping a close eye on the money and the bitch that always went and got it, Pinky. It had been weeks since she had been in the boss's bed and she silently prayed her work would be paid off with long deep strokes.

"That's the last one," Baseem said as he wrapped and placed the stack of hundreds in the bag.

"I'm hungry and tired as fuck," Wise said as he stretched his long frame.

"Word. I need a meal, a shower, some neck, and a nap. In that fucking order." He counted his list one finger at a time.

"My nigga. I'm with you when you right." Wise put his fist out.

Baseem tapped his fist on Wise's smiling widely at the thought of all the nasty shit he was about to get into.

"You need anything else?" Wise looked over at Kayson.

"Nah, I'm about to treat myself," he said with a straight face as he rose to his feet.

"Somebody about to be in trouble," Wise joked as he counted the bags.

"Let's get this shit ready for the pick-up." Baseem headed to the stash.

The men followed suit zipping everything closed and placing them near the door.

"We are done as well," Pinky said letting out a loud sigh.

"I'll put them over there, you can take a break," Tiny offered as she got up and began taking the packed bags to the door.

"I'll get this, then I'ma hit the shower real quick and get this shit off me before we roll."

"Cool," Tiny said as a surge rose in her stomach. It was her moment she needed to get close to the boss.

Pinky collected all the utensils and placed them on the tray, then put them back in place. She reached in her bag, pulled out some bleach spray, and wiped everything down. When she was done, she secured her items, then pulled a spare outfit and toiletry bag from her backpack and headed to the bathroom.

"You good, Boss?" Tiny asked as she set the last bag on the cold tile.

"Yeah, I'm good. Thank you for all your help." He pulled her into his arms and squeezed her tightly.

"No thanks needed." She held him close as she inhaled his scent.

Just as Tiny began to rest into his embrace a knock rang out on the door. Kayson released her from his grip, then reached for his heat. "Wait in the living room," he instructed as he turned to Baseem and Wise who also got into position.

After checking the credentials, they eased their weapons. Baseem opened the door letting his street team enter. Tiny walked back to the living room feeling like a deflated balloon as her moment was stolen once again by his loyalty to duty. She plopped down on the couch and gathered her things as she tried to mask her feelings with a slight smile.

"I gotta pee. I'll say my hellos in a minute," Red said as she hurried past the team.

"Where the fuck you get her from yo'?" Wise turned to Baseem.

"I don't know. God be blessing a nigga sometimes." He chuckled as he continued to pass out the work.

"Niggas," Aldeen slurred as he closed and locked the door.

"Glad you made it back safely." Kayson met Aldeen halfway and the two grabbed fists and bumped shoulders.

"Glad to be back," Aldeen responded as he followed suit giving each of his brothers the greeting.

"How was your trip?" Wise asked, then waited to feel his energy.

"It was solid." Aldeen left it at that and turned his energy to Kayson.

"They can begin rolling out," Kayson ordered pointing at the bags.

The men got into action grabbing the duffels and backpacks, then with a few minute's distances between them, they began rolling out.

"Y'all look tired as shit," Red said as she moved between Wise and Baseem.

"And you look like you need to not to be in grown men's business," Baseem shot back as he looked down at all that sexy in a dark red bodysuit.

"Grown men business, huh? I'ma need you to define that for me when I see you again," she shot back looking at him from head to toe stopping for a few seconds to check out that print in his black sweatpants.

"See me again. You see me now. Talk your shit." He rubbed his hands together enjoying her playful banter.

"Sir, I am here on a domestic capacity. I will have to rain check this small work." She again looked him up and down.

"Kay, let Tiny roll with the boys. I need to hold onto this one for a minute," he said not taking his eyes off Red.

"This nigga," Kayson responded as he watched the handoff of the last two bags.

"Heyyy…my love," Pinky sang out as she walked through the living room headed in Red's direction.

"Heyyy…Poo, I missed you. I see they been putting a bitch on the stroll?" she joked as she looked at what was leaving the building.

"You know how it is when a real nigga gotta secure the bag."

"Hell yeah, he came to get a real bitch," Red finished her sentence as the ladies slapped hands mid-air.

Pinky and Red sat down and caught each other up as the men did the same just inches away from them. Tiny sat anxious in her seat as she watched the dynamic of the room change.

"Tiny," Kayson called out jolting her from her reverie.

"Yes." She turned in his direction.

"Let me holla at you." He walked over to the kitchen.

Tiny got up from her chair and walked over to where he stood, her stomach did flip flops with every step.

"Kay, I ordered some shit to eat. It will be up here in about thirty minutes!" Pinky yelled, then went back into her conversation.

The last bags left the room as the food entered. Aldeen took the tray and set it on the dining table, then headed back to where Kayson stood.

Kayson didn't respond to Pinky as he turned to Aldeen. "Report." He went right to business.

"All pickups were made. Once these drop-offs are complete the team are going to tuck in and just watch the action."

"Who is making the run down to D.C.?"

"Ebony ol' girl from Jersey."

"Can she handle that by herself?" Kayson's brow ruffled as he thought of a female alone on the road.

"Yeah, she got it, that's the one that rides with them three big ass rottweilers and that .38 in the glove box. She good." He chuckled. "Plus, when she hits the city line, we have a crew that will trail her until she is out of the city."

"Make sure of it." Kayson held a firm gaze as he passed out his order.

"Done."

"Anything else."

"Not right now. I'll sit down with you when we get back." Aldeen leaned in, shook his hand, and bump his shoulder, then turned to exit.

"Tiny, I need you to go with Al," he passed out his orders, then turned his attention back to Aldeen. "Y'all handle this shit. See you in the am." They bumped fists.

"I got you," Aldeen confirmed. "Come on lil' mama." He nodded his head toward the door.

"You good?" he asked, looking down into her pretty brown eyes.

"Always." Tiny picked her heart up off the floor. She struggled to keep it together as she headed to do what she did best, get the boss his money.

"Let's go handle this work." Aldeen squeezed her arm reassuring her it was all good.

Tiny nodded her understanding, she was in her feelings but tucked that shit and threw on her gangsta. She knew one thing for sure, having them muthafuckas on your sleeve in the field could earn you a grave badge.

Kayson followed them to the door, then closed and locked it behind them. He headed back to the living room with a strong mission on his mind. He needed to work off some tension between Pinky's tight, slippery walls.

"You straight?" he asked looking down at all that ass poking out at him through the thin material she called a dress.

"Yeah, I'm straight," Pinky responded as she straightened the kitchen and placed all food to the side. "All you have to do is heat this up and y'all should be good to go." She moved from one side to the other.

"Can I heat this up?" He grabbed her ass in his hand, stopping her in her tracks.

"I think the boss has plenty to heat up." She gently moved his hand while staring back at him through her low glossy eyes.

"Is that right?" He shot her that sexy grin.

"Yes, it's right." She twisted her lips trying to force a little attitude.

"You are so sexy."

"Oh, am I?" She pouted.

"Let me holla at you." He put his hands on her waist and placed her on the counter, then stepped between her legs.

"Y'all niggas foul. Why you ain't order me anything to eat?" Red yelled over to Kayson and Pinky.

"Your sister about to feed me. You should ask Bas to put something in your mouth," Kayson spoke slick as he watched Red straddle Baseem's lap placing the blunt backward in her mouth.

"That's what type of shit y'all on?" she asked, as she blew thick smoke into Baseem's mouth.

"Kay, they don't want this smoke," Baseem spat blowing high into the air.

"Talk your shit," Red responded as she grinded to the music.

Baseem sat back and watched the show as she popped that fat cat back against his now rising dick.

Kayson was tied up with some work of his own as he played between Pinky's thighs. Pinky moved Kayson's hands each time he slid them on the side of her thong.

"Stop it," she mouthed as her eyes opened wide.

"Shhhh…" Kayson put his finger up to his lips as he slipped his hand past the lace, then pushed deep inside her.

"Kay don't," she again whispered placing her hand on his as he began to move his finger against her spot.

"Shhh…let this shit happen," he mouthed back as he stared into her eyes. "Cum for me." He picked up a little speed. He put his hand at the small of her back and went to work.

Pinky braced her hands on the counter and just let the boss have what he wanted. Kayson leaned in and bit into her neck as he felt her juices flowing between her lips.

Red watched as Kayson set Pinky's body on fire. She pulled hard on the haze. As the smoke left her mouth, she put her lips on Baseem's, sucked his tongue, and grinded against him while she watched Pinky's body submit to Kayson's power.

Kayson let Pinky recover as he pulled the string of his sweatpants and released the beast. He eased her to the edge and slowly pushed between her gripping walls.

"Ssss…Kay, not here," she panted, trying to slide back.

"I'm only in control of how my pussy gets wet," Kayson slurred as he pulled her into his push. The Enforcer wanted his treat and he wanted it now.

Pinky reached over and grabbed the remote turning the volume up high as Kayson slowly stroked to her pleasure. She dropped it on the counter, then wrapped her hands around his head.

"Cum on this dick," he mouthed as he pulled her back and forth along his steel.

Red was on fire as she watched the show. She had been in the house with Pinky many times hearing through the walls how good the boss's dick was but to see him fucking her good only feet away had her body filled with so much heat she felt as if she would explode.

"I need to feel you," Red whispered in Baseem's ear.

"Lift up," Baseem slurred as he pulled at her jeans.

Red leaned back as he pulled them off her feet, then her panties. Baseem stared down at her fat, pink lips, and of course, he had to bless her. He pulled her pussy up to his mouth, placed her clit between his lips, and gave her a quick fit.

It was now Kayson's turn to watch a show. Red put her hands on Baseem's knees and fed him his pussy as she winded her waist into his face. Kayson put his arms under Pinky's legs, lifted her from the counter, and pulled her up and down his length as she wiggled and came each time the Enforcer asked for it.

Red released sticky heat all over Baseem's mouth as she watched Kayson's dick slid in and out of Pinky's pussy, thick and slippery as he too stared down at the same pretty sight enjoying the wet view.

Baseem pulled his shirt over his head wiped his face then tossed it on the chair and unzipped his jeans. He released the one-eyed monster from his cage, then pulled her onto the head and eased her down slow. Red positioned her feet into the cushion and bounced her ass as she gripped her kitty around him. She put her hands on the back of the couch and rocked until he was deep, then rode the pole as she watched Kayson walk and fuck Pinky from one end of the kitchen to the next.

"Take me in the room, I need you deep in your pussy," Pinky moaned as she again rained all over him.

"I can have it any way I want it?" he continued to stroke.

"Pleaseeee...." she purred as she bit into that sweet spot at the base of his throat.

Kayson's knees weakened and he gripped her ass in both hands as she gyrated her pelvis, squeezing tightly around the Enforcer. "You tryna get fucked."

"In every position, you can get me in." She began riding up and down as he headed to the back bedroom.

"Don't run," he teased with a wicked grin.

"I won't." She rode and moaned as he pushed deeper.

"Punch in, nigga. It's boss hour," Kayson said to Baseem as he walked out of the room with Pinky tightly wrapped to his waist.

Baseem stood up, turned Red around, bent her over the couch, and positioned himself right between her cheeks. Red arched her back as he spread her cheeks wide. "You heard the boss. Clock in," Baseem growled and parted her lips with something thick.

Red rocked back as he pulled her faster and faster along his length. Kayson had given the order and they were about to show no mercy.

Chapter 43

Dark Hearted

Kayson opened his truck door, tucked his gun, and headed toward the back entrance of the club. He slipped the bouncer a few hundreds, moved past the small crowd surrounding the door, and headed to the booth he booked in the far dark corner. A waitress walked over to him, took his order, then promptly returned with his shot of Bourbon. He leaned back and stalked the area waiting for his opportunity. The music bumped hard in the background as the bodies moved in sync rubbing together in a sea of heat and passion putting in place future contracts to rub skin-on-skin. Kayson moved through the crowd searching for the right spot to post up and watch his mark. A waitress approached him offering a drink.

Kayson declined, then leaned in and whispered in her ear, "I can hear that pussy purring."

She giggled shyly as she listened to the venom ooze from Kayson's lips.

"You are dangerous, sir. Let me know if you need anything." She rubbed her hand over his shoulder, then moved off back through the crowd.

Kayson just watched all that ass switch off in those tiny, black shorts and thin tee then took note of the woman's energy and cataloged it if needed for a future endeavor. He posted up against the wall in a shadow and just watched as the club filled what seemed to be way past capacity. Kayson watched all the movement as he searched for his target. The music pumped loudly causing big bodies to sway and bounce. He played eye contact with a few women until his eyes set on a back corner of the room where his target had just left a space open allowing him a better sight on the prey and laid low.

****

KoKo pulled up at the end of the block, tipped her driver, then stepped hard along the concrete blocks to her destination with five-hundred thoughts clouding her mind. There was an enemy they had yet to discover and all she needed was a small window with a peek at who the trader was and her gun would show no mercy. She ticked on plotting her plan. When KoKo reached the parking lot across from the club she eased between the sea of cars until she reached the entrance.

"Oh, shit, that's you KoKo?" the tall security guard asked as he reached out to unlatch the velvet rope.

"It's not another bitch alive you can confuse me with," she responded as she put her hands to the side.

"Talk that shit, ma." He smiled at her cocky attitude as he moved the security wand along her body. "Go ahead, you, good." He waved her by ignoring the beeping near her waist.

KoKo dropped her arms and walked through the doors trying to adjust her vision between the flashing lights. The club was not her thing, but she had to admit the music was hitting her soul. She walked over to the bar, ordered a tall Guinness, and took it to her lips. As she walked through the sea of hips and ass popping, her mood went from fun to what the fuck in five seconds flat. KoKo stood bopping and searching the room for the nigga her informant had told her about. She set her eyes on a VIP section over by the stage and zoomed in to see who was in attendance. Her eyes adjusted to a low squint.

Ha'Roo unaware of the two sets of stalking eyes on him conducted his business as usual. The woman on his lap was playing her role as well. She jiggled and danced against his dick as the guests in the section cheered and popped bottles celebrating the night. Ha'Roo placed his hands on her hips holding her place as he leaned in and whispered in her ear.

KoKo slid past security and moved calculated through the crowd. She stopped briefly to talk to a few guys in attendance, then kept on to the bar. She posted up near the bar and laid low watching the scene. As her eyes rolled back past the DJ booth she froze when she looked up and saw Ha'Roo in a far corner with a bitch on his lap. Her blood began to boil as the woman touched and kissed his face. She tightened her fists and her teeth clenched together.

Ha'Roo confident in his surroundings touched and tasted a few things himself. KoKo's body flooded with emotion, she began to slowly move toward her unexpecting victims. Before KoKo reached the end of the bar she grabbed a tall Guinness bottle and tightened her grip around the handle. The voice of *Wu-Tang Clan's C.R.E.A.M*, blared through the speakers as she closed the space between them. *Only way, I begin to G off was drug loot. And let's start it like this son, rollin' with this one. And that one, pullin' out gats for fun, but it was just a dream for the teen, who was a fiend. Started smokin' woolas at sixteen.*

Just as she stepped out of the shadows, Ha'Roo looked up to see her hand raised, his eyes widened when he saw the glass figure crash into the side of the woman's face. She flew to the floor and Ha'Roo jumped up to grab KoKo's hand before she went to work on her.

"Get the fuck off me!" KoKo barked as security rushed over to where they were.

"Cut it the fuck out before you start some shit we don't need."

"Fuck you." She snatched her arm away, then headed to the exit over by the bar.

Ha'Roo followed closely behind her while his team helped the woman out of the front of the club and into a truck just by the exit.

KoKo moved through the crowd with Ha'Roo behind her copping his plea.

371

"Come the fuck on, KoKo! You know these bitches gotta handle shit for me," he said grabbing her arm and turning her to face him.

"I don't give a fuck if these bitches are sucking your dick every night at nine on prime time."

"You saw me trying to get her up."

"Well, if you hurry you can still help her. Cause your bitch on the ground," KoKo hurled back as she kept moving to the exit.

Kayson sat back in the booth eyeing the interaction. He moved his head from side-to-side to see the woman who was causing his target so much attention, but the crowd moved in front of his view.

When security headed in their direction, he pushed his hood down over his eyes and eased toward to front door.

KoKo stormed out the side door and into the parking lot with Ha'Roo pushing through the crowd close on her heels. He sped up catching her just before she put too much distance between them.

"Where the fuck you goin'?" Ha'Roo grabbed her arm turning her body to face him.

"Get the fuck off me." KoKo snatched away from his firm grip and stepped back with her fist balled up tight. "Don't fucking touch me," she said choking back the tears.

"I'm not fucking letting you walk off into the fucking night." He moved closer to her.

"You ain't got no fucking choice," KoKo huffed in and out as she tried to catch her composure. She was ready to slap her steel across his face.

The two of them stood locked in place with unwavering eyes and heated hearts ready to explode.

Shakka and Lex ran up behind Ha'Roo with five hundred questions wanting to calm their heated exchange.

"We need to get up outta here," Shakka said as he moved toward the truck.

"You ready?"

"Hold up," Ha'Roo responded, then turned his attention back to KoKo. "I need you to come with me." He slightly adjusted his attitude.

KoKo stood with her bloody fist clutched tightly while trying to contain herself. She was done with all the emotions Ha'Roo had been taking her through and today she had vowed to reverse this shit.

"Nah, I'm good. Always have been. Go find out what them bitches is doing." She turned and began jogging through the parked cars until she got to the exit, then she took off running dashing in and out of traffic until she hit an alleyway, she tucked herself in a corner.

"KoKo. KoKo!" he yelled as he rotated his attention between watching her and the blue flashing lights approaching the club. He walked over to Shakka's car jumped in and slammed the door closed. "Drive around the block," he ordered.

KoKo stayed put until she saw a few cars go by. "You wanna play muthafucka. Let's play," she growled through clenched teeth.

After she thought the dust had settled, she tossed her hood over her head and ducked through the streets. Love, she tucked it. Hate, she fueled it. Fear, she instilled it. From this day forward there was an iceberg in the place of her heart.

****

Night sat patiently in the cut watching as the figure of KoKo dipped off into the darkness.

Kayson opened the car door and hopped inside. "Did you see that shit? Ol' boy got bitches holding him up in the parking lot," he said scanning the parking lot.

"Yeah, I saw it. Homie got a lot of shit going on." His mind played out the next move. "We need to ride on these niggas before they wake up."

"Nah, we gonna be patient and ride this wave. We gonna move all our shit around and tuck in, the way they movin' they

373

gonna fuck around and kill each other." Kayson made his orders clear.

"Copy," Night responded as he backed out of the parking spot.

The two men rode off with a whole new perspective of the opposition and they were about to deal with it accordingly.

****

KoKo was fuming, and before she knew it, she had walked clear across town. She was ready to put hands and bullets on the first person who gave her a reason. She dug in her pocket and pulled a twenty sack out, sniffed it, then pushed it back down deep. KoKo scanned the area for a corner store, then headed in its direction. Just when KoKo thought the universe was fucking with her, she turned the corner and was rewarded with the target she needed. KoKo ducked behind a big tree and watched the woman with the animated gestures explain her plight.

"Yo,' I had to get the fuck up outta there. When I was leaving, I heard shots ring out. I didn't even turn around, niggas started pushing and running I got the fuck outta there."

"Shooting? Who the fuck started shooting?"

"I don't fucking know," she panted as she tried to recall what she heard. "I can't say, but it didn't sound like love was in the air." She tried to lighten the mood.

"You good, though?" The man looked her over and his eyes settled on her forehead.

"Yeah, I'm good, we just gotta be careful," she said as the severity of the situation sunk in.

"Damn. This shit is fucked up." He sat thinking for a few seconds. "Go ahead and get to the spot I'ma ride around and see what's going on."

"Okay. Let me run in this store and get some shit. See you at the spot." She put her fist out to his.

Aldeen knocked fist with hers, then eased away from the curb. KoKo read off the plate and yes it was that nigga and yes that was the bitch feeding him information. She waited for Mercedez to disappear into the store, then moved swift to the door entering right behind her.

Mercedez looked over the chips, grabbed a bag of hot fries and a Pepsi before heading to the register. She placed her items on the counter ready to pay and go when she felt the heat coming her way from her left side.

She turned and looked over at KoKo and rolled her eyes. "Da fuck wrong with this bitch?" she mumbled, then reached in her pocket.

KoKo's body began to heat up, conversation level had passed it was time for that work. She reached around her back and gripped her gun, she was ready to let go of some hot shit but the smug ass look on her face said she needed some footwork. She pulled out and rested it at her side, then headed right to where Mercedez was standing.

"Do you fucking know me?" Mercedez spat as she locked eyes with the very bitch she had been warned about.

"Nah, bitch you don't know me but you about to." She set her gun on the counter. "Here, Papi, hold this I'ma give this bitch these paws".

"Bitc..." was all Mercedez could get out of her mouth before her head snapped back.

KoKo hit Mercedez again busting her top lip. "Yeah, bitch let's fuckin' go." KoKo stepped back in her boxing stance ready to give this grimy bitch some hand and footwork.

"Yeah, let's go." Mercedez wiped the blood from her lip and squared up.

KoKo didn't give her a chance to swing first, she took the show right to the theater. She threw jab after jab connecting face shots with every punch. Mercedez didn't hesitate to return the heat she exchanged punches landing a few in between the many that were snapping her neck back. KoKo served her that work until she saw Mercedez getting drunk on her feet she charged her, grabbing her in the collar, then slammed her on the ice cream freezer. She grabbed her hair and banged her head on the glass causing it to shatter beneath her.

Mercedez felt the glass pushing into her scalp, she struggled to hold her balance as KoKo tried to force her head through the door. Mercedez kneed KoKo in the stomach only causing more fury. KoKo rained fists down on her until she saw the blood pouring from her nostrils and above her left eye. She picked her up and slammed her to the floor. Mercedez scrambled backward as KoKo's foot connected with her face when KoKo reached in her bra and pulled out her blade Mercedez slid over to the potato chip rack and pulled herself to her feet.

She lifted her hands trying to focus through the thick paste running down her face just as she cleared her vision the fright of KoKo coming at her with the sharp object paralyzed her in place. KoKo grabbed her throat with one hand and went to work with the other. Mercedez screamed as she swung her arms to stop the blade. KoKo forced her backward to the door punching and slicing with every hit. The force of both of their weight against the glass caused them to crash through it and onto the ground. KoKo straddled her chest, dropped the blade, put her hands around Mercedez's throat, and squeezed with malice intent until she heard her gurgle and cough on her blood, spit bubbled on her lips as she tried to scream.

KoKo blacked out as she tightened her grip. Mercedez grabbed at KoKo's hands. KoKo released one hand long enough to grab her blade. Mercedez's horror peered back at her through the bloody slits as KoKo brought her arm toward her.

"Yeah, bitch, run your mouth through this hole." KoKo slit her throat with one hard swipe pushing the blade deeper as she raked it through flesh and bone.

Mercedez's hands clawed at her neck as she felt her life seep between her fingers. She gurgled and choked struggling to bring air into her lungs as they filled with fluid.

KoKo stood staring down at her victim as venom fueled her rage, she was ready to stomp her into the pavement. She pulled her foot up prepared to print that Timberland sign in the middle of her forehead.

"KoKo!" The voice snapped her back, her foot crashed inches from Mercedez's temple. "You gotta go. Here." Papi shoved her gun in her waist, then whistled for his brother to bring around the car.

Sirens blared in the distance as he snatched open the car door and put KoKo in the back seat. "You are bleeding, mami." He looked down at KoKo's lap.

"Shit." She looked down at the flood between her legs. "Take me to the hospital," she panted as sharp pains began to pinch her gut.

****

KoKo opened and closed her eyes as the bright lights of the emergency room ceiling pierced her vision, severe pain cut into her stomach as the gurney rushed through the halls and big doors. They pulled her into a room and began undressing and probing at her stomach, she winced in pain as the nurses pressed on different sides of her abdomen.

"Ma'am, what happened? Have you been attacked?" The senior nurse asked as she looked at the blood flowing between KoKo's thighs.

"I'm pregnant," she whispered as the fever in her body began to take hold.

"Ma'am, if we can save your baby do you want us to try?"

KoKo shifted in and out of consciousness as the reality of the hour at hand sunk into her soul. Were her prayers answered or had she condemned her child to hell. "Yes, please save my baby," she moaned as she felt a prick in her arm. The liquid coursed through her veins and before she could fight the wave that was taking her away, her eyes fluttered and closed.

Chapter 44

Bend Don't Break

Red and Pinky's car doors were opened for them and they stepped out onto the concrete staring at all the people waiting in line to enter the club. Red was true to her name dressed in a bright red, strapless, body dress rested right at her thighs, with red hair and Red Bottoms to match. Pinky held to her post as well in a Hot pink bodysuit with a low back. All eyes were on them as they adjusted their clothes and their attitudes.

"Let's give these bitches fever," Red said to her sister taking the lead walking to the door.

"You already know."

Tiny and Dee Dee stepped out of the back seat shooting hot stares from the chicks waiting to enter a place they already had access to. They strutted past the gawking eyes walking right up behind Pinky and Red, leaned in, and gave their names and party that was expecting them. After security checked the guests' list the velvet rope was removed allowing them access to the venue.

The ladies came through the door like they owned the place patterning their sexy strut with the loud music.

"This shit is lit!" Dee Dee yelled over the music, then adjusted her perky C cups in her form-fitting, black leather mini dress.

Tiny was like a kid at Disney World, her eyes bounced from one area to the next, then over at the stage where women were twisting their half-naked bodies around the shiny gold poles.

Pinky's eyes went to a low squint as they walked into the flashing and strobe light effects. Red scanned the VIP sections for her Chinky eyed friend and his crew. Just as they began to move through the crowd, she felt a hand touch her shoulder. When she looked up, there he was with those sexy eyes and a soft, pouty lip smile.

"Y'all ready?" he asked looking down at all that sexy wrapped in a pretty Red bow.

Red nodded slowly, then grabbed his arm as he led the way. Pinky did a little dance as she sauntered behind them ready to turn up and add some new niggas to her roster. Dee Dee and Tiny walked as if the runway were calling their names. When they reached a VIP section next to the stage, they were directed to some empty seats and their glasses were filled with Champagne. They sat sipping and bouncing to the beat as they scouted the club for all the right marks. Red took a seat on Chinkz's lap giving him the opportunity to feel all that soft booty gyrating against his thighs.

Chinkz gripped her hips enjoying every movement of her hips. He nibbled the middle of her back as she gave him the energy he was looking for. Pinky and Dee Dee mingled with the guys in his section as they danced to the music blaring from the speaker only inches away from them. One of the guys stood up and waved over a waitress, who took his order, then returned minutes later with three other girls carrying a bottle in each hand. When the drinks hit the table, the night began to progress fast from there, blunts and brown liquor cyphered from one end of the section to the other as they moved in sync with every song.

"Yessss...bitch, yesssss..." Pinky yelled as she watched her sister put the heat on Chinkz.

Tiny carefully looked on as her crew whispered in these niggas ears while spending their money and enjoying all the party favors. Her eyes shot open when the music dropped, and *Wu-Tang Clan* hit the stage with their hit song *'Protect Your Neck'*. She stood up waving her hands and singing along when it got to her favorite part. She sang loudly matching every word as if she wrote it, "I

380

smoke on the mic like smoking Joe Frazier! The hell-raiser, raising hell with the flavor!" She was in her glory. She watched her favorite member *Method Man* do his thing. "This my shit!" She turned to Pinky with the biggest smile on her face.

Pinky smiled back loving that Tiny was coming out of her shell. She watched her team enjoying themselves and for once everything felt like it was lining up. She kept her eyes on this new nigga and his team as they entertained her crew. She watched like an overprotective mother ready to get busy if shit got nasty. After Wu-Tang left the stage there was a special guest performance from a new group called *Mobb Deep*.

Once the live entertainment stopped, they shared a few more bottles, then Chinkz and his boys summoned the bill paid up and escorted the ladies out of the club strutting by all the gawking eyes, they smiled and switched to the beat giving them hos fever as they went by. When they stepped into the crisp summer air, they scanned the parking lot for their cars with the men close behind them.

"Damn that shit was lit," Red said to Chinkz looking up into his sexy gaze.

"I wanted you and your little crew to have a good time," he teased back staring down at her.

"*Little crew?* Don't hate on bad bitches it'll make your dick shrink," Red replied crossing her arms over her chest.

"That you are," he agreed as his eyes roamed over her frame. "And you ain't gotta worry about him." He grabbed a hand full of that pipe. "He only shrinks after he spits."

"Pop ya shit playa," she joked as they proceeded to the car.

"Let's enjoy the rest of the night," he said deviously as he envisioned all that ass smacking his thighs.

They walked toward the vehicles and just as the men pulled the doors open for them to get in, bullets ripped through the night air hitting Chinkz, then Red. A few more moved through the steel of the vehicle door striking three of his boys and putting one in Pinky's leg. Tiny and Dee Dee hit the pavement trying to seek cover but were both struck as they screamed and slithered along

381

the pavement. The figure moved low behind vehicles angling just right and filling their bodies with hot lead.

Chinkz pulled his gun from his waist and shot in the direction of the heat hitting only glass and metal, several shots came back in his direction. He slid down the side of Pinky's car with his hand on the hole in his stomach. He pushed at his organs like he was trying to put them back in as blood seeped through the cracks of his fingers. Chinkz sat growing in pain as he attempted to slide to the back of the vehicle. His heart raced as he watched his reaper get closer to where he lay. Blood trickled from the sides of his mouth as he struggled to get to a safer place. The sounds of screams and feet scattering in the background played along with the agony of his guests and friends.

"You should have stayed out of family business. Hell awaits you." The final shot robbed his lungs of all breath as the bullet ate through his throat. As he took his last breath his mind played the horror of the night and the look in his attacker's eyes.

Chinkz gurgled on his blood as he tried to speak his final words. Just as the breath left his body so did his soul as his assassin's bullet entered the front of his head blowing the back into the side of the car. The killer tucked the gun and walked off into the night with screams of terror cascading in the background.

Security ran to where they all lay scurrying from one body to the next. They applied pressure to the open wounds as they awaited emergency services.

"Just hang in there!" the man standing over Pinky yelled as he watched blood ooze from her side.

"Nooooooo…" Dee Dee yelled as she cradled Tiny's bullet-riddled body against hers.

Tiny held her hand to her neck trying to stop the leaking. Dee Dee put her hand over Tiny's applying as much pressure as her weary body could muster.

"Please help us!" Dee Dee screamed from the bottom of her stomach.

Red drug her body over the black gravel trying to get to her sister. She winced in pain as the earth beneath her dug into her bloody wounds. She reached her hand out grabbing Pinky by the ankle just as the sounds of sirens drowned out the screams. She looked at her sister's lifeless body as the men pumped on her chest and breathed into her mouth. Tears streamed down her face as she gripped tighter to the only person she had in the world. She said a silent prayer hoping the things they had done would not clog the ears of God and instead grant them the mercy they showed their victims.

Chaos erupted as several EMS and police vehicles pulled to the scene hustling around them and asking questions to whoever could fill in the blanks. Red just laid her head on the cold ground and closed her eyes again and prayed but this time it was that none of this was real.

****

Lady pulled up to Monique's house, grabbed her purse and a few grocery bags from the back seat, and headed up the steps. She became winded as she approached the door stopping to sit down before she rang the bell. She was just catching her breath when she heard the locks click, she looked up to see Monique popping her head out of the front door.

"You okay?" she asked as she walked over to where Lady sat.

"Yeah, I'm good, just got a little winded. This baby is taking up space these days." She chuckled.

"Oh, yes, I remember those days. Let me get one of these bags." She reached down and grabbed one of the brown paper bags, then headed back into the house.

Lady stood up, picked up the other bag and her purse, and followed behind Monique closing the door behind her. "It smells so good in here," Lady said as she took in all the aromas coming from the kitchen.

"Just a little something I put together," Monique stated humbly as she washed her hands and grabbed a spoon from the holder to stir the sauce.

"Where do you want me to put this?" Lady asked as she looked around the kitchen.

"You can put that right in the counter over there she pointed to the right.

Lady sat the bag down, then reached into her handbag and grabbed the small jewelry box Kayson had given her.

"Here drink something, relax for a minute." Monique handed her a glass of cold water.

"Thank you." Lady took a few sips, then handed Monique the small jewelry box Kayson had given her.

"Awww…my son is so special," she cooed as she took the gift into her hands. She opened the box and her mouth fell open with it. "Wow," she said as the diamonds smiled back at her. "Here help me put this on." She handed Lady the box.

Lady walked over to where she stood, took the Ruby and Diamond bracelet from the case, and fastened it to her tiny wrist. "This is beautiful," Lady said impressed with the bling Kayson had adorned his mother with.

"Yes, I will always be his number one." Monique turned her wrist from side to side adoring her precious gems.

"Well, you may have to share that spot." She smiled rubbing her belly.

"That's the difference between me and you sweetie." She looked her right in the eyes. "My spot will always be sold. I'm the only one he will never replace." She now smiled.

The phone rang just as the conversation was heating past no return.

"Excuse me, Mrs. Wells. You have a very important call." Her assistant came to the door with a cordless phone.

"Thank you." She took the phone then walked out of the room.

"Fucking bitch," Lady mumbled as she sat heated, fighting hard to hold back the heat coursing through her body. She swallowed the bile that was rising in her throat as she tried to breathe through all the emotions. She wanted to get up and run out of the room, but her body would not allow her to move from

384

the spot it was planted in. When Monique returned to the room, she was just settling her soul and ready to speak her mind.

"My driver will take you home I have to go," Monique announced with her clutch tucked under her arm and a mission firm in her mind. She turned and walked out of the room not waiting for Lady to respond.

Lady let out the air she was holding in her lungs, then reached over and grabbed her Chanel and rose to her feet. By the time she got down the steps a car was waiting with the door open. She walked down the steps and got into the back seat, then she let all the emotions go. Tears streamed down her face as she replayed the disgusting words that left Mo's lips. They say the truth hurts but in this case the truth kills. The truth had just killed everything she liked about Monique and some of what she loved about Kayson.

Sharp pains lit her abdomen as she digested Monique's silent threats. Lady rubbed her belly as the driver zipped through the streets. She closed her eyes and tried to relax as the pain increased. The driver pulled up to the gate and Lady opened her eyes long enough to punch in her code. When she eased in front of the mansion her head was spinning, the door opened, and the fresh air offered a small amount of relief just enough for her to gather herself and step out.

"You okay, ma'am?"

"Yes, I got it," she forced a response, then walked up the steps.

Lady gripped the doorknob while turning the key in the lock she felt a sharp stabbing pain at the bottom of her stomach. Her knees began to buckle and weaken with each feeble movement. She opened the door wide, then closed it and slowly walked toward the living room as she gripped the bottom of her stomach. She fell onto the couch and hugged her belly, trying to stay awake through the severe pain stabbing her gut.

"Oh, my God. No, please no," she cried as she reached over to the end table grabbing the phone with what felt like the last strength she had. Lady dialed 911 and put the phone to her ear.

"Hello, I need help," she mumbled as she tried to control her breathing. Her mind raced as the woman on the other end asked her one question after the next. She moaned out the address, then closed her eyes as her body began to shake in pain.

Lady's head began to spin as the room seemed to go with it. She leaned forward violently vomiting all over the side of the couch. She fell to her knees causing the phone to slide across the floor, she crawled back to the door to unlock it.

****

Kayson pulled into the visitor parking and found a spot in the back of the lot. Battled with his emotions as he turned off the engine and popped the locks. He stepped out into the summer heat hoofing quickly to the hospital entrance. He walked through the doors and up to the directory when he found the floors, he wanted to hit he located the elevators and moved toward security.

"May I help you, sir?" the officer asked as he approached,

"Headed to the cafeteria."

"Do you have ID?"

"Indeed." He reached for his wallet and pulled out his license.

"Keith Brown," The man read off the words, then looked up at Kayson's face. "Take the elevator over there." He held out the ID keeping his gaze on him.

"Thanks." Kayson held eye contact as he took the card from his hands.

"Have a nice day, Mr. Brown," the man spat with a smirk dressing his lips.

Kayson didn't respond he just turned to the elevators and kept it pushing.

As the silver box rode from one floor to the next a sinking feeling filled Kayson's belly as he thought about the gravity of the situation he was about to walk into. He held his breath between floors as he battled with the words he would need to say to make any part of this tragedy painless. He walked out of the elevator just as the doors parted and headed to the waiting area at the far end of the hallway. Kayson pushed the double doors open then scanned the room for his boy.

Baseem stood up and headed in his direction. The men met over by the patio door then stepped out closing the door behind them.

"What's the temperature?" Kayson asked as he looked out over the sea of cars in the parking lot.

"That shit is intense. Lady is empty. I sent Dee up there with some flowers and bears and shit to her and Red. That's all I could do at the moment. Their family been coming and going I just keep one man on a four-hour-shift, I'll do whatever you suggest next." Baseem stood rubbing one hand in the other.

"I'll get with you when I come out of here," Kayson spoke from an injured soul.

"Cool. I'll be out here on watch."

Kayson again didn't respond, he just walked back inside battling with the pain and loss coursing hot through his veins.

****

Maternity Ward 7ᵗʰ Floor: 7:00 pm

Kayson walked along the corridor taking one heavy step after the other. He scanned the doors until he came to room 725. He took a deep breath, then knocked twice as he pushed the door open. He looked over at Lady who was blankly staring at the window. He glanced over all the cards and balloons, then moved closer to the bed and Lady slid closer to the edge. She kept her gaze at the window not even wanting to see his face.

"Baby, I'm sorry this is happening to you," he spoke a little above a whisper.

Lady didn't respond afraid of what her words would produce.

"Did you see him?" he asked now experiencing the same fear.

Again, Lady sat silent as she thought about her baby on the way to the morgue instead of safe in her belly. The water she had just gained control of disobeyed her and left her eyes streaming down on the pillow below.

"I guess it all worked out in your favor," she too spoke softly.

"Favor?" Kayson's brow wrinkled with confusion. "Why would you think I would want this hurt for you.?"

Lady laid silent for a few seconds choosing her words, her heart wanted to turn and comfort him but the piercing pain her loss had just created blocked all love. "I should have walked away." She took a deep breath before continuing, "The night I met you, I saw the signs. I saw who you were, and I ran toward the darkness with both eyes shut." Tears rolled down her face warm and steady.

"Saw who I was? You know who I am. I have not changed from the day I met you, baby."

"It's not who you are, it's what you are. And what you are I don't want any parts of."

Kayson ignored the heat that was rising off her words, then spoke some of his own, "If I could wear your pain I would. All I can do is try to make it up to you." He reached out to her.

"Don't!" Lady based stopping Kayson in his place. "Don't ever touch me again." She choked on her words as they left her lips. "This pain…this pain that I carry you can't purchase, nor can you erase it. I just want out." She turned her head back to the window.

"Lady, let me…"

"Leave. Please, just leave." She turned her whole body this time. "After tonight I don't want to see your face."

Lady's words hit his chest hard and for the first time, he had no words to fix or change the anguish she was living in. When he thought he had found a few words to speak into her spirit he was interrupted.

"Lady." Monique walked into the room with Baseem and Lady's best friend Octavia flanking her, each holding arms full of white, long stem roses in rose tint crystal vases.

Lady's whole body cringed when she heard Monique's voice. She wanted to blink her eyes and disappear but there would be no such blessing.

"I came as soon as I could." She walked over to the window and sat the vases down. "Put those here," she instructed as they approached her.

Octavia and Baseem followed suit then positioned themselves in the very uncomfortable space around the room.

"Sis, sorry for your loss," Baseem humbly offered his condolences, then walked over and kissed Lady on the forehead. "Here if you need anything." He reached in his back pocket, pulled out an envelope, and passed it to her then stepped out of the way so Octavia could get a little closer. Lady just nodded.

"Awwww…friend. I wish I could make this all better." She leaned in and hugged her friend as tight as she could. "I love you, mama. Hang in there," she whispered in her ear before releasing her from her grip. "I spoke to your mom and sister they have a flight scheduled for the morning. I'll pick them up from the airport for you," she offered, then walked over to the chair and took a seat.

"Thank you." Lady tried to put a slight curve to her lips.

"No worries best friend I got you," she vowed as she looked over at Kayson and his overbearing mother.

"If you need anything just let me know," Monique said as she prepared to leave the room. The energy had shifted, and she didn't want her words to tip the scales.

Lady just shook her head as her eyes began to flutter.

"Maybe we need to let her get some rest," Octavia asserted seeing her friend began to drift from her consciousness.

"Yes, let her rest." Monique shot Octavia a look that said stay in your place. She walked over and placed an envelope on Lady's lap then stroked her hair. "If you need anything I'm here." headed to the door. "Kay, I'll meet you downstairs." She looked over at Baseem then headed out the door.

"Feel better, sis." Baseem humbly stated before heading to the door. "Be outside, Boss."

389

"Do you need me to get anything for you?" Kayson asked as he looked down at this broken woman.

"No, I don't want anything from you," Lady answered, then closed her eyes and pulled the covers up to her eyes.

"I'll come back in the morning. Try to get some sleep." He walked over to where she had turned. Kayson leaned in, wrapped his arms around her, and cradled her in his arms. "I'm sorry," he whispered as he held her in his arms and just breathed.

Lady laid limp in his arms depleted of emotion and energy. She had lost all her fight and now she had lost the very thing she thought would save her, her baby. Kayson held her for a few more seconds then released her and kissed her lips before pulling the blanket back up then kissed her again before preparing to leave.

"If she needs anything call me first." He looked over at Octavia then walked over and handed her a wad of money.

Octavia took it in her hand while shaking her head in disgust. She rose to her feet and looked Kayson in the eyes. "You can't throw money at every problem. Some things require your presence, not your presents." She choked back her tears as she walked over and climbed into the bed next to her friend.

Kayson watched as Octavia nuzzled next to Lady. He knew he needed to be the one there with her, but on the other side of that wall a war had been waged and he needed to make sure he did not lose anything else precious.

"I'll see y'all in the morning."

Neither woman spoke a word. Lady just rested against the soft fabric as the tears streamed from her eyes onto the pillow. Kayson grabbed the extra blanket from the chair and placed it over Octavia's body. He stepped closer to the door then turned to give her one last look.

"I got you." Octavia squeezed Lady as she began to hear faint cries leave her lips.

When Kayson heard the sniffles, his heart sank to his feet, he turned and walked out of the room. He had just lost his son, there was no way he could make up for that.

Monique stood at the end of the hall waiting for her Kayson to emerge from the room, when she saw him dragging a long spirit appearing to be defeated, she forced a smile to her face in an attempt to comfort his weary soul. She walked up to meet him at the elevator as she prepared her next words.

"You okay?" She placed her hand on his arm.

"She don't deserve this." He looked down at his mother.

"She is strong, she will be fine," Monique kept her comments short.

"Yeah, but even the strongest person breaks into a million pieces, as they watch what they wanted crumble." The weight of Lady's pain combined with his own was tugging at the water he was keeping from rolling out of his eyes.

"This is the life she chose. Just like us." She gave him a firm glare. "The only thing this game recognizes is sacrifice. And when you are the boss that shit ain't pretty, but it's always necessary," she reminded her son who the fuck he was.

Kayson pushed the down button before he responded, "Let's see what our enemies are willing to sacrifice." He confirmed his understanding of his mother's words.

The doors opened and they stepped inside riding in silence there were no more words left to say. His mother had said it all, they were at war and sacrifice was essential to win, he would just build with whoever was left standing.

****

Ha'Roo stood in the doorway of KoKo's hospital room filled with immense grief. He stared at her for a while as she slept peacefully feet away from him nervous and afraid than hurt to know she had just lost their child. His heart filled with sadness as the thought of him not knowing that the only woman he had ever loved, was carrying and then lost his first baby. KoKo wasn't just another chick, she was his best friend, his confidant, the only person he trusted, and to see her lying there helpless, had his head in a fog of confusion. He was prepared to just stand there and watch her not wanting to wake her from her slumber.

KoKo began to stir as she felt the heat coming from the doorway. She forced her eyelids open and tried to focus on the image, but the blur of her vision prevented her from seeing who was staring back at her. Ha'Roo moved a little closer hesitation filling his gut, he didn't want to say or do the wrong thing. Slowly he approached the bed then stood by her side looking at the tubes from her arm to the bags hanging from the pole.

KoKo's eyes fluttered back and forth as she tried to focus on his face. Ha'Roo grabbed the chair next to the bed and slide it over then sat down. He put his hand in hers and she gave it a light squeeze. He placed his other hand on top and then placed his forehead on their hands. KoKo slowly lifted her other hand and placed it on the back of his head and rubbed back and forth giving him a small amount of peace in the middle of their trauma.

Warm tears rolled down onto her hand as the reality of the loss sank in. He had only known for hours that he was about to be a father and within seconds that joy was stolen. He couldn't lift his head to look at her thinking of the last time they spoke and the venom that filled the air between them.

"It's okay," she spoke a little over a whisper. KoKo rubbed his head a little more before her arm became too weak to hold up. Her hand slid down and her eyes closed as the morphine took over her body.

"I love you," he confirmed as he just held her hand in his.

"I love you, too," she confessed barely able to hold her lids open.

Ha'Roo sat there in that seat for hours just watching KoKo rest. When KoKo finally was able to open her eyes, she looked over at the clock on the wall that read 5:00 a.m. She then looked at the chair where he slept, she forced a smile to the crease of her lips as she now watched him fast asleep. KoKo stared at him a few minutes more than drifted back off feeling safe and at peace. As the sun crept through the curtain KoKo opened her eyes again and this time she was alone.

She rested her hands on her belly and the heart ached at the now empty feeling in her gut caused a flood to her eyes. "I'm sorry." She looked up at the ceiling, then closed her eyes. Darkness now her shield and if she had any mercy left, it had just died right along with her baby. "Tell your grandfather I love him. I might see y'all soon."

Chapter 45

Deadly Reign

Ha'Roo got out of his car with his mind heavy on his KoKo. He scanned the area as he began walking to the sidewalk thinking of how to make everything right. He had a plan in place but executing it was going to be a challenge. He stepped swift along the pavement headed to the side alley until he got to the back door of the house. He twisted his keys in the lock and just as he was about to open the door, he heard a rattle off to his right. Ha'Roo reached into his jacket and in one turn pulled his heat ready to fire.

"Aaahhh…muthafucka!" He winced as he felt a blade dig repeatedly into his chest.

"This is a big boy's game. And your shit is canceled," the voice barked as the man pinned him to the door and gave him a prison-style shanking. The steel pushed into his flesh digging deeper with each thrust of the blade.

Ha'Roo squeezed the trigger as he tussled in the doorway. The husky man showed no mercy he jabbed Ha'Roo in the abdomen and chest causing his body to quiver with every strike. Blood ran from the corner of his mouth as his lungs filled causing him to gasp for breath. Using the last energy, he had left, he grabbed the man by his collar and lunged forward head butting the man in the face, infuriating him causing the man to stab Ha'Roo in the throat.

Ha'Roo gurgled as he fell to his knees. The man stared down at him watching his hidden enemy now exposed. The man threw

Ha'Roo to the ground and stepped back wiping at his broken nose. He tucked his blade, then moved back toward the way he came leaving his enemy to die in a puddle of his own blood.

****

Baseem got out of his truck and adjusted his gun in his jacket pocket before popping the trunk and retrieving a few bags, then headed to the back entrance of Red and Pinky's house. When he was safe inside, he locked the door and headed upstairs. He could hear the faint sound of smooth R&B playing as he turned the knob. When he opened the door, he walked into the living room where Red sat on the couch in an oversized sweatshirt and her hair disheveled. Baseem's eyes settled on the bandage on her leg and bruises on her face and arm. He shook back his emotions as he felt heat forming in his palms.

"Hey, Ma," Baseem said as he emerged from the doorway.

"Hey, Bas," she responded forcing a broken smile.

"How you feeling?" he asked as he placed the bags on the table.

"Fucked up," she responded grabbing a tissue from the box.

Baseem took a seat next to her and placed his hand on her knee. "You know this shit is already handled," he assured her.

"I know you got me," she spoke through the tears.

"Is there anything you need me to do for you?"

"Nah, I appreciate everything. Once your team gets here, they can just pack everything up for me. I don't want to be here. Whatever is here will go in storage." She took in some air. "When I leave, I'm just taking me." She looked into his eyes.

"I understand, Ma. So, sorry for your loss." He rubbed her leg in an attempt to comfort her. "Everything is taken care of. When you are ready to go the boys will be outside to take you to the airport."

"I can't believe she is gone." She wiped her face as what felt like sharp daggers tore at her heart. "I just want to spend a little more time in our space." Again, her face flooded with water. She grabbed a few more tissues from the box and dried her cheeks.

Baseem sat silent allowing the soft sounds of the music in the background crowd the space. He allowed Red to get her composure, then he went after the answers he needed to make the devil pay for what he took off his shelf.

"I know this shit is hard, but I gotta ask you a few questions. Where did that nigga come from?"

Red snapped back to the here and now as the question left his mouth. She thought back to the day they were all in the house talking shit and Pinky revealed she had met this nigga. "I don't really know where he came from. She met him and he invited us out to the club. I know we should have peeped some shit, but she thought he…I don't know." She rubbed her head. "I think we just needed a night. Some regular shit, we let our guards down. I let them down, I am always on point. I fucked up." She shook her head in disgust.

"Nah, Ma, don't do that to yourself." He reached in and placed his hand on her shoulder. "This is my fault. I'ma make it right." He tried to take some of her pain.

"Nothing can make this right. I'ma be out here in this world by myself." She let out a hard sigh placing both hands on her chest.

"You're not alone, Ma. I got you." Baseem pulled her into his arms and placed her on his lap.

He cradled her against his chest as she released her pain. Red cried from the depths of her soul to the tips of her toes and Baseem just squeezed tighter. After she released the flood of emotion that was rocking her core, she laid her head on his shoulder and steadied her breathing.

"Thank you," she mumbled as her body settled against his.

"Whatever you need, I'm here." He confirmed his loyalty.

Red wrapped her arms around his neck and nuzzled her nose against the side of his jaw allowing his cologne to ease up her nostrils. "Right now, I just need you," she whispered as she turned her body and straddled his lap.

Baseem didn't respond with words instead he allowed the dick to speak. Red lifted herself to her feet and pulled at Baseem's sweatpants until she released the heat. She pulled her panties to the side and slid down on him without care or caution. Baseem grabbed her ass cheeks with both hands and guided her as she bounced up and down his length.

"Just hold me," she whined as she twisted her waist wetting every inch of him. "Just hold me," she moaned as tears rolled down her face.

"I got you, baby. Get that shit," he moaned as he bit into her neck.

Red rode and cried, then shivered against his chest, she had gotten exactly what she needed. Baseem just held her close, kept that dick rock, and let her have all she wanted. When she had filled some of the emptiness inside her, she sat and kissed his lips savoring the last of what she knew they would share. Nothing would be the same from this day forward.

"Thank you, Bas," she uttered, then hugged him tightly around the neck.

"I told you I got you."

Red smiled for the first time in a week. "Come help me get ready."

They got up and headed upstairs to shower and change before the crew got there. They plotted and planned as Red gathered a few important things and emptied her safes. She placed everything in a small leather Fendi travel bag before giving her bedroom a once over. It was about to be a long-ass night and they needed to have their head in the whole game because losing another one of the family wasn't something they were willing to sacrifice.

"You ready?" Baseem interrupted her thoughts.

"As ready as I'm going to be." She inhaled, threw on some shades, then headed down the hall.

Baseem grabbed the bags following close behind her and as she hit the lights and locked the doors. The new hell, she now lived in took over her soul.

Today there was another tragedy in Brooklyn, what appears to have been a home invasion turned deadly. A man had been fatally injured no word on a suspect or a motive at this time. We will keep you updated as the information comes in from the police. Back to you Fred.

KoKo snatched the IV's from her arm and swung her legs over the bed. KoKo grabbed the two towels next to the bed and wrapped one around her arm then rushed into the bathroom with hate and revenge coursing through her veins. She showered then headed to the closet and looked for her clothes. KoKo pulled at the bags to see everything she came in there with covered in blood. She frantically looked around the room until she found a gown in the drawer next to the bed. She put it on like a coat and eased to the door and peeked out to see what was moving.

When the nurse got up to attend to a patient she slid out of the door and to the staircase, then hurried down the flights to the bottom. As KoKo got to the last step she felt fuzzy feelings in her head. She gripped the banister and adjusted her vision before moving to the door. Once she had a firm footing, she pushed the emergency exit open setting off the alarm. KoKo didn't look back, she dashed through the adjoining parking lot and onto the street in need of a cab.

Tears filled her eyes as the pain began to take over her belly. She gripped her side as she waved her arm at the oncoming traffic. Several black and yellows sped past her blowing their horns leaving only smoke in their place. KoKo's heart raced as she tried to fight the pain both in her body and her heart. She was ready to say fuck it and walk when she heard the sound of a voice in the distance.

"Ce'Asia!"

KoKo turned to see who was calling her by her real name and was blinded by the lights.

Pashion stepped out the back-passenger door extending her hand. "I got you, come with me."

For the first time KoKo felt helpless, she was ass out and without her gun in the presence of a stranger who knew her real name. She tossed a mental coin and when heads was the verdict she slowly walked to the vehicle.

"It's okay. You will be fine. Come with me. Give me your hand."

KoKo extended her arm and just as she was about to take another step she collapsed to her knees.

Pashion rushed to her side. "Help me get her into the car!" she yelled to the driver.

The two placed KoKo into the back seat hopped in the front and drove off. Pashion stared at KoKo as they proceeded into traffic. "Take me to the Hills," she ordered, then turned and stared out the front window. For years she could do nothing and today she was at the right place at the right time but was it the time to reveal all.

When KoKo opened her vision, she forced her focus on the brightness that peered through the window. She rubbed her eyes as she looked up at the sheer drapes extending from the canopy above. She sat straight up stretching her arms then swung her legs over the edge of the huge bed and planted her feet on the thick furry rug below. KoKo looked down at the silk pajama pants and tank top then rubbed her hand over her arm stopping at the Band-Aids where the IVs were hours ago.

She rubbed over her belly and tears formed in her eyes and as the salty stream eased down her face, she thought about Ha'Roo and how she had just lost them both. KoKo looked around the room for some clothes and her eyes settled on a few bags on a suede bench in the corner. She walked over and sifted through them pulling the fresh pair of black Girbaud jeans, a pack of white t-shirts, and a long sleeve Long John, there was a Victoria Secrets bag containing panties and bras. KoKo laid everything on the bed, then grabbed the last two bags pulling a North Face vest and a box of black Timberlands from inside. She shook her head at the idea of this stranger knowing exactly what to get her.

KoKo opened one last box to find her gun fully loaded with two extra clips lying next to it and a fat blunt and lighter. "This bitch is crazy." She chuckled shaking her head. KoKo lit the end and inhaled the smoke deep into her lungs. She pushed peace into her heart as she tried to ready her mind. She smoked the blunt down to half then put it out.

KoKo walked over to the bathroom and sat on the toilet, she was cramping and felt weak and defeated, but she knew she needed to get out on the streets and make some heads swell for what just happened to Ha'Roo. KoKo flushed then got up to wash her hands, she stared in the mirror at the stress on her face. She had bags under her eyes and agony in her heart, she grabbed a towel and washcloth then turned on the shower and hopped in the hot water. She needed to wipe away all the agony she had been in for the last few days.

KoKo stayed in the steam and just closed her eyes allowing her mind to flow free, she began to see a little clearer and began the plot that would throw a wrench in every plot her enemies had on the table. She stayed in the hot water until her fingers pruned, she stepped out onto the bathmat, grabbed a new toothbrush from the medicine cabinet, brushed her teeth, then headed to the room to get dressed. Once she had her clothes on, she tucked her gun then headed downstairs to face the music.

When KoKo emerged in the doorway Pashion was ready and waiting to unload the information KoKo needed to operate among the snakes. She watched as this beautiful chocolate woman moved gracefully around the kitchen while preparing her coffee. She looked at her silky gown flowing and then smells of early morning caressed her nostrils causing a bit of nostalgia to rise in her chest.

"Did you rest well?" she asked as she sat her coffee cup on the kitchen table.

"I'm good, but how did you know where to find me?" KoKo got right to the point.

"Well, you rejected my invitation, so I had to come see you. Plus, I always know where you are." She pulled a chair out and sat at the table. "Have a seat."

"I'm good. Talk."

Pashion took a deep breath then smiled at the beast staring back at her. "Sit," she asserted this time leaving no room for interpretation.

KoKo stood her ground for a few seconds then walked over to the table, pulled out a chair, and took a seat. "Speak," she spoke firm as her patience was wearing thin.

"Listen, princess. I know you think you got this shit. However, there would be none of this without the people behind you keeping you safe."

"I do a pretty good job of that." KoKo sat forward in her chair.

"That you do. I must admit you do take care of yourself and others." She reached under the placemat and pulled some photos out, then tossed them in front of her.

KoKo looked down at the massacred images of her victims. "Why the fuck you showing me this?" KoKo feigned ignorance looking straight into Pashion's eyes.

"Don't play with me. I've been doing this before you were a twinkle in your daddy's nut." Pashion now sat forward. "Listen, I'm not trying to get in your way. I'm just here to help." She put her hands out to the side.

"What do you want?"

"I just want what I have always wanted." She picked up the cup and put it to her lips. After a small swig, she continued, "I want you to be smart and to be safe."

"Is there a reason why I won't be safe?" KoKo's brow creased.

"You are Malik's daughter you will never be safe."

"Don't put my father's name on your tongue." KoKo stood up sending her chair crashing to the floor.

"Relax, child. You don't rule up in this muthafucka," Pashion growled back.

'You know what, let me go. I appreciate the ride and hospitality." KoKo turned to leave.

"You are just like him. He didn't fuckin' listen and neither do you." She too rose to her feet. "You want to be the best at this shit, learn how to fuckin' listen," she asserted.

KoKo turned back to face the music Pashion was playing and planned on adding a few tunes, "I'm out here by myself. I don't fucking know you. The past has been chasing me my whole life and I have been smacking the shit outta that bitch every time she shows up."

"Is that right?" Pashion spat with a slight smirk on her lips.

KoKo cringed as she heard that infamous phrase. "I want you and the rest of those bum ass skeletons in my dad's closet to stay the fuck away from me. I won't ask twice." KoKo turned this time not stopping, she just kept on toward the door.

"This is the last time I will reach out to you." She became unsettled in her spirit that KoKo would do something they all would regret. "Remember this, princess, sometimes you gotta follow before you can lead."

KoKo grabbed the knob as she unlatched the locks. "Even when a nigga thinks he's leading me, just know I gave that nigga permission." She snatched open the door.

"Just let it come to you, KoKo!" Pashion yelled as the door slammed shut. "Shit!" Pashion sat hard in the chair then smacked her palm on the table.

****

Night stepped out of his C-class, hit the alarm then headed to the front entrance of Macy's. He moved along dressed sharp in his crisp dark blue jeans, black Long John shirt, and black boots. When he got to the makeup counter, the woman standing with a bottle of cologne in one hand and a sample in the other, locked eyes with him.

"Damn," she mumbled under her breath as all that chocolate headed in her direction. "Can I interest you in anything?" She smiled widely.

Night held her gaze, then winked. "Nah, I'm good, Ma." He looked her over from head to toe his eyes teased by her full breasts peeking through her blouse and all that ass squeezed into that pencil skirt.

"I get all the exclusives, so if you need anything at all just let me know." She grabbed a pen from the counter and jotted her digits on the back of the little white sample card then slid it into his hand. "You can hit me anytime."

"You gonna fuck around and make a nigga arch that," he spat looked at her small waist as he slid off.

"I hope so." She chuckled, switching off giving him something he could feel as she walked away.

Night looked back one last time taking notes on that business he was going to handle. He shook his head, then pushed on to the men's athletic department. When he saw Kayson. He walked over to where he was, ready to discuss how he wanted to handle the rising rebellion.

"What's good, boss man?" He extended his hand.

"You know the math. Same shit different fuckin' day." Kayson bumped shoulders with Night shaking his hand before he prepared to pass out his orders.

"I believe we nipped some of the problem in the bud with that nigga," Night confirmed.

"I thought the same shit. But from my intel, it's way bigger than him." Kayson thumbed through the hoodies.

"I know all these niggas got somebody to answer to. I think if we lean a little harder, we can flush that nigga out."

"Yeah, but with each head, we knock off that's more money off my table."

"So, what you want to do?"

"Call a meeting it's time to sit down with the heads of this dragon."

"You sure?" Night rubbed his hands together.

Kayson thought about his question, then confirmed his orders, "Yeah, I'm sure. It's time to move the Kings from one throne to the other."

Night nodded in agreement then left the same way he came. It was time to make the piper pay and only the reaper could persuade them.

****

"Pull up over there." KoKo slid some money in the slot, then slid down in the back seat. "Turn off the engine and just roll down my window," she ordered, then watched the detectives move back and forth between the black and yellow tape in front of Ha'Roo's house.

She noted each man on the team recording their features. As she took inventory, she noticed a black BMW with Georgia plates pulling up to the crime scene. The man walked confidently up to the scene, hands in the pockets of his Armani suit.

"How's it going?" Rock asked as he approached the men.

"Look what the fucking dog drug in on a rainy night," Detective Bergen joked as Rock approached.

"Fuck you, girl scout." Rock put up his middle finger.

The men erupted in laughter as they shook hands. "This is Detective…" Bergen tried to make the introductions.

"You can just call me, Rock."

"Welcome to our home," Detective Lawrence extended the greetings.

"Yeah, he's up from the dirty." Bergen looked around at his partners. "He will be here on assignment for a few weeks while he's here. Feel free to pick his brain, he is one of the best."

"We need to get him on this case, these dumb muthafuckas been leaving a trail of breadcrumbs behind enough to make a pie," Lawrence joined in.

"Anything I can do to help I'm here," Rock agreed as he looked around at the area.

KoKo slid further down as she watched the men talk their shit. She had to admit the lady was right it was time to listen and follow.

****

Kayson tapped lightly on the apartment door, waited, then tapped a little harder. He stood in the brightly lit hallway, head down and soul in turmoil. When he heard the chain slide and locks click, he raised his head prepared to see his Angel. The door eased open and there she was, the only one who understood him and the only one he knew he could be himself with.

"Kay, why are you here?" She turned quickly closing her robe and tightening the strings.

"I needed to be in your presence," he confessed closing and locking the door behind him.

"Kay…you can't be here." She put a little more space between them moving closer to the window.

"Why you not answering my calls?" he asked following behind her.

"I have a lot going on. I really don't have time for what you may be going through." Lisa felt the pain emitting from his soul and became conflicted with her choices but, then gave in. "What do you need from my life?" she asked yet afraid of the answer.

Kayson walked along the shiny, hardwood floors of the upper Eastside loft looking around at the huge paintings on the walls, antique crystal vases adorning the room with the many bouquets he sent her, and nodded his approval as he approached. "You've always had the best taste."

"In some things," she uttered keeping her back to him.

"Baby, I need you." He placed his hand on her shoulder.

Lisa turned quickly with fury in her eyes. "Why? Why do you need me? What? All the little ratchet ass legs you climb between weren't open when you stopped by?" She based as the very thought of him with other women turned her stomach.

"What the fuck?" Kayson looked down at her belly.

Lisa crossed her arms at the waist as if she could hide her growing midsection, his reaction to the revelation broke her down as the energy in the room shifted. "Please say what you have to say and leave. I can't have you here when he comes home."

Kayson ignored her words as he stood right in front of her staring intensely. He reached his hand out and rested it on her stomach as his chest tightened with emotion. He swallowed what spit he had left in his mouth as he processed the moment. Lisa brought her hands to her face and covered it just as the tears began to flow.

"Is this my baby?" He looked down at her, then placed his finger under her chin lifting her head to face the music.

Lisa stared back at him wanting to just blink and disappear but there would be no such luck, her greatest love and biggest regret was right there in front of her. "I just want to live my life," she mumbled through her tears.

"That's not what I asked you," he calmly uttered.

"If you love me just let me be free," she answered with a plea.

"Answer my question." He raised one brow not backing down.

Lisa slowly nodded her head up and down as the water she had been holding for months began to fall rapidly down her cheeks. "But I need you to let me live my life."

"You know I can't do that."

"Why? You have your fiancé and your baby on the way. Go play house with them. I want my son to be safe and away from the evil that is haunting you." Her chest heaved up and down as she spoke reality into his spirit.

"Son," he repeated, and as the words left his mouth a knot formed in his throat taking his breath.

Lisa immediately regretted her reveal as she watched the overwhelming emotion take over Kayson's mood. She placed her hand on his cheek and looked into his eyes. "Just walk away."

"You know me better than that. You know I would never walk away from my son."

"But you can walk away from me?" she asked offended by his statement.

"I never walked away from you. I honored your request and let you have some regular shit as you put it."

"Then honor this request and allow me to continue living my life," she pleaded.

"I can't," he confirmed.

"Kayson, I'm happy. You need to be happy for me and let me raise this baby with peace of mind."

"You know a son of mine will never be safe." He rested his hand on her belly. "Please don't shut me out." He placed his other hand on her belly and as the warmth of his hands settled on her skin the baby moved sending chills up his spine. "See he needs us both." He looked at her grief-stricken face, then leaned in and kissed her lips.

"I'm scared," she whispered as all the love she felt for him took over her rational thoughts.

"I got you," he vowed and pulled her into his arms.

"I wanted to tell you," she uttered as she rested against his chest.

"Well, I know now. And now I have to put you somewhere safe."

"Somewhere safe? I don't want to leave." She pushed back.

"There is no other choice. Like you said he needs to be safe."

Lisa stared at him for a change in mood, but he did not budge. "What about my parents? My mom, she is ready for him to be here."

"When it's time I'll send for her. Until then, don't say anything," he gave the orders then looked around for the house phone. Kayson picked up the receiver and placed a call. "Hello. Yeah, come back and get me and come upstairs," he instructed Night then hung up.

"Kayson, this is crazy. We need to sit down and think about this." She shook her head no. "I can't just walk away from my life."

"And I'm not walking away from you. You are the only woman I will ever love. I can't lose you twice."

"What about…"

"Just get what's important we will handle the rest. Hurry up Night will be here in a minute" He looked down at his watch.

"This is fucked up." She turned to walk to her room. She knew that saying no was not going to be an option.

Kayson walked over to the refrigerator and grabbed a bottle of water then posted up as he processed what had just been revealed.

Lisa went to her closet and began stacking underwear and bras, then her comfortable jogging suites along with a few other items of clothes. Once she had her essentials packed, she moved to the safes and dumped her jewelry, money, credit cards, and passport in a cosmetic bag. She then moved into her office emptied the file cabinet of all paperwork then grabbed her laptop and purse. Lisa placed everything by the bedroom door then dropped her robe to the floor and hopped in the shower. Quickly she lathered her skin as she thought about the man, she loved in one room and the man she had grown to love only hours away from walking into an empty house.

Tears again formed in her eyes, then ran down her face. She was ruining lives all to save a life that had yet to enter the world, and to be honest she wanted no part of what he was being born into. Lisa rinsed her skin then stepped out rushing around the bathroom oiling her skin. She entered her bedroom jumped in velour Liz Claiborne and tracksuit and sneakers. When she turned to walk out of the room, she saw Kayson standing there with a look of pride on his face.

"You know I got you right?" he asked moving a little closer.

"Yes, I know you got me. But what if something happens to you?" She looked up into those hazel eyes.

"I can't change who I am. But I can promise you that no matter what you and my son will be safe."

"What about your little girlfriend. You gonna just walk away from her and that baby to be with us?" she asked needing more than answers.

Kayson hesitated then began his spill, "We broke up. She lost the baby. That's why I can't lose y'all."

"Oh, my God!" Lisa screeched then grabbed Kayson into her arms. "Baby, I'm so sorry," she caressed his back.

"I guess it's my punishment," he confessed and for the first time, he was honest with his demons.

"God is not punishing you. You have us," she whispered in his ear.

Kayson gripped her tighter as an onslaught of thoughts crowed his head and his heart. He did not respond with words he just held her and enjoyed the moment of calm before the storm. Lisa closed her eyes also taking in the good vibes as she accepted that there was not an out, Kayson wasn't letting her go and she wasn't willing to walk away from him either. She was now all in the game and the sacrifice would be whatever it is.

A pattern of knocks on the door jolted them back to reality. "Finish getting ready, I'ma run these bags to Night." Kayson turned to grab her bags then headed to the front door.

"What's good, Boss?" Night asked with urgency in his voice.

Kayson looked down at the gun rested against his leg and quickly put him at ease. "I'm good. You can relax."

Night put the gun in his waist then closed the door behind him. "What you need me to do?"

"I need you to take Lisa overseas." He handed him the bags.

"What about the meeting. I need to be there with you."

"Nah, I got it. Baseem will make the meeting with me. I'm putting my world in your hands." He looked Night square in the eyes.

"Copy," he confirmed.

Lisa walked up behind the two men while pulling her arms into her sweater. "I'm ready." She took a deep breath and one last look around the apartment. She walked over to the end table and scribed a note folded it over and placed it down. She felt so fucked up leaving like she was, and no words could comfort the trail of pain she was leaving behind, but she had to say something.

"This is Night. He is the only one I trust with my life and you can trust him with yours." Kayson broke her train of thought.

"When will I see you again?" she asked with a heavy heart.

"Couple of days. I just have to tie up some loose ends." Kayson put his hand out to her.

"I'm so scared." She placed her hand in his then stepped into his arms. She stood right against him inhaling his scent.

"Don't be. I got you, Ma." Night cut in. "Come on I'll get you something to eat on the way to the airport."

Kayson nodded his head in agreement. He reached in his jacket pocket and pulled out a stack of hundreds and handed it to Lisa. She took it into her grasp then brought it to her chest.

"Don't make me do this by myself," she pleaded as she rubbed her belly.

Kayson leaned over and kissed her stomach then planted a few on her lips. "Never," he vowed then lead her over to Night and out the door.

Chapter 46

The Penalty Is Death

Monique stood at the bottom of the cold slab looking at Chinkz's body. She stared at the hole in his head and vomit rose to the top of her throat. She choked it back down along with her regret. Tears rose in her eyes then slid down her cheeks. Monique wiped her face with the back of her hand.

"I'm sorry, my friend," she whispered as she tried to gather her emotions.

Monique closed her eyes and silently prayed for his soul and the souls of his family as they had to walk this journey. She was snapped out of her reverie by the door opening behind her. She turned and looked back only to see a ghost from her past. The man slid up next to her and took a place by her side.

"You didn't have to make this trip," Monique said softly keeping her eyes on Chinkz.

"I put him in motion. It was a must," Scarie's low Caribbean tone eased from his lips as he looked at the gap in Chinkz's head.

"Don't mistake my mercy for actual care for your life." She looked over at her adversary.

"I am very grateful for the deal you gave me. I am not in your way…" He paused looking down into her weary eyes. "I am just here for support."

"Go back up top. Because when the day comes that she learns who you are," she then paused her brow lowered and creased as she continued. "I cannot and will not save you."

"I accept that," he chose his words carefully. "But who is going to save you when Malik's children grow to learn your hands are not clean?"

Monique chuckled and shook her head at Scarie's ignorance. "Don't worry about my hands. Blood washes off very easy with hundred-dollar bills."

"I guess we will all be waiting to see what the future holds."

"It only holds my power," she spat dropping the smirk from her lips.

"Yes, sir Boss Lady," his thick Jamaican accent dripped with contempt as he tipped his hat and bowed his head.

"Hurry up and leave. I don't want your stink to rise in their nostrils. As I said, I won't save you." She turned to the door, walking out of the room leaving Scarie standing at the foot of the dead, a place he was not too far off from joining.

"Greedy bitch," he mumbled as he turned to his soldier to pay his final respect. "Sleep well. You will have plenty of company soon." He touched Chinkz's leg then settled his emotions and left the room with Monique's threats at the front of his mind.

****

It's Never Over...

Baseem pulled up to the other vehicles and deaded his engine. Kayson scoped the area trying to identify the players on the scene and only one car stood out.

"Ain't that the car of the nigga we were trailing?" Baseem said what Kayson was thinking.

"Yeah, that's the one," he confirmed.

"I don't know about this shit, Boss." Baseem reached in his armrest and pulled out his gun and checked the chamber.

"Nah, them niggas ain't that crazy, plus Mo secured our safety."

"Well, the first nigga that breath wrong, I'ma secure our safety," Baseem vowed.

"You always wanna kill some shit." Kayson chuckled. "Come on."

The men stepped out into the night in all black with ruthless guns at their sides ready to negotiate. Keeping their head on a swivel they approached security and extended their arms. After being cleared to enter, they moved past the men and into the open area.

"What the fuck?" Baseem based through clenched teeth as he reached for his strap.

Kayson's eyes widened as he set his eyes on the carnage before him.

"Aht. Aht." Magnum wagged his finger. "Be easy, my nigga."

"Nigga you must be tired of livin'?" Baseem pulled one in the chamber ready to match blood for blood.

The sound of several weapons locking bullets echoed in the distance. Baseem and Kayson looked up around the walls to see men heavily armed with red sensors pointing right at them.

Kayson put his hand on Baseem's arm. "This is business gentlemen lets conduct it as such." He directed his words at Magnum as he watched the connect's heads leak out onto the table.

"This *is* business," Magnum barked back, crossing hands behind his back.

Baseem's breathing quickened as he looked at the woman, he had just held in his arms only days ago tied to a chair beaten and bloody. Kayson cut his eyes over at Baseem while silently praying this nigga didn't give them a reason.

"So, what is this about?" Kayson kept his inquiry short.

"Oh, this? Well, that right there." He pointed at Red's dead body. "That is a gift for my boss. You know, a life for a life." He smirked at the position his enemies were now standing in. "And these trader ass muthafuckas are a gift from my boss to you." He waved his hand over Don Anibello, Miguel, and Mr. Lu and their first in command's bodies.

"A gift for me?" Kayson now chuckled as well. "Is that right?"

415

"Yeah, just a little peace offering from the reaper, take it in good faith," Magnum continued. "In a few days, you will get a visitor that person will put you with the new connect, cause tonight we change all hands."

Baseem was heating up, ready to just start hitting whatever his bullets could connect with. "Tell your boss he only gets one time to touch mine," Baseem threw his threat on the table.

"From the looks of it, it's the last time you get to touch her also." Magnum dug the knife in a little deeper.

Baseem's trigga finger became itchier by the second but he had to remain calm, he was ready to die every day but to put Kayson's life in danger was not an option. So, he took a deep breath and conceded to the power that be.

"Indeed." He tucked his gun causing the temperature to go from one hundred to one.

"Now if there is nothing else, I got shit to do. You're excused." Magnum got cockier by the minute.

"I guess we will wait on the visitor," Kayson spoke calmly holding firm eye contact with Magnum.

"Yeah, you do that." Magnum accepted his surrender.

Kayson tapped Baseem on the shoulder, then turned to the door, he eyed the men with guns on him and recorded each face as he passed by. There was no settling with the house tonight. Each man had a target on his forehead, and he was going to fill them with something hot. Baseem and Kayson hoofed it to the truck and hopped inside, they were on fire.

"What the fuck?" Baseem yelled as the doors closed.

"Just chill, I'm already all over this shit." Kayson's lips tightened to a scowl as he started his engine and peeled out of the parking lot.

"I'ma chill cause you here. You know a nigga ready to let off some heat." He turned his gun back and forth.

"Nah, let them niggas breath..." he paused for a minute. "What did they say that bitch's name was?"

"KoKo," Baseem sang looking over at Kayson. "Let me do that bitch."

32

92

148

"Nah, I want you back on the streets. With Miguel gone Edwin will have that work. I need you on the reup. I'ma put Aldeen and Wise on her, she gonna be for me."

"Nigga, that bitch a killah. You can't just put dick between you and the bitch like that. Gonna fuck around and lose a few inches," Baseem joked.

"Dick is a bonus."

"And Pussy is a trap." He looked over at his friend.

"Yeah, that's why I just gotta make her love me." He looked at his comrade confident in his ability.

"Indeed." Baseem sat back and just stared out the window as Kayson pushed on to their destiny.

****

When Magnum confirmed that the men were gone, he signaled to his team to clean up the scene then headed toward the back of the building. He pushed open the exit doors and inhaled deeply taking in the New York night. Magnum walked over to the awaiting vehicle and hopped in the front seat.

"Everything good?" KoKo asked from her reclined position.

"Yeah, had them niggas shook. That dark skin nigga is a bitch." Magnum laughed as he thought about the look on his face when he saw Red.

"Fuck them niggas. Now them bitches work for us," Link chimed in.

"So, all bases are covered?" KoKo asked as her finger caressed her trigger.

"Yes, we covered all bases." Magnum nodded in agreement.

"Where to, boss? We need to celebrate this victory," Link said as he started the engine.

"The shit that gets me. They play that nigga Kayson real big time, and that nigga didn't even flinch." Magnum pulled a blunt from his pocket. "Rest easy, my nigga, this shit is for you Roo!" he shouted as he put fire to the end and pulled the smoke deep into his lungs. He took a few more pulls, then passed it to KoKo.

"So, you ready for the transition." She took in the sweet smoke.

"Hell yeah. We family can't nothing change that." He confirmed his loyalty. "Blood in Blood out." Magnum rubbed his hands together as his chest filled with pride. "Damn, Ma pass that shit." He turned around and was met with a bullet in each eye.

"What the fuck...?" Link screeched, before he could finish his thought KoKo cleared his mind.

"Family Ain't Family. Blood Ain't Blood," she uttered wiping the thick crimson from her face.

KoKo hopped out of the back seat tossing the gun in the front. "Burn them bitches they ain't worthy of open coffins," KoKo gave her orders as the men approached her.

"Copy." The men moved to clean the scene. "You need us to take you somewhere?"

"Nah, where I'ma end up, no man wants to go." KoKo pulled her hood over her head and jogged off the pier with evil intent in every step.

****

KoKo staggered through the tombstones holding on to the ones she could reach as she passed them. She tripped and stumbled along the way to the mausoleum, pulled the door open wide, then continued inside. KoKo rubbed her eyes to focus on the light, then walked slowly to Malik's tomb. When she got to the wall where he laid, she rested her back and slid down to the floor. She rested her head against the cold slab, closed her eyes, and let the water make its way down her cheeks.

"Why you leave me out here by myself?" she whispered as the weight of the hour sat heavy on her soul. "I'm tired, I don't want to do this alone," she confessed as she reached in her jacket pocket.

KoKo pulled her gun out and sat it next to her, then reached back in and grabbed a blunt and lighter and set it ablaze. As she inhaled both smoke and cold air her lungs gave way sending loud coughs through the empty space. She took one long pull after the next trying to numb her pain but the reality of where she sat would not allow it.

"Daddy, I don't know what to do. I need you," she cried between the smoke that left her lungs. "I'm fucked up." She brought the Philly back to her lips.

KoKo sat and sobbed as she took in all the loss, she had suffered. Her heart was empty and the only thing she had to fill it with was hate. She closed her eyes and focused on the pictures she had seen of her mom and dad using them as a catalyst for her revenge. "Don't worry dad, I may bend but I won't break." She wiped her nose then took another hit. "Take care of my angel. There was no place on earth for that sweet soul." Tears again streamed down her face.

"I knew I would find you here," the husky voice based in her direction.

KoKo pulled her weapon pointing it right at the intruder.

"Whoa, I'm on your side." Fred threw his hands in the air.

"Everything on this side of the green is suspect." She eased her weapon down allowing Fred to get a little closer.

"May I?" he asked waving at the bench across from her.

KoKo nodded her acceptance then put the smoke back to her lips.

"Damn, I miss your dad. He would stop by and talk his shit, drop a little on my table, and be gone like he never stopped by." He smiled at the memory.

"I miss him, too. But no worries, I'ma keep sending him company until their graves are as full as mine." She eased her fingers over the letters of Malik's name.

"I guess you set the records straight tonight." He sat back and crossed his legs at the knee.

"I do what I can," KoKo slurred as she locked eyes with Fred.

"Sorry about Tiny," he offered her condolences.

"She was a casualty, no condolences needed," she smugly stated.

"Well, she knew the job." Fred reached in his pocket and pulled out his flask, twisted the top, and put it to his lips. "Will you need another inside man?" he asked taking a few swigs.

"Nah, I got it. I'm about to make things right."

"When are you going to stop. At some point, you need to rest that gun." He took another sip.

"I can't, Fred. Ain't no stopping, all gas no breaks." She became slightly aggravated with his direction.

"KoKo, you know I love you, and I am saying this out of love. You gotta try to live. Let the dead comfort each other. You are too young to not live."

"*Live?*" She sat up straight. "How the fuck do you live when they took everything you love?"

"Baby girl, there is still love here on this side. Don't miss out chasing ghosts."

"They drew first blood." She rose to her feet. "I'm just going to let it flow." She headed to the door. It was time to go, KoKo had her moment of weakness it was time to turn off and turn up.

"Don't retaliate. Just sit back everything will come to you," Fred echoed the words Pashion had also uttered.

KoKo looked over her shoulder at Fred as the words left his mouth and for the first time, she held her cards. She could see the dealer and the players were on the same team and she needed to protect her queen until she had the right pawn to sacrifice.

"No worries. Everything that is supposed to happen will happen and every enemy of my father will die," she spoke her peace. "I'll give you the same mercy I gave everyone else." She noted the concern on Fred's face. "Stay out the way." She tucked her gun, then walked out of the building plan firm in mind.

****

One Year Later...

"Yo, are y'all muthafuckas working or what? I ain't running a got damn babysitting service. Do some shit or get the fuck off the block."

Niggas got busy doing whatever their job was. People were coming up whispering in her ear trying to let her know the daily count and that Kayson was present. She looked up, spat on the ground, and headed toward Kayson and Aldeen.

"Who the fuck is that?" Kayson said to Aldeen.

"That's KoKo," Aldeen said with a smile. He was interested in what Kayson was going to do next. "We got a fucking dyke out here running shit?"

KoKo could hear him, so she answered the question, "I eat a lot of things, but pussy ain't one of them."

Aldeen busted out laughing because he knew that shit was getting ready to get really interesting.

"Is that right?" Kayson responded.

"Does a bear shit in the woods?" She put her hand out then said, "I'm, KoKo."

Kayson put his hand out to make the introduction. "Well, I'm Kayson, the Boss." Neither one of them blinked.

Then KoKo responded, "Oh, that's what they call you?"

"They...what you mean by they?'" Kayson shot back.

"I'm just saying. The way I see it, we work in goods and services. You provide the goods. We provide the service. If you didn't have us, you would be out here yo' damn self-hoofing and sweating. So, my motto is, fair exchange ain't no robbery."

Kayson looked at Aldeen. Aldeen shrugged. "So, wait a minute, if I ain't the Boss then who the fuck am I?"

"You are going to have to do some soul searching or some shit for that one."

Chapter 47

The Vow

Present Day...

KoKo sat staring out at the open sea as the waves crashed and wailed. She thought about all that had taken place and all that had taken lives. She inhaled deeply as the warm breeze swept over the balcony. KoKo grabbed her glass bringing the warm beverage to her lips, she swallowed one gulp after the next until the glass was empty before placing it back on the small table next to her. She had buried enemies and friends and now she just needed to sit still and regroup while planning the last stages of her plan.

"How are you feeling?" Kayson asked placing a hand on her shoulder.

"Being here always brings me so much peace." She looked up into his gaze.

"This is the only place we are able to just be us."

"Nothing exists outside of us and the family we have created. Thank you for protecting us." She took his hand into hers and placed a single kiss on the backside.

Kayson choked back the heavy emotions that were weighing on his chest, then he spoke, "My whole life has been to protect this family. And I plan to destroy everyone who may be able to stand in the way of that." He squeezed her hand tightly in his.

"Me too," she confirmed, then stared back off into the distance. As she watched the moon dance on the water, she confirmed her vows and accept every sacrifice it would take to hold them.

"Boss, the plane is ready," Baseem announced as he stepped out onto the balcony.

Kayson turned and looked in his direction then down at KoKo. "I'll just be a few days gotta get back to the city and see what the fall out produced."

"Be careful, baby." She looked up into his eyes.

"You already know." He leaned in and kissed her lips ever so gently savoring all the love she had left to give. "I love you."

"I love you, too. Always and forever," she vowed, rubbing his face.

Kayson kissed her palm enjoying her touch as he stood locked in their trance not wanting to leave his family. "Be good." He kissed her again then walked to the sliding doors.

"Yeah, be good," Baseem joked as he exited the balcony with Kayson close behind.

"Don't get fucked up, I still got these hands." KoKo returned his humor, then put her views back out into the distance.

"I don't want no problems." He threw his hands up in surrender.

"Don't make her have to touch you up." Kayson chuckled as they walked off the balcony.

KoKo set her vision back out over the water, with Kayson and Baseem's laughter tickled her ears as they ascended the stairs, she sat thinking about the day she began twisting the knife of revenge right in the hearts of her enemies.

"Them niggas are headed this way." Buck slid into the front passenger seat. "And them niggas are fucked up this should be an easy lick." He nodded his head ready to put in work.

"A'ight y'all get in place. If they breathe one breath too heavy, don't hesitate," KoKo gave her orders.

"Got you, Boss." Buck jumped out of the car and ran across to the street to get in position.

KoKo looked out the front window of the car anticipating the emergence of her marks. She thought about the level she was entering and what she would have to sacrifice if shit didn't go right. She tossed around the plan with the few seconds she had left, then was distracted by her confidant speaking.

"You ready to release evil?" He looked over at her.

"I was born ready," KoKo confirmed. "But change of plans, kill the decoy, and move on to plan B."

"You sure?" His brow wrinkled as he realized the call she had just made.

"On the soul of our father." She looked over, locking eyes with him, solidifying their agreement."

"Watch your fucking back." He extended his hand grabbing hers and pulling her into his arms. "It's just us," he confirmed before letting her go.

"Just us," she repeated taking a deep breath to fit her tears. KoKo swallowed her fears and stepped into the dark side.

The man got out of the back seat heading to the position of the strike. He looked back at KoKo one last time as he heard his mark's voices approaching in the distance. He winked at her and shot her a quick smile with the last part of his soul that was not cold. He quickly tucked the love moving to his spot.

"You sure these niggas gonna bite?"

"There is one thing you can count on with a real nigga." KoKo stated smoothly.

"What's that?"

"Loyalty. Earn it and you rise! Cross it and you die. Show him loyalty." She looked over at him.

"I will give them the same justice they gave our father."

"I don't want justice. I just want pain," she calmly stated.

"Then pain they shall receive." Baseem nodded his head as he exited the vehicle.

KoKo rolled down her window to give one last order. "Bas...." He turned quickly. "Make him love you." She rolled the window up and slide down in the seat.

"Abso-fucking-lutely." Baseem eased into the shadows and waited.

****

"Oh shit, hold me up," Kayson said to Aldeen.

425

"Shit, I'll put one hand on your back, but if I got to hold your dick, you going home pissy tonight."

The unsuspected men started to laugh again their voices carrying into the night until they heard a faint argument in the background. This woke them up. All they could hear was a voice saying, "Y'all niggas thought that I was a punk?"

Kayson put his dick back and zipped his pants. They peeked around the corner and saw this black ass nigga holding two guns, one in each hand, and pointing at two cats who looked like they were deer caught in headlights. One responded to the question.

"Nah, my dude, we were just checking your status. We never saw you before."

"Well, y'all need a better welcoming party because this nigga hit me with a gotdamn bottle. That shit felt more like a threat on my life."

Just then, Kayson noticed a nigga creeping up from the corner and coming up behind the guy with the guns. Kayson reached for his gat and put one in the trigger. He usually didn't get in other nigga's business, but from what he could hear, if they hit this nigga with a bottle and he was able to remain standing and get to his guns, then turn the tables on them, he might have run up on a hitman for hire. Kayson was always looking for talent so he could step farther back.

When it looked like it might be over for Baseem, Kayson bust off catching the guy in the head. Baseem immediately put one in the throat of the guy on his left, and one between the eyes of the guy on his right. They both fell like a deck of cards. Baseem turned his attention to Kayson and Aldeen, realizing that they had just saved his life. He went over to them and gave them dap.

"Thanks for having a nigga's back," Baseem said, apparently very grateful.

"I have a proposition for you. Let's get the fuck outta here, then we can talk," Kayson said as he walked off toward the limo.

The men followed now with a new adversary in their corner and from what Kayson witnessed Baseem was about to be a hell of an asset and was about to give him a proposition he knew he would not deny.

KoKo watched as they pulled off from the curb she had to smile as she watched Baseem ride away with her opposition. While all, them niggas was *focused on pussy bringing them down, she slid a dick between them and made him bring her the crown.*

"*King Me.*"

KoKo stood up, walked to the edge of the balcony, and watched as the children ran out onto the beach moving quickly to the fire pit with the nannies, graham crackers, chocolate, and marshmallows in each hand. She formed a smile on her face, which felt like were the last few smiles she would have. She watched her legacy laugh and play free of worry, and fear. Now with Goldie's son added to her nest, her trifecta was complete. It was now time to get back to the states. She had a few more kills in her gun and this time the blood on her hands would trickle between her enemies, friends, and family.

"Just gotta make them love me." She chuckled, then turned to prepare her bags, there were traps to set and she going to be the dangerous pussy at the center of them all.

ALSO AVAILABLE BY NENE CAPRI PRESENTS

NeNe Capri Presents